THE VIEW FROM GALLOWS HILL

A novel of Witchcraft, Magick and Demons
based on the Pendle Witch Trials of 1612

NICK STEAD

COPYRIGHT

DEDICATIONS

This one is for my mum for first introducing magic into my life, and for Sara for introducing me to the Pendle witches.

I would also like to thank my beta readers, Hannah, Jo, Joanna, Owen, Gemma and Vivien. Your feedback was invaluable in making the story the very best it could be.

And finally, thanks to the other two founding fathers at Twisted Fate Publishing, Chris for believing in this novel right from the first draft all the way through to this published version, plus Gareth for the usual hard work on the cover design and feedback on the final edit. And thanks to Jayne for drawing the cover art amidst a busy weekend - the manuscript would still be sat on my PC without you three!

Nick

AUTHOR'S NOTE

I feel like this novel needs a quick introduction with it being based on true historical events. The key phrase here is 'based on' – history buffs will recognise some scenes as being taken straight from our records of the time, but it's important to remember this is a work of fiction. Many scenes came directly from my imagination.

It started off as a short piece for the Huddersfield Authors' Circle annual President's competition in 2015, for which the theme was 'based on a true story'. My friend and fellow member (and president that year), Sara Burgess, is as fascinated by witchcraft as I am werewolves, so it's no surprise the Pendle wise women placed her under their spell. I still remember sitting in the pub, listening to her recount the story of Old Demdike and her family over a few pints. It seems the cunning folk bewitched me that night as well, because the deadline for the competition was looming and I still needed something to enter into the new 'novel opening chapter' category she'd introduced that year, and I remember lying awake listening to fierce winds whip across the fields and batter the house, and the opening scene atop Pendle Hill beginning to take shape.

My entry won first place in the opening chapter category and the immediate question on the group's lips was "Are you going to carry on with it?" I told them I would but I needed to write more of my Hybrid series first, so it was

2017 before I sat down to continue the story I'd started in that short opening.

Delving into historical fiction presented new challenges – more than I think I first anticipated. I've put more research into this story than I've needed to in any books in my Hybrid series, not just on the 1612 witch trials and the practices of the cunning folk, but also on the early seventeenth century period in general to get the setting as true to life as I possibly could. I have deliberately changed some details as I wanted to put my own spin on the story, but I hope anyone interested in all things Pendle witch trials will still recognise the strong characters Thomas Potts immortalised in his 'The Wonderful Discovery of Witches in the County of Lancaster', and their story as we understand it.

CONTENTS

PART FOUR - 1612

PROLOGUE

Rope creaked with the strain of a dead weight. Icy tears rolled down cold, pale flesh, following the tracks made in those final moments on this earthly plane. But these were nature's tears. These were the tears of the heavens, falling from above and landing on dull eyes staring sightlessly into the night. Eyes which no longer blinked away the sting of the foreign liquid nor squinted against the downpour. Devoid of emotion, there was only the emptiness of death now. Their real tears had long since dried up.

Left hanging as a cruel warning by their executioners, the corpses danced and twisted at the mercy of the storm's breath. There would be no resting in peace for these three souls rotting atop Pendle Hill, not if the 'good' Christian folk had their way. And so the land wept.

Thick clouds smothered any natural light in the sky above. The three bodies were barely visible, no more than silhouettes with the vague likeness of human forms. And if any had been there to stand witness, they might just have made out a fourth figure making her way over to them, moving with a confidence and surety that was at odds with the blackness of her surroundings.

A flash of lightning rent the night. The one they called Demdike came to a stop before her sister wise women and bowed her head. 'Twas a terrible crime to be different, and these three had paid the ultimate price. Yet the fool villagers hadn't minded the cunning folk in their midst when they'd come seeking cures to their ailments or advice through divination, not so long ago. Then came King James with his religious ideas, and there was only one place left in Pendle for suspected witches – the end of a hangman's noose.

The old woman looked back up at the Puritans' grisly message, her eyes ablaze with all that the dead gazes lacked as she struggled with the conflicting emotions that raged within. Strongest was her dark desire for revenge. Blood must be paid with blood, death with death. But with an effort, she suppressed the curses that so naturally came to her lips. It was not the time, not yet. First she must ensure the three women found the peace the Christians would otherwise deny them, a peace they would never know without this last act of kindness. Not after the torment they'd endured in their final days in this mortal life.

Demdike knelt and unwrapped the tools she'd brought with her. She picked up all but one of the old human bones and placed them in a large circle, moving quickly, yet treating them with respect. The remaining femur resting on the scrap of black cloth was larger than the other bones and had symbols of power carved into it.

Alongside the femur lay a ceremonial knife, several candles and a pendant in the likeness of a pentagram which had belonged to her mother. With wizened fingers, she placed each of the candles around the circle of bones, then lifted the carved femur, handling it with the tenderness reserved for her most prized possessions.

She began to chant the words of the ritual, first using the old bone to channel power into sealing the circle she'd created. Flames burst into life at the end of each candle wick, and though the storm still raged, once burning the flames could not be extinguished.

With the circle sealed, she reverently placed the femur back on the scrap of material, her cold, bony fingers closing on the ceremonial blade now. Her other hand shot out with the speed of a much younger woman, as if the magic of the ritual had given her body new strength that transcended her years. Squeals of terror were all but drowned out by the gale raging around them as the unfortunate rodent wriggled in her grasp. Yet despite its best efforts, it could not fight free of the fleshy prison that had so suddenly closed around it, not even after it bit the wrinkled skin.

Demdike ignored the sudden, sharp pain where the rat had drawn blood and brought her hands up to the edge of the circle. She drew the knife over the rodent's throat and it soon went still, a crimson fountain spraying forth. The power intensified, becoming a charged force tingling across her skin. She placed the blade back in her makeshift pack and traded it for both the femur and the pendant this time, all the while continuing to chant.

The old wise woman sensed the magic reaching new heights with the life force she'd fed it, small though that life had been. Her voice rose with it. The circle still appeared empty but, as one, the flames went out and the hillside was plunged into sudden darkness once more, until there came another flash of lightning. And for the briefest of moments, the one she'd summoned was revealed.

Robes as dark as the night itself billowed about him, as

if he wore the very shadows around them. Within his cowl grinned every mortal man's worst nightmare, the eye sockets as empty and emotionless as the corpses swinging beside them in the wind. Skeletal fingers gripped a scythe, the tool humming with a power of its own.

"Why do you summon me here?" Death asked.

Demdike looked into the terrible emptiness of those eye sockets as boldly as she would look into the eyes of any human. "These three have been wronged; I feel their souls' suffering. I'll not see them trapped here for eternity while I still have the power to do something about it."

"I can do nothing so long as you contain me within this circle," Death said.

Thus came the dangerous part of the summoning, but one that was necessary if she wanted the Reaper's aid. Aware that she was relinquishing her only protection against one of the universe's greatest forces, Demdike nudged one of the bones, breaking the circle. Once free, Death's power hit her as if it were a physical force. She felt her old heart flutter in response and had to grip her tools tighter in a struggle to keep her hold on this life. Only through her force of will did her heart regain its rhythm and the strength of its beat.

"You will guide these three into the next life," she ordered him.

"You dare command me, mortal?" Death thundered, his voice seeming to come not from one place, but from all around her now. "Are you so arrogant as to believe your magic grants you any hold over me – that it will let you conquer death?"

"I am no fool. I know I am but an old woman who has lived too long already. When you come for me, I will not fight you. But that time is not now. You are not here for my soul, you are here because I summoned you. And the ritual grants me one wish, so you will see these three laid to rest in whatever afterlife awaits them." She gestured at the hanged women.

Death considered her. There was no magic strong enough to bind him by any rules; even the ritual circle would have collapsed eventually if she'd left him trapped there. Demdike sensed his resentment at having to obey her commands, but he was a part of the balance of the universe. If he took her soul before her time, it could have catastrophic consequences on the other forces he worked with to maintain equilibrium. And to leave the souls of mortals trapped in the earthly realm could also upset that balance. He had only one choice, and they both knew it.

"Very well."

Demdike nodded, then closed her eyes and focused on the bond she shared with her familiar – the spirit she'd made a pact with all those years ago. Through that bond, she was able to reach him without the need for tools or rituals, but whether Tibb chose to respond was another matter. She opened her eyes to find that night he had answered her call in the form of a large black dog with eyes that burned with the fires of the place Christians would call Hell.

Tibb looked up at her with the same faithful patience as any mortal dog. Demdike couldn't help but smile as she met his gaze. Then she gestured to the hanged women. "See that they make it safely to the next life."

Death seemed to grow taller at that, and his next words came out as a hiss. "Now you doubt my word?"

A pain shot through Demdike's chest. She gasped and gripped her tools tighter. The sharp sensation of the pentagram digging into her palm helped her focus – that and

Tibb's rumbling growl, fierce yet comforting. She thought it a pity that he couldn't take the tormented spirits to peace on his own, but only Death had the power to free them from the weak grasp on their old life. Still, she would feel better knowing Tibb was with them. Death might not care where they ended up, so long as they went to one of the astral planes where they now belonged. The last thing she wanted was for them to escape one hell, only to find themselves in another.

Those empty sockets continued to glare at her from the gloom of the cowl. Demdike bowed her head, choosing her next words with care. "Forgive me. I merely wish to know that their souls are at peace, and I would not trouble you again simply to hear the answer to that question."

There was a long moment of silence, somehow more terrible than the sound of his voice. "I will not forget your treatment of me this night, Elizabeth Southerns."

A shudder ran through Demdike as he uttered her real name, but she said "I fear thee not, Death. When next you come for me, I will welcome you with open arms."

The empty eye sockets remained fixed on her for what seemed an eternity, until finally the skeletal figure turned away, facing the hanged women. Without another word, he swung his scythe across the chest of each corpse, creating a deep gash that went through each of their hearts. Thus severing the ties between the tormented spirits and their earthly remains, he commanded the ghostly forms of the three women to follow him. The spirits never once looked at Demdike, unaware of her in their current state, but Tibb looked back and nodded before disappearing with the others.

Then they were gone, and she was alone once more. She knelt to gather her tools and wrap them in the scrap of cloth, but as she stood she became aware of a man approaching, his lantern bobbing up and down like some illuminous spirit flitting over the moors. Demdike was confident he wouldn't notice the evidence of her magic in the limited visibility so black and miserable a night afforded, but she readied a curse to strike him down just in case.

The man stopped just short of her and raised his lantern, revealing a middle-aged face made stern by piety. A dark goatee framed his thin mouth, set in its usual position of contempt. His grey eyes squinted at her through the rain. "What are you doing up here, hag?"

Demdike felt her own face hardening in response. "I could ask you the same, Richard."

"My business is no concern of yours. Tread carefully, pagan, or you might find yourself joining your fellow whores."

The darker emotions she had struggled to suppress were quick to rise to the surface, filling her every being in a tidal wave of anger. Richard was so blinded by his own hate that he failed to see the fury in her eyes.

"Murdering innocents," he continued, finding passion in his own self-righteousness. "It isn't right what you folk did to Master Sawyers and all those others, causing their deaths so suddenly like that."

"There is less blood on these old hands than on your young Christian ones."

Richard laughed at the absurdity of that statement. Then he noticed his hands were no longer wet with just the rainfall.

A crimson flow ran down his skin and dripped from the ends of his fingers to pool in the mud. He opened his mouth to scream, but only a gurgle sounded from his throat. To his horror, he found himself choking as blood vessels burst and the red wave frothed up, spilling from his mouth in painful racking coughs and leaking from the various orifices in his body. He fell to his knees and reached up towards Demdike as if for help, terrified as the seconds trickled by in which he couldn't breathe, drowning in his own blood. The warmth of his flesh ebbed on that red tide and he began to shiver uncontrollably. Then came the lightheadedness which signalled he was on the verge of passing out.

Demdike stood over him, rage coursing through her and fuelling the curse she'd placed him under with barely a conscious thought. It would be so easy to kill the self-righteous fool, but something held her back. With effort, she forced her anger back into submission and severed the link to the spirits providing the flow of dark energy, leaving him gasping and shaking in the mud. She turned away without another word, and started back towards the small cottage the villagers had christened Malkin Tower. There would be a time for revenge later, but at a moment of her choosing, rather than in the heat of anger. And not without Tibb. He was central to her dark plan, and she had no doubt he would delight in playing the role she had in mind for him.

It took some time before Richard's pain and dizziness left him, and he felt able to pick himself up from the mud. Still he shivered in his sodden, blood-soaked clothes, anger creeping in again now that his life was no longer in danger and the terror had drained away. He glared in the direction he guessed Demdike had gone, though he could see nothing of the old crone in the blackness, the comforting glow of his lantern lost to him now. He must have dropped it and the fall had doused its flame – that or it was the witch's doing.

Bad enough that she'd caught him out here, but to humiliate him and cause him such pain demanded retribution. It would not be the last they saw of each other, and Richard Baldwin vowed there would be a reckoning when next they met.

PART ONE - 1609

ONE

N ew light spilled across the Forest of Pendle,
revealing the natural beauty of the surrounding
farmland that made up the area Demdike called
home. Pendle Hill was but a distant shape on the horizon
now, grey and indistinct at a distance. Yet there was no
mistaking that shape for any other hill. It towered above
the untamed greens and browns of the moorlands like the
back of one of the great sea creatures of legend, striking,
and perhaps even sinister to visitors from more civilised
lands. To Demdike it was a comforting presence. She need
never feel lost so long as the earthen giant was there,
watching over her.

The warmth of the early morning sun was a welcome
sensation on her skin, the darkness of the night's events
almost reduced to naught but a bad dream. Almost, but not
quite. For while the storm had passed and the sky was now
clear, the night's chill lingered on through the clothes still
clinging to her body with an uncomfortable wetness. The
need for revenge also remained.

She hadn't been back at the cottage long before the first

signs of life reached her ears from within. The door creaked open, and she turned to meet her daughter's lopsided gaze. Demdike was well aware of the gossip and the sneers that followed her family wherever they went, her daughter's disfigurement a long standing source of amusement for many in the community. But Elizabeth Device would always be her daughter, and in her eyes she was no less beautiful for the left eye which drooped lower than her right.

"What are you still doing out there, Mam? Come on in before you catch your death of cold."

"Don't fret, girl – 'tis a pleasant morning."

"Well at least come and change out of those wet clothes."

Demdike snorted. "Change into what? Unless you've found a way to conjure any fresh up, my other set is still to wash."

"Come by the fire then; you'll dry quicker than out here."

"I'm not so old as to need you fussing over me yet," Demdike admonished. Elizabeth retreated back inside without another word, but she supposed her daughter was right and followed her in.

The brightness of the natural world gave way to the gloom of their humble home. A shiver ran through Demdike then. The cool dampness of the fabric on her skin was much more noticeable now she was out of the sun.

Elizabeth was already lighting the fire. Demdike set the bundle of tools back in its place atop a wooden chest and stripped down to her shift, then settled on a stool by the hearth. New warmth slid over the exposed areas of her bare flesh, pleasant and welcome.

Her eyes fixed on the flames, but her thoughts were

back on the moors with her sisters, and in her mind she couldn't help but replay all she'd seen and experienced that night. She could at least take comfort in the knowledge that the hanged women's spirits would find peace, her trust in Tibb absolute. The eternal rest she'd arranged for them was a small mercy, yet it was all she had to offer. If she could have saved them from the noose she would have, but alas, she had been too late. There was nothing more to be done other than honour their memories and find a way to prevent any more deaths. Demdike swore to herself then that when the god-fearing villagers next convicted anyone of witchcraft, she would not fail them as she had those three.

Then there was the matter of Richard Baldwin. She'd never had any love for that pious fool, his attitude towards her family calling to the darker desires she nursed deep within. Born of the injustices all those branded 'witch' had suffered, her anger had grown too strong to allow for any acts of forgiveness. But she shouldn't have lost control during that last encounter, no matter how briefly. She would have to guard her emotions more carefully in the future. Age had taught the wisdom of patience, and patience dictated she wait for the right opportunity to strike back at the men who deserved it. Better to plan ahead and weigh up all the risks when turning to the dark arts. Calling on them out of anger was never going to end well – they would only guide her down the path to her own destruction.

She did wonder what the miller had been doing out on the moors though. No Christian she'd ever met would wander the land after nightfall, not by choice. What business could have been so pressing that it drew him from the safety of his home?

An excited cry cut through the old woman's thoughts as the youngest member of their family squealed "Granny!"

Jennet came rushing in, her eyes alight with the joy of those yet to lose the innocence of childhood. At six years old, she still found much wonder in the world and that sense of awe small children felt in the presence of their elders, curiosity often leading to numerous questions on everything from the workings of nature to her family's personal trade. Demdike treasured that innocence and welcomed little Jennet with open arms, knowing it would soon be taken from her granddaughter. The day would come when the harsh life they led forced the child to grow up and find wisdom far beyond her years. But that day was not upon them yet.

"Now, lass, where have you been this morning?"

"Alizon promised to show me a spell before we go begging later."

Her other granddaughter appeared in the doorway, looking across at them with a mixture of respect and defiance. Having reached adolescence, Alizon had already begun to develop from a child into a young woman who was not displeasing on the eye, unlike their mother with her strange disfigurement. Demdike smiled, seeing a reflection of her younger self standing there, before age had snatched her beauty.

Father Time had been cruel in that regard, blackening her teeth and etching her face with the lines of her many hard years, and planting hairs on the already unsightly mark she bore on her left side. There were as many stories told about that as about her daughter's mismatched eyes. A mark made by the devil himself, they said. The brand of a witch, her neighbours whispered. In truth she had been born with it, yet no one wanted to believe something so mundane from a woman well known to be skilled in the arts of spells and divination. The stories had only grown with her reputation.

Her eldest grandchild slunk in just behind Alizon, his face sullen and his eyes burning with an even greater temper than his sister. James was not far off a man, and he was of an age where he believed himself to be right in all matters, rebelling against any who challenged him and his views. An air of impatience hung about him that morning, as if he thought there were better uses of his time than humouring his old grandmother. He stood there with his arms crossed, sighing heavily to make his point and refusing to look at any of them.

His attitude might have angered Demdike if he'd been anyone else's grandson. But her blood ran through each of the youngsters' veins, forming a bond just as powerful as she shared with her Tibb. That rebellious streak, and the strength each of the adolescents was beginning to discover, came directly from the old wise woman herself. She couldn't help but feel a sense of pride that they'd inherited such traits, and again she was reminded of the girl she'd been in her mid-teens. When her time in this world came to an end, she could at least leave it knowing her legacy lived on.

"Breakfast," Elizabeth interrupted, handing each of them a lump of hard bread. The meagre offering was tough on Demdike's teeth but she chewed it without complaint, though it did little to fill the ache of hunger in their bellies.

"Will you show me more magic, Granny?" Jennet asked between mouthfuls.

"Hush now, child, there'll be time for that later. These old bones need a rest before setting them back to work."

"Later?" Elizabeth said. "I hope you mean back here and

not round Pendle Forest. I know what you were doing out there last night, Mam. It's not safe for us anymore."

"Who is it that's put such fear into you, my girl? There will always be those that abhor and even turn on us when their tolerance runs too thin. But there are still people that recognise the power of the old ways and the help only we of the cunning folk can bring. Or those who grow desperate enough when their prayers fail them and no mortal medicine will provide the cure they seek. Winter will soon be here, and what would you have us do then? Begging and such work as carding wool can only put so much food on our tables; if we want to see another year through we must practise our craft, or go hungry."

Elizabeth opened her mouth as if to argue, but then gave a small shake of her head and bit into her breakfast. She forced the mouthful down with a grimace. "So why did you summon us to meet you and our Alizon here, Mam?"

Demdike nudged Jennet off her lap. "Alizon, go take your sister back outside to play."

Alizon's brow furrowed with indignation. "Why do I have to go? I'm only two years younger than him!"

"Two years too young. Go on, lass; your time will come soon enough."

The adolescent girl huffed and stormed out, barking at her half-sister to follow. Jennet ran after her, impervious to her bad mood.

"Not too far, mind!" Demdike called after them. "We've not long before we need to set about the day's tasks!"

"Well?" Elizabeth asked again, once the girls were out of the way.

Demdike's eyes grew firm as she turned them back on her daughter. "I called you both here because I feel it is time James had a familiar of his own."

All traces of surliness left James's face. Excitement took over, but Elizabeth said "Mam, no! He's too young to make the pact."

"He's almost a man now, and with so many against us, we each need all the protection we can get. Spells calling on unbound spirits can only do so much; you know as well as I the real power lies in the pact, and there is no greater defence against folk that wish us ill than the bond of a familiar. You have your Ball and I have my Tibb. Now James must find his companion."

Again, Elizabeth opened her mouth as if to argue, but then she winced and her shoulders slumped in resignation. "When do we perform the ritual?"

"Summer is ending and Samhain will soon be here. It must be before then or the risk is too great. You know what happens when the veil weakens. Only fools or those afflicted by madness attempt a binding with the veil at its thinnest. Besides, the ingredients we need must be fresh. Better to act now while the plants we want are still plentiful."

Elizabeth nodded. "Tonight, then?"

"Aye, here at twilight."

"I'm ready," James said eagerly. "How will I know which spirit is my familiar?"

"It works two ways – the spirit chooses you as much as you choose him. It may be that you have met him already, or he may come through for the first time tonight, a stranger to us all. All will make sense tonight, lad. Now be off with you to Carr Hall and see what you can do for the Towneleys today."

James nodded and set off with more of a spring in his step than usual. Demdike watched him make his way down the path with a fond smile and a slight shake of her head. Elizabeth continued to radiate worry beside her.

"I hope you're right about this, Mam," she said once he was out of earshot. "He's so quick to anger at the moment. Should we really be binding that temper to the power of a spirit?" Her eyes tracked back and forth, and for a moment it was as if they'd managed to turn back the years. There was a desperation in the way she searched Demdike's face for reassurance, one Demdike hadn't seen since she was James's age. "I fear this can only end in tragedy."

Demdike gave her daughter's arm a loving squeeze. She couldn't really blame Elizabeth for having doubts, but she had been the same age as her grandson when she'd first made the pact with Tibb, all those years ago. The boy was old enough, and she'd feel better knowing he had his own spirit watching over him when she or Tibb couldn't be there to keep an eye on him themselves. That had been all too often of late. At least with Alizon helping out round Malkin Tower she needn't worry too much about her eldest granddaughter, and at such a young age, Jennet was still closely watched over by Elizabeth. But it was all too easy to imagine the trouble her grandson might get himself into. With few friends in the community, he may well have need of an otherworldly companion before long.

The ritual was not without its risks though. There was a reason they'd made the boy wait till he was on the cusp of manhood, but they couldn't protect him from the dangers of their craft forever. If he was to be a cunning man then he had to make the pact sooner or later. Demdike could only pray she had read the signs correctly. If she was wrong, her daughter may well never speak to her again.

Laughter sounded from outside, temporarily banishing such misgivings. Jennet came running in, a daisy chain bouncing around her neck and more flowers in her hair. Alizon was not far behind, her bad mood still apparent in the frown on her face and the rigidity of her body posture as she stood crossing her arms. The girls must have seen their brother leaving and taken it as their cue to return.

Demdike paused a moment longer to watch her youngest granddaughter dancing around the room, before finally giving an answer to the fears Elizabeth had voiced before the interruption. "Have I ever led this family astray, girl? Now let us be about our business as well. We have much to prepare and there is work to be done around the village. You know what to do."

Elizabeth nodded. "Come on, Jennet."

"But, Mam, I want to stay with Granny and Alizon! Can I go begging with them today, please?"

Her daughter looked to her for help, but Demdike didn't mind taking the little girl with them. She had no intention of getting into anything more dangerous than Elizabeth or James, at least not that day. "Aye, lass, you can come with us."

Later that morning, Demdike found herself back out in the sun with her granddaughters. It was a beautiful autumn's morning, yet there was a dreariness to their destination the light couldn't touch. Even Jennet's childish happiness and excitement was sullied by the mood that hung over Wheathead.

Foreboding crept upon them with every step they took. Demdike soon felt Jennet tugging on her arm. It was a silent plea to turn back, and who could blame the girl? The people here had no love for the old ways. Unfortunately, this was the only field where she knew henbane to grow. They couldn't turn back now.

Up the path ahead, there loomed a monument of misery and malice. Bleak and uninviting, the mill itself might have been enough to repel most unwanted visitors. Most, but not she. For Demdike was no stranger to such loathing and had long since hardened to it. Even so, an involuntary shudder ran through her. And there was the bitter man himself, Richard Baldwin, casting the dirtiest of looks their way. No doubt he'd been seething all night. Still, her curse had done one thing. He appeared to be keeping his distance, for the time being at least.

Jennet seemed to take strength from that. The tugging on Demdike's arm stopped as they reached the gate to the mill, and there was a glimmer of fresh excitement in the girl's eyes.

Demdike released Jennet's hand and gripped her shoulder. "Now, listen carefully." She glanced at Alizon, then back down at Jennet. "I want you two to keep watch for me while I gather some plants that grow round these parts. The Baldwins don't much like our family, so you two need to keep an eye on them and let me know if it looks like trouble. Understood?"

Jennet beamed. "Can I help you pick the plants, Granny?"

Demdike laughed and pulled the youngster into a brief hug. "Nay, lass, 'tis not safe for little girls. These flowers are poisonous. You stay close by your sister and warn me if Master Baldwin over there finds the courage to approach."

Alizon said nothing, but she took her little sister's hand, standing alert by the gate to the mill as she'd been asked. Demdike felt Baldwin's eyes following her as she made her way along the wall enclosing his land, treading the same path she'd walked two decades before in the days leading up to her daughter's pact. She felt certain she'd still find the henbane growing in this area, the land changing little over the years. Wheathead didn't disappoint. Pale yellow flowers waved in invitation, their long stalks swaying gently in the breeze. An air of deceptive harmlessness clung to them, one that had taken the life of many an unsuspecting victim.

She paused by the plant to glare at Baldwin, daring him to interfere in matters he could never understand. It wasn't that she particularly feared the man himself. Not when she could easily bring him to his knees again, just as she had out on the moors. No, the real danger was that someone would report her to Roger Nowell, the Justice of the Peace, who would gladly brand her entire family witches and send them to the assizes. And a trial could only ever have one ending, if Nowell had his way. Yet as long as Demdike drew breath, she remained determined that was not to be the fate of her family. She cared less for herself, but those she loved would not hang, as so many had before them – not while she still lived.

Their gazes locked in a brief battle of wills, Baldwin's hate digging its claws into the flint of her defiance. No doubt he called on his god to give him strength against the devilry he perceived in her family, but Demdike was unyielding and after a moment he looked away. He had the grace then to retreat back inside, perhaps to gather his own family and make certain they kept away from the pagans at their gate.

She couldn't help but feel a flash of triumph at Baldwin's retreat, though she knew her victory would likely be short-lived if they lingered on the edge of his land. So she turned her attention back to the henbane and the leaves she needed.

Her concentration was fixed solely on the plants now. One deep breath and their scent could very well lure her into deep sleep, a sleep which there may be no waking from. A fool way to die.

Demdike took great care as she pulled off several leaves and placed them in the basket she carried. Her respect for the natural world and all its dangers served her well. The henbane's poisonous perfume failed to ensnare her and she returned to her grandchildren with a sense of destiny. Events had been set in motion that would forever shape the lives of the people of Pendle Forest, not just in the here and now, but for many decades to come. She could feel it. Come midnight, her grandson would prove himself worthy of taking up the mantle of cunning man, and so would begin the next great chapter in their family's legacy.

The trio retraced their steps from Wheathead, but it wasn't time to go home yet. Demdike led them past the path leading up to Malkin Tower, into Newchurch and towards St Mary's, taking no notice of the reactions of many of their neighbours as they passed.

Jennet was full of questions as they walked. "Why do they make that sign, Granny?"

Demdike glanced at one of the women crossing herself on instinct. Many still worshipped the old religion; not the old ways of the cunning folk, but the Catholic faith they'd been brought up on before King Henry brought this new branch of Christianity which King James now embraced and enforced on the land. And so they warded themselves in the only way they knew how; all those daft enough to share in Baldwin's belief that the cunning folk aligned themselves with the devil and set out to cause harm to everyone they laid eyes upon. Demdike wasn't worried. The Christians would see it differently when they had need of their magic again.

How to explain that to her six-year-old granddaughter, though? "Because they fear us, child. You will understand when you're older."

"Will you put a spell on them?"

Demdike laughed. "Maybe, if they don't keep out of our way."

"Can I help?"

"Not with cursing folk, you're too young."

"But I want to learn magic too! You promised you'd show me more, and it's been hours already since I first asked."

"Indeed I did. Very well then, I'll tell you more about our craft as we walk, and perhaps we'll work a spell together when the preparations are in place for tonight. Agreed?"

"Agreed!"

Demdike took a moment to collect her thoughts. "There are two types of magic in this world. White magic comes from the force of nature, the power held within every rock and tree, earth and water, fire and wind. 'Tis good for protection, removing curses, healing and fertility, and bolstering the land we live on to bring greater harvests and healthier livestock. These are the things men would call blessings from god, but men are fools full of self-importance and silly ideas of power. Their god is nothing, yet they worship him all the same. Those with authority need to believe they are above the rest of us, you see. They need to believe some divine being appointed them because otherwise a king is just a man, a priest just a superstitious fool following rules that hold no real meaning. Nature is where the real power lies, if they weren't so blind to see it.

"But sometimes white magic is not enough. Then you must make a choice, for there is also black magic, darker and more powerful, used to bend the laws of nature and break them as one sees fit. Yet going against nature should not be done lightly, and there is always a price.

"We can also call on spirits to grant us power, both dark and light. And that is what we will be doing later with your brother, and one day for you, when you come of age. Until then you must be patient and make do with the spells and charms fit for young wise women."

How much the little girl understood didn't really matter. She listened intently, the talk of magic casting a spell of its own that seduced and called to many a mortal, and for those brought up around it, how could one so young not find fascination in what others would consider witchcraft? Still, Demdike would be careful not to expose her to anything dangerous at such a tender age. There was no harm in teaching her charms of protection and the like, as she had with the other two at Jennet's age, but black magic and invoking spirits was strictly for when they reached adulthood. And even then she would counsel against the dark arts as much as possible.

Alizon frowned. "I thought you said all magic came from spirits." It was the first time she'd spoken since leaving Malkin Tower.

"Most does, but there is a big difference between a charm which asks the spirits of nature to grant their blessing to heal or protect, and a ritual to invoke a specific spirit to perform something more complicated."

"Why do you need to invoke other spirits when you have a familiar?" There was a light in Alizon's eye then, a sure sign the girl's curiosity had awoken and was now beginning to override her sullen silence.

"Because different spirits have different skills, just like people, and the same goes for our familiars. Hellhounds like my Tibb are fiercely protective, yet they lack the healing touch of other races."

"I want a familiar to play with," Jennet said.

Demdike smiled down at her youngest. "When you are older, lambkin."

A thread of fear entered Alizon's voice. "Gran."

The girl had come to a stop. Her eyes were fixed on something up ahead, something that had brought a tremble to her limbs and drained the colour from her face.

Demdike followed her granddaughter's gaze and felt herself go cold. Her heart quickened, and sweat beaded on her skin. It was the girls she feared for, if only there'd still been time to get them to safety. But it was too late to turn back now, and besides, they needed to visit the church.

There was just time to offer up a quick prayer to the Goddess and the Horned One. Whether they were listening remained to be seen.

CHAPTER
TWO

L ike the henbane flowers, the approaching danger was deceptively harmless to any who didn't know better. She came in the frail form of a woman the equal of Demdike's years, but in this case Father Time had been beyond cruel. Where Demdike stood tall and in good health for her age, Old Chattox had been bent and twisted, her body withered and decrepit. Yet there was nothing weak about those eyes glaring out of the gaunt face.

From the corner of her eye, Demdike caught Alizon taking a step back, pulling Jennet along with her. If it hadn't been for the risk of the girls being struck down by some curse while they ran, Demdike would have bid them return to Malkin Tower, where they'd be safe behind the protective charms she'd laid about the place. Since that wasn't an option, she'd just have to protect them herself as best she could.

"What are you doing here?" Chattox hissed. "Come to steal more work from us, have you?"

"Not today. We have business at St Mary's. Let us pass

and you have my word we will not bother you or get in your way."

"A likely story, Demdike. You think I don't see through you after all these years? One word of a sick cow and you or your family are there before any of us even has a chance."

"Believe what you want but it is the truth, and you will either let us pass or we will be forced to turn our magic on each other, and what good can come of that? It is a fight I think we would both rather avoid."

Chattox laughed, a sound more like a rasping cough. "A fight you would rather avoid maybe. I welcome the chance to put an end to our rivalry."

The words had barely left those thin lips before her eyes took on a faraway look, concentrating on either a curse or summoning her familiar, or both. Her mouth was still moving with muttered words too low for Demdike's old ears to catch, but she didn't need to hear them to know they came from the dark arts. She reached out to her own familiar, begging him both mentally and with a whispered plea. "Tibb, I bid thee, do not forsake me now. Answer my call or I fear we are doomed."

With her inner eye, she could see a dark force building around Chattox. It was as though her rival had stepped into shadow, despite the sun still shining bright overhead.

Tibb!

Demdike called out again with her mind, a desperate cry for his protection.

"I will give you one chance to flee," Chattox said, breaking her chant. And yet her hold on the power never faltered, the darkness around her remaining just as strong. "Run back to your Malkin Tower, and your granddaughters needn't be harmed this day."

Much as it would have wounded her pride, Demdike

might have been tempted to take her up on that offer, if she'd trusted Old Chattox to keep her word. They had till nightfall to return for what they needed from the church, after all. But she was too convinced her rival would attack the moment their backs were turned. "I cannot. Either let us pass or we must fight."

"As you wish."

Chattox resumed her chanting. Demdike frantically began her own spell, settling on one for protection not for herself, but for Alizon and Jennet. A crowd had begun to form around them by that point, morbid fascination bringing even the most fearful of Christians to witness this encounter between the two most notorious figures in Pendle. They might not have understood the danger Demdike and her granddaughters were in, but they had to at least sense the dark power building, even if they couldn't put into words exactly what was causing their unease.

Still Tibb remained absent, even as Chattox's curse began to take hold. A sudden pain racked Demdike's body from head to toe. Her nerves felt like they'd been set alight, tearing a scream from her throat and forcing her hands into tight fists.

Salvation came from an unlikely source. She noticed a man pushing his way through the throng, his stern features set in grim determination. In many ways he was just another familiar about to enter the struggle, bound not to one of the cunning folk but to the resident Justice of the Peace. And the JP's hound shared his master's hatred of witches.

"Anne," Demdike said. The words did not come easy through the pain, but she had to try to reason with her opponent one last time. "Trouble approaches. Our rivalry must wait for another time."

"Trouble? More like you have turned coward and wish to talk your way out," Chattox sneered, breaking the incantation a second time and granting Demdike a temporary reprieve.

"Do not be a fool, Anne. After all these years, you should know me better than that. It is Constable Hargrieves. If he catches us, we will have far worse to fight than each other. You know as well as I where the law stands on witchcraft."

"Let him take us; my Fancie will crush them all before they can hang the likes of me."

"And what then? You would live out the rest of your days an outlaw, forever hunted by all those that would see us dead. Perhaps the King himself would take an interest, and as powerful as your familiar is, even he could not protect you from the entirety of the King's forces."

Chattox scowled, but the darkness around her faded as if it had never been. "Very well, I will leave you be, for now. But be assured this is not the last of it, Demdike."

The decrepit old woman slunk back in the direction of her cottage at West Close, the crowd parting for her like water around a sea serpent. She looked back just once, making Demdike tense again and prepare to start chanting a curse of her own. But the moment passed and her rival continued on her way.

"Come, girls," she said. "We do not need yonder hound sniffing about our business, today of all days."

"What hound?" Jennet scanned the crowd.

"She means the constable," Alizon answered. "We can find a dog to play with later – come on."

The three slipped away before Hargrieves caught up with them. Demdike could hear the muttering as the crowd dispersed, but none of the villagers wanted to be caught up in any dealings with the constable. She felt certain they had successfully evaded him for the time being. Still, it had been a lucky escape, and she remained wary as they continued on their way to St Mary's, especially when one last call for Tibb went unanswered. She would have liked the comfort of his presence with so many threats around, but such was the way of spirits – they came when they saw fit, pact or no.

She was still on edge as they approached the church, the stone tower standing silent vigil over the graves of the Christians buried within its consecrated grounds. It looked more inviting than the likes of Baldwin's mill, and yet there was a cold emptiness as they entered its shadow. Christ was not home.

The Goddess and the Horned One were all around them though. They could be heard in the voices of their children singing in the trees surrounding the graveyard and snorting from the fields. Pendle Hill was concealed behind the slope St Mary's occupied, but the view from the churchyard gate offered a vision of a landscape almost as impressive.

Demdike paused to look out across the acres of fields that dipped and rose in green waves rolling out all the way to the horizon. Did those distant hills bear similar testaments to the cruelty of men as her beloved Pendle Hill with its ghastly token of Puritan injustice?

The moment passed, and she continued along the church path.

Such a place might seem an odd destination for three pagans, but this was not the first time Demdike had been given cause to visit hallowed land. The absent god they worshipped here might not be everything the Christians believed him to be, yet there was power in the faith of the stout believers themselves. It was possible to draw on that power during certain spells and rituals.

That day was not about borrowing from the faith of the

Christians, however. There was even greater power to be had than the relics contained within the church, though this was something which she knew full well could get her in infinitely more trouble. Taking a cross or communion bread was one thing, but this was something else entirely.

"Alizon, I need you to take your sister inside the church now and see what offerings you can beg from the vicar. 'Tis of the utmost importance you keep him and anyone else in there busy while I see to things out here. Can I trust you with this?"

"I'm not a child anymore, Gran; I know the dangers!"

"I should think so, or it will be your corpse I next tend to out on the moors."

"I'm not hanging just so James can get his familiar. Why can't he do all this himself?"

"He will have his own trials to face tonight, just as you will when your time comes. Trust me, lass, you don't live to my age by being careless. But it is my neck at risk if we're caught, so take your sister inside the church and distract them while I tend to things out here."

Her granddaughter muttered something unintelligible and grabbed Jennet's hand, stamping into the church as instructed. Demdike waited until she heard them speaking with the vicar, then she turned her attention to the real purpose of their visit.

Tibb might not have deigned to respond to her summons that morning but there were plenty of other spirits around. She could sense them as she moved through the graveyard, all the ghosts of those who had passed but found no peace in death. Reduced to shadows of their former selves, they would pace restlessly until the end of time. They made her hair stand on end, not from fear, but rather the energy they gave off. It was a power all of its own, though one that paled in comparison to that of the otherworldly spirit creatures like her familiar. And Fancie. They'd been lucky he had not chosen to show himself either. If he had, Chattox may not have been persuaded to surrender before the constable so easily.

Demdike pushed such thoughts aside. There was no sense dwelling on what might have been. Chattox and her familiar were a problem for another day, and the dead were no threat. There was only the living to fear at present. And despite the distraction of her granddaughters for those inside the church, there was still one of the living she must deal with herself.

In the far corner of the graveyard he stood, his cruel whip the bane of many a hungry dog come scavenging for a morsel. By his feet lay the treasure Demdike sought – a macabre heap of off-white pieces evicted from their resting places to make room for newer residents. She just had to convince the whipper-out to allow her to take what she needed.

A flicker of panic passed through the young man's eyes when he saw her coming. He seemed to waver for a moment, like he was on the verge of deserting his post, but he soon found new strength. No doubt his position with the Church gave him the feeling of importance he needed. Demdike almost admired the way he straightened up and brandished the length of leather with all the menace he could muster. "Be gone, pest! The Church does not recognise your heathen ways; we have nothing for you here."

"There is something I need and I will not leave here empty handed, so you might as well stand aside now, lad, and let me take my prize."

The boy looked puzzled, so Demdike turned her gaze on

the pile of bones by his feet. His face paled, his grip tightening on the whip as he muttered "Lord protect us."

"Come now, lad, there be no law against taking a few old bones, so long as they are just lying there and no grave robbery is committed."

"These poor souls are at rest. How in good conscience can I let you take them to use for your evil purposes? Think of their living relatives if naught else!"

"Don't talk nonsense, lad; their relatives are long since in the ground themselves. The graveyard is already overrun with any who might have mourned them, the people they once were long since passed from living memory. None will miss the scalps I've come for."

"And what of their souls? I'll not let you disturb their peace for the sake of some wicked spell."

"Then you leave me no choice, Jack Robinson. I will call their spirits to rise up here and now and strike you down, and I will have what I came for."

The young man paled further. It was a matter of seconds before his nerve failed him and he began to back away, hands raised and whip drooping harmlessly at his side. "Take them then; I don't want no trouble."

Demdike smiled to herself and knelt beside the grim mound. She'd had no real intention of hurting the lad, who was only trying to do the job he was paid for. Often the mere threat of a curse was all it took.

She began to sift through the remains, careful not to damage any of them. Her wrinkled hands passed over each one with respect while she felt around with that sense which went far beyond the physical realm. It was skulls she needed, or scalps as they often called them. So she focused on the energy of each and every one the pile had to offer, searching for the strongest. Three stood out, echoes of the lives they'd led still resonating within the craniums which once housed all they'd been as flesh and blood.

She claimed all three, hiding them in her basket beneath a scrap of material, safe from any prying eyes. "You may return to your duties now, lad. The Church need never know these old scalps went astray on your watch."

The young man didn't look happy, but he kept quiet. Demdike made her way back through the graves, confident he wouldn't cause her any more trouble, for the time being at least. The girls emerged from the church just ahead of her. She re-joined them, pleased to see the vicar had taken pity on her family that day. It wasn't much, but in the basket Alizon carried there was now an onion, a lump of cheese and more bread – enough to keep all three of them going till their evening meal.

There was just one ingredient left, then it was up to her daughter to fulfil her role and bring the most important piece, the main focus of power to allow James to see into the spirit realm and find the one who would be guide, companion and protector. If Elizabeth failed to obtain that focus, they would have no option other than to wait a while longer. But Demdike felt sure fate was on their side.

Again she felt a sense of destiny as she led her grand-daughters to the area of forest around Newchurch, nibbling at the vicar's offerings as they walked. This last plant shouldn't pose too much trouble at least. It grew on the very edge of the forest where the tree cover wasn't so dense, sparing them the need to face any further danger that day.

Demdike located the distinctive orange berries with relative ease, though it was the root she really needed. As with the henbane, the plant appeared harmless, but it was so steeped in superstition that few dared go anywhere near it. She'd worked with the plant often enough to know the dangers were greatly overexaggerated, but her grand-daughters were wary.

Their disappointment was plain to see when she pulled the mandrake from its bed of dirt to reveal an ordinary root. With a bit of imagination, it was possible to see the human figure the girls were looking for, yet it was distinctly lacking in a mouth sounding the deadly scream of folktales. That didn't mean it couldn't kill though, and she placed it straight into her basket with the other pieces she'd gathered before either of her granddaughters could get too close.

Their part in the day's preparations done, the trio spent the rest of the day begging until the sun began its descent, signalling the time had come to return to Malkin Tower. For it was there the real work would begin.

"Granny, you promised!"

"So I did. Come then, child, let us work a quick charm while we wait for your mother." Demdike smiled at her youngest granddaughter's eagerness to learn their craft, patting the bench for Jennet to sit at the table beside her. The little girl didn't need to be told twice. "Alizon, be a dear and get the pottage on for when James and your mother return."

Her eldest granddaughter let out an almighty sigh, but she did as asked, trudging out to fill the pot with fresh water from the nearby stream. Demdike paid no mind to Alizon's attitude, retrieving her tools from where she'd left them earlier and unwrapping the bundle. She took out the pendant and held it up to the light still streaming through the window so little Jennet could see. Silver glinted as it spun on its string, worth more than all their other belongings put together. "This belonged to my mam, and her mother before her, and her mother before that. It has been passed down through the generations of this family, from mother to daughter, father to son, so that each of us may draw strength from all those that came before us. One day it will pass to one of you, when my body returns to the earth and you have greater need of it than I."

The young girl had already seen enough death to understand what was meant by that. Her eyes filled with tears. "But, Granny, I don't ever want you to die!"

"'Tis the way of life, child. Dry your eyes now and enjoy the time we have, and take comfort that when we are parted it will not be a true parting of ways, for I shall still watch over you in spirit, till your own time comes and we are reunited on the other side."

Jennet sniffed. "Promise?"

"Aye, lass, I promise. And fear not, I do not think life is done with me just yet. Now, till such a time comes when the pendant may pass to you, we will see about making you your own charm. But not today."

"Then what are we going to do today, Granny?"

Demdike placed the silver pentagram in her granddaughter's hand. "I will teach you a spell of protection against evil spirits, and you can use the family pendant for now."

"But I thought you said I was too young for working with spirits."

"Yes, child, but sometimes spirits seek us out whether we want them to or not, and with Samhain drawing closer, it is as well you have some protection for if the worst should happen. Now repeat after me:

"Spirits of earth and spirits of air,
Ancient spirits of nature's beauty and fair,
By the power in this charm I call on thee,
Grant this favour asked by me,
Watch over me this night of danger and threat,
Protect me from dark spirits and demons met,
Keep me from harm while at risk I remain,
Spare me from sorrow and grievous pain."

The little girl did her best to memorise the verse while Alizon returned with the pot full of water and set about making their dinner. Running footsteps soon reached their ears. It was James rushing back for the ritual he'd been promised, a stupid, excited grin plastered firmly on his face. Elizabeth wasn't far behind.

Demdike sensed her grandson was burning with questions, but he restrained himself while they ate. The pottage had little flavour that day, each spoonful bland on their tongues. But the mix of water, grain and vegetables at least had a warmth that chased the chill creeping into the air as the sunlight faded. And it was better than nothing at all, which was what came all too often of the days and weeks where begging was less fruitful and work was harder to come by. No doubt they had more of that to look forward to during the winter months.

Once their bowls were empty, Jennet was sent to bed and Alizon was tasked with rinsing out the dishes. Again her eldest granddaughter seemed disgruntled with her chores, not least because it meant missing out on more of the adult affairs. But she did so without argument. It wouldn't keep her busy for long, but it gave time for the words that needed to be said.

The moment the two younger siblings were out of the

way, it was as if a dam broke within James, a flood of questions bursting from his mouth.

"So how does it work?"

"I'm not going to lie to you, lad. Making the pact is dangerous – it could cost you your life," Demdike answered. "Some spirits will certainly try to take your soul, but whatever you do, you must not enter that kind of bargain. You will be made many offers, but only you will know the right spirit to call familiar. Choose wisely and do not jump into the first deal you are offered. You're searching for the spirit you feel the strongest connection with."

"My soul? I thought it was only during Samhain demons can come through?"

"Demons will always come through if given the chance. There will just be less of them than during Samhain."

"How do the spirits come through? Will I be able to see them? Do we have to conjure them?"

"There is a ritual, but we won't be conjuring them so much as we'll be calling to them and seeing who answers. They won't physically manifest in the room for you, so we have gathered the ingredients to help you see."

James seemed to think about that and opened his mouth to ask something else, but Demdike shook her head. "No more questions now. We have a potion to brew and a rite to prepare." She turned to her daughter. "You have them?"

"Yes," Elizabeth answered.

"Then let us begin."

CHAPTER

THREE

Alone figure made its way up to Malkin Tower, shivering in the bitter air that slithered through daylight's gate and ensnared the land in the cold of night. That evening it was especially crisp, given strength by the clear skies overhead.

Under cover of darkness, he remained unseen by the eyes of fellow mortals, though that brought him little comfort as he picked his away across the fields. Only fools ventured out at night, or those with evil intent. And then there were the dangers of things worse than men – all manner of foul beasts and agents of the Devil. Foulds could only pray for the Lord's protection from the many risks to both his life and his soul, not least of which awaited in that dread building to which he must go.

Strange sounds carried on the wind, and more than once he jumped at the sensation of something brushing against his skin. There came the cry of some unnatural creature and the splash of goblins dragging a poor unfortunate soul down to a watery grave. His heart thundered an unnatural rhythm and sweat trickled over his flesh, despite the night's chill.

No lantern marked his progress. Foulds preferred to slip through the shadows and avoid the less savoury characters he might otherwise have met – a decision he was beginning to regret. Several times he stumbled on the uneven ground, cursing. If it weren't for the greater fear of what would become of him if he failed in his task, he wouldn't be out at all, and it was that fear that drove him on.

By the Lord's grace, he reached his destination without coming to any harm, for which he thanked God profusely. Yet the worst was still to come, and so he took a moment to say another prayer, asking for further protection from the witches and any curses they might have laid around their home. The prayer did little for his nerves, and he could only hope the Demdike clan would not hear the pounding in his chest as he crouched by the window, peering cautiously through the translucent, oil-soaked linen. He felt sure they would see him there, but again God was on his side. It seemed they were far too caught up in whatever devilry they were currently working to pay him any heed, and a moment later he braved peeling back the edge of the linen where it had frayed away from its wooden frame.

The old crone was a dark figure moving round the family's table in the glow from the fire. Squinting Lizzie followed her lead, while the two older grandchildren sat and watched. Their voices sounded loud and clear in his ears as Demdike said "We're not far off ready now. Alizon, go watch over your sister. Should you sense any spirits taking an interest in either of you girls, I need you to speak the charms to ward them off."

"But I want to watch James make his pact!"

"You've seen enough for tonight, lass. You will get your turn, in time."

"Yes, Alizon, you're too young for this," James taunted.

"None of that now," Demdike answered sharply. "Go on, Alizon. Keep Jennet safe and I'll teach you something new on the morrow."

The granddaughter's face was the very picture of youthful frustration, but she did as she was told, stamping out of the room with a loud sigh.

Foulds couldn't see much of what the two older women were working at, the table obscured by their vile bodies, though if he had to guess he would have said they were crushing something. He dreaded to think what this pact was the young witch had just referred to. A pact with the Devil perhaps?

His patience began to run thin as the minutes wore on. The night's chill continued its assault on his face and hands, and his nerves stretched tauter at every rustle of grass or crunch of dead leaves. He was just about ready to return to the safety of his home, thinking to make up some story about the witches for his master, when finally Old Demdike shifted to the side, revealing what they'd been working on.

Plant juices stained a mortar and pestle, shining in the candlelight where they were still fresh. Three skulls grinned their macabre smiles beside the mortar, and to his horror, the hags set about grinding each of them into a powder as well. Only the teeth survived the process. Put to one side for later use, perhaps? Then the whore with her monstrous deformity, no better for the shadows which partially concealed her face, took a knife to a living bat and bled its wing. Where the animal came from, Foulds couldn't say, but it seemed to him that she had conjured it from thin air.

These ghoulish parts all went into a cup, his stomach turning at the very thought of drinking such a foul potion.

"I know you have already begun to learn how to work with spirits," Demdike said to her grandson. "But tonight we will open your inner eye, and once you have made the pact, you will see much more than you ever could without it."

She nodded at Squinting Lizzie, who produced the final items, wrapped in a filthy rag. They handled the bundle with such care that Foulds could only assume it was something rare and of great value, not as easily obtained as the other ingredients they'd gathered. Excitement filled him when he realised it might be stolen. If he could give his master evidence of theft as well as witchcraft, he may just be rewarded, or at the very least, if they could convict the family, he would never have to do this again. Thus he watched them peel back the shroud with bated breath. But when the witches exposed their treasure, it was all Foulds could do not to cry out. For there on the table sat a pair of human eyes, wide and seemingly staring straight at him. Red tendrils had crept through the whites, surrounding the blue like a nest of thorns, while gruesome pink fetters trailed behind each one where they'd been cut from the skull.

Foulds almost baulked and ran at the sight of them, especially when the older hag crushed them as if they were no more than another kind of plant and added them to their devilish brew. But morbid fascination kept him at the window, and so he continued to bear witness to this strange and abhorrent rite.

The smell of tallow reached his nostrils as Demdike lit three candles, intoning:

"Coming of age and coming of power,
A spirit he seeks in this great hour,
A familiar to call on when in need,
Who will this summons heed?"

She repeated the verse three times, then held the potion out to her grandson and bid him "Drink."

The boy grimaced and hesitated to accept the cup from his grandmother.

"You must drink it. 'Tis the only way you will find the spirit that calls to you most strongly, the one you will make a pact with. Drain the contents and see through the veil."

James seemed to be fighting an inner battle with himself, no doubt his lust for power wrestling with his revulsion. In the end, the desire for power won out, and the young witch did as instructed, though he wore a look of disgust the instant the potion touched his tongue. It looked like he was having to force it down. Foulds almost felt sorry for the lad, who might have grown to be a Christian if he hadn't been unfortunate enough to be born into the Demdike clan.

A part of him wanted to leave the witches then, thinking he'd seen enough. But he hesitated long enough to see James's skin turn as pale as a corpse and bead with sweat. The cup fell from the boy's hands, then the young witch's eyes rolled up into the back of his head, so only the whites showed, and it was as if Foulds had also been placed under an enchantment.

Foulds's hand moved in the sign of the cross, but there was an absentmindedness to it. His eyes refused to wander, as though bewitched. He could only stand and continue to watch through the window that offered a mere glimpse into this blasphemous world he could never understand.

CHAPTER
FOUR

D emdike couldn't blame her grandson for his reluctance to drink. She remembered all too well the horrible taste of the potion to open the inner eye. When it took effect and his sight passed from the physical world through to the spiritual, she was taken back to the night she'd made her pact. The night she'd first met Tibb.

Her throat convulsed as she forced herself to swallow the thick mixture she'd been given. It felt to be fighting her every inch of the way down, and she struggled against the urge to cough and retch, and bring it back up. Willpower alone made her keep drinking until she'd drained the cup. Then she gave one final, mighty swallow, and gripped the arms of the chair against the nausea.

"That's it, my girl. Keep it down, and find your familiar."

A steeliness entered her eyes as Demdike raised them to meet her mother's gaze. Except it didn't seem to be her mother anymore.

The walls of their humble home looked to be fading

away. A kind of mist crept over their surroundings, obscuring everything and turning her mother from the woman she knew so well to an indistinct shape, one she felt had become intangible. Even that faded. Soon Demdike was alone in the thick fog bank – an endless expanse of it. There was nothing looming in the grey, no buildings or people or even trees. Not even her beloved Pendle Hill. Nor were there any sounds echoing within its dismal depths. She was alone.

Oddly, she didn't feel particularly scared. Confident as ever, Demdike rose from the chair to find that too had faded, and started forward. Drinking the potion would help her see through the veil, her mam had said. Did that mean this mist was the veil? She could only assume so. The mist was the veil, which the potion had given her the ability to see. It was down to her to cross the rest of the way through now.

Another step, and another, and another. Demdike lost count of how many she'd taken. The mist showed no signs of thinning, her surroundings as grey and apparently empty as ever. But a prickle of the hairs at the back of her neck brought the sudden suggestion that she was no longer alone.

Demdike turned slowly and scanned the grey. Still there was nothing to see. She resumed her journey onward, and with each new step, her conviction something was watching strengthened.

A sense of foreboding crept into her heart. This was not the experience her mam had described. Where were the spirits lining up to offer her a pact? Why was she caught in the veil, alone but for this unseen thing watching and waiting for the Goddess knew what? The first stab of fear did go through her then. What if her body was rejecting the potion? What if her physical self was retching and heaving the liquid she'd had to fight so hard to swallow, and it had left her here, trapped between worlds? What if her mam was trying to wake her, trying and failing while she remained here, at the mercy of whatever lurked in the mist?

No. Giving in to panic would get her nowhere. Demdike drew herself to her full height, and the steeliness returned to her gaze.

"Show yourself."

She poured all her will into those two words, all the confidence that came from the simple knowledge she was of the blood of some of the most powerful cunning folk ever to walk the earth. And she waited.

There was no response, yet her certainty she was not alone remained. Something was taking an interest in her. Something altogether too dark and sinister. She could feel it now. No, not it. **Him.** He forced himself into her consciousness like the pressure of a coming storm, a build up of villainous energy reaching into her mind and flooding her with new thoughts, new feelings. But he was powerful. So powerful. And the things she could do with such power – she could be the greatest wise woman in all of history, if only she would reach out and take his hand, and accept all the gifts he would bestow upon her. Gifts of magic far beyond the comprehension of other cunning folk, gifts fit for a god. The things she could do with such gifts. No one need ever die on her watch, or suffer, or struggle to eke a living when the weather turned harsh and crop yields were low. Her family need never know hunger or sickness, or even the cruel touch of time. They could have eternity, young and beautiful until the end of time. All she had to give him in return was her soul.

Doubt niggled at the back of her mind. Demdike

ignored it. There was a shape in the mist, something not quite human, though she couldn't have said why she thought that. His arm was outstretched and she reached toward him, striding boldly forward.

"Look for the spirit you feel the strongest connection with, but don't lose sight of what is most precious." The words rose through the building darkness, and for a moment she was looking at her mam's face, grave as she spoke her warning but not completely devoid of the loving warmth Demdike knew so well.

"Power?" Demdike had asked.

Her mam tutted. "Power? Nay, I've brought you up better than that. I'm talking about your soul, girl. Do not agree to anything that costs your soul."

The memory broke through the power's seductive pull and Demdike came to her senses, her fingers mere inches from touching the spirit's. Fresh fear swept through her. Fear and shame. Whoever this spirit was, he had almost claimed her as his own, in this life and the next. And all it had taken was a few promises of power. Thank the Goddess her mam wasn't here to see. The thought of that disappointment was almost too much to bear.

Demdike dropped her arm to her side and balled her hands into fists, clenching them as she struggled to gather her will. The thoughts of her mam had helped push back the darkness, but the spirit's hold was still strong. Her mind was far from clear.

"My soul is my own!" she all but screamed, and wrenched herself from his grasp with all the strength she could muster, turning away and forcing her feet in the opposite direction. It was enough. The promises of power and all she could accomplish with it turned from deafening thoughts to the barest of suggestive whispers, then they faded away and the fog began to recede with them, revealing the moors she knew so well. The rest of the spirits came flooding in.

It was overwhelming at first, like she'd entered an overcrowded room full of voices all clamouring to be heard. It was as though she were moving through that room, guided only by instinct as she pushed her way through the throng. Many of the spirits tried to grab her as she passed, especially those of a darker nature, but none had the same power as the being she'd broken free from. She struggled on without becoming ensnared again until she saw the face of a bald man with fiery eyes, glinting like gemstones. She might have mistaken him for human if it hadn't been for those eyes, the pupils like two slits gouged by claws. Then he spoke, and his voice thundered so loudly it seemed as though it should be coming from a much larger chest.

"I offer knowledge and wealth, if you will bind yourself to me." Those eyes fixed on her, and she had a sense of something ancient in the otherwise youthful-looking, hairless face.

Wariness seized her. Her mam had said the spirit would bind itself to her, not the other way around. She tried her best to shield her emotions from him, careful to show the respect he deserved. "I am honoured one so great would come through to offer his aid for a mere mortal such as I, but I fear you are not the familiar I seek."

The man resonated calm indifference at that, his human skin shedding as his body swelled to take on the shape of something huge. Wariness gave way to shock. This was not a demon or an animal spirit like her mother's. No, he was a creature of stories, a thing of legend. He was a dragon.

She very nearly changed her mind at the sight of so

magnificent a beast, almost called out to him that yes, she would bind herself to him. But again she found the strength to resist temptation.

A second spirit drew her over, though this one was not in the guise of a man. The bear offered strength and courage at a much lower cost, yet instinct told her that this pact was still not the right one. So again she turned the deal down and pressed on, only to find herself facing another powerful creature. This third one didn't speak; he simply turned his predatory gaze on her, and she felt an instant connection as their eyes met.

He was considerably smaller than the dragon, yet no less breathtaking. Fur the black of night covered his body, rather than the tawny colour she'd heard described in stories. It thickened into an impressive mane around his feline head, neck, shoulders and chest, and his eyes blazed red. Here were two more flames she was in danger of falling into. Demdike almost reached out to touch him, but still something held her back.

A clawed hand reached out to her the moment she turned away. That was practically all she could see of this fourth spirit, his body shrouded in darkness. All but his eyes: twin orbs of malice which etched themselves so deeply in her memory that she would never forget the way they glowed from within the shadows. Devilish cruelty and promises of pain for all those that crossed him burned through his gaze.

Demdike felt the same power she'd turned down once pulling at her again. She found herself drawn towards him as though in a trance, and she was unable to resist now. His proposition came in a seductive tone oozing temptation.

"I offer dark magic the likes of which you have never seen." His voice hummed with that same great force which had been there right from the start of her spirit journey, and again his thoughts seeped into her mind. "None shall stand against you so long as I am by your side. You already know what I ask in return, if you are willing."

Here was power far beyond anything the others had to give. Why wouldn't she say yes? Her fingers reached for the outstretched hand once more.

"Power?" Her mam tutted in the back of her mind. "Nay, I've brought you up better than that. I'm talking about your soul, girl. Do not agree to anything that costs your soul."

The thought of her mam's disappointment returned. Demdike's voice came out weak and shaking, but she came to a stop, and she managed the words "I am not."

There was a narrowing to the demon's eyes, but the gleam in them suggested he was smiling, not scowling. "Take a moment to consider it. I do not make this offer lightly, and it is not for just any wise woman. We could do great things together, you and I."

"I do not doubt that, but the price is too high." Demdike's voice regained its strength. "I cannot accept your offer."

The spirit did scowl then, and he growled his displeasure. Darkness began peeling back from his features. Demdike's resolve hardened and she turned away a second time, sparing herself the sight of his true face. She was still left shaken by the experience, however, to the point where a weaker-willed woman might have backed out of making the pact at all. But she was the wise woman destined to become Demdike of Pendle Forest, and she would not flee back to the physical world without achieving what she'd set out to do. She would find her true familiar, or die trying.

Those clawed hands made a grab for her as she moved on. But she was ready for it, for his attempt to claim her and keep her in the spirit realm, while her body died to the effects of the potion and her mam looked helplessly on. The dangers of seeking a familiar had been impressed on her in the days spent preparing. She knew so powerful a demon wouldn't allow her to simply walk away, and she ducked his grasping fingers, and ran. Only when she'd slipped through the evil spirit's clutches did *he* appear to her.

Stepping out from the crowd in his human form, he smiled at her with youthful features pleasing on the eye. That face felt like one she knew of old, as if he were a friend she'd once been close to, but had long since lost touch with over the years. And yet she couldn't remember ever meeting him before.

His green eyes were filled with a warmth to rival those of her mam, twinkling invitingly beneath his head of black hair. Demdike was not fooled. She sensed he was another dark spirit behind that familiar, friendly smile, and much more than just a man. But dark is not the same as evil. It was not the same quality of darkness as the demon she'd turned down, nor was this man ruled by the same malevolent nature all demons burned with. No, what she sensed of him was all she could hope for in a spirit companion, and when he spoke, she knew he would be hers.

"I offer loyalty and strength. None shall harm you and yours so long as it is within my power to protect you, and should any enemies cause you grief, I will bring vengeance."

He didn't resonate the same power as the others, but in him she felt a similar kind of connection as with companion animals like dogs and cats, different to the feral nature of the bear and the lion. It was that as much as anything that resounded so deeply within her. She didn't doubt his promise of loyalty, and it would come as no surprise to learn of his hellhound form.

Demdike felt a smile tugging at the corners of her mouth. The blow to her confidence was already forgotten. "What would you have of me in return?"

"I ask only to be allowed to feed from time to time, when I am in need of your strength."

Her smile didn't falter. "To feed?"

"To sup at your blood, if I may."

She nodded. "That seems fair. I accept your offer."

"Then bleed for me now, to seal the pact and bind me to you forever more."

She couldn't explain what happened next. Somehow a cut opened up on her palm, even though no blade had come near her flesh. She held up that bleeding hand and Tibb mirrored her, an identical gash running through his own skin which he pressed to hers. Their blood mingled in a passionate rush, until she was jolted back into the waking world, her clothes damp with sweat and her breathing ragged. The ignorant might have tried to tell her it had been no more than a dream caused by the henbane and mandrake root, but then she heard the spirit's voice again, and there could be no doubt.

"You may call me Tibb."

Tibb. She smiled at that. Yes. Her Tibb, loyal and fierce and a companion like no other, from now until the end of time.

That same voice spoke to her from beyond her memories, and Demdike was brought firmly back to the present.

"You are not alone."

"A fine time for you to show up," she answered, turning to look at the handsome, black-haired man. "Where were you earlier when I had need of your protection?"

"I am here now, and I come with the warning: you are not alone. You are being watched."

"Let them watch; wouldn't be the first time," she replied, though she dropped her voice to a low whisper.

"He has seen the eyes. There will be talk of murder."

She sighed, inwardly cursing the villagers for sticking their noses into her business. Why couldn't they just let them be? No one had died by her hand. 'Twas the hangman who'd claimed the life of the thief, not their family. By the time Elizabeth had gotten to the body, the condemned man would have had no further use for his eyes. Her daughter had committed no crimes, and yet they would be judged as though they too were criminals if they didn't keep tongues from wagging. Even though her daughter would not have been the only one to claim a prize from the gallows that day.

Tibb's gaze remained steady and unwavering, patient and loyal as ever. "What would you have me do?"

"Put such fear in him that he dare not speak out against us, nor share what he has seen. But do him no harm – it will only make matters worse if he suffers any injury or sickness on this patch of land we call home."

Tibb bowed his head, though she sensed his disappointment. "As you wish."

With that, he vanished, only to reappear somewhere outside as the black hellhound again. In her mind, she was presented with an image sent through his link to her, a vision of the land as he saw it. She could hear the beat of the intruder's heart running fast as a stag before a wolf, and his breathing made ragged and shallow in fear's glen, this weak mortal man who was nothing but prey to so mighty a beast as he. She felt Tibb's hunger for blood, a deep ache in her belly worse than that of her own hunger, and his longing to tear into soft flesh. Yet the man's face was hidden to her. His form was murky to her inner eye, despite her familiar's greater night vision. She focused on the image, willing it into clarity.

"Mam!" Her daughter's voice cut through the vision, breaking her concentration. The images faded to nothingness. "Should he not have returned to us by now? Is there naught we can do to help him back?"

Demdike suppressed a sigh and looked across at Elizabeth's worried face. Dread threatened to take hold as she turned to look at James's still form, sitting upright in the chair with only the whites of his eyes staring sightlessly ahead. Demdike pushed the dread aside. She needed to be strong for the both of them.

"He must find his own way back, same as it was for you the night of your pact. Fear not, girl, our blood – our strength – runs through him. He will return to us, in time."

She made her voice as reassuring as she could, yet as the minutes wore on with no change in her grandson, she began to feel doubt creeping in, and the dread returned. She'd been so sure James was ready for this, but it was taking much longer than it had for Elizabeth, and longer than she felt it had been when she'd drank the potion herself. Had she been wrong to try and lead him deeper into the world of spirits that night? Was he too young after all, just as Elizabeth had feared?

Demdike offered up a silent prayer then, beseeching help from the ancient Goddess of her ancestors, whom Christian men had tried so hard to bury in the sands of time. If they'd had their way, her family would have been converted to Catholicism long ago. But the old ways were too important to simply be forgotten. The cunning folk knew their duties, and so they had kept them alive through the ages, against all the odds. Did the Goddess recognise that? Of course she did. She valued the worship of her loyal servants, and she would lend her aid to those who truly needed it, when she could. There was every chance the Goddess would choose to intervene on this occasion as well, and guide James back if he needed it.

Still there was no change. Just as Demdike feared her prayers would go unanswered, finally a cut appeared on her grandson's hand and he began to stir. His eyes rolled forward to look out on the mortal world once more, and a name formed on his lips.

"Dandy."

"James!" Elizabeth cried, rushing to his side.

Demdike felt the same sense of relief as her daughter, but she merely smiled at her grandson, unwilling to let them see she'd ever doubted his return. There also came the flash of triumph that once again their blood had withstood the spirits' test and found new power through the pact.

A large black dog slid into view, similar to her Tibb. He gave James's hand a quick nuzzle, and then he was gone. Her pride swelled.

"Welcome back, lad," she said. "Dandy is the name he bid you call him by, I take it?"

"Yes."

"Be careful who you share that name with now. Some folk would try to claim him as their own given half the chance, and if they know his name they can call on him just as you do."

"Is that not what the pact is for, to bind him to me?"

"Names are powerful things. If your Dandy proves to be a loyal spirit he will honour the deal you just made. But if another calls on him and gives him a better offer then he may well make a new pact. Better to be safe and keep his name in the family for now."

"Yes, Gran."

"No doubt you will be excited to work with him, but you must be careful. Spirits have a will of their own, and those of a darker nature love nothing better than to exact revenge on those that cross us. Guard your thoughts against ill wishes made in anger, or Dandy may well take an action you come to regret."

James nodded and pushed his mother away. "Will I be able to talk with him same as you with Tibb?"

"Aye, lad, now your inner eye is open you will have no trouble speaking with your Dandy, though it will take time and practice before your bond is as strong as mine and Tibb's. But enough for now. 'Tis late and time we were in bed. You two can sleep here again tonight, if you wish."

James shook his head. "I can't sleep yet. I think I'll walk back home and clear my head."

Elizabeth looked like she wanted to stop him, but Demdike whispered "Let him go, lass. Dandy will protect him."

Her daughter looked like she wanted to argue but again she held her tongue. They watched James make his way down the path, a new confidence to his stride now. He was swallowed by the night within minutes.

Elizabeth shook her head. "I still say he was too young for the pact. That temper of his will be the death of us."

"And I still say you worry too much, girl. There's enough brains in that head of his to keep him out of trouble."

Silence fell between them as they retreated to the bedroom. It was cramped for the whole family, and if James had stayed, one of them would have been forced to sleep as best they could at the table. In his absence there was just enough room for them to squeeze on the mattresses. Jennet was already asleep, but Alizon had kept watch over her little sister, though her resentment at being left out was still plain to see.

"You've done well, lass," Demdike said. "In the morning, I'll teach you that new thing I promised."

"I bet it's not as good as getting a familiar spirit," Alizon huffed.

"Perhaps not, but it might go some way to make up for having to wait."

With that, Demdike settled down to rest. Sleep came much easier than in her youth and she was soon in a dream world herself, where she would remain until the dawning of the new day.

CHAPTER FIVE

That same night, sleep remained elusive for Richard Baldwin. No matter how he tossed and turned, all he could see were the eyes of the Devil's wenches fixing him in their glare and holding him in torment. It was as though he were still trapped out there on the moors, still caught in the hex the old hag had placed on him. And then she'd had the audacity to come to his land. The way she'd looked at him with such defiance, it set his blood boiling just thinking about it.

He dreaded to think what she'd been doing out there; teaching her granddaughters some of her strange and unholy customs, no doubt, so they could continue her unnatural work once she finally had the decency to shuffle off the mortal coil and leave him be. But what if it was more than that? He grew uneasy at the thought she might have come back to finish what she'd started out by the hanged women. Perhaps she had been cursing the land so that all he had worked so hard to accomplish in life would crumble around him, his family withering away until he was left with nothing.

His heart quickened as such dark suspicions played through his mind. But what could he do? He wanted to believe the God he had devoted his life to would protect him from Satan and his servants, yet his faith alone had not been enough to keep him from Demdike's wicked clutches. It seemed he would have to take matters into his own hands then, because one thing was clear: the witches had to go. Their stain needed removing from society for the sake of all of Pendle.

There was a sigh, and movement in the bed beside him. "What troubles you, husband?"

"'Tis naught you need concern yourself with. Go back to sleep."

His wife snorted. "And how am I to sleep with you turning so restlessly beside me? It's the witches again, isn't it."

He didn't answer, staring up at the ceiling where those accursed eyes continued to glower back.

"You still haven't told me what you were doing out there in the first place. You ought to know better than to wander the moors at night, Richard Baldwin."

"Christ, woman, can't you leave it be? There's little wonder I'm laid awake with your infernal questions plaguing me, as if the witches aren't enough!"

He couldn't see her face in the darkness, but he sensed the anger he'd ignited in her once more. It seemed she was opting to give him the silent treatment as no answer was forthcoming, which he thought to be an improvement on the ruins of their relationship. None could know the reason he'd braved the night and all its dangers, and doubtless would do again, least of all his wife. He had yet to think up a convincing lie for her though, so her questions were best avoided altogether. If only it hadn't been for that fated meeting with Demdike, she might not have discovered he'd been out there at all. But there was no hiding the blood-stained clothes from her prying eyes. He'd been forced to admit to going out and being hexed then, for what other reason could he have given for all the blood?

Sleep became all the harder for the brief exchange with Jenneta, and before long the weak light of dawn was just starting to seep in through the window. He resigned himself to another day spent with no rest, climbing out of the bed and dressing himself. It was a little earlier than he needed to be up, but there was no sense in lying there when sleep continued to evade him. And it would not do to nod off and oversleep that morning, of all mornings. Not when it was a market day.

Still seething, Richard went out and loaded the grain he had to trade onto a cart. He was in no mood for dealing with Jenneta again that morning, or even his daughters, and he headed straight off for Colne without even giving them so much as a goodbye. He would be one of the first there but that didn't bother him – he welcomed the solitude for as long as it lasted.

Market day was always lively, and this one would be no different. That morning saw all manner of people who lived in and around Colne bustling through the town. Among them were none other than those whores who'd haunted his night. To Richard's disgust, they preyed on the Godly folk in the crowd, using their powers to trick any they spoke with into parting with their hard-earned money or goods. He wondered that the Justices hadn't dealt with these pests sooner, but none stopped them as they went about their begging.

The presence of the witches did nothing for his bad mood. And then she caught him looking and fixed him with her stare again, the worst of them, that wrinkled old hag. Her gaze was so piercing he imagined she could see right through him.

Richard felt a sudden stab of fear. ***She knew.*** It wasn't enough that she had such power over men through witch-craft, but now she'd learnt his secret and so gained power over him in that way as well.

Panic gripped him at the thought of the damage she could do with such knowledge. If word got out, it would be the end of him. His good standing with his neighbours would be dragged through the mud, and his marriage would be over. All he had worked hard for would decay around him as surely as if the witch had cursed the land as he'd first feared. And the shame it would bring. He feared that above all else.

Finally the old crone looked away, but the sense of doom hanging over Richard remained, even after the whores moved on and out of sight. He remained on edge for the rest of the day, paranoia turning even the friend-liest of smiles into knowing smirks, and every conversa-tion he wasn't privy to becoming malicious gossip. What if the old witch had already started spreading rumours about him? How could he continue to live and work in the area if his secret got out, when all respect he'd earned would be gone, his good name besmirched and his reputa-tion left in tatters, and his sins laid bare for all to see? And yet he couldn't just abandon his mill and his family. He might be trapped in an unhappy marriage, but he still cared deeply for his beautiful daughters. Being parted from them would wound him greater than anything else he stood to lose.

The day passed without any further incident, though that did nothing to ease Richard's mind. When the market came to a close, he found he still couldn't face his family. He had to make the long walk back to Wheathead to drop off the cart and his goods, but instead of joining them for dinner he continued on to the local alehouse. He didn't know what he would find there – a warm welcome from friends or icy stares and angry muttering – but he wanted ale while he contemplated his next move, and he found it preferable to the idea of yet another confrontation with his wife. Even if it meant braving the dangers of night once more.

Again he took a lantern with him to part the suffocating depths of the shadows. The small flame flickering in its cage did little to reveal the countryside around it, however. Its dim glow was just enough to show a small patch of land directly in front of him, allowing the miller to pick his way across the uneven ground without stumbling. But anything lurking in the darkness remained cloaked in shadow. Wariness ruled him until he reached the safety of the alehouse.

That night it was crowded, full of villagers persuaded to risk the journey by the lure of gossip. Richard braced himself as he entered. But he stepped in to find his fears were unfounded, the source of their chatter the very wretches who plagued him so. He scowled when he realised even here he wouldn't be able to escape that hated family. Only his thirst for ale was enough to persuade him to stay. He made his way to the bar and ordered a tankard of the local ale.

Taking a sip, he looked around at the animated faces occupying the dingy interior of Widow Sawyers' home.

How she could endure these evenings of endless, witch-filled conversation was beyond him. Not when it was witchcraft that had taken her husband from her. Yet she continued to brew her own ale and open her doors for all who wanted to drink it. And there was never any shortage of people wanting a drink. It took a moment for him to notice a man at one of the tables beckoning him over.

Miles Nutter watched his approach with a hint of amusement. "Now then, Dick. What brings you here?"

Richard scowled. "Can a man not enjoy a drink?" There was no room on the bench beside Miles so he remained standing, but he set his lantern down on the table top.

"Aye that he can, but by the looks of it, you're not finding it all that enjoyable. What's the matter, too much merriment going on for you?"

"I would remind you that I am a steward of the Church and I will be treated with respect."

"All right, no need for that tone. We were just discussing Old Demdike and her family."

"So I heard," Richard growled.

"What's the matter, they been causing you trouble?"

"They are pagans and Devil worshippers and I will not suffer them on my land!"

The corners of Miles's mouth twitched. "They can't be all that bad. They've helped many a family round here with their healing and protection magic."

Richard shook his head in disgust. "Faith in the Lord is the only protection any of us need. It is time we rid ourselves of these blasphemous ways and stamped out witchcraft!"

Miles snorted. "You might see it differently if one of your daughters got sick."

"I would not let that family within a hundred miles of

my girls if I had my way, sick or no. Do not pretend they haven't caused as much harm with their heathen ways as they've helped folk when it's suited them. How many have to die before you are all persuaded to put a stop to them?"

Richard's voice rose with the passion of his hatred, and he suddenly became aware that all eyes were on him. Pride puffed out his chest. Rather than the unwanted attention he'd been worrying the witches would bring down on him, this was the kind he enjoyed.

"And are we all forgetting that period of madness that lasted eight weeks after Demdike conspired with one of her demons?" he continued. "How can we trust a woman like that when she can't even protect herself from her own black magic?"

There were a few nods from the audience.

"Hear me now if you value your souls. No man is safe so long as they walk this land. We must unite against them and weed them out before their poison can spread to any more of this community."

All hints of amusement drained from Miles's eyes. "You might want to tread carefully there, Dick. Old Chattox could easily hold her own against Demdike, but I trust that one even less. Just yesterday they were on the verge of some magical battle, till one of them spied the constable approaching and lost her nerve. Or so I've heard."

A few voices shouted their agreement, one man crying "It's true, I was there!"

Richard allowed himself a callous smile. "Then let them curse each other and free us from their blight."

"Aye, that may well be the outcome. Best not get involved and let the witches deal with each other, eh?"

The men began to talk amongst themselves again and Richard knew his moment had passed. One of them caught his eye and cocked his head ever so slightly in invitation. Richard nodded, though he didn't immediately follow the other man out. He waited a few minutes, savouring the rest of his ale before taking his leave.

Outside, the darkness felt even more unsavoury after the candlelit alehouse. The miller's lantern floundered weakly in the crushing weight of the night, and it was with a sense of growing unease that he walked onto the moors, just as he had two nights ago. Paranoia still preyed on his thoughts to the point where he fully expected to cross paths with Demdike once again. Perhaps she would be lying in wait to curse him a second time, no doubt commanded by Satan himself to deliver the souls of good Christians straight to Hell. And for all his sins, Richard still considered himself a man of God.

The night air was still and dry, but on the edge of the dull glow from his lantern he could just make out the shapes of the hanged women left rotting on the end of their ropes. His mind flashed back to the encounter with Demdike and he remembered her ridiculous statement that there was more blood on his honest hands than on her aged, evil claws. He had played his part in sending suspected witches to the gallows, of course, among other criminals who had acted against God, but it had never once occurred to him that any of those poor souls might have been innocent. As far as he was concerned he had never done anything but the Lord's work. He had helped bring justice to Pendle and continued to do everything in his power to protect honest men and women from the threat of pagans and heathens who would drag them all down to Hell if given the chance. The same could not be said for the old crone who delighted in cursing any who would cross her.

The witches continued their reign of terror over his thoughts and soul as the miller pressed on, even after he'd left the hanged women behind. No amount of prayer could clear his mind of the hags, and it was not until he reached his destination that they were finally driven out of his skull, if only temporarily. For inside the old, currently unused barn waited the younger man he'd come to meet – a farm labourer who went by the name of Rob.

Richard glanced around before stepping inside. "Are you sure you weren't followed?"

"Yes," Rob answered.

He nodded his approval and strode over to the labourer, grabbing him in a rough embrace and kissing his shameful secret. There was a time when he'd loved his wife and enjoyed the beauty of her naked body. But over the years, his love for Jenetta had waned, and she alone could no longer satiate his appetites.

At first he'd thought God was testing him. Temptresses danced and flirted at every turn, and his gaze began to stray more and more, taking in every pleasing curve, every wicked smile. It had shamed him deeply to be failing the Lord's test, yet he couldn't seem to resist. He'd taken his pleasure of all the pretty girls who took his fancy, and loathed himself for it. But then there came a point where even they would not satisfy.

Richard couldn't remember the exact moment he'd been drawn to other men. For reasons he couldn't explain, their handsome features began attracting his gaze more than the temptresses, and he found his sinful urges taking a far more sinister turn. The sheen of muscular bodies working the fields, the rugged good looks of labourers, and the refined masculinity of the gentry – he found himself beginning to note it all, try as he might to fight it. And then he knew it was not God's doing at all, but the witches'. They'd cursed him with these unnatural desires. How else could he have lost all control over his flesh?

But now Demdike had discovered the identity of his lover, and was probably already plotting to use it against him. He knew then that he should end the affair. If rumours spread, nosy neighbours might try to determine the truth of it for themselves. The risk of being caught was growing.

Questing fingers found the buttons at the top of his britches and fumbled with the fastenings. Richard's Christian morals nagged at him that he should be trying harder to resist these urges, if not for the sake of his family and his reputation, then for the sake of his soul. But even the cold of the night couldn't touch the heat of their passions now. That familiar throb of excitement pulsed through his loins, and Richard Baldwin was lost.

CHAPTER
SIX

Two months passed. October was drawing to a close and Samhain was upon them. That time of year when the line between life and death began to blur, the realms of spirit and earth merging so that death's shroud became something patchy and easily passed through. Demdike sensed the change to the veil – the normally dense fog had already become a fine mist. Soon it would be too thin to keep all but the weakest spirits out. They had but one day left to prepare before it reached its thinnest.

She tasked her granddaughter with making charms to ward off evil beings. These they would offer to any with enough sense to accept the protection of the cunning folk. Many would turn them away, preferring to rely solely on Christ. But it was their duty. As far as she was concerned, they were honour bound to aid their neighbours on this most dangerous of nights. So they would make the same offer they did every year, and if the Christian families refused their help then so be it, let them see where it got them as the shadows lengthened and the spirits worked their mischief. It also didn't hurt that there was some profit to be made during Samhain, and with winter fast approaching, they needed every last scrap of worth they could lay their hands on.

There were also their own defences to reinforce. This Demdike would entrust to no one but herself, not with such high stakes. Their very lives might depend on the strength of the protective spells laid about their home, and so she recited the ancient rites and incantations with the utmost care.

The hour was late when they went to bed. But it was the next day when the real work would begin, and her sense of duty would not allow her to sleep through the morning. She awoke at the first touch of sunlight filtering through the linen-covered window, the importance of the day sweeping aside her body's need for rest.

Alizon was still deep in slumber, her breathing slow and steady. Demdike sat up and took a moment to enjoy the sight of her granddaughter's pretty face in a state of such peace. On any other day she might have left the girl to rest a while longer, but the spirits would wait for no woman. Come dusk, the dead would cross into the earthly plane, whether the living were ready for them or no.

She rose and placed a gentle hand on Alizon's shoulder. The girl stirred and her eyelids fluttered, her features settling into a disgruntled frown and a groan escaping her lips.

"Time we were up now, sweetheart."

"Not yet, Gran," Alizon mumbled.

"Sorry, lass, but there is still much to be done. There are folk relying on us to keep them safe, and you know I can't do it all alone."

The girl grumbled something unintelligible but did as

she was told, throwing back the blanket with a loud sigh and swinging herself upright. She trudged through to the kitchen for a bowl without needing to be told, and the door creaked open and shut a moment later.

Demdike gathered the necessary tools of their craft needed for the day ahead of them while she waited for her granddaughter to fetch the fresh water. It didn't take long for Alizon to return. The clear liquid was cold yet refreshing as she dipped her hands in and splashed her face. A quick rub down with a cloth took care of the rest of the grime, then it was time to be on their way.

The autumn sun was weak that morning and did little to ward off the chill of winter's bite creeping into the air, and there seemed to be a dullness to the land that went beyond the grey skies overhead. The squeak of an empty wheelbarrow marked their progress down the path. If all went well, it wouldn't be empty for long.

There was no sense making the trip up to Wheathead, given the reception they were likely to receive from the Baldwins and their associates. So the two went in the opposite direction, towards Roughlee. The Nutters had always been open to the use of their arts and would likely accept their aid. Unless Richard Baldwin had finally succeeded in turning the family against them, there was no reason why that should have changed.

The farms were a flurry of activity around Samhain time as workers busied themselves with preparing for the winter months, and the Nutters' estate was no different. The labourers took little notice of Demdike and her granddaughter making their way along the path to the farmhouse, and they reached the door without incident. A brief knock was all it took to summon one of the residents. The thick wood creaked open to reveal a woman similar to

Demdike in age, though their circumstances had placed them worlds apart.

Alice Nutter made for a noble and dignified figure as she stood there in the doorway, in spite of all the hardships she'd suffered since her husband had passed away, leaving her to raise their five children and run the farm. Being part of a relatively wealthy family helped, of course, but life had not been easy. A sense of respect existed between the two women, born of a widow's struggles.

"Alice," Demdike said. "The time has come again. We offer renewed protection for your home, in readiness for tonight."

Alice nodded. "Come in."

The Nutters' home was far grander than their humble Malkin Tower, and Demdike sensed her granddaughter was more than a little jealous as she abandoned the wheelbarrow just outside the entrance and stepped inside. But then Demdike supposed she would have felt no different at Alizon's age, before she'd learnt to be content with her lot in life. Someday the girl would come to appreciate what little they had, when she'd found a man to call her own and started a family.

Alice showed them to the kitchen. They set their tools on the table and Demdike wasted no time in setting to work. She unwrapped the human femur imbued with the power of the runes, more candles, the pentagram pendant, an incense burner and some incense. Passing both candles and incense to her granddaughter, she asked "Can I trust you with the cleansing again?"

Alizon nodded and lifted the burner on its chain. She glanced at Alice as if seeking permission, then approached the fire dancing merrily in the hearth, well fed with the onset of winter. The girl held the end of one of the candles to the flames until a new one spawned at the tip of the wick. Then she used that to light the charcoal inside the incense burner and sprinkled the scented grains on top. Under the watchful eye of the two older women, she walked slowly around the kitchen, and then passed through the doorway, back into the hall. Alice chose to follow her as she made her way from room to room, beating back the negative energy in the house with the candle's purity and the incense's sweet fumes twisting through the air. Dark energy attracted dark spirits. The cleansing was an added precaution to the spell Demdike was about to work.

Taking the femur in one hand and the pentagram pendant in the other, she began to chant another charm similar to the one she'd taught little Jennet the night James had made his pact with Dandy. Both objects grew warm with the power channelling through them and her sense of the spirit world heightened. She could feel the spirits pushing at the veil in their eagerness to cross over to the mortal realm.

The spell's energy grew and angry whispers filled her ears. Undeterred, she kept chanting and strengthening the unseen barrier around the house. This was a shield against demons and other malevolent beings, one far more effective than its physical walls. And the demons knew it. Their whispering grew louder and more intense, full of promises of blood and suffering if she didn't cease her efforts to keep them out. Demdike paid them little heed. They couldn't actually harm her as long as the defensive spells held.

Once the incantation was done and the magic had been woven into the very fabric of the Nutters' home, the spirits grew quiet again. But Demdike could still sense other-worldly eyes on her. Come twilight, they would be seeking the perfect opportunity to take revenge for her meddling on this one night that belonged to them and them alone.

Moments later her granddaughter returned, both candles and incense extinguished now the cleansing was complete. Alice wasn't far behind. In her youth, Demdike might have taken offence at the woman's lack of trust, but as it was, she'd long since grown used to such attitudes towards her family. They had never taken anything they didn't have a right to and Demdike prided herself on that, no matter what other folk might think.

"'Tis done," she said. "As last year and the year before that, the spell won't keep every spirit out, but it will protect you from the worst of them entering the house without an invitation. The rest is up to you. Take this fresh charm crafted under last night's moon for added protection, and be careful who you welcome in later."

"Thank you," Alice replied, accepting the small stone with its defensive symbol carved on either side. One of her sons was approaching just as she was showing them out, and she called "Miles! See these two are given fair payment for their services, please."

Fresh death was thick in the air as they were led back through the estate. The smell of blood marked the end for the unfortunate livestock selected to provide meat for the winter months. It was a call the darker spirits were sure to answer come nightfall, and Demdike pitied any who were fool enough to venture from the safety of their homes. She was given another brief sense of the things waiting to cross over to their world – dark shapes pacing restlessly, glimpsed with her inner eye. Miles brought her back to the physical realm.

"Here," he said, handing them a piggin of milk, a few vegetables and a sliver of meat.

A whole piggin of milk was always welcome, though the wooden bucket was awkward and heavy to handle, even for Alizon's young arms. The creamy liquid was in danger of slopping over the sides when she lifted it into the wheelbarrow, and their progress along the path slowed. It was already midday before they'd finished working the rest of the Roughlee area, and from there they continued on to Newchurch, laden with more goods.

They had just started towards Moss End Farm when a familiar voice sounded from behind. "Mistress."

Demdike turned to find Tibb in his guise of a man. Apparently he'd chosen to show himself only to her, because Alizon continued on a few paces before realising anything was amiss. Not that there was anything unusual in that – materialising for all to see took far greater energy, hence the need for the cunning folk to open their third eye in the first place.

Tibb's expression was grim. "You are needed at Carr Hall."

Demdike frowned. "Carr Hall, what for? Elizabeth is quite capable of sorting the Towneleys' protection, or James for that matter – if they'll even accept it!"

"You should go to Carr Hall," Tibb insisted. "There is trouble for your kin there."

"What is it, Gran?" Alizon asked.

"Change of plans, lass." Demdike turned back to her granddaughter, still frowning slightly. "Seems we're wanted at Carr Hall."

"But won't Mam and James be working there?"

"Tibb says they have need of our help and I trust him, so we go. The Bulcocks will have to wait."

She glanced back to the patch of land where her familiar had stood just seconds ago, but already he had vanished. It seemed she would have to find out for herself what manner of danger awaited at Carr Hall. She wished Tibb would have stayed with her on the road to the Towneley's estate though, even if he'd said all he was willing to. What if they were about to clash with Chattox a second time? Or worse, her rival's familiar, Fancie?

"No!" Alizon clenched her fists. "I don't want to go to Carr Hall, I **want** to help the Bulcocks. You go rescue James from the trouble he's got himself into – I'm going to see my friend John."

"Alizon Device, you will come with me this instant or so help me I will slap your scalp so hard it will knock more than just sense into you!"

Her granddaughter glared at her, but after a moment she submitted, cursing as she struggled to keep up with the wheelbarrow, awkward and unruly on the uneven ground. The movement turned the calm surface of the rich white lake in its piggin basin to storm-tossed waters. Milky waves were at even greater risk of crashing over the sides, but preserving as much as they could of the nutritious liquid didn't seem so important then. Not with more immediate problems than famine to contend with.

The Towneley's estate was far more impressive than Richard Baldwin's mill, yet it felt much more approachable than the miller's land. Demdike was unsure what to expect as they neared the hall, but she was grateful not to sense any curses at work. If Chattox was threatening Elizabeth and James, at least she had arrived in time to help protect them from her rival's dark magic.

The servants and labourers were every bit as hard at work as those on the Nutters' land, though several stopped to watch the old woman and her granddaughter rush past. Such was her reputation, Demdike was able to pass through them without being challenged. But she had no need to march all the way up to the hall. Raised voices sounded from the back of the property where the outhouses were situated, and she realised then the nature of the trouble Tibb had warned of.

"What is the meaning of this?"

"I'm only strengthening the protection round your home. What's wrong with that?"

"I've told you before, I'll not have any witchcraft performed on my land. Your pagan ways are not welcome here!"

"And I've told you before, it's not witchcraft and I'm no witch!"

Demdike rushed round the property to find the situation was far graver than most mortals could comprehend. Her grandson's temper was almost a tangible force, so strong did those fires burn with the indignation of the accusations being made against him. His hands had balled into fists, shaking with what little restraint he had left. Anne Towneley was a murky reflection in comparison, though her usual dignified air had been clouded somewhat by a weaker flame, her face burning red with it.

Dandy was by James's side, lips pulled back into a fierce snarl and eyes blazing with the energy of his human's rage. The real danger. He had not revealed himself to his unsuspecting victim, but Demdike could feel how close he was to lashing out at the perceived threat to his master – an action sure to have disastrous consequences.

"Mistress Towneley, is there a problem here?" Demdike asked, trying to keep her voice as level as possible.

"More witches! I will not have your kind tainting our family's good name. Be off with you! You are not welcome here anymore."

"Very well, we will not trouble you again. Come, James."

Her grandson showed no signs of backing off. Dandy took a step forward.

"James!"

"No, not till she pays us what she owes."

"Do you want to be arrested?" she hissed in his ear. "'Tis not worth it, lad. Time to seek work elsewhere, before the day is lost."

"Why?" He turned to look at her and gestured angrily at the noblewoman. "She has no power against our magic. Why suffer these injustices they bring against us?"

The red in Anne Towneley's face deepened further still. Demdike glanced at her and raised her voice. "Because wealth has a power of its own. You would do well to respect that power. Even our familiars cannot protect us from the noose."

Fear crept into those angry features, dousing the fires with its icy chill. James went pale.

Triumph flashed in Anne Towneley's eyes. "Listen to your grandmother, boy. There are enough here to act as witnesses, should anything unnatural befall me."

"Fear not, Mistress Towneley, we are leaving." Demdike placed a firm hand on her grandson's shoulder and steered James away, beckoning Alizon to follow. There came a rush of relief when Dandy, so solid and muscular to her inner eye, simply faded away, presumably retreating to his own realm now the threat to his master had passed. Once they were out of Anne Towneley's earshot, she asked her grandson "Where's your mam?"

"Round Laund Farm last I saw, working the protective spells for Samhain like you taught us."

"Good. Do you want to tell me what that was about?"

"I wasn't performing any witchcraft, Gran, I swear! I know the dark arts are dangerous. I was just trying to add more protection for the Towneleys. I thought they might give me a little extra for it, but then Mistress Towneley caught me and started accusing me of witchcraft!"

Demdike sighed. "Have you no brains in that scalp of yours? If Mistress Towneley did not take kindly to the use of magic last time you tried performing a spell on their land, what made you think she would suddenly change her mind? Foolish boy. Best keep away from Carr Hall for now until this all dies down, then perhaps we might find you more work there if we are lucky."

"Sorry, Gran," he muttered, looking sheepish.

"Go see if Master Duckworth has any work for you."

He turned and slunk away. Demdike watched him go, thinking at least he seemed to have realised he'd made a mistake. Hopefully he would learn from it.

"I still don't see why he gets to have a familiar before me," Alizon said. "Mam was right, he wasn't ready."

"Perhaps not, but it is too late now."

"I would not make such stupid mistakes."

Demdike couldn't help but laugh. "I should hope not! But that does not make you old enough for the pact."

Her granddaughter only huffed at that and returned to her sullen silence.

The rest of the day passed uneventfully in comparison. Demdike made her way around the families who would still accept their help, and Alizon trailed behind with an increasingly heavy wheelbarrow. They did go to the Bulcocks' farm at Moss End, only to find Elizabeth had incorporated it into her rounds that year.

Sweet tendrils of incense twisted through the doorway. Elizabeth's eyes were half closed in concentration, her lips moving with a muttered chant. A huge, brown-furred dog padded faithfully by her side. Elizabeth was too busy with her work to notice her mam and daughter, but Ball met Demdike's gaze and gave her a nod. Demdike nodded back. She watched them for a moment, pleased to note the hum of the threshold building with every word her daughter uttered.

Childish laughter sounded from behind. Demdike turned her attention back to the farmyard and the pitter-patter of little feet. Jennet ran into view, squealing with delight as the Bulcocks' niece gave chase. Isobell began to close the distance between them, her longer legs carrying her closer and closer to her quarry. She stretched out her hand. Jennet squealed again and twisted away, then she caught sight of Demdike and the game was instantly forgotten.

"Gran!"

Demdike smiled and knelt as Jennet sprinted over, opening her arms in invitation for a hug. The six year old barrelled into her with surprising force and Demdike fell backwards with a startled laugh. Jennet landed on top of her, beaming from ear to ear.

Isobell watched with growing impatience. "Come on, Jennet. It's your turn to chase."

Jennet turned to look at her friend, but she didn't let go of Demdike. "No it's not, you still haven't caught me."

Demdike chuckled and planted a kiss on her grand-daughter's cheek. "Go on, lambkin, enjoy your game while your sister and I finish our rounds."

"Aw, Gran. Come join us!"

"Not today, lass. You go back to your friend and we'll play another day." She kissed Jennet again. "Your sister and I have work elsewhere."

Alizon's laughter cut through the scene. She had abandoned the wheelbarrow to talk to John, laughing with him as if her bad mood had never been. Demdike stood and smiled to herself, remembering the first time she'd felt that giddiness around a man. Jennet glanced across at her older sister with a puzzled expression.

"Why is she acting so strange, Gran?"

Demdike ruffled her hair. "'Tis naught for you to worry about, lass. Go on now."

Jennet frowned, but then Isobell started running. "Your turn to chase, Jennet!"

"No, no fair! You haven't caught me yet." Jennet sprinted after her and Demdike looked across at Alizon again. There was a blush to the girl's cheeks as she gave John a sideways look and a bashful smile, her fingers fidgeting with her dress. Young Master Bulcock did not show any signs of being caught in the same rush of emotions, his smile firmly one of friendship. Demdike sighed. She feared her granddaughter was doomed to experience the one pain she could not protect her from.

"Time we were leaving, Alizon. Your mam has everything in hand here, and there are still plenty of other families in need of our aid."

She expected more arguments, but her granddaughter chose to come willingly, perhaps not wishing to cause a scene in front of John. Demdike made no comment on the matter. She felt sure Alizon would talk to her about it when she was ready. Until then, any advice she tried to give the lass would no doubt fall on deaf ears.

They continued to call round each of their neighbours, working their spells of protection where it was wanted and accepting more gifts in return. It was already nearing daylight's gate when they finally trudged back up the path to Malkin Tower, weary with more than just the physical hardships of a hard day's work. There was a weight to the shadows lengthening across the land, a sense of foreboding settling over the Forest of Pendle to crush even the highest of spirits. And with the fading of the sun's light came more than just the darkness.

A foul odour permeated the dusk, heralding the fall of that final defence standing between the worlds of the living and the dead. The scent of the grave wreathed the villagers in its sickly stink, made up of death and decay and the earth the deceased would have been resting in at any other time of year. But not that night.

Christians had their own way of giving the dead their due. The sombre tolling of St Mary's bells rang loud and clear across the moors as Demdike opened the door for Alizon and followed her inside, then made her way over to the window. She knew it was a mark of respect for the lost loved ones they would honour during Allhallowtide. Such customs would go some way towards appeasing the wandering souls crossing through the veil, but they were no substitute for the proper protection granted through the old ways. All the prayers in the world would not save the Christian folk when the malevolent spirits came calling.

Demdike pitied the fools led astray by the likes of the Baldwins. Her world might be one of injustice, but many of the families were innocent of the wrongs wrought upon those of her craft. Many of them didn't deserve the evils that would soon visit. They didn't deserve it, and yet they'd been left blind to it by their misplaced faith.

The sound of wood on wood brought Demdike back to her own family's concerns as Alizon set the table and began to dish up a sizeable portion on each plate. Usually they would have rationed out their takings from the day's work, making the food stretch over as many meals as possible. But Samhain was not a time for pottage or meagre pickings. No, this was one of but four nights of the year where they would feast, perhaps not like kings or the gentry, but at least like yeomen. This was a night for meat with their bread and cheese, and other rare treats.

There was something else that would have seemed out of the ordinary to any who'd forgotten the old ways – the feast was not shared between two plates, but three. The Christians would have disapproved, had any been there to see. Demdike knew all too well what conclusions they would have drawn from this custom.

Her granddaughter came to join her by the window once the food was laid out, and together they peered into the darkness. It didn't take the opening of one's third eye to sense what was out there.

An impenetrable wall of blackness surrounded their home. A ghastly procession of all the earth's dead could have been marching on Malkin Tower, and they would have utterly failed to see it. Still they kept watch. Cunning folk or no, they were only human after all. Instinct demanded it of them. Even with hunger beating its nauseating fists against their stomachs, the two women stayed by their post.

Alizon shifted restlessly, youth stunting her patience into something short and weak. Demdike felt her lips lifting into a smile. Her granddaughter would learn the value of such things over the years, just as she had, but it was really a lesson only age could teach.

She supposed the wait might have been easier if they'd had more of a sense of what was happening outside. The night was too quiet, the shadows too still. There was only that ethereal caress to make their hairs stand on end, reinforcing what they already knew to be true.

Then came the thing they were waiting for – a knock on the door, just as the last of Alizon's patience seemed about to fail. It came without warning. Even Demdike jumped, her heart galloping in her chest as she turned away from the window.

A second knock sounded. Silver bit into wrinkled skin where she clutched her pendant tight, muttering the words of the strongest protection charms she knew. Her legs turned to lead. It was a short walk across the room, but a difficult one.

The wooden barrier separating their home from the outside world seemed inadequate then. Demdike paused with her hand on the doorknob. Had it been any other night, she might have demanded the visitor identify themselves, or she might have refused to open the door at all. But the spirits would not be denied. Not answering could have far greater consequences than dealing with whoever or whatever waited on the other side. So she turned the knob and peeked outside.

SEVEN

The night yawned dark and foreboding beyond the entrance to St Mary's Church. Foulds glanced around at the other Puritans filing into the pews. None paid him any heed. The last thing he wanted was to leave the safety of God's house this All Hallows' Eve, but he was more afraid of what would happen to him if he didn't.

He gritted his teeth and stepped out into the gloom, shutting the door as carefully and quietly as he could. Rows of tombstones greeted him on the other side. Foulds shivered with more than the cold autumn air. The church grounds were empty, but that didn't mean he was alone.

Treading carefully, Foulds made his way to the grave where he was supposed to meet the one he'd been tricked into serving. It wasn't hard to find. The headstone had already begun to crack and fade, weathering faster than the surrounding graves. Foulds liked to think it was a sign God had denied his not so dearly departed father entry to Heaven, something he would usually have found a grim pleasure in. Not that night. He glanced back at the church. More candles than he could count had been lit for the evening service, and the windows were alight with the welcoming glow. A draft caused them to flicker, beckoning him back into their fold. He swallowed and turned away again. Not yet.

Dread of more than just his master filled him, knowing full well this was the night for the dead to return; a night for witches and demons; a night filled with more dangers than any other. The hairs on the back of his neck raised with the feeling he was being watched, and for a moment he was afraid his dad might rise up and give him another beating. But the presence he sensed was not his father stirring in the earth beneath his feet. It was in fact the one Foulds had come to meet, which was perhaps not all that much better.

He prowled between the graves like he owned the place, this thing like unto a Christian man. In appearance, he was no different to any of Foulds's neighbours. His lined face gave the impression of years of toil, framed by dark hair and a beard kept neat and trimmed. Clothes both clean and respectable hid the well-proportioned body beneath, and his hands looked human, the palms as rough as any other labourer's, and the nails blunt and short. Yet all those who had the misfortune of dealing with him were left with the sense he was something more than human, something far worse than any mortal man could ever be. What that something truly was none could say. There was only that feeling of terror he inspired in those around him, and the knowledge that it was not natural for any man to affect his fellows so.

Foulds knelt and bowed his head. "Master."

"Arise." There was an air of impatience to the dread thing's command. "What knowledge do you bring?"

"I have watched the witch clan like you asked of me,"

Foulds began, wishing his legs would stop shaking. "And a more unwholesome and wicked family I have never seen. I have witnessed deeds most terrible and blasphemous; it makes my blood cold just thinking about it."

"Yes, yes. Do not mistake me for that fool in Read Hall or a court in need of swaying. Dispense with the theatre and tell me what you have learnt."

"I have seen them using scalps for their Devil worship and bat's blood. They have candles and incense they no doubt stole from the church and herbs they pick from the land without a care for who it belongs to."

His master scowled at him as Foulds launched into a rant about the evil he had witnessed. It didn't take him long to falter, the words dying to the thunderous expression on his master's face. He could see rage building in those terrible eyes glaring out at him from the otherwise handsome face, eyes that betrayed the monster lurking within the shape of a man. They were never quite human at the best of times. Devoid of the empathy that should have been at the heart of all good men, instead they glittered with a malevolence Foulds had never encountered in anyone else.

Drops of red appeared at the corner of each eyeball, spreading through the white until they appeared completely bloodshot. Yet its taint didn't stop there. No, it not only surrounded the two discs of natural colour at its centre but crept into each iris and turned them the same shade of crimson. Only two black dots in a sea of blood remained, twin vortexes sucking unsuspecting victims into the blackened soul beneath.

Foulds might not have been the greatest of thinkers, but he was far from simple. He looked into those eyes with new fear, realising there was a very real possibility that his master might kill him if he didn't give the creature what he wanted. He'd been saving his greatest discovery for last, but he knew then his only hope was to skip ahead and pray it was enough.

"And eyeballs!" he blurted. "They had a pair of human eyeballs. They mixed all the ingredients in some foul concoction and James Device drank it, then he went into some kind of unholy trance."

Mercifully, the blood tide in those eyes began to recede until they returned to their former state, appearing almost human again. "The pact? Did he make the pact?"

"I think so. I mean, I heard them talk of a pact and spirits and something about opening an inner eye. Please, that's all I could find out before one of their beasts drove me off. I know not where they got the eyes, but they were human, and they were fresh."

"You have proved useful after all. You may go now."

"Will you arrest them?"

"You mistake me for the law again. I have other interests, which are no concern of yours."

"Of course, I didn't mean to pry. Please don't kill me."

"Oh, you will meet an unnatural end," his master said. Those inhuman eyes seemed to gape with a terrible emptiness which he thought he might fall into, never again to see the light of day. Foulds tore his gaze away from the end they promised, only to feel a fresh wave of horror when he noticed the name on the nearest headstone had changed. It no longer bore the name of his father, but his own. "But not by my hand. Now go."

With an involuntary whimper, Foulds backed away from the portent of doom. The urge to flee gripped him but he wouldn't turn and run until he was confident his master was not going to follow. The dread thing merely watched, the corner of his mouth twitching. Cruel amusement gleamed in his eyes. Foulds couldn't meet that gaze any longer. He turned and ran.

St Mary's beckoned him with greater urgency now. He sprinted all the way to the door, never once looking back till he was slipping through it and into the light's embrace. Only then did he peer back out, to find the evil in the grave-yard was gone. Somehow that wasn't as comforting as it should have been. Not even his faith in Christ could calm the panic seizing hold at the core of his very soul.

Foulds collapsed onto the nearest pew and joined the prayers to keep evil spirits at bay, his tongue forming each verse with barely a conscious thought. But in his head he saw only his own grave, his master's parting words whispering through his mind until he felt trapped by the grim fate awaiting him. The Reaper was near, and there was no escape.

EIGHT

A sliver of night was visible through the crack in the doorway. Demdike peered round for a glimpse of the visitor and was just able to make out a dark figure on the doorstep.

"It's me, Betsy," the visitor said. He bore no lantern, his face utterly hidden in shadow. But there was no mistaking that voice.

"Tom..."

Emotions stirred in her old heart, a deep ache running through scars long healed. It was like losing him all over again. Fresh grief filled her and a longing for what once had been. A widow's pain. It took possession of her soul, just as it had on the night of his passing. Demdike fought it, blinking back the tears threatening to spill down her cheeks. The pain went on regardless. Even the family pendant couldn't keep it at bay.

"It's me, Betsy," he repeated. "Will you not let me in while we are permitted this one more night together? Our time will be brief enough as it is."

Demdike wanted to believe that truly was her husband

come back to her to share in their Samhain feast. She wanted it with all her heart. But she knew better. It didn't matter that his presence didn't feel malicious or demonic at all. The best of them could hide their true natures, and she was not about to invite him in without examining him properly.

Gripping the pentagram tighter still, Demdike opened the door wider so the candlelight spilled across his face. Another ache went through her. For he looked exactly as she remembered him in his final days on the earth, when he had been strong and muscular from working the fields, his rugged handsomeness the bane of many a young lass. Yet that was only the illusion of spirit. With her gifts of sight, she was able to look deeper until she saw the truth of him, and was as certain as she could be that this was not a trick.

"Yes, there is a place for you at our table this Samhain." She stood aside to grant him entry. "I invite you to share the warmth and comfort of our hearth and home, such as it is."

Tom smiled as he stepped inside, his gaze meeting the wide eyes of their granddaughter.

"Who is it, Gran?" Alizon asked.

"Alizon, meet your grandfather. Put aside your doubts and fear now, child. He will not hurt us."

"I'm not afraid!"

The quiver in her voice said otherwise, but Demdike chose not to comment, her own reservations receding once the spirit had seated himself at the table. She took her place beside him.

Their granddaughter joined them after a moment's hesitation, and they began to tuck in to the feast laid out before them; even the dead man. A look of ecstasy settled over his handsome features.

"It is good to finally meet you, Alizon," Tom said

between mouthfuls. "I can see you have the same fire in your soul as your gran. You will need it in the times to come."

Alizon didn't seem to know what to say to that. Instead she asked "Were you a cunning man as well, Grandfather?"

Tom laughed. "Nay, lass, these hands of mine were always far too rough for practising much of the craft. I would have made a poor healer! Besides, your grandmother has skill enough for us both. I made my living as a labourer, much like your brother and your father in his time on this earth."

Alizon dropped her gaze to her plate, sadness creeping into her young features. "I still miss Dad, but I can barely remember his face now. I wish he would come to visit one Samhain."

"That is the way of life. The memory fades till the dead are naught but a name carved in stone, then the day comes when that too is gone and it is as if we had never been. And yet we live on." Tom reached across to cup her chin, gently lifting it so their eyes met again. "Take comfort in knowing your dad is still with you, Alizon, even if he cannot be here with us in a more physical form tonight."

Demdike kept quiet while the two talked, though her gaze never left her husband. He still wore an expression of happiness as he ate, his face never once betraying the disappointment he must have felt to be given only a weak reminder of what it was to be flesh and blood. For she knew the bitter truth of his return.

Each mouthful barely touched his tongue before it began to decay. Rotting food turned to dust, dust to nothingness. It was as though it had as little substance as the being consuming it. Others had told her as much in previous years. And yet she continued offering them a share of the annual feast, for the sake of the brief taste they were allowed from each bite. For who was she to deny them what precious little of life's pleasures they were granted in death, on this one night of the year when the boundaries between the two began to blur? Even when times had been hard and food scarce, she had been careful to uphold tradition.

She felt for the spirits, certain they must miss the pleasures of the flesh. Why else would they choose to cross back into the mortal realm during Samhain? But she had never felt so strongly for any of them as she did that night.

His talk of memories rang true for the most part, his words full of a wisdom gained from the other side. But the dead were not always condemned to utter obscurity as he had suggested, living memory not always doomed to failure. Though why some faces remained clearer than others Demdike could not say. She only knew that her ability to recall his features more perfectly than even the most talented of painters could have depicted them had never waned. Remembering all that she had loved in him was no harder after all this time.

Such memories were with her again while they ate. There was much she wanted to say to her husband, but not in front of Alizon.

Silence fell as they each cleared their plates. Demdike waited for Alizon to wash it down with the rest of her ale, then bid her granddaughter go to bed and allow her some time alone with Tom. She half expected the girl to make some indignant retort, but for once Alizon complied without argument.

Tom was the first to break the silence after their granddaughter left the room, his hand reaching for hers as he said "Ah, Betsy, I have missed you."

Demdike slid her hand back towards herself so he couldn't grasp it as he meant to. "Then why has it taken so long for you to come back to me, Tom? Near forty years it's been since you left me alone in this world, with not even a whisper of your spirit nearby."

He sighed and got to his feet, walking round the table to stand just behind her chair. Those rough hands stroked the side of her face with more tenderness than they looked capable of, love creating a magic all of its own. Demdike lost herself in the moment as she leant into his touch.

His hands were almost warm with life, and she was young and beautiful, as she had been when they were first courting. Her body had been shapely then, her features pretty enough to win his heart without the need for love charms.

"Because I knew my coming back would do you more harm than good. Is the pain not made fresh by my being here?"

"It is," she admitted, twisting round to look at him. "And yet here you are. What makes this year so different?"

Tom's hand dropped back down to his side and the spell was broken, the grim truth of their mortality restored. Clearly her husband hadn't wanted to get into the reason for his visit so early in the night, but his shoulders slumped in defeat and he answered "I come with a warning. There is trouble for you, my love."

"Ha, when is there not trouble? My whole life has been dealing with one trouble or another."

"There will be a death tonight. You know as well as I they'll suspect any known witches of having a hand in it, and there are none more infamous than you in these parts."

"There's Chattox."

99

"This is serious, Betsy. They will blame you for this, and it will set events in motion that can only end in misery."

"I am well aware of the fate the gentry would deal me if given the chance. Let them try – it will be their undoing."

"Yes, I know what you mean to do and I understand your need for justice. But I beg you to turn away from this dark path you have set your eyes upon, before it is too late. It can only end in tragedy."

"I know the risks, Tom. I have seen the signs. And yet I am prepared to give my life when the time comes, if that is the price that must be paid."

"You know I can see far more from this side than any cunning man or wise woman ever could. I have seen, and I tell you the price is too high."

"If you have seen then tell me plain and tell me true. No more riddles."

"You know it does not work like that. There are rules, and I am bound to them as any other spirit is bound. My love for you cannot change that, though I wish it could be otherwise. All I can do is warn you of the dangers you face and make my plea once more – turn back, before it is too late."

"I will think on it and look deeper into what I can glean of my future. But enough talk of death and coming darkness. I would make the best we can of this time together, before you must leave me again."

"You still blame me for making a widow of you?"

She paused, her mind casting back to that terrible day when they'd first parted ways. There he lay on the bed, reduced to a pale phantom of the man he had been, so weak and frail in the grip of mortality. The sickness had been quick to take hold and brutal in its assault on his body. Yet she could have saved him. If only she'd ignored his wishes to leave his fate in the hands of a higher power, they need never have parted ways. It still pained her to know he had feared her magic more than his own death. Out of love she'd done as he'd asked, leaving nature to take its course. She'd regretted the decision ever since.

But that was not her only regret. He might never have fallen ill in the first place, if it hadn't been for her own moment of weakness. Demdike had no doubt now that it was that fool choice which had left him susceptible for all those years, and that it had only been a matter of time before sickness struck. Not that the knowledge did her any good. She would have given anything to have taken it back if only that was the way of things, but of course it was not, even for cunning folk.

"No more than I blame myself," she finally replied.

"Oh, Betsy," he said, gentle but firm as he pulled her to her feet and into his embrace. And as if he knew what was going through her mind, he added "You mustn't think like that."

She didn't answer, allowing him to hold her and wishing she could return to the past again as she had at his first touch. The illusion of youth and life was just a lie, she knew that, yet it was so much kinder than the cruel truth of their current forms. Demdike didn't often lament the loss of her beauty and the desirable body she'd been gifted in her prime, before the years had eroded her flesh until it slipped and sagged into something grotesque. For old age comes to all. But that night she found herself mourning the pretty young woman she had been, and the man Tom had been in life when he was still hers, before death had laid claim to him.

"I did forgive you, you know, even if I couldn't bring

myself to give the boy my name," he told her. "Christopher might have his own life now, but the lad's done you proud."

And there it was. Her son born of adultery, the wound that had scarred Tom's heart. Whatever he said, she didn't think he'd ever fully recovered from the pain her infidelity had inflicted.

"I don't deserve your forgiveness," she answered.

In response he pulled away so he could look her in the eye, then leant in for a kiss. And despite what her inner eye showed her, Demdike did not flinch from the display of affection. Instead she tried to concentrate on the image her physical sense of sight tried to present her with. She tried to focus on that Samhain deception of soft lips brushing against hers just as they had in life; tried to let love and memories restore all that death had taken. But there was no closing her inner eye to the truth of him once she'd taken that first look, and there was only the unpleasant sensation of hard bones bumping against her mouth, all flesh from the area long since turned to dust. He was more complete than his physical remains would truly have been, with just enough patchy tissue left to give the impression of the features she used to know so well. But there was nothing to hide that skeletal grin or cushion the discomfort of the feel of it against her wrinkled flesh.

Then came the scream, not so much heard as felt, like an echo reverberating through the soul. The couple broke apart, and the lipless mouth formed the words "It has begun."

CHAPTER NINE

P rayer and the strength of the parish's belief resonated within St Mary's, encircling the building and forming a shield for the faithful. Their voices rang out with such fervour that the power of it began to seep into the very walls. Richard felt such pride to see so many of the community adhering to the true Protestant faith, especially at a time like this. It was the night Satan's wolves were free to hunt in all their guises, and so it was only right that they of the Lord's flock should shelter together in His house and seek protection, not just in God, but in their own numbers. Richard truly believed nothing could harm them so long as they stayed together and remained true to their religion – not even those vile witches.

Jenneta stood beside him and their children took up the rest of the front pew, a family united in the light of Christ. For all their failings as a couple, the bonds of marriage still held together whatever was left of their broken relationship, and the one time Richard felt remotely close to his wife was within that sacred hall. It seemed the darkness could not touch them whilst surrounded by the glow of the candles. And how strongly they burned that night! Even the slight disturbance of one of the congregation slipping in partway through the service could not weaken the Lord's presence. Yet it still irked Richard that anyone would show such disrespect. He resisted the temptation to turn and look, but inwardly promised himself he'd investigate the matter later and fine the culprit accordingly for their sins.

His mind returned to their holy vigil, until the service came to a close with the offering of a final prayer. In times of old, the night would have been as much about the lost souls trapped in purgatory as warding off the agents of the Devil. But such fancies were nothing more than the misguided idea of Catholics influenced by earlier pagan beliefs. They had no place in the one true religion.

The room emptied from the back. Richard scanned the rows of faces while he waited to take his place at the rear, forming a mental list of which families were present and which were missing. A flash of anger coursed through him when he noticed some of the Nutters of Roughlee had failed to present themselves. Were they among the stubborn individuals still clinging to the old faith? Had they chosen to neglect the All Hallows' service in favour of holding a secret Mass? Richard snorted to himself at the very thought. If the Catholic fools had gotten their way they would have been lighting candles on graves and souling; ridiculous superstitions little better than the heathen practices the witches were no doubt observing. It had fallen to him to show the Forest of Pendle the way, and he intended to do just that, through whatever harsh methods were required of him. They would all thank him when their judgement came and their souls were granted salvation, no matter how unfair this new doctrine might seem to them in life.

But the Nutters weren't entirely a lost cause. It pleased Richard to see John and Agnes Nutter of Bull Hole Farm making efforts to embrace the new religion, and it seemed they had persuaded a few relatives to join them. Yet there was still much work to be done. Perhaps he could enlist the help of these enlightened few in bringing the rest of their family to the true faith, if the witches hadn't already dug their claws in. It certainly merited looking into.

One particular face stood out, Richard's eyes lingering over him much longer than any of the others. There was something unwholesome about those grizzled features. He couldn't say what exactly it was that unnerved him so – maybe it was nothing more than the fact this man was a stranger. That in itself was unusual at Allhallowtide. After all, most avoided travelling at a time deemed so perilous to their immortal souls. But what other reason could there be for the outsider's presence?

The stranger's eyes briefly met his, and Richard felt a chill run through him. He might have feared more witch-craft if they hadn't been in God's house. Surely the Lord would not have suffered an agent of the Devil to enter His domain? But something was at work which went beyond any natural feelings of instant dislike and wariness. Then the stranger turned his gaze on the door and filed outside with the rest, and Richard breathed a sigh of relief.

Moments later, the miller was ushering his family along their pew and to the back of the procession, and they made their way out of the church. Each grabbed a candle as they passed back into the darkness. Richard took comfort in the knowledge that Christ went with them, the tiny flames symbolic of His presence. Otherwise, he might never have dared brave the walk to John Nutter's farmland.

Rob was also part of the throng. The young farm labourer seemed to have hung back so he could get closer to Richard and his family, but Richard was careful not to make eye contact with his shameful secret, even when Rob's candle went out and a look of real panic passed over his youthful features. The miller didn't trust himself to remain strong in the face of his desires, so he ignored the source of sin as best he could.

"Lord, give me strength," he muttered under his breath, wrapping an arm around Jenneta's shoulders. "Let me resist these unnatural feelings, at least while there are so many to see. Let me avoid the shame I would bring, that I might keep a hold of their respect and continue to deliver them from the blasphemous folk traditions I've been working so hard to stamp out, for you, in your name. Please, Lord. Give me strength."

That night, it seemed his prayer was answered. When next he risked chancing a glance in Rob's direction, the farm labourer had been swallowed back into the crowd. He was safe.

"Hmm? Did you say something, husband?"

"Nothing you need trouble yourself with, dear. I was merely asking the Lord to keep watch over us while we make our way to the feast."

Jenneta snorted. "Dear. You are in a good mood tonight."

Richard squeezed her shoulder, digging his nails in. "Careful, *dear.* The Lord is watching."

Jenneta gave a hiss of pain. "And half of Pendle. I know my duty."

"Then keep your vicious thoughts to yourself."

They made the rest of the way across Bull Hole Farm in silence. A large barn awaited, soon to be a fresh light in the darkness. Plates lined the large table within. The procession made their way inside, setting their candles down alongside the walls. Agnes and John lit more candles on the table, drawing everyone's eyes to the banquet they'd laid out. Richard's daughters gave a happy squeal and ran straight for the food.

Richard was appalled. "Girls! Mind your manners!"

"Let them be children this one night, Richard."

"Nonsense! Look – it's a wonder Ellena didn't just knock poor Agnes over."

Jenneta's face suddenly seemed haggard in the candle-light, yet there was a defiance in her eyes. "Is this not a time for celebration as much as fear?"

Ellena came sprinting back, her excitement turned to disappointment. "Father, where's the meat?"

"Have I taught you nothing, child? The flesh of animals is a temptation evil can't resist. Whether cooked or raw, it would be sure to lure evil into our fold. We must abstain."

Jenneta shot him a sideways glare. Her gaze softened as she met her daughter's eyes again. "There will be plenty of meat tomorrow, sweetheart, when we celebrate All Saints' Day."

Ellena's eyes shone with new excitement. Richard watched her run off again with more disapproval.

"Let them be, Richard. Please, just this once."

He grunted as they also made their way to the food. The feast was large enough to feed the entire village, and he helped himself to a huge portion of the fruit, vegetables, cheese and bread without fear of gluttony. Then he turned away from the table to survey the crowd. It was time to mingle.

Jenneta allowed him to steer her through the throng without complaint. They wound their way to speak with other members of standing in the community, keeping up the pretence of a happily married couple. His daughters sought him out again as he stopped to thank John and Agnes for the use of their barn.

"Please, Father, can we play now?"

Richard flashed the two Nutters a weary smile and looked down at the children. "Yes, you may play. But no running in the barn! Remember your manners and don't go bothering any of these good folk."

"Yes, Father," they chimed.

He watched them hurry away at a fast walk, his sternness giving way to a warm fondness. They were good children, for the most part. They just needed reminding of how to behave once in a while.

With the mood turned almost festive, it was easy to forget the dangers waiting beyond the light. Richard was far more concerned with avoiding the one man who could very well be his undoing. He strategically worked his way through the crowd so that there were plenty of bodies between him and Rob, but he was so focused on the young labourer, he failed to notice the nearness of the stranger from St Mary's. He soon found himself face to face with the man.

Richard narrowed his eyes. "I do not know you, sir. What brings you to Pendle?"

The outsider looked at him with an expression that was far too mischievous for Richard's liking. "Blood."

He felt his temper rising again. "Blood? Speak plainly, man. Do you mean family?"

"If you like," the stranger smirked, slipping away before Richard could ask anything else.

The miller was left feeling more confused as to who the man might be and what business he might have than he'd first felt in the church. He shared an uneasy glance with Jenneta and turned to Henry Bulcock.

"Henry, that man there. Do you know who he is?"

"Him? Can't say that I do, no, but I heard him asking if he might join the procession tonight, and of course our Reverend was all too happy to invite him in. Why?"

Richard shook his head. "I'm sure it's nothing."

Yet his doubts and uneasiness remained.

A scream tore through the pleasant conversation filling the barn, a terrible sound born of pain and despair. In its wake, there was only that dread-filled silence in which hearts pound and ears strain for further signs of danger. Somehow the silence was worse than the scream. It allowed room for the knowledge that something terrible had befallen one of them to seep in.

Dread turned to panic when Richard scanned the crowd and saw no child-sized shapes among them.

"Where are the girls?"

Shocked faces turned to look at him, but no answer was forthcoming.

"Where are our children?" Richard bellowed.

He replayed the scream in his head, but his memory of it was neither a definitively male or female voice, nor was it distinguishable between an adult's and a child's. Only the grim touch of a horrific fate was certain, and the worrying absence of his daughters. He tried not to think about what he might find if the scream had been one of the children. But the mind is a treacherous thing. Images took shape in his skull, images of his little girls lying in the dirt, their eyes gaping and mouths slack.

Around him, he could see expressions settling into reflections of his own as the same fears spread through the gathered villagers. Yet none of them made a move to go searching for the missing children, each caught between the fear for their beloved offspring and the fear of what lay beyond the safety of the barn. Richard knew then it was up to him to show them the way once again; to be their light to lead them through the blackness.

"Christopher and Henry Bulcock, Mytton, and three of you Robinsons with me; the rest of you keep vigil here until we return." He turned towards the barn door when a hand gripped his arm.

"Don't be a fool, Dick," John Nutter cautioned him. "You know as well as I what evil visits this night."

"You would do the same if it were your children out there," he answered, pulling free of the other man's grasp.

The men he'd picked seemed to take strength from his resolve. Again they took up a candle so their Lord might go with them, finding comfort in the light, small as it was. But the group hesitated on that perceived threshold between good and evil, light and dark, holy and unholy. The square patch of night might as well have been a gateway to another world, ominous in its obscurity and leering with the threat of the unknown. Once they passed back into Satan's shadow, there was no telling what might happen or what they might encounter. Each man knew it could well be his own cry that next resounded through the night.

"Lord, preserve us," Richard intoned. "Preserve our

souls and those of our loved ones, and let us find our children alive and unharmed. Don't let my harsh words be the last I will ever speak to them!"

He steeled himself for the evils they were about to face, then took that first step into the blackness. The others followed.

They split into two pairs and one group of three, checking around the farm first. But the area was utterly devoid of any childish laughter. Richard soon resigned himself to having to lead the search party further afield. Yet no matter how he strained his senses for any hint of the whereabouts of his daughters or for any warning of the approach of malicious spirits, he could detect neither. The night seemed oddly quiet. He found that more unnerving than any of the usual noises his ears might have otherwise picked up. It was as if the land had been muted by the evil that had descended upon it, allowing demons to hide in shadowy silence. There they would lie in wait for unsuspecting mortals to capture and torment. Like his innocent little girls.

Richard quickened his pace. His own fears guided him back down the path from Bull Hole Farm, and the rest of the men followed. They had just passed through the farmland's gates when the comforting glow of their candles vanished, snuffed out in a single instant as if by the breath of the Devil himself.

"Faith, brothers!" Richard cried. "We must go on if we want to see our children again in this life."

He forged on before the other men could panic and run back for the safety of the barn, though his heart danced just as fast to the song of fear. Only the thought of his daughters kept him moving onwards. Satan would not steal them away from God's grace, not as long as there was life enough in his body to fight the evil threatening their very souls.

Gradually his eyes began to adjust, but in some ways that made the fear worse. He struggled to remember if the shape to his right had been there when last they'd passed that way, or if the thing he could make out just ahead was one of the buildings he thought he knew so well. The feel of the night's chill grew ever more sinister on his skin, the foul stench on the air suffocatingly strong in his nostrils. And as the minutes wore on, the darkness only seemed to grow stronger, and it took on a malevolent nature, as if the very shadows had a demonic quality given a life of its own. Richard sensed his men's courage failing. Even the fear for their children could not drive them any deeper into the night. Their bravery hung by fraying threads, and all it took was another cry to send it plummeting.

This cry was made all the worse for their muted surroundings. But this was not the scream of human prey. Its hellish shriek was enough to melt all rational thought, leaving the men little more than mindless beasts in the grip of blind panic. There was only one response to such primal terror. They ran.

To his shame, Richard found himself now leading them in their cowardice. He could not find the strength to stop and face the darkness a second time, let alone to rally his group to join him. Shelter was the only thing on his mind.

Back down the path and through Bull Hole's gates they ran. The farm buildings loomed ahead, the light spilling from the barn a beacon.

Figures slid into view, blocking their path. Richard felt sure then that the old hag and her family had seen fit to destroy him once and for all that night. No doubt they had given their satanic lord dominion over his once godly soul so that the demonic forces about the land might snatch him from the Heaven he should have known and doom him to Hell. He skidded to a stop and sank to his knees in despair, crying for mercy even though he knew such creatures had none.

"Richard!" Christopher Bulcock said, giving him a rough shake. "Richard, look!"

He flinched at the physical contact, but just about registered the words his fellow Christian spoke. His gaze returned to the demons ahead, and a shock ran through him. They weren't demons after all but the missing children they'd risked their souls for. It took a moment for this happy truth to sink in, then he was back up on his feet and running to embrace his girls in a wave of relief.

"Where's Ellena?"

Wordlessly, the girls pointed to the cart shed behind them. Fresh dread filled him as he broke away and bade the men to keep watch while he went to investigate. The two Bulcocks opted to go with him, though he was barely aware of them following. He was too caught between fear and a glimmer of hope – hope that all might not yet be lost.

The building's archway was just visible. A gateway to grief and despair, nothing good could ever come of passing through it. Part of him wanted simply to turn away from the heartbreak he was sure lurked within, but he had to know. He had to find out what had become of his sweet little girl. So he plunged inside.

Darkness concealed the truth of the scene he'd entered, impenetrable shadows like a shroud over his eyes. Richard stretched his arms outwards and began to shuffle forwards. But no warm softness of living flesh greeted his reaching fingers, nor did his feet find any lumps on the floor to indicate the worst. Once again, his ears failed to pick up any signs of life. It was his nose which found the first clue as to what awaited him here.

A new stench slithered through the air. It was instantly recognisable as the odour of fresh death, characterised by a mix of blood and worse.

"Ellena?" he called with rising desperation.

The cart shed was not a particularly large building, and Richard did not have to suffer the unknown for long. Just as his hand brushed something standing before him, two flames burst into life on either side of the room. He recoiled from the sudden brightness on pure reflex, repelled by the fire's otherworldliness as much as the glare itself. And a terrible thought wormed its way through his skull – what if the children outside had not been their children at all but demons in disguise, pointing him into a trap?

That dreadful notion was almost too much to bear. The only thing that kept him from running was the figure he'd touched.

Recognition dawned as his vision cleared. With new relief, he looked on this one source of innocence and purity lost in the circle of Hell. She was alive! His little girl was alive and seemingly unharmed, and their family were not to suffer the pain of loss after all. But what had she been doing in the shed in the first place? And if not his daughter, then who had met an unfortunate end at the hands of the evil spirits about the land?

"Ellena!" he said, moving to embrace her as he had his other daughters. She made no move to hug him back. He realised she'd been standing as if staring at what lay at the back of the shed, even though she couldn't possibly have seen any more than he had before the flames lit up the scene. "Come away now, Ellena."

Richard steered his daughter outside and over to the

rest of his girls, amidst horrified gasps from the two Bulcocks. The men made no move to follow him back out. They were too busy staring at the source of the odour, as Ellena had been.

Once satisfied all the children were accounted for, Richard instructed the men to return them to the safety of the barn, then hastened back inside the cart shed. His sense of duty insisted on it. And besides, whoever this poor soul was – this victim taken by the demons – they were still caught between the unnatural flames. He could not in good conscience leave them there to damnation. Even if there was nothing more to be done to save that most divine piece of them, he had to at least try.

The awful stench resumed its assault on his nostrils the moment he stepped back through the archway. Richard raised a hand to cover his nose and squinted against the glare of the flames. Neither of the Bulcocks had moved. They continued to stare at the body propped up against the far wall of the shed. Richard followed their gaze.

Blood framed the grim piece, pooled around the corpse and soaked into every inch of the victim's clothes. His shirt had been torn open, as had the skin beneath, revealing the broken, gore-streaked cage where his most precious of organs should have been: that which was the pump of life itself. But worst of all were the twin craters in his face. They seemed impossibly large in features Richard was so used to seeing with muscle and skin and, most of all, eyes in the sockets. Yet all that was gone now. Everything the man had been, all of who he was, obliterated by some satanic rite, and his heart and soul stolen by forces of evil.

That was not what brought true horror for Richard, however. No, for him there was a deeper shock than the ghastly manner of the man's brutal end, and with it came the feeling his own heart had been ripped from his body. The terrible realisation brought him to his knees, unable to tear his eyes away from the grisly remains as if he could will it to not be so. But there was no mistaking that empty shell. It was his lover. It was Rob.

TEN

"Gran, what was that?" Alizon asked, rushing in from the bedroom.

Demdike didn't answer. She looked at Tom, certain that the scream heralded the death he'd been alluding to and hoping he'd elaborate on the warning he'd already given.

"Best you look and see for yourself," he said.

The old wise woman sighed and crossed the room to where she kept her tools for divination. There were various methods of peering into the future for a glimpse of one's fortunes, but that night was more about scrying current events from the safety of their own home. And there was only one tool in her possession that would allow her to work that kind of magic.

Dull and every bit as unremarkable as any household item, the blade-bone of a sheep might have seemed an unlikely tool for scrying. No runes were carved into its smooth surface, nor had it been altered in any way since the animal it once belonged to had died. But Demdike knew how to change it from something worthless into a magic mirror.

She brushed its surface with oil until it took on a new shine. Thus transformed, it now caught the glow from the fire, revealing shapes along its length. Creating the mirror was the easy part, however. Any fool could do the same, cunning folk or no, but only those skilled at their craft could actually use it. And even with years of practice, it still took a good deal of focus to look beyond the reflection from the flames and change it again from a mirror to a window.

"Mirror of seeing, mirror of knowledge,
I search thee now, I seek thy truth,
Give me answers, grant me clarity,
Of things I would know, events I would see,
Show me the fate of the one who screamed,
Show me what led to this evil deed."

The words acted as a focus while Demdike opened herself to the energy of the world around them, allowing her to channel her intent and pour that energy into the bone. New shapes took form in the oily surface, shapes independent of the flames or anything else in the room. She concentrated, willing them to become something more tangible.

A vague human outline turned into the image of a person, taking on the likeness of one of the villagers. This must surely be the identity of the victim. His face was recognisable as one she'd seen around the area, a young farm labourer. But it was not one she knew particularly well. So she looked deeper, searching for the events leading up to this man's death.

A scene began to build, visible only to herself and made

possible by the use of the tool combined with her third eye. She soon realised she was looking at a vision of the graveyard at St Mary's. The headstones appeared much clearer than they would have been in the darkness, had she truly been standing there watching what was about to take place. Amidst them stood the man who was doomed to die screaming, the focus of the image. What was his name? Foulds, that was it. Robert Foulds.

There was someone standing facing him, as if in conversation. Demdike tried to concentrate on the second figure, yet it remained oddly murky. She frowned and poured more energy into the spell, focusing the entirety of her will on that one image. Nothing changed. She could think of only one reason for that. There must be a greater power than hers hiding the figure's identity.

There was no sound to the vision, no sense of what they might have talked about. Frustration and worry threatened to break Demdike's concentration. She fought to keep her mind clear as the image began to ripple and blur, forcing her emotions aside for the time being. The vision cleared again and she watched Foulds begin to back away. He broke into a run moments later, the scene moving with him so that she couldn't see what happened to the one he'd met.

The image changed and became a reflection of the interior of St Mary's. It was filled with Christians apparently deep in prayer, though it was as if she were standing at the back with Foulds because she could only see the families from behind. One or two turned round to see who had dared to disturb the peace of their god's house, but most chose not to react. Only when the prayers had finished was she given a glimpse at the faces of those present as they filed out of the building.

One face in particular stood out from all the rest. It

wasn't just that he was a stranger – the mere image of him raised the hairs on Demdike's neck and sent a chill tingling down her spine. It was only as he passed that she was granted an insight into the truth of him.

A dead face looked out of the oil, his skin blackened and leathery, no more than a thin membrane clinging ineffectively to his skull. His nose and lips were long gone, but the eye sockets weren't empty. No, they still housed two cloudy orbs, burning with a cold fury. Demdike felt certain then she knew what had come to pass, and she fought back a wave of sadness. Foulds needn't have died that night.

Soon they were back outside. Foulds was slow to make his way into the candlelit procession, and Demdike was given the impression he was waiting for someone. She didn't have to wait long to find out who. It was Baldwin he was trying to make eye contact with, yet the miller was clearly being careful to ignore the younger man. That was curious. Especially when the farm labourer's candle went out and his features settled into a wordless plea for help. Even then, Baldwin still would not look at him or offer any words or prayers of comfort. Again, Demdike could only think of one reason for what she was seeing. They had to share a secret of some kind, one Baldwin was perfectly happy for the poor lad to take to the grave. But she didn't have time to wonder at that for long. For soon they were in a barn at Bull Hole Farm, where the customary feast had been laid out for the entire congregation.

She saw John and Agnes Nutter among the crowd, trying to embrace the new religion but clearly not happy at the Puritan way of doing things. Demdike suspected they'd have been happier to stay in their home with the protection she herself had seen to earlier that day. It didn't take much to guess who had bullied them into not only going along with the Puritan customs, but providing the space for the feast.

The vision remained centred around Foulds, but she watched the others carefully, or as much as she was permitted to with the limitations of the magic mirror. There wasn't much to see. Foulds's evening in the barn had been largely uneventful.

Then that dead face reappeared in the crowd. He moved with purpose towards his victim, like a cat closing in for the kill. And something about the vengeful spirit must have spooked Foulds because he saw what was coming for him and recognised it for the threat it posed. His terror was plain to see.

New scenes formed, first outside the barn and then within the cart shed as Foulds ran into what was to be his deathbed. The dead man followed him in, clearly a soul who'd been wronged if not by the young farm labourer himself then by his family, though why the spirit had chosen that year to seek revenge was anyone's guess. Demdike did not recognise the stranger as someone who had passed in all her years living in the area. She could only assume his death had been before her time, which begged the question – why wait so long to return to settle an old score? She was aware that time passed differently on the other side, and what could well have been decades or even centuries for mortals might have seemed but a fleeting moment for the spirit. Nevertheless, it was unusual for the dead to come for blood so long after their passing.

The mirror had no answers beyond the glimpse it allowed into these events. She was left to wonder as the spectre advanced towards Foulds, who suddenly seemed to realise he was trapped. Whether he had thought to hide in there she could not say, or perhaps blind panic had simply robbed him of his senses. Whatever the reason, he was soon backed against the wall with nowhere left to run.

Demdike took no pleasure in the vision of the young man's death, especially not one which was so cruel and agonising. The lad was not among those who had wronged her or any other cunning folk as far as she knew, and she bore him no ill will. She was glad of the lack of sound as the spirit dug its hands into Foulds's chest and pulled apart his ribcage, glad not to have to hear the sickening crack of bone breaking or that terrible scream. Experiencing it once had been enough.

Silently he sounded his cry as all he had been in his earthly life and all he might have grown to be exploded in a shower of gore. The vengeful spectre didn't even have to use the physical form it had been granted through the power of Samhain – it was more akin to something from the craft where the dead man simply willed it, and it was. Both eyes and heart burst with that malevolent will, the body that had once been Foulds sliding to the floor. And even with all that she had seen in her years working with spirits, Demdike couldn't suppress a shudder at the image filling the mirror now.

The spectre's dead face twisted into such dark satisfaction that it could almost have been demonic. Then the being faded and returned to the realm whence it came. Whoever the stranger had been in life, and whatever injustice he had suffered, it seemed it was now resolved. He was unlikely to cross the veil again in all the Samhains to come.

Yet the vision did not end there, and as Demdike continued to stare into the bone's glistening surface, she saw someone else enter the cart shed and approach the corpse. The murkiness of the image suggested it was the same being she'd seen before in the graveyard, but even that much remained unclear to her. She could only watch and wonder as the human-shaped figure knelt beside the cadaver. For a moment, the figure appeared to be admiring the vengeful spirit's handiwork, then it began to reposition the body so that it was sat upright rather than slumped over. It seemed to take great care to ensure that the wounds could clearly be seen. With that done, the figure stood and left the shed. But still the vision continued.

This glimpse into Foulds's fate was beginning to raise more questions than it had answered. Demdike held on to her concentration, watching for whatever there was left to see in connection with the death. She didn't have to wait long before the being reappeared, this time leading someone in with him. It should have been too dark to see the face of the child now in the building with them, but the vision still remained clearer than the reality would have been. She could see the girl was none other than Ellena Baldwin, standing there with an air of uncertainty. The child's nose wrinkled at the stench the corpse must have given off, while the murky figure remained as shrouded in mystery as ever. But it appeared to whisper something in the girl's ear. The figure vanished a moment later, as if it had never been.

The likeness of Richard soon appeared and two flames sprang into life on either side of the corpse. Demdike had to wonder if that was the murky figure's doing, for she was now in no doubt that no matter how human its form had been, it was something otherworldly. Had the creature brought the girl inside simply to lure Master Baldwin to the grisly spectacle within? It seemed likely, but why? If the murky figure had killed the young man itself, she might have assumed it was a message. But it had been the work of a vengeful spirit, unrelated to whatever the creature was.

Perhaps it was something to do with the secret between the two men? There were no clear answers, not even after she'd watched Dick usher his daughter away from the ghoulish scene, and then return to discover the identity of the corpse.

His reaction once he recognised the young man was most telling. She'd seen enough of loss to know a broken heart when she saw one and she understood then what their secret was. No wonder the Puritan had steeped himself so deeply in his religion. He must have become so bent on stamping out all sin in the area in an attempt to atone for his own acts against his god. But why would that forbidden love interest the otherworldly creature?

With that final revelation, the vision came to an end, the images in the oil fading until there was nothing but the reflection of the flames once more. She wiped the bone clean and returned it to its place among her various tools for divination, then seated herself back at the table and thought over all that the magic mirror had shown her. One thing was certain based on what she'd seen: Tom was right in that the death would bring more trouble their way. If Baldwin had truly just lost someone close to his heart, he was likely to lash out in his grief and maybe even blame her for the death. After all, there was no escaping the fact Foulds had died to something unnatural. There would be those who'd suspect witchcraft, and they had no real way of proving otherwise, which meant they were going to have to tread carefully in the days to come.

"What is it, Gran? Are we in danger?" Alizon asked.

"Not tonight, child," she answered.

"What did you see?" Tom said.

"Do you not already know?"

"Then let me rephrase: how much did you see?"

"Vengeful spirits at work," she answered with a wave of her hand, not wishing to discuss it too deeply in front of her granddaughter and worry the girl unduly. "Why, is there anything more you can tell me?"

"Did you see the connection with Richard Baldwin?"

"Yes."

"Do not underestimate him. Events have been set in motion, events which will bring more conflict between the two of you. Do not give him any more reason to drag our family in front of Nowell than he has already. That is as much as I can say."

Demdike closed her eyes and took a deep breath in an attempt to push back another wave of frustration. She knew the future wasn't set in stone – any mortal had the power to change the course of destiny if given the chance, as long as they had the will to make different choices and turn from their current path. And she knew her husband was trying to give her as much guidance as he could to allow her to do just that. But she needed more than vague warnings and pieces of advice any fool could see for themselves. She needed insight into the milestones of the destiny she was set on, something to help her recognise the key points along the way so that she might take a different turn and forge a new fate.

Alizon snorted. "Why should we have anything to fear from that Christian idiot?"

"We have everything to fear from the likes of him. He has the respect of the community and the ear of the gentry, and if he thinks he can find proof of our family harming anyone with witchcraft we will all be for the gallows. Your grandfather is right, we should not underestimate him. But there is nothing more to be gained by talking about these matters tonight. Back to bed with you."

"You need your rest as well, Betsy," Tom pointed out.

Demdike found she couldn't really argue with that, and so she allowed him to lead her into the bedroom, as he had so often in life. But there could be no physical confirmation of the love between them that night, no giving in to lustful desires like they might once have done all those years ago. Not with Alizon in the same room, and besides, such things were only for the living. For what was sex but the ultimate feeling of being alive, the very act of creating new life and enjoying the pleasures of the flesh? It was not for those beyond the grave, those with no more life to give. It was no longer for her Tom.

And yet, the line between life and death had blurred, even if the barrier had not completely broken. What was left of her husband climbed into bed beside her and wrapped his arms around her frame, holding her close one last time. She shivered against that cold, skeletal body, but didn't push him away. It had been a long time since she'd known the comfort of another. In that moment, she felt she would sell her soul to the next demon she dealt with just to know it again, for however many years were left to her in that life. Even if it was only the cold shade of what they'd once had, it would be better than nothing, better than being alone on a night but for her granddaughter. And Alizon was long past the age of cuddling in bed.

She fought against sleep for as long as she could, unwilling to let the night end. But time was one of the things it was not within her power to control. Samhain could not last and her body could not manage without sleep for much longer, and there was nothing she could do to change that. Somewhere in the early hours she nodded off, resigned to the fact her husband would soon leave her again.

ELEVEN

D emdike awoke with a shiver. Light streamed through the oil-soaked linen, but the chill of the grave lingered on. Her groggy thoughts groped for why that was. Tom!

There was no cold body lying beside her now. She rolled over to find the blankets much cooler than usual on the side where he'd lain, but no other sign of him. Her heart sank. Had he left her again so soon?

The sound of hushed voices filtered in from the cottage's main living area. Demdike's heart rose in a surge of hope. She threw back the covers and swung herself upright and onto her feet.

Old bones ached in the cool air. Alizon stirred in the bed across from her and an eye peeked out from between the covers. It vanished behind tightly shut lids a moment later. Demdike smiled to herself but gave no indication she'd seen the girl wake. Let Alizon feign sleep. The veil would not be fully restored until the sun set that evening, and until then, Malkin Tower remained the safest place for both of them. She saw no harm in letting her granddaughter stay in bed, just this once.

Ignoring the discomfort of her aged limbs, Demdike went through to the next room. Mixed emotions rushed through her when she saw one of the voices was indeed Tom. Chief among them was a feeling of relief that he was still here, but she also couldn't help the hint of anger that he'd let her believe he'd gone while she'd slept. She might have said something to him if their time together hadn't been so limited. And then there was the matter of the second man sitting across the table from him.

"Tibb," she said. "What business do you have with my husband?"

Those green eyes regarded her with more in the way of worry than their usual warmth. "We fear for you, Mistress."

"And what good to me is your fear?" she snapped. "What good to me are your mutterings of danger and trouble when they lack the substance needed to do anything about it?"

"Forgive us, Betsy," Tom answered. "You know we would tell you everything if we could."

"Sometimes I wonder. Is this just a game to you spirits?"

Tom shook his head. "Of course not. I promise you, my love, we are here to help."

"There is more you need to see," Tibb said. "And perhaps then you will let me take revenge on our enemies, before it is too late."

"Revenge is not the answer," Tom argued.

Demdike sighed. "Enough. I have already told you both, I will make my move when I am ready. What would you have of me now, Tibb, more scrying?"

"No," Tibb said. "Scrying is too limited, and there are

happenings taking place at this very moment which we would have you forewarned of. Let me be your eyes and ears. That is why I come this morning. Believe me when I tell you I am here to serve, as always."

"Then prove it. Show me something useful."

Her familiar bowed his head and got to his feet. Seconds later he was dropping to all fours, a hellhound once more. Demdike couldn't help but think – and not for the first time – how such a drastic transformation from human to animal should be more awkward and painful. She had to remind herself he was a spirit. No matter how solid his body appeared to her senses, he was not really there in a physical sense and he could manifest as he saw fit. And yet, of the three hellhounds bound to their family, he alone had shown the ability to shapeshift. There had to be some difficulty to it.

Tibb's change was seamless. His shape simply collapsed and reformed with no more effort than it took most people to change their clothes, and it was over so quickly her eyes could barely track the process.

The hellhound looked up at her expectantly. She seated herself beside her husband and met Tibb's now blazing eyes, opening her mind to his through the power of their pact. But that was the easy part.

She could feel Tibb there alongside all that made her who she was – his emotions, the darkness at his core, his desire for mischief and revenge. One might say their souls touched and began to mingle. Yet she could never hear his thoughts, unless he specifically projected them to her.

It was not his thoughts she needed though. It was his eyes and ears, as he'd said himself. And to experience the world through his senses, she would have to go further than merely brushing against his mind. She would have to follow that connection all the way through and into Tibb's skull, leaving her own body vulnerable while her soul occupied another. It was a risk, but one she believed was worth it. Merely sharing memories was not as powerful as being in the moment, and visions were too easily broken, like the one on the night of her grandson's pact. Tom would watch over her physical self while her soul went with Tibb.

Her familiar offered no resistance as she reached out for his mind, her soul clawing its way across that connection the pact had given them. Her sense of her body faded. She could no longer feel the warmth of her limbs or the hardness of the wood she was sitting on. There came the disconcerting feeling of being nothing more than a spirit herself, her soul free of its fleshy tether to the earth and seemingly in danger of floating away to wherever the astral realm might take her. But she kept her sights solely on the hellhound until she found herself in his head, looking out through eyes that saw so much more than a human. In some ways, it was similar to opening her inner eye. Similar, though Tibb's sight was far greater than that.

It was almost like opening her eyes on a strange new land, one so full of swirling colours and twisting shapes it was dizzying. But perhaps strangest of all was looking at her own body slumped in the chair, with its slack expression and vacant eyes. There was something deeply disturbing about seeing her physical self like that, and if she'd been in her own body, she might have shuddered. Tibb didn't have that same reflex, however.

Demdike had witnessed a true possession only twice in her career as a wise woman, and this power to enter Tibb was not that. True possession meant completely taking control of the host. Demdike doubted she could accomplish such a feat with her familiar, even if she'd wanted to. She made no attempt to take the reins as the hellhound turned his head to look at her husband.

"Take care of her," Tom said.

"Always," Tibb answered.

She'd barely felt him speak the words when he decided to take his leave, vanishing and reappearing elsewhere as only spirits could. In this instance, he'd reappeared just outside Read Hall. As far as Demdike was aware, it had been instantaneous, so that one moment they'd been in Malkin Tower and the next they were looking at the grand building that was home to Roger Nowell, with no sense of anything in between. It might have been disorientating if she'd experienced such an unnatural leap in her own body, but to Tibb it was nothing and her soul was merely along for the ride. The usual rules didn't apply.

Approaching footsteps reached the hellhound's sensitive ears, his head turning so that they were looking over at the path leading towards the estate. There was no sense of alarm from him. It seemed he'd been expecting the Nowells' visitor, or perhaps he was merely confident in the knowledge no mortal could hurt him. Either way, he was content to sit and wait for the man to appear at the gate, giving her no option but to wait with him.

Richard Baldwin strode into view. Demdike supposed she shouldn't have been surprised. Of all the Puritans that might pose a threat to them, had it not been him specifically she'd been warned of? Yet the very sight of the hated man stirred her darker emotions, made stronger for the closer connection she currently shared with her familiar, his hunger for violence mixing with her desire for revenge. A growl started to rumble deep in Tibb's throat. The Puritan didn't even flinch, utterly oblivious to the danger he was in.

There came that feeling of time slowing while the

rhythm of Baldwin's heart filled Tibb's ears. Demdike could feel her familiar's longing to taste their enemy's blood. Except now it was her longing too. The beat almost seemed to be calling to them, calling to set its precious fluid free. Their combined darkness strained to answer. She felt Tibb tense, ready to lunge at their prey.

But Baldwin had his own darkness. Beneath those haggard features it lurked, a soul raw and bleeding with the fresh loss suffered through the night. His heart festered with a dangerous concoction of grief, hate and rising anger. The miller was doing an admirable job of concealing such emotions behind his fleshy mask, but there was no hiding the ugly nature of his soul from Tibb's eyes. Visible as a murky shape just under the surface, that ghostly shadow bore the pain of the gaping wound in his heart. Pain that made him all the more desirable as prey to the hellhound.

One mighty leap and it would all be over. Her familiar's sights remained locked on the Puritan, lips curled back in a fierce snarl. They could end the threat he posed there and then, and perhaps set destiny on a new course before it was too late – before the fate the spirits had foreseen was sealed. Or his death could prove to be their undoing.

Demdike sensed Tibb was about to make his move when the miller came to a sudden stop, his head snapping to the left where the hellhound crouched. What happened next should not have been possible. Whether it was the darkness currently ruling him feeling the same pull as Tibb's she couldn't say, but Baldwin's eyes met the hell-hound's and he seemed to sense the spirit watching him, and perhaps even her presence as well.

In all her years as a wise woman, Demdike had never once known her familiar to suffer from the same doubts or uncertainty that so often ruled mortal hearts. But he was less sure of himself then. The dark tide that had been so quick to crash through their connected minds ebbed away, leaving only wariness.

It seemed an age before Baldwin looked away and resumed his walk to the mansion. Only then did Demdike feel Tibb relax, though he remained cautious as he followed the Puritan into the hall. His mind was guarded now. Guarded, but not completely closed off to her, for that would have pushed her out and back into her own body. And she still hadn't seen whatever he'd brought her to see.

Baldwin was shown into the study where Roger Nowell was at work at his desk. Stacks of official-looking papers covered the oaken surface, rising up on either side of the JP like miniature versions of Pendle Hill. Behind him hung a portrait of some long-dead relative looking down with apparent disapproval on them all.

Tibb padded into the middle of the room, seating himself just to the side of the two men, on an ornate rug. It covered most of the wooden floor, resplendent with its beautiful patterns and delicate intricacies. Even the walls were more decorative than the bare stone Demdike was used to, framed with their wooden panels, and the window was made of glass.

There was more furniture in that one room than she owned in the entirety of Malkin Tower, including numerous chairs. Some were padded for greater comfort. They looked more inviting than the hard stools and benches she was used to, yet Baldwin remained standing.

Her familiar focused his gaze on the two men, so Demdike could clearly see and hear everything about to pass between them. And for as long as she looked out on the land with her familiar's eyes, the secrets of a man's core were hers to see. Nowell was no different – no amount of power gained in the world of men could shield him from the greater forces at work in the Otherworld, or the hold its agents so often had over mortals. But the JP's darkness was not quite the same as the miller's, his soul not made ugly by the emotional sores Richard bore. There was corruption there, born of his position in the social hierarchy. Yet that darkness did not rule him. No, to Demdike he looked much lighter than Baldwin, with only patches of shadow betraying the taint in his heart. In her younger days, she might have hoped that meant there was enough good left in him to be reasoned with. The years had long since eroded any such naivety. She need only cast her mind back to that night two months past to remind herself of Nowell's tolerance for perceived witches.

"Richard. Am I to presume this is about the unfortunate events of last night?"

"Unfortunate? A man lies dead, murdered by witchcraft no less, and you call that unfortunate?"

Baldwin seemed to be struggling to maintain his mask, his spirit self rising to the surface so that it distorted his mortal face. To Nowell, it would have been no more than Baldwin's emotions bleeding into his features. Only Demdike and her familiar could see the true manifestation of his pain. Like the shadow of a demon or a gargoyle it was, merging with his flesh and blood self into something truly grotesque.

"Careful now, Richard, lest your feelings betray you. I am sure you would not wish the whole of Pendle to learn of your indecencies with the victim."

Shock cut through Baldwin's uglier emotions. His darkness fell away in an instant, back down to the gaping wound in his heart.

"You knew?"

"Of course. It is my job to know the secrets of all those I must preside over, for how else am I to keep the people of Pendle on the right side of the law?"

"But how?"

"That is not important. You needn't worry, Richard. You are an otherwise upstanding member of the community, and your assistance in unmasking the Devil's agents has been most valuable. And that is precisely why you have come seeking an audience today, is it not?"

Baldwin let out an angry snort, his hatred rising again. "I do not understand why you have not yet arrested that old crone and her wretched family. It is past time they were tried in the assizes for their foul deeds! Aside from all the hurt they have caused through witchcraft, are they not a nuisance to us all when they come begging and leeching off honest men? And now they have caused yet another death right under our noses! They make fools of us, Roger. One need only look at the body to see the evidence of the unnatural and the devilry at work here. Rob was murdered and we both know who is to blame."

Nowell regarded the other man. "Perhaps. But you know as well as I that I cannot send anyone to the assizes without some kind of evidence. And I have seen no proof that Old Demdike or any of her family are the witches behind this."

"Everyone round here knows the hag hates me. She put me under some kind of curse one night when we had the misfortune of crossing paths, till the blood leaked out of my body and I started to faint. I still have the ruined shirt to prove it! Doubtless she sought to deal me further harm by murdering someone I care about."

"And what were you doing out at night that would lead to such an encounter?"

Richard's gaze dropped to the floor, the darkness in him receding a second time. Demdike didn't need any gifts of insight to pick up on the shame replacing his anger. "I was going to see him."

"I thought as much. So unless you want to risk every soul in these parts – including your wife and daughters, I might add – finding out your sins, we must look for something else to take before the assizes."

Defeated, the miller turned away and shuffled over to the door without another word. Nowell watched him leave the room, his face betraying nothing of his thoughts as Tibb stood and made his exit, vanishing and reappearing a second time without any warning. Demdike's last glimpse of the JP showed him returning to his work. A second later, she found herself looking at an entirely different scene, though it was not the inside of Malkin Tower.

They were somewhere outside again. That was as much as she knew, for she could see no immediately recognisable landmarks to place exactly where Tibb had brought her now.

She was still trying to get her bearings when she felt something crash into Tibb's flank. Pain burst through him as he was dragged to the floor. He didn't bleed like a mortal beast, but the stinging was there to indicate the presence of a nasty gash down his thigh.

A second wound opened up across his ribcage. Fear took hold of Demdike. They could see nothing of their attacker, and she couldn't determine any clues as to who or what it might be through Tibb's other senses. If there was any recognition from her familiar, she didn't sense it, though everything was happening so fast there wasn't much time for thinking. Tibb was reacting purely on instinct, fangs bared in a defensive snarl.

She was painfully aware of how vulnerable he was lying there on the floor, utterly at the mercy of the other creature. But she was powerless to help. This was his battle, and she was no more than a spectator urging him on.

Tibb tried to pick himself up a second time. He almost succeeded when something collided with his skull. It plunged him into darkness and the connection was severed. Demdike's head snapped up, her soul firmly back in her own body. But her fear remained.

TWELVE

"Betsy? What is it, my love?"

Eyes wide, Demdike stared at her husband without really seeing him. Her thoughts remained solely with Tibb.

She tried reaching out to the hellhound. Nothing. There was no sense of that spiritual binding they'd entered into. Worse, it was as if it had never been. No matter how she cried out to him with her mind or begged him to answer her summons, he gave no reply.

Her thoughts turned to the worst. Some rational part of her mind tried to reason that he could not truly be dead because he had never been alive – not in the mortal sense of the word. It did nothing to abate her worries. Tibb could have been ripped and torn until he simply ceased to be.

"Betsy?" Tom tried again.

The cold touch of his hand brought him into focus. She looked from his worried face to her granddaughter, now up and dressed and sitting across the table. The familiar walls of Malkin Tower surrounded them.

"It's Tibb," she said. "Something hurt my Tibb and

there is nothing to be done whilst we must shelter in here till the veil is restored."

"Is that even possible?" Alizon asked.

"Only spirits can harm other spirits, but I do not know what attacked us or why. I was forced out of his mind before I could see anything."

Her husband seemed to be debating something with himself, and it didn't take the craft to guess what.

"No, Tom," she said. "I would not lose you as well."

"We both know my time here is limited. In a few hours we must part, whether we would choose to or no. The risk is not so great for those of us already among the dead."

"And if whatever hurt Tibb attacks you as well? I could not live with the knowledge your soul had been destroyed."

"What other choice do we have? Scrying might not give enough answers."

"Then let me conjure a spirit to go in your stead."

"Think about what you are saying, Betsy. Summoning spirits without Tibb to protect you carries just as much risk as going out there yourself. There is no other way."

"'Tis too dangerous. Stay, for what precious little time we have left together."

He shook his head as he stood and walked round to embrace Alizon with a sad smile.

"Will we see you again, Grandfather?" Alizon asked.

He kissed her cheek. "Not in this life, child. But take comfort in the knowledge I will always be with you."

Demdike stood as well. "Stay with us."

"No, Betsy. Let me do this for you."

She knew there was nothing she could say to persuade him otherwise. Death looked to have made no impact on that stubborn streak she'd found both frustrating and endearing in their time on the earth. But she wasn't happy with his decision. Knowing he was doing it out of love for her did nothing to change that.

Her own stubbornness made her stiffen when he pulled her into another hug. The deep affection they shared took over a moment later. She melted into his arms.

"Don't go," she tried one last time.

A skeletal hand stroked her hair as he whispered "I must. But fear not, for this is not the last goodbye – I will be waiting when your time comes."

"Promise me. Promise me you won't go anywhere near Tibb's attacker, if it is indeed still out there."

He didn't answer her with words, instead drawing her into another kiss. And though all warmth was gone from what little of his flesh remained, the echoes of their love reverberated across the grave, bringing a heat of its own. Then the moment passed, and he was pulling away and taking his leave. Demdike felt the same void open up in her heart as she'd struggled to fill the last time they'd parted. An ache took hold deep in her chest, and she turned away from the table so Alizon would not see the tears spilling down her cheeks.

"Gran?"

The old wise woman wanted nothing more than to be alone with her pain then, but somehow she found the strength to dry her eyes and face her granddaughter. "Yes, child?"

"Will Grandfather not return, even if only to report back to us what he found out there? Dusk is still hours away yet."

Demdike shook her head. "He will send us a message, if he can."

"But why?"

"Because he believes he will be sparing us the pain of a

second goodbye if he is successful. And if not, I fear there will not be enough left of him to come back to us."

There was another reason her husband was leaving earlier than Samhain's end dictated, though Demdike did her best not to think about it – about what would become of him at daylight's gate. Deep down she knew it was for the best Tom had elected to spare them that added pain, yet she couldn't help but resent him a little for leaving so early in the day. She shared none of this with her granddaughter, however. Alizon might be starting to develop feelings for the Bulcock boy, but she had yet to truly discover any of the trials of the heart. She wouldn't understand until she did.

"Is there nothing we can do to help?" Alizon asked.

The question took Demdike by surprise, but it was what she needed to pull her back up from the pain-filled depths of her grief and fears, at least for the time being. She felt slightly ashamed that she had not thought of helping Tom herself. "Aye, lass, we will seek protection on his behalf. But only the most powerful aid will suffice this time. Calling on the spirits will not be enough."

"You mean we need to work some dark magic?"

"No!" she snapped, uneasy at the eagerness in the girl's voice. "The dark arts should only ever be a last resort, when white magic is simply not enough."

Alizon's tone turned sullen. "Well what then, if not a white protection spell from the spirits?"

"We must keep to the white arts, especially while Tibb is missing. I simply mean to call on the most powerful of beings and request their aid. Whether they give it remains to be seen."

She could see understanding dawn in her granddaughter's face, and without another word Alizon abandoned her place at the table in favour of helping prepare for the ritual they were about to work. It was simple enough to perform but one which was used rarely, as the help of such forces was less reliable than the other spirits they would usually work with. It was safer than dealing with those associated with the dark arts though, for there was no price to be paid. Either the beings they were about to reach out to would choose to help, or they would not. There was nothing more to it.

With her granddaughter's help, Demdike soon had the tools she needed laid out before her. A small flame danced atop its pillar, pure and burning with a kind of life of its own, one born of the very forces cunning folk relied so greatly on. The smooth surface of the old human femur gleamed in its light, her most powerful aid in imbuing the spell with her intent. Demdike wrapped her fingers around it and gathered her thoughts. The greatest of strength was needed to ensure she was heard above the clamour of every other living thing under the care of the ones who could be considered the essence of nature and life itself. So she poured every ounce of her will into the rite as she spoke the ancient verse:

"Goddess of life, Goddess of nature,
Goddess of fire, air and water,
Please accept this offering of the flame,
This candle I light in thy honour and thy name,
Hear my prayer, hear my plea,
I ask only this of thee,
Protect the soul known as Thomas Ingham,
Protect and keep him free from harm,
Protect him until the danger has passed,
And by my will this spell is cast."

Smoke twisted and curled from a second offering of incense, and she held the candle to a small pile of herbs until they too began to smoulder in their metal dish. This third offering was symbolic not only of the natural world but also the destruction their Goddess stood for. Life and death, creation and destruction, birth and slaughter – all part of the same balance, flip sides to the same coin. And the Goddess embodied all. She, and her male counterpart, the one Demdike would now invoke in her second verse. The ceremonial blade glinted with the light of the candle as she raised it in her other hand, readying the final offering.

> *"Lord of the hunt, Lord of the wild,*
> *Horned One, hear your child,*
> *Accept these offerings of root, flower and flame,*
> *And this blood I spill in thy name,*
> *Feel my heart beat for you,*
> *Your daughter, forever true,*
> *And grant this blessing if you will,*
> *Oh mighty Horned God, take your fill,*
> *Revel in the blood of enemies, make them thy prey,*
> *Hunt any foolish enough to stand in thy way,*
> *Keep Thomas Ingham free from danger,*
> *Kill any seeking to be his hunter."*

Crimson tears dripped from the tip of her finger, spattering the herbs and fuelling the power of the spell. The allure of her life force was sure to be too strong for the mightiest of all hunters to ignore.

Demdike repeated the last two lines of the first verse to finish the spell, and no sooner had the word 'cast' left her lips than the herbs burst into open flame. Her voice had been heard. Whether the protection for her husband would be granted only the deities themselves knew, but she took comfort in the knowledge that her words had at least reached them. The rest was up to Tom now.

She sat waiting for the fire to burn out and the power to fade, the blaze surprisingly strong, even with the power she'd fed it. It was when that flame began to darken she knew something was wrong, the orange glow dimming into blackness. The shape of the flame was still visible, yet instead of giving off light as it should have done, it cast only shadow, the kitchen turning gloomier as a result. Fresh fear stabbed through her then.

"Who intrudes on our sacred rite?" she said, not so much asking as demanding an answer. She succeeded in keeping her voice strong and commanding, though she knew her act was not fooling any spirits, especially not the kind of beings who fed on emotions such as fear.

No answer was forthcoming so she asked again "Who interrupts this ritual?"

A rush of power surged across her vulnerable body, a tingling feeling that made her hairs stand on end and her skin crawl. The flame flickered and died, allowing more shadows to rush in. And in that darkness she could just make out the outline of something vaguely human in shape only, its true nature wreathed in a malice and cruelty that went far beyond any evil born of the human heart. That presence filled her with fresh dread and instinctively she called out for Tibb, yet still he remained lost to her. Instead, she was answered by the dark spirit.

His malevolent laugh bypassed her ears so that it sounded directly in her head, audible to her only. With Alizon's third eye not yet open, her granddaughter would not be able to see or hear such spirits unless they chose to fully manifest in the mortal realm.

But Alizon was far from simple, clearly recognising that something was amiss. "Gran, what's wrong?"

Demdike opened her mouth to answer, but the words would not come. Her tongue felt heavy in her mouth and unresponsive, no matter how much will she poured into resisting the dread thing and vocalising her thoughts. She gripped the old pentagram amulet, fighting to keep her hold on the physical world and regain command of her own flesh. It was no use. Without Tibb's protection she was weak to all manner of spiritual attacks, and both she and the demon knew it.

The room was growing darker still as her vision began to fade, her soul beginning to slip away. Panic gripped her at the demon's strength. She continued to fight with everything she had, but it simply wasn't enough.

Her greatest fears then were what would become of her daughter and grandchildren. Would the demon take them too? Elizabeth and James had their familiars to protect them, but for how long? In her heart, she knew this was the same entity who had attacked and defeated Tibb with relative ease. It was doubtful Ball and Dandy would fare any better if the creature faced them one on one.

"Gran!" Alizon cried, rushing forward to catch her as she fell to her knees. "Speak to me, Gran; tell me what to do."

Demdike's body was completely beyond her control now, the demon rendering her incapable of communicating through any gestures she might have made, let alone speech. Her granddaughter's voice sounded so far away, almost drowned out by that malicious laugh still echoing in her skull. Death would soon be coming for her, the fight all but lost. In but a matter of moments she would die there in Alizon's arms, utterly helpless and stripped of the power so many had feared and respected over the years. She could only hope the demon would be content with her soul and leave her granddaughter unscathed, and perhaps warier of the dark arts in the future.

Just as she was on the verge of passing out, she felt a fresh surge of strength course through her veins. Alizon's voice grew louder, while the laughter in her head receded somewhat, so that she could recognise the words her granddaughter spoke. A sense of pride beat back the fear and restored her will to fight. Demdike's vision began to clear a moment later as Alizon chanted spells of protection, driving back the darkness.

Still it wasn't enough. The demon renewed his attack and Demdike remained at his mercy. Her body continued its refusal to obey her commands.

A growl sounded from somewhere behind. Fresh hope filled Demdike's heart. Tibb was alive! Alive and returned to her, stronger than ever.

The hellhound charged past, brown and leaner than the spirit beast she'd made her pact with, though no less fierce and protective not just of his mistress, but of all those her daughter bid him watch over. Ball showed no hesitation in lunging at the demon, snarling his fury as he sank his fangs into the dread thing's arm and shaking his head with greater savagery than any earthly animal. Before the demon could shake him off, a second beast appeared, this one black and more muscular, yet still not the hellhound Demdike was hoping to see. Nevertheless, Dandy was also a welcome sight.

Dandy latched onto the demon's leg, forcing the malevolent being to deal with the two hellhounds. The demon's hold on Demdike's soul slipped. Her muscles, so heavy and akin to stone under the dark spirit's power, regained what suppleness age hadn't already taken. The temporary paralysis lifted and her ability to speak was restored.

Demdike added her voice to her granddaughter's. Together they chanted the words of protection and called on any spirits who would grant them aid. The demon's laughter turned to growls of frustration. Powerful as he clearly was, it seemed even he could not overpower both the familiars and resist the protection magic of two cunning folk all at once. He succeeded in shaking off Dandy but Ball refused to let go.

Black smoke twisted and curled in place of the blood the hellhounds would have torn from mortal beings. Demdike sensed a great reluctance from the creature to have to retreat, but the hellhounds were leaving him with little choice. Once Dandy was back on his feet and snapping at the dark spirit's other leg, the struggle was over, the demon vanishing as swiftly as he'd appeared. The unnatural darkness retreated, the room seeming much brighter in its absence.

Demdike nodded her thanks to the two hellhounds. They seemed to have come out of the encounter unscathed, and moments later they too were gone, leaving her to wonder why they'd appeared in the first place. Not that she wasn't grateful, but it was unlikely either Elizabeth or James had known how badly she'd needed their help.

"What just happened, Gran?" Alizon asked, her eyes a little too wide and her voice a little too high.

"I'm not entirely sure, lass." Demdike winced as she picked herself up, her body complaining at being made to lie on the hard floor. "No doubt you sensed a presence, and what I can tell you is the thing you sensed was a demon, but what kind of demon or what name he goes by I cannot say. I wasn't able to see him clearly. Nor could I tell you why he came through during the rite, or what his interest in us might be. He was a powerful one, though. So now you might understand why I caution against the use of the dark arts, except for when there really is no other option. Demons are dangerous enough without making deals with them."

"Yes, Gran, I know. You don't have to keep lecturing me."

"See that you take heed of my advice then, and stop asking to work dark magic."

"But what about the rite for Grandfather, did it work?"

"Yes, our plea was heard." She seated herself back at the table with a tired sigh. "We can only hope the Goddess and the Horned One grant him their blessing and keep him safe from the likes of that demon."

They fell silent, and so began the long hours of waiting. That afternoon was one of the hardest Demdike had ever endured, her fear for Tibb equalled only by her fear for Tom. She wasn't sure what form a message from her husband might take, but the closer dusk drew with no word from him, the greater her worries became.

Alizon set out the evening meal. Demdike dipped her spoon into the pottage with little enthusiasm. There was only nausea in the place where her usual appetite would be.

"Come on, Gran. You need to keep your strength up." Alizon took a big spoonful of her own pottage and feigned more enjoyment than the bland meal had any right to.

Demdike couldn't help smiling, though she made no move to bring her spoon up to her mouth. "Oh, you're taking care of me now, are you? As if your mam fussing over me isn't enough."

Alizon grimaced and stared down at her bowl. "I'm just trying to help."

"By treating me like a child?" She reached across to gently lift her granddaughter's chin. "Don't you worry about me, lass. I won't be wasting away anytime soon."

Alizon gave a half smile, but Demdike could see worry alongside the usual sullenness. "Maybe not, but you really should try and eat. It's been a long day."

Demdike sighed. Her granddaughter was right. She dipped her spoon in the bowl again and raised it to her lips, barely swallowing it down before Tom's messenger appeared.

"Mistress," Ball said. "I bring news of your husband's search for Tibb, though there is not much of it."

"I would hear whatever he has learnt, no matter how little."

"Your husband went to where the fight took place, but there was no sight of Tibb, nor the creature that attacked him. Tom searched the area and looked as far beyond the veil as he could see without crossing back over, but he found no hint of where Tibb might have gone. Then he saw the danger coming for you and hastened over to the Device household."

"And that is all he said?"

Ball nodded, a strange gesture on his animal frame.

She sighed and dropped her spoon back into the bowl. "Thank you, Ball. You may go, unless you would like a share of our food. I've no appetite this evening."

Ball raised his nose to the air and snorted at the mix of vegetables and grains. "Has Tibb taught you nothing of our tastes?"

Demdike opened her mouth to answer, but the hell-hound had already disappeared. She sighed, her heart heavier with the lack of news. At least Tom was safe, and she had her answer as to how her daughter and grandson had known to send Ball and Dandy to her aid earlier. But what of Tibb?

The last of the day's light faded and the veil was restored. The threat of wandering spirits came to an end for another year. Demdike's thoughts turned to her husband, her comfort in the knowledge he hadn't also succumbed to Tibb's attacker replaced by the sadness that she would never see him again in that life. But it was more than the aching in her heart to lie with him again through the night. It was more than the aching to simply feel the warmth of his living body and be held in the arms of the one man she had only ever known true unconditional love with. This fresh pain was born as much from the thought of what was happening to him at that very moment as it was her fresh grief.

She tried not to think of her Tom's handsome face sloughing from his skull in a stinking, rotting mess of congealing blood and decaying tissue. She tried to fight the mental image of his muscular frame slipping from his bones until there was nothing but his skeleton left. She tried, and failed.

The gruesome scenes played out with a clarity that came from having witnessed the same thing happening to other spirits in previous years. She had seen the physical forms granted through the power of Samhain disintegrate into nothing. She had witnessed flesh and organs turn to a kind of grisly soup, watched as eyes had collapsed into pools of sludge and tongues had slid from between bare jaws like pink snakes slithering out from bony crevices.

Even the bones would turn to dust, and the disgusting puddle of decomposing tissue would vanish. Only the ethereal part of the spirit was left behind to wander the lands of the dead once more.

Perhaps it was as well Tom had departed early. She had been all too aware the deception of life could not last beyond nightfall, but even with her gift of sight breaking through that illusion, she had still found herself wishing for more. It broke her heart to lose him a second time.

She hid her pain from her granddaughter as best she could, but when Alizon began to ask more questions about her grandfather, it all became too much. Demdike went to bed early that night. There she lay until dawn, hugging her pillow and weeping silent tears.

CHAPTER
THIRTEEN

F or many, time may be the greatest of healers, but for Demdike the passing weeks only made her pain worse. She visited her daughter more often, trying to distract herself from it with the added company of Elizabeth and her other two grandchildren, though even little Jennet's youthful innocence could not completely take it away.

"Why are you so sad, Granny?" the little girl asked while Elizabeth was busy washing their clothes down by the river. Alizon was also preoccupied with her attempts at divination, probably seeking answers to the one question she was currently obsessed with – did she have any hope of a future with young Master Bulcock? As for James, he had business elsewhere.

"'Tis nothing for you to worry about, child. I miss my Tibb and your grandfather, that's all."

"But Grandfather isn't really gone. He said he'd still be watching over us from the other side, even if we can't see him now Samhain is over. Just like you promised to do when you die, remember, Granny?"

"Yes, child, and so I shall."

"I like Grandfather. He told me I would be a wise woman as well someday, and I'll have a dog familiar of my own. I wish he hadn't had to go back to the spirit world when Samhain ended."

Demdike smiled through fresh tears and hugged her youngest granddaughter tight. "I wish he could have stayed as well."

"Granny?"

"Yes, lass?"

"Is Grandfather in Hell?"

Shock made Demdike pull back, her hands on Jennet's arms as she studied her face. "What would make you think that?"

"Isobell says all those that don't go to church go to Hell when they die; the vicar said so in his sermon last Sunday!"

Demdike snorted and waved that away. "Nature is more complicated than the Christians would have us believe with their ideas of light and dark, god and satan, heaven and hell. There are the realms we call the Heavens and those we know as Hell, but not like in their Bible, which twists the truth into the story that most pleases them. I would rather not talk of such things at the moment, child. And besides, your grandfather did go to church."

Jennet seemed to be thinking about that.

Demdike gave her an affectionate tap on the nose, making Jennet laugh. "How about I tell you of the importance of Samhain and the coming winter solstice?"

"I'm not that little, Granny – I already know why Samhain is important. It's when spirits like Grandfather come back to visit us."

"Indeed it is." Demdike hugged Jennet close again. "And soon we shall celebrate the winter solstice, which is a time of death and rebirth. Then we will be looking to Beltane and the summer solstice, both times of year to celebrate new life and fertility. Beltane is another important time for magic and protecting against the mischievous fae with the great Beltane fire, or at least it was before the Puritans put a stop to the old ways. Even the Catholics had their May Day celebrations as they danced round the May Pole. But we will still observe the old traditions, even if our neighbours will no longer join us in such things."

"Why does Chattox hate us?"

The suddenness of this question made Demdike pull back a second time. "I would rather not speak of that either, child."

"But why were you and Alizon so afraid of her that day James made his pact?"

"Because she turned to the dark arts long ago, and she thinks nothing of using black magic to hurt those she holds a grudge against. It was she and her familiar – Fancie – who murdered James' and Alizon's father."

"Why?"

"Not tonight, lass. Someday you will understand."

"What happened to my father?"

"Best not to speak of him either. Your mam does not need reminding of that good-for-nothing mongrel, and she might come back in at any moment. Broke her heart, he did, with all his promises while her husband lay on his deathbed."

"Will you show me more magic?"

"Aye, lass, I will teach you some fortune telling if you wish, like Alizon's doing."

She took a small lump of lead from amongst Elizabeth's tools and melted it over a candle. Next, she poured it into water so they could study the shapes it solidified into, explaining to her youngest granddaughter what each one meant as she did so. And thus passed the shortening days with her family while she struggled through the pain left in the wake of that fateful Samhain.

The onset of winter brought greater hardships. Demdike sat beside her granddaughter in front of the fire, nibbling a much smaller piece of hard bread for breakfast than in weeks past. Crop yields had been low that year, limiting the amount of food to go around the community. None felt the constant snapping of hunger more than the poor, but even the wealthier families were struggling.

Alizon finished her bread and her stomach rumbled for more. She looked thoroughly miserable, staring glumly into the hearth.

Demdike took one of Alizon's hands in hers, firm but gentle, and pressed the rest of her bread into the girl's palm. "Here you are, lass – take the rest of mine. I've no appetite again this morning."

Alizon's eyebrows shot up in surprise. "Gran, no! You need your strength as much as I do."

"How many times?" Demdike fixed her with a steely gaze, determined that her granddaughter should be allowed this one kindness. "Don't you worry about me. I just wish I had more to offer you."

Her granddaughter maintained her gaze for a moment, but made no move to eat the bread. Demdike was just beginning to think she had another argument on her hands, when Alizon finally looked away and took a tentative nibble. Those young eyes darted back to meet

Demdike's a moment later. The girl opened her mouth, then closed it again.

"Speak your mind, lass. I'm not about to punish you for having thoughts of your own." The corners of Demdike's mouth twitched. "Tell you what a fool idea it may be, yes, but never punish you."

Alizon hesitated a second or two longer, then her gaze hardened. "If you don't want to see me going hungry, then why aren't we working more of the craft? There's plenty of sick animals we could be helping."

Demdike gave her a sharp look, until the girl looked away again. "I've told you, it's too risky without Tibb. When he comes back—"

"But what if he isn't coming back?" That fiery temper sparked into life, all sense of Alizon's doubts and worries gone in an instant. "It's been weeks, Gran. Can't you make the pact with a new spirit?"

"I'm not abandoning my Tibb!" The words came out harsher than Demdike intended, and it brought her no pleasure to see Alizon flinch. But this was one argument she would not suffer. "We don't know for certain he's dead, and until we do, I'm not giving up on him. Now finish your breakfast and let us be about whatever work our neighbours have for us."

All traces of the youthful temper withered beneath those words. Alizon returned to staring into the hearth. The room all but fell into silence, save for the crackle of the fire and the girl's absentminded chewing on the rest of the bread. A sudden knock on the door made them both jump.

They shared a glance, then Demdike rose and answered it to find Christopher Bulcock on their doorstep. His face was lined with greater concerns than the stresses of winter.

"Come, quick!" Christopher panted, his chest heaving

as though he'd run all the way from Moss End Farm. "His fever won't break and he's growing weaker by the day. He needs your help!"

"Slow down, lad. Who is sick?"

"Is it John?" Alizon asked, rushing over to the door.

"Aye. He's been bedridden for three days past and this morning is worse still. Please, you have to come help him. We fear he is bewitched, or possessed by a demon."

The hairs on the back of Demdike's neck raised at the word 'demon'. Could this be the return of the dark intruder who'd attacked at Samhain – the very thing she'd been trying to avoid? Now she was the one to hesitate. The word 'no' hovered on her lips.

Her mind's eye took her back to the night of John's birth, helping while Jane strained to bring him into the world. He'd been beautiful from the moment she'd delivered him. That babe might have long since grown, but she couldn't just leave him to die. The Bulcocks had always been good to her family. And then there were her granddaughter's feelings to consider. Alizon's eyes were so full of pleading, Demdike fancied she'd have to be as heartless as Chattox to say no.

Her resolve strengthening, Demdike straightened up and promised "I will do what I can." She turned to grab her tools, taking them in a basket this time. "Alizon, see what work you can find elsewhere. I will send for you if I need you."

"But I can help!" Alizon said.

"I will do all I can for your friend, but we must care for ourselves as well. I am relying on you to bring more food home for our stores."

Alizon opened her mouth to argue, but Demdike rushed down the path before the girl could say anything more.

Christopher hurried after her. In truth, Demdike was more worried about the demon than their food stores. Better not to risk Alizon's soul as well.

Through Roughlee they hurried, down the muddy road twisting alongside Pendle water, bordered by a wall of trees on either side. The trees gave the illusion of straying into the forest, but this was not the untamed land it appeared to be. Their forefathers had shaped it into farmland long ago.

They followed that road into Newchurch, and just beyond there lay the farm known as Moss End.

There was no immediate sense of black magic hanging over the area as they passed through the fence and into the Bulcocks' land. That did nothing for Demdike's nerves. She remained tense on the walk down the path to the humble farmhouse the Bulcocks called home. Humble, but still larger than her single-storey cottage.

Christopher led her into a similar living space to her own, though it carried the grander name of hall. A doorway led through to the parlour, but they went straight past it and on to the staircase at the other end of the room. Christopher continued to lead the way up to John's bedroom.

Wordlessly, he stopped by the doorway and gestured for Demdike to go in. She took a deep breath. Part of her wanted to turn and run back to Malkin Tower, and the safety of the charms woven into its walls. Another part of her wrestled with the idea of sending Christopher for Elizabeth and Ball. No. Losing Tibb had been a harsh reminder of the fact their familiars did not make them invulnerable to demons and other dark spirits. She would not risk losing Elizabeth and Ball as well.

Demdike plunged through the doorway. A grim sight awaited within. John lay in his bed, pale and still as a corpse. Sweat beaded his brow and his breathing was too slow, too wheezy. Then there was the rolling of his eyes beneath closed lids, and the twitching of the muscles across his face – sure signs of the fevered dreams he was trapped in.

Jane Bulcock sat beside the bed, mopping her son's brow and saying something in a low voice. Age had long since dulled Demdike's hearing, her ears not sharp enough to catch the words. Whether John heard them or not she couldn't say, but his troubled dreams continued regardless.

Jane looked up as Demdike entered. Relief smoothed the lines of her face, and her eyes lit up with hope. "Thank the heavens! You keep fighting, John. Help is at hand." Jane gripped his arm as if to transfer some of her own strength into his weakened body, but her eyes were locked on Demdike's. "You will help him, won't you?"

"I will do what I can." Demdike gave the most reassuring smile she could manage. "Better you leave me alone with him now. I will call you back if there's any change, or if I have need of either of you."

The worry returned to Jane's face. She looked back down at John and squeezed his arm, but made no move to get up. Christopher placed a grateful hand on Demdike's shoulder as he made his way into the room and over to the bed.

"Come on, love. Let us wait downstairs while Demdike works her magic." He took Jane's hands in his and gently pulled her to her feet. She allowed herself to be led away, turning for one last look at her son on her way out. John's face contorted into a grimace and Jane let out a whimper. Then they were gone, giving Demdike the space she needed.

She made her way over to the chair by John's bedside

and seated herself beside him, gently placing her basket of tools on the floor by her feet. John wheezed and grimaced again. The rolling of his eyes became more frantic and his fingers dug into the damp sheets beneath him.

His muscles relaxed a moment later. Demdike drew in another deep breath and placed a hand on his clammy brow. Nothing. No crackling of dark energy, no sense of a malevolent presence possessing the boy. But she had to be sure.

Concentrating on her breathing, Demdike took several long breaths in and out until her mind cleared and her heart steadied. She focused on John's sick body, his laboured breathing and his weak limbs, until her vision moved beyond the earthly and she was able to fix him with the gaze of her inner eye. A faint aura came into view. The last time she'd seen it, the aura had been a vibrant, deep red, full of energy and strength. This was but a pale imitation. The red was so washed-out it might have been mistaken for pink, and it was much duller than before. Demdike's heart sank. John was losing the battle with his sickness.

There was no second aura to indicate John was possessed. Slowly, Demdike shifted her gaze from John's face down towards the foot of the bed. No spirits came into view. She ran her Sight over the rest of the room, and found nothing.

With a sigh of relief, Demdike reached for her basket of tools and took out the old femur. She kept one hand on John's forehead and gripped the femur with her other, muttering:

"Magic dark and magic foul,
Be that what makes the Reaper prowl?
If this is a curse, I would know,
If bewitched, make this bone glow."

The femur remained the same chalky white it had always been. The lad's sickness was of natural causes after all.

John began to twitch more violently, his entire body racked with convulsions. Demdike summoned his parents back into the bedroom then. Her heart went out to them when they saw the deterioration in their son's condition. It was all too easy to imagine it was Alizon lying fighting for her life, and after Samhain Demdike felt their pain more keenly than ever before. But that only strengthened her resolve to save their son.

"It may bring you some comfort to know this sickness is not the work of demons or dark magic, yet your son's condition is no less dire. I have herbs with me to help reduce his fever, but I need you to set some water boiling over the fire so I can mix them into a tea."

"Of course," Christopher said. "Anything you need to save our John."

Casting more worried glances at the boy as they retreated from the room, the couple hastened to prepare the water as instructed. Demdike began a healing rite while she waited, digging in her basket for savory and salt.

"Spirits, I beseech of ye,
Help heal this young body,
Take his fever, make him well,
Let them not ring the death knell,
Give back his strength, I beg of ye,
Spirits, lend your energy."

John's convulsions began to ease again as she chanted. She took advantage of that and placed the dried herbs on each of his wrists, then sprinkled the salt over the same area. To finish the rite, she took some chervil and ran downstairs to throw it in the fire. John's eyes were open when she returned to his bedside, and he sat bolt upright, looking around wildly.

"Easy now, lad," Demdike soothed. "Come back to us."

Christopher had followed her upstairs, his face lighting up when he saw his son had awoken. "John!"

"He's not out of danger yet," Demdike warned. "The water, is it ready?"

"Oh yes, it's on the boil now."

"Good. Watch him while I go mix the herbs in."

She made her way down into the hall once again, where Jane was still keeping an eye on the pot of boiling water.

"John's awake, but the danger has not yet passed. Return to his bedside if you wish. I will be along shortly with the tea for his fever."

Jane grasped Demdike's hands. "Thank you."

Demdike nodded and watched her run back to her son's room.

Making the tea was simple enough. Demdike added the herbs and let it stew before straining the contents into a cup, which she then carried up to her patient. The boy didn't even look at her as she re-entered his room. He still showed no signs of having escaped the dream he'd been caught in, seemingly unaware of his parents and even his surroundings, as familiar and comforting as it should all have been.

Demdike pressed the cup to his lips while Jane held him, noting how he appeared to be swallowing on reflex rather than of his own free will. She was able to get him to drink about half of the brew before his eyes widened and fixed on something only he could see. His lips mouthed wordlessly with new fear, then his eyes rolled upwards and he went limp in Jane's arms.

"John?" Jane looked up at Demdike, her face filling with panic. "What's happening?"

"The sickness is strong. I will keep on trying all I know to help him fight it, but it will be a hard battle," Demdike answered, feeling his forehead again while she spoke. His temperature burned hotter than ever.

She gripped her pentagram amulet and chanted another healing incantation, channelling all the energy the room had to offer and pouring it into John. His parents were healthy and had plenty to spare, and she sensed a benevolent spirit answering her call and lending his aid. Still John's fever refused to break.

Hours passed without any changes for the better. Eventually Demdike was forced to admit all she was really doing was delaying the inevitable. When John's time came, the Reaper would not be denied, and there was nothing more she could do to cheat Death of his prize. Not without resorting to black magic, and accepting the price that inevitably came with it. A price she was not willing to pay.

The light began to fade and the shadows lengthened. Demdike rose, defeated. "I have done all I can. His life is in the hands of the Goddess now."

FOURTEEN

A pair of eyes watched Moss End Farm from within the murk of daylight's gate. Those same eyes had looked upon the inside of Malkin Tower, one of the few spirits ever to do so uninvited. And they looked upon the mistress of the 'tower' now, tracking Demdike's movements down the path as she made her way back there.

The demon wore the shadows about him like a cloak, unseen by even the cunning folk and their familiars if he chose to remain hidden. Darkness was his hunting grounds, an endless plain filled with prey to torture and torment. He lived for the suffering of others.

On any other night, he'd have been revelling in the Bulcocks' misery. But not that night. He had business elsewhere.

In his guise of a Christian man, the demon turned his thoughts to the human he had dealings with, and her equally humble home. The blackness of the countryside gave way to the dim glow of candles flickering in a draughty room. He was back inside the kitchen and living area of the Whittle's cottage. All it had taken was an effort of will.

Chattox appeared to have been waiting for him, muttering to herself, as was her wont. Her lips had rarely been still in recent years. The fool mortals believed it to be the madness of her twilight years, or something altogether more sinister. But in this case, the demon knew she was merely cursing with the impatience seen in most humans. He supposed he couldn't blame them when their time as flesh and blood beings was so short, yet he found it tiresome nevertheless.

"Well?" Chattox asked him. "Lord knows you were gone long enough – what have you learnt?"

He gave her his most charming smile. "The Bulcock boy is sick. You would do well to pay the family a visit."

"What do I care about some farmer's brat I have no quarrel with? What of Demdike and her wretched brood, have you no news of them? And that accursed Moore family are becoming a problem again. What of them?"

"If you would avenge yourself of the Moores, you know the easiest way to strike them down. Make another clay image of each of those you wish to kill and crumble it into dust."

"Yes, yes, I know how to bewitch them to death."

"Indeed, you do not need my help with such curses after all these years. But I do have news of Demdike, if you still wish for my aid in her downfall – she who is not so easily bewitched."

"You know I want her gone, then perhaps folk will come to me and my daughters with their problems, and we might not be going hungry so often."

"Then I tell you again, the Bulcock boy is sick."

"Stop playing games, Fancie. Did you not succeed in killing Tibb? Is this not the time to strike, before she makes a new pact?"

The familiar smirked. It was almost too easy; once again, he barely had to do any work to manipulate the humans he'd chosen as his pawns. She still believed herself to be his mistress, completely failing to see it was he who pulled all the strings. But they did share some dark desires, or he would never have offered her the pact, he who was older and far more powerful than the likes of hellhounds and animal guides.

"Tibb is gone," he confirmed. "And my intrusion during Samhain has put her on edge, as hoped. Yet she is not entirely defenceless. Perhaps we could bewitch her, and perhaps not. There is still Ball and Dandy to contend with. They may be no match for me in a fair fight, but do not underestimate your rivals. It will be harder to take them by surprise after the last attack, and we cannot simply curse the family so long as those two stand in our way."

He waited with the patience mortals lacked while she muttered to herself again. It went on for several minutes but that was nothing to one as ancient as he, and only once she was ready to listen did he continue.

"There is a way to take some revenge on Demdike. It will not lead to her death, not yet, but it will weaken her."

"Tell me," Chattox commanded.

"Go to the Bulcocks. Their boy will die if no one practised in the dark arts intervenes. Demdike was not willing to pay the price, so you shall pay it in her stead, and she will suffer the consequences."

Understanding finally dawned. He could feel it through their connection. She needed no more convincing to visit

Moss End Farm, gathering her tools without further argument and calling to her daughter that she would be back later that night. He walked her to the farm, lest any were foolish enough to try anything, but once she was safely inside he left her to work her magic. She knew what had to be done.

FIFTEEN

"Demdike!"

The cry cut through the old wise woman's dreams and her eyes snapped open. A shape lurked at her bedside. Its identity was mostly concealed in the darkened room, though she could just make out enough to recognise it as a hound of some description. Relief surged through her. Tibb had finally returned.

"Demdike," the hellhound repeated. "My mistress requires your urgent assistance. It's Jennet!"

It was not Tibb after all. Demdike's sleepy mind took a moment to place the voice and recognise it as Ball, but his words didn't leave much room for disappointment or fresh grief. Relief quickly turned to dread.

"What's happened?" she asked, pulling back the covers and climbing out of bed.

"It's Jennet," Ball repeated. "She's fallen sick."

"Let Elizabeth know we will be with you shortly."

Ball bowed his head and then disappeared without a trace, as only creatures of spirit could. A sense of foreboding was left in his wake, and Demdike hastened to dress, anxious to get over to the Device home her daughter had married into.

Movement from the opposite bed signalled Alizon was stirring. Her voice was thick with the remnants of a deep sleep as she mumbled "I thought I heard voices."

"Aye, lass, that you did. Your sister is ill and your mother needs our help to nurse her back to health. You can come with me today – Jennet may well need the whole family around her if she's caught anything as nasty as the Bulcock lad."

Alizon groaned in wordless protest, but she got herself up and started to dress. Demdike checked her basket while she waited, topping up the herbs from the stash she kept in the kitchen in case Elizabeth didn't have what was needed. Moments later, they were making their way down the path from Malkin Tower in the cold, dim rays of the early morning light.

A fierce wind made the walk harder going than usual, the force of the gale stealing their breath as they fought against it. It was as if the very land had turned on them.

Some might even have said it was the wrath of their Goddess and the Horned One blowing across the moors. Demdike rejected that notion. She could not believe the deities she had respected and worshipped all her life would betray her so. Nor could she accept the thought that Jennet's illness might also be of their making. No, she was more inclined to share the worries of the Bulcocks from the previous day – that either a malevolent spirit or a witch had brought this latest misfortune to her family.

The wind alone was not enough to keep the two from reaching their destination. Demdike tried the door without bothering to knock first. It opened to the cry of "Mam! Through here, quickly!"

"Steady now, lass," she answered, making her way into the bedroom. The scene awaiting her was just like that of the previous day, her daughter almost as pale as the little girl in the bed. Tears leaked from those mismatched eyes as Elizabeth looked down at Jennet with dismay. "We have to stay calm for Jennet's sake. Tell me what happened."

"Oh, Mam, I don't know! She woke early and one minute she was running around, then the next she was lying on the floor with a fever. I can't wake her and she feels so hot, but nothing seems to help. I didn't know what else to do, so I asked Ball to bring you here."

"And you're sure it came on so suddenly – there was nothing to indicate she was starting with it yesterday or through the night?"

"Yes, she was fine until she collapsed just now!"

"Then it is as I feared; there is dark magic at work here."

"But who would want to hurt an innocent little girl?"

"I can guess. Yesterday I treated John Bulcock for fevered dreams he would not wake from, but neither my healing charms nor my herbs could cure him. Today Jennet shows signs of the exact same illness. This can only be the work of a witch; one who is not only prepared to pay the price of such black magic, but to use it to harm us in the process."

"Chattox?"

"Who else? We both know the easiest way to cure the incurable is to transfer the sickness to another being. You know I'm not willing to make that wicked trade. Chattox must have heard of John's sickness and stepped in after I failed."

"Then send it back to her," Elizabeth hissed. "If there is anyone deserving of such evil it is she."

"Nay, lass, it might be the easiest cure but 'tis still a dangerous one. Transferring the sickness to a specific target is considerably less easy, and it could just as readily strike any one of us down instead."

"But you just said healing charms and herbs aren't enough! We have to cure her, Mam, we have to – my heart could not bear it if we lost her at so tender an age."

"Nor mine. Fear not, my child, I will save her. Best you and Alizon wait outside now, and make sure James does not come in either, if he's still about."

Elizabeth scowled, but did as she was told. Demdike turned to Jennet with grim resolve. One way or another, this battle would be won. The sickness would be vanquished. Not transferred as Chattox had done, but taken away as if it had never been. Then Jennet's health would be restored without having to make the vile trade for the health of another.

Jennet began to convulse just as John had done the day before, her limbs twitching and jerking to the cruel song of the fever. The pitiful sight was enough to spur Demdike into action, her hands steady as they pulled the necessary tools from her basket. Fear had no place in her heart this time. She was too confident in the powers she was about to call on. They wouldn't fail her, so long as she paid their price.

She created a circle of bones much as she had the night she'd summoned Death, placing candles around it and the incense burner at its centre. A different incantation was required to invoke these beings whose aid she needed, but the carved femur remained her focus of choice to channel the power into the ritual.

Once again, flames sprung into being on the end of each candle wick, conjured through the magic she poured into the rite. Those fiery points danced to the rhythm of her chanting. They swayed in the draughty room, but refused to succumb to the might of the gale outside.

Winter's chill already invaded the house, but the room grew colder still with the opening of a gateway to the Otherworld. Demdike ceased her chanting and gripped her Pentagram. "I call forth a demon with the power to heal. Who will answer my call?"

Silence.

"I seek the aid of any who can cure my granddaughter. Are there none willing to answer my call?"

Still the room was quiet, though there came the tickly sensation of her hairs standing to the command of more than just the cold. A similar, unnatural gloom to that which she and Alizon had experienced during Samhain took hold. It was a dimness even the sunlight filtering through from outside couldn't touch, let alone the glow of the candles. Demdike knew then that something had come through, whether it deigned to speak or not.

All but one of the flames winked out of existence. The gateway closed with them. Demdike turned slowly, concentrating on her Sight as she scanned the room.

Something slid across the edge of her vision. There was enough of a glimpse to draw her eye, yet the moment she tried to fix it in her gaze, it twisted away. Inwardly she cursed herself. She should have known better than to try looking directly at a thing only half seen in the shadows.

It wasn't long before the demon slithered back into the corner of her eye. She fought the instinct to look in its direction a second time. The trick was to try and hold it there, on the very edge of her vision. It would only keep on dancing out of sight otherwise. And who knew what mischief it would wreak if left unchecked?

"I know you are there," Demdike said. "Who answers? Show yourself!"

Silver bit into her palm as she clutched her pendant tight. The beat of her heart quickened and her nerves grew taut. Yet her voice remained as commanding as ever, even though she was well aware she had no real control over the situation. The demon would not be made a servant of, and the ritual gave her no real hold over it. Whether it revealed itself was entirely up to the spirit, and all she could do to entice it out of the shadows was to make a deal.

Just as it was beginning to seem she would have to do something to persuade the thing to come forward, its shadowy form became more solid and it stepped into view. "I answer."

"You?"

"I answer," he repeated, his eyes an unnatural sea of red in an otherwise human-looking face.

"I know you. Are you not bound to another?"

"Yes, we have a pact, Anne Whittle and I. But I am so much more than your Tibb, and no pact with a mortal is so absolute in its binding for one such as I. I may deal with whoever I choose, enemy of Chattox or no."

"And why would you choose to deal with me now, after all these years serving Anne?"

"Does it matter? Your granddaughter will die if one of us does not intervene soon. You could try calling on another, but I tell you now she does not have long left. It is I who chose to answer, and so it is I you must deal with. Or will fear cost you her life?"

"I won't deny my fear of you, nor my distrust. But if it is you I must deal with, then so be it. Name your price."

Fancie smiled, an expression which twisted his human mask into the very face of malice. "Your soul."

Demdike did not flinch in the presence of such evil, and his answer did not really surprise her, though her suspicions were rising. Had this been her enemies' plan all along – to lay claim to her soul? But what did Chattox stand to gain from that? It was a great prize for any demon, but worthless to mortals. Not that it mattered. Jennet was dying, and Fancie had the power to save her.

She smiled back. "My soul is my own, and not for the likes of you, demon. But I have other things to offer. Let us bargain."

CHAPTER
SIXTEEN

L ong were the hours in which Demdike waited for the miracle she had bought. Her granddaughter remained very much in the grip of the sickness and showed no signs of improvement as yet. Fancie's word was all he'd given in return for the sacrifice she'd made, but such was the way with demons. They did things in their own time and in their own way.

Of course, Demdike would not have hesitated to give up her soul had Fancie not settled for anything less. But she had not been about to accept the first offer he made her either. It always paid to barter. The part of herself she'd given was of far less worth than that most precious piece at the heart of all living creatures.

It was long after nightfall before the little girl's sickness finally abated. Demdike sat in darkness, waiting with a patience and confidence her daughter and other two grand-children lacked. She could not see anything of her family, yet she was aware of them fretting beside her all the same.

Jennet's breathing returned to normal just moments before Elizabeth exclaimed "Jennet!"

"Mam, what happened?" Jennet asked. "I'm hungry."

"Oh, lambkin, you had us all so worried. You were really sick, but you're all better now, thanks to your granny. Come give her a hug."

Demdike heard her granddaughter climb across the bed and onto her knee, the small body a warm and welcome weight on her lap. She wrapped her arms around the little girl but Jennet didn't hug her back, pulling away with a gasp.

"Granny, your eyes!"

"Hush now, child," she said, gently pulling her granddaughter back into the embrace. "There is always a price, but I pay it gladly if it buys you a long and happy life."

Yet in spite of her words, inwardly she began to weep for this latest loss. Condemned to a lifetime of blackness for whatever years remained to her, she would never again see the faces of the grandchildren she loved so deeply, nor the beauty of the world around her. Fancie had denied her the joy of watching the children continue to grow and develop into adulthood, of seeing the fine people she hoped they would become. The demon had taken away her right to that as a grandparent. And though it was better than losing the child altogether, she felt a sense of grief for the vision she had always taken for granted. Ideally, she would have liked to have held onto it just long enough to share in the happy sight of Jennet waking up. But that was not the deal she'd made, and what was done could not be undone.

Sensing her granddaughter's confusion, she added "You will understand someday, lass. Until then, let us not speak of dark things. You are returned to us, and that is all that matters."

She cuddled Jennet for a few minutes longer, love temporarily washing away her sorrow as she held the little girl close. The moment soon passed. Jennet broke away to go with Elizabeth into the kitchen for some supper, and James retired to his room. Demdike was left to grieve in the dark cage of her blindness.

"Gran, are you well?" Alizon asked.

She could hear the doubt in her granddaughter's voice, even if she could no longer see the worry on that pretty young face. "Aye, lass, do not fear for me. The demon's price was a high one, but it could have been far worse, and the lives of you three youngsters are worth more than any piece of this old body of mine. I will adapt to the loss of my sight."

"You won't have to do it alone," Alizon replied, with conviction. "I'll be here to help, I swear it. I can be your eyes when you need them."

"Thank you, child. You will never know how much that means to me."

The girl did not reply out loud, but Demdike could hear her gathering the tools used for the summoning and returning them to the basket. She felt Alizon take hold of her a moment later, and her granddaughter began to lead her by the arm at a measured pace, apparently taking great care to keep her from stumbling or bumping into the walls or furniture. In this fashion, they made their way back to Malkin Tower, though their progress was much slower than it would otherwise have been. The sudden blindness was going to take some getting used to. More than once, Demdike stumbled on the uneven surface of the roads and paths winding through the countryside. But her granddaughter never once complained.

As they carefully picked their way along the path, Demdike became aware of lights floating in the darkness – flashes of colour she was sure could not really be there. She supposed she must be trying to strain her now useless eyes out of habit, and it was causing her to see things. The random lights were distracting, but she was used to maintaining focus when working her craft. It didn't stop her from listening to her other senses.

The wind had died down to a light breeze carrying the bite of winter. It was enough to raise the hairs on Demdike's skin and cause the blackened teeth in her mouth to chatter, much like those of her rival behind the cracked lips that were never still. Demdike's thoughts turned to Chattox and her familiar. Again she wondered if her enemies had manipulated the recent events in revenge for past altercations. They might not have succeeded in robbing her of her soul, but they had dealt her a devastating blow nevertheless and they were surely celebrating even as she continued her struggle back home. Her gaze hardened. It was an attack she could not allow to go unchallenged. They would only strike again otherwise.

Her phantom lights continued to flash across the empty painting of her vision, the focus she'd been so careful to maintain on her other senses beginning to slip. There were two lights in particular vying for her attention. These were different to the others in that they remained static and unchanging, and refused to fade into the nothingness after a brief existence like all the others experienced.

Demdike found herself staring at those two lights, transfixed by them for reasons she couldn't quite fathom. The cold stab of dread went through her as she realised why they held her attention so. It was when the lights began to move towards her that her fears were confirmed.

She stopped walking, planting her feet firmly on the ground. Alizon was forced to stop beside her.

"What is it?" Alizon whispered.

"Spirits."

For they were not lights at all but a pair of fiery eyes, seen with that sense not even Fancie could take away from her.

As the eyes came closer, the thing they belonged to started to take shape amongst the flashing colours. Big and muscular, it prowled towards her with all the feral confidence of a mighty hunter. Dark energy radiated from the thing. Demdike's fingers instinctively returned to the pentagram about her neck, though the charm felt inadequate in the face of such power.

Alizon's breathing came a little faster and Demdike felt her turning on the spot, as though she were looking for the danger. She would never see it coming until it was too late, until unseen fangs ripped into her flesh and her life leaked out on a crimson tide.

Planting her feet more firmly on the uneven ground, Demdike started chanting, calling on any spirit who would aid her. The thing spoke before she could finish.

"I am returned," he said. "And I ask for but a taste this night."

She stared, trying to make sense of those words. His request she understood well enough. The taste he wanted could only be one thing, but who was he to ask this sacrifice of her?

He drew closer still. She could see now he was a hellhound with fur black as night, and though a part of her had to wonder if this was real or some kind of cruel illusion, she could not help but laugh.

"What is it, Gran, what's happening?" Alizon asked, her voice a mix of fear and confusion.

"Tibb," Demdike replied, fresh tears in her eyes. "Tibb has come back."

And she laughed again even as she rolled back her sleeve and offered her familiar the sustenance he required, only briefly grimacing at the pain of his teeth piercing her skin. She could not explain how he was back after so many weeks with no sight or sound of him, or even that sixth sense granted through the bond they shared, but none of that mattered. The hellhound's tongue licked across the blood welling up from the puncture wounds he'd made, and their connection leapt back into life, forged anew and stronger than ever.

Their pact resealed, Tibb backed off and fell into step beside her as they continued their journey home, Demdike still laughing. Her enemies might have taken her sight, but Tibb's return felt like an even greater victory. More than that, it brought her hope. Tibb was back and she could resume her practice of the craft. All would be well.

PART TWO - 1610

SEVENTEEN

He sat alone.

Around him, the alehouse swam in and out of focus, the other villagers glimpsed through a drunken haze. Someone bumped into the table and Richard glared after them. They didn't even have the decency to turn round and apologise on their way to the bar. He stared back down at his tankard a moment later. That was all that mattered now.

The emptiness of his lover's passing gaped as wide as ever, and Richard allowed himself a bitter smile at the particular cruelty of his fate. First they'd cursed him with this unnatural, blasphemous attraction to another man, and then they'd taken that very man from him. But was that the end of his curse? Would they at least allow him that relief after everything else they'd done? No, of course not. The unholy craving for male flesh remained as strong as ever. Women would simply not do anymore, try as he might to reignite old passions for the female form.

Richard raised the tankard to his lips and took another gulp, finding little comfort in the bitter liquid he'd come to rely so heavily on. There was little comfort left to be had in any aspect of his cursed life. Especially not the teachings of the Bible he used to take such pride immersing himself in, nor in God Himself. How could he take solace from the divine being he used to worship so, when that being had allowed him to become the plaything of witches and devils? Even his children brought him little joy now. But alcohol would at least help him sleep at night, and it had the power to make him forget, even if only temporarily.

Time began to blur. The days bled into each other so that he had trouble recalling where one week had ended and the next had begun. The change of the seasons barely registered in his troubled mind. When he'd been left as cold as the winter snows, there was little wonder he hardly noticed the icy temperatures of those harsh months. And yet, when the land gradually grew lighter and warmer again, it was as if the sunlight could not touch him, for he was not really aware of that either. He might as well have been living his days in a dream, so detached from reality had he become.

Aware of it or not, time continued to pass as it always had and winter gave way to early spring. The world had entered another year, though the dawning of 1610 brought no fresh hope or joy for Richard's tormented soul, nor did the promise of summer's return. There was only his nightly reprieve in the dregs of one ale too many, where he nursed his hatred for the witches and cursed that fool, Nowell, for failing to act after Rob's death.

The thud of a second tankard on the table and the scrape of one of the few empty chairs brought Richard out of his dark musings. He looked up to see a man sitting across from him. Distaste curled his lip as he recognised this newcomer as companion of Chattox, she who was every bit as foul as the hag who constantly plagued him so.

"Go away," he growled, still scowling. "I have no business with the likes of you."

"Come now, Richard," the heathen said. "Is that any way to speak to the one man in all of Pendle who can offer a chance at your heart's only desire?"

"The witches took my heart. Go away."

The heathen laughed. "Oh no, Dick, I think you will find it is Rob's heart which was taken. You still have one, trust me – even if it is shrivelled and blackened and no longer has room for love."

"Trust you? Consort of witches and perhaps even versed in the dark arts yourself? I would rather gouge out my own eyes than be seen conversing with you, let alone give you my trust. Be gone, fiend!"

"I think you will want to hear what I have to say. I won't deny my bond with Chattox, but would you not see the entire Demdike clan dead at any cost?"

"I would see Pendle rid of all witches, Chattox included."

"And one day you may get your wish. But is Demdike not the biggest thorn in your side?" the heathen pressed.

Richard glared at the strange man while he wrestled with his morals. Of course he wanted Demdike and her family gone. But if he accepted the heathen's help, he would be soliciting the very devilry he had been fighting so hard to stamp out.

Had he not been so strongly under the influence of the beer – a type of devilry all in itself – Richard might have answered differently. Or perhaps it was inevitable by then that his hatred for Demdike would win out. Either way, he found himself unable to turn down the heathen's aid.

"I'm listening," he said, though it came out somewhat reluctantly.

"Then listen closely. There will be an incident involving the Towneleys and James Device tomorrow. It could lead to a trial, and there is the possibility for that trial to end at the gallows, but only if you can persuade Henry Towneley to testify."

"And how can you possibly know this?"

"I think you have had enough experience to know the power of witchcraft by now. I have looked down the course fate is currently set on, and I have seen what will come to pass. As long as that course is not altered then it will result in the outcome you have been praying for. But only if you can bring Nowell the evidence he requires to put together a strong case."

"And if you know so much about the future, why do you not go to him yourself?"

"Because you already have his ear. He trusts you, does he not? While I am considered a witch, or worse, by the entirety of Pendle and will only be met with suspicion."

Richard couldn't deny the truth of that, though he felt there was far more to it than the man was telling him. Still, if acting on the heathen's advice meant the execution of the most hated witches in the area then he had to do it. He could always find a way to build a case against Chattox and the rest at a later date.

"Very well. I will bring the incident to Roger's attention."

"Give it a week for events to play out. And remember, Henry Towneley is key. You must convince him to testify or everything will fall apart. Fate will take a new direction and Demdike's family will continue to live on."

"Understood." Richard lifted his tankard and dipped his

head in thanks for the information. The pewter drinking vessel continued toward his lips as though it had a life of its own, but something made him pause before it touched them. "What if I need to find you? I don't even know your name."

Charm entered the heathen's smile. "You can call me Fancie."

Richard frowned. It seemed an odd name even for a witch, and he almost commented on it. The fear of offending the man held him back. That, and the call of his drink. He tilted his head and guzzled the rest of his ale, but when he set the tankard down on the table again, it was to find the strange man had vanished.

Confused, Richard stood and scanned the room for Fancie's retreating back. There was no sign of him.

A chill crept down Richard's spine. How could anyone disappear like that? It simply wasn't natural. He looked longingly at the second tankard. The ale called to him, virtually untouched by the man who may not truly be a man at all. No. There was something sinister at work here, and the time had come to take his leave.

He pushed his way through the press of bodies and out into the night. Fancie was still nowhere to be seen, so Richard staggered back home and to his bed, mulling over this latest turn of events along the way.

The question on his lips was not could he trust the man but should he trust him? Probably not. Yet the rivalry between Demdike and Chattox was no secret, so he supposed the information could be genuine. In any case, there was nothing more to be done that night, and he resolved to see what the morning would bring. Then he could decide on the wisdom of following a pagan's counsel.

EIGHTEEN

It wasn't easy being the son of Squinting Lizzie. James sat apart from the other farm labourers and bit into his meagre lunch, grimacing at the taste of stale bread. One of them glanced over at him, and their eyes met for a second. The older man quickly looked away and muttered something to the others. James paid them little mind. Furtive glances and muttered suspicions followed him wherever he went, but he'd grown to enjoy being regarded with something akin to reverence.

Things weren't all James had hoped they'd be though. After making the pact, he'd thought his days of hard bread and cheese were over. He'd thought he'd be saving his neighbours from witches and dark spirits, and handsomely rewarded for his troubles. Duckworth was a fair employer, all things considered, but he wasn't the wealthiest of yeomen. Helping around his farm was hardly the kind of work befitting the grandson of Old Demdike, especially for such modest pay.

James's thoughts turned to Carr Hall, and all the Towneleys had to offer, if they hadn't been so stupid as to mistake him for a witch. He'd not been back to their estate since his altercation with Mistress Towneley, but he suddenly found himself tempted to go back then. Maybe if he could sneak into the kitchen he might be able to persuade one of the cooks to give him something more satisfying for his lunch – perhaps even a bit of meat to keep him going through the afternoon. The thought of that was too much to resist.

Young as he was, James was no fool. He knew better than to march up to the front of the hall where there was more chance of being seen by the Towneleys, so he avoided the path from Laund Farm and made his way down to the river. There he followed its bank a little way until he came to the crossing.

He took great care not to lose his footing as he made his way to the other side. Such places had a natural magic all of their own, and his grandmother had warned him often enough of the water spirits who delighted in luring men to their doom. But once he'd made it safely across, a new feeling of confidence came over him and a swagger crept into his step.

A dark shadow flitted between the trees as he continued along the bank, and he glimpsed a large black dog which could only be Dandy. The hellhound glanced across at him, and for a brief moment James felt their minds touch in a flash of dark desires and unfailing loyalty. Then Dandy's mind broke away again, leaving James gasping at the intensity of it.

The connection they'd made through the pact remained – James could sense it. But most of the time it was as if there was a distance between them he hadn't yet learnt how to cross. Dandy lurked on the edges of his consciousness like an elusive thought he was struggling to grasp. It would take years before he could fully sense his familiar or communicate with him through their minds. James wasn't worried. The mere sight of the spirit animal gave him a feeling of such power that he felt untouchable. Surely none would dare attack a cunning man with the blood of Old Demdike herself, and even if they did, what of it? They would soon feel his wrath.

Such was his mood as he approached the Towneley estate, even after Dandy disappeared. He entered the grounds to the rear of the hall where there were less prying eyes, weaving between the outbuildings and heading straight for the kitchen. A few labourers gave him disapproving looks along the way but none dared to challenge him outright. That only fed his ego as he stepped inside.

Food covered every work surface. Mouth watering at the sight of it all, James took a moment to watch the women in the kitchen preparing more for one meal than he would eat in an entire week.

The kitchen workers barely glanced at him. That suited James just fine. He advanced towards a tray of freshly baked buns like a wolf stalking its prey, hand reaching for his prize when a voice snapped "James Device, just what do you think you're doing in here? Get your hands off those buns right now and be off with you afore Mistress Towneley sees."

He turned to face the head cook, giving her his best roguish grin as he slipped a bun from the tray and held it behind his back. The risk of being caught didn't bother him. What were they going to do, report him to their mistress? He'd like to see them try. One growl from Dandy and the women would be begging for mercy. They knew better than to cross him. The worst the Towneleys could do was sack them; he could curse any one of them if they gave him reason to.

"But, Mary, I've been toiling in the fields all day and you know Master Duckworth doesn't pay us well enough for the work we put in. A man's got to eat."

"That is no concern of the Towneleys. Get thee back to the farm, or you will have more to contend with than an empty belly!"

"Wound me, you all do," he said with his other hand on his heart. "Would you really see me starve when the Towneleys have all this food going spare? Besides, Anne Towneley still owes me for the magical protection I was good enough to give them last Samhain."

"You know as well as I she doesn't want anything to do with your magic, Master Device. Take your charms and medicines elsewhere, and don't be spelling any of my girls either."

His attention was already drifting from the older woman to one of the maids who never failed to catch his eye. Maggie was the very definition of beauty. His mind wandered to the soft flesh beneath her bodice, imagining peeling back the fabric to the delights underneath. "Too late for that, Mary, but it isn't the magic of the cunning folk at work here. I don't need love charms to win your girls' hearts."

James couldn't help grinning like the lovesick idiot he was fast becoming, completely oblivious to the fact that the other workers were suddenly very focused on their tasks.

"You!" a familiar voice yelled. "Did I not tell you once before you are no longer welcome here?"

That brought him crashing firmly back to reality. His gaze darted from beauty to beast, locking with the blood-shot orbs of the old bat who called the place home. Her lined, spiteful face was enough to turn Cupid's arrow to ash. Lust gave way to anger.

"All right, I'm going," he growled. "I was merely hoping for a bite to eat as payment owed for my services at Samhain."

"I owe you nothing! Your magic is not wanted here and if I catch you round Carr Hall again, I'll have one of the lads fetch the constable."

"Fetch him! Practising magic is no crime; only using it to harm others is. And I told you before I'm no witch – I'm no practitioner of the dark arts and I take no part in curses that put people on their deathbeds. I know the law and you have no proof I've done anything to break it."

"Be that as it may, I want you off my land this instant, or I will have him investigate my missing turves. I know it was you and that ugly mother of yours, so don't you dare deny it!"

The accusation of theft incensed James more than anything else. "Let him! We merely took what we were owed for all that work we did; we never stole anything!"

"Well there will be no further payment from me. Your services are not wanted and I will not pay for work I haven't asked for. Now get off my land or I will send for Constable Hargrieves, and we will see what he has to say about my turves."

James could feel his control slipping, his hands already balled into fists and his teeth gritted so hard his jaw hurt. It took all his self-restraint to rein in his temper. He was well aware of what would happen if he lost his hold on the situation.

"I'm going," he growled again, turning his back on Anne and striding over to the same door he'd used to come in. "I have better things to do than listen to these accusations anyway. Some of the folks in these parts still realise the importance of the craft, even if most of you are too ignorant to see it."

James grabbed the door handle and felt a blow from behind, right between his shoulders.

"I will have that insolent tongue ripped from your foul mouth if you come here again! Never have I encountered such disrespect. I will not be spoken to in that manner, least of all in my own home! Get thee out of my sight this instant."

He could feel his face burning. Bad enough to be physically struck by a woman, but to suffer such humiliation from one no greater than his equal? The fact it had happened in front of Maggie only added to the shame of it, and his rage blazed all the stronger.

It took all his self-control to keep walking. He didn't even turn round to glare at the evil hag who saw fit to treat him so unfairly. She was watching him leave though – he could feel her eyes on him. James clenched his jaw. He had done nothing but work hard for the Towneleys, even helping without being asked at times, and in return for what? All they'd ever given him were harsh words and pitiful payments, whether in the form of coin, food or useful items like turves for the fire. And now she dared strike *him*? He who was the son of Squinting Lizzie, grandson of the great Demdike, and master of Dandy? He should not have to endure such treatment from the likes of Anne Towneley. She should consider herself lucky he had shown such self-restraint in the face of this injustice.

James reached the edge of the Towneleys' estate and made his way back to the river. The banks and surrounding woodland were still and quiet, save for the odd burst of birdsong or the splash of a fish coming up to the surface to feed. Dandy was nowhere to be seen. That seemed odd. The spirit had been all too willing to take action when James had last argued with Anne Towneley, so what had changed? There were none to counsel against doing anything rash this time. He would have expected the hellhound to be jumping at another chance to take revenge.

Laund Farm was exactly as James had left it. If the other farm labourers had noticed his absence, they made no mention of it, and they continued to keep their distance as they went about their tasks. James wasn't complaining. He was happy to be alone with his anger as he worked, and his temper continued to simmer long after the day was done. The night brought no rest, his mind replaying the altercation again and again. It wasn't long before he started wishing the ungrateful bitch dead. But what could he do without Dandy there to help?

Both his mother and his gran had been careful to avoid teaching him anything in the way of black magic, and James had not yet sought to gain any of that forbidden knowledge through his pact with Dandy. No one had taught him how to channel his anger into the form of a curse capable of causing harm. If he'd allowed himself to completely lose control earlier, he fully believed Dandy would have appeared and Anne would be a corpse already. But he had no idea how to strike her down without the hellhound's aid.

"Come on, Dandy," he whispered into the night. "Where the hell are you?"

James was in no better mood come morning.

"Breakfast!" his mam called.

He finished dressing and stomped into the kitchen. His mam was just sitting down to her portion of stale bread. There was a second plate on the table waiting for him, and the crumbs on a third plate indicated Jennet had already eaten hers and run off somewhere. James sat at the place set for him and took a bite.

"Morning." There was a warm twinkle in his mam's drooping eye, and a loving smile on her face.

James glanced at her and stared down at his plate again. "Morning."

He could feel the frown without looking up a second time. "Is something the matter, love? Is it Master Duckworth? Is he not paying you fairly?"

James just grunted.

"Oh, don't tell me you've had a falling out with Master Duckworth now as well. You haven't–"

Jennet chose that moment to rush back in. "Mam! Mam! There's a kitten outside. Can we keep it, Mam? Can I give it some cheese?"

James took advantage of the distraction to slip away, taking his stale bread with him. The kitten froze at the sight of him and turned tail, bolting for cover. James snorted. "Stupid animal. It's not you I want to hurt."

He tried concentrating on Dandy as he walked, fixing an image of the hellhound in his mind and trying to make his thoughts heard. It was no use. There was no sign of his familiar anywhere, nor even the sound of Dandy's voice. James was beginning to think the hellhound had abandoned him for some other master. Was that possible? He remembered what his gran had told him the night of the pact – that if other cunning folk knew Dandy's name they might be able to tempt him to serve them instead. But he had kept the hellhound's name in the family, just as his gran had said, and besides, he'd only ever sensed loyalty from the spirit. So why wasn't Dandy answering?

Maybe he should seek out his grandmother for advice. It was no use asking his mam when she worried all the time, but his gran might help him deepen the bond with his familiar and learn how to fully use the connection they shared. Would she guess at why he was showing a sudden interest in such things though? Possibly. The demon she'd dealt with to save Jennet might have taken her sight, but her mind remained as sharp as ever. James couldn't take that risk.

News of the row with Anne Towneley had already begun to spread. James rounded the path leading to Roughlee and spied a group of his neighbours deep in conversation. They went quiet the moment they realised he was coming into earshot, but he heard them muttering again once he'd passed by. And they weren't the only ones. He didn't catch any of what these groups were saying, but he felt sure they were laughing at him behind his back. It could only be the reputation of his family protecting him from being openly taunted and teased as he went about his business.

A sudden thought occurred to James – a consequence of the falling out he hadn't considered until then. He'd allowed Mistress Towneley to hit him and live to tell the tale. Would his family's reputation hold if he let that challenge go unanswered? He doubted it. Surely, then, it was his duty to seek some form of magical retaliation?

The whispers and the staring suddenly made James uncomfortable. It was enough to drive him from the path and back along the river, where there were none but the animals to watch as he passed.

"I could really use your help with this, Dandy. Does our pact no longer stand?"

Could Dandy even hear him? He tried thinking the words instead, and felt even less sure they'd reached his familiar. But he had to keep trying. It was either that, or do nothing at all.

A male voice called out from behind. "You are seeking vengeance against the one who wronged you yesterday?"

James came to a stop. There was something familiar about that voice, something that raised the hairs on the back of his neck. It could only be a spirit. He began muttering a charm of protection as he slowly turned.

The glare of the early morning sun hid most of the creature. It stood upright and looked human in shape, but James wasn't fooled. "What of it? You are not bound to me."

"No, but I can still help."

The cunning man squinted, struggling to put a name to that voice. Then the shadow of something inhuman became visible to his inner eye, something dark and winged. He regarded the creature with a new wariness.

"You're Chattox's familiar," he said. "Fancie."

"Indeed I am." The spirit gave a mock bow.

"And why would you help me, grandson of the sworn enemy of your mistress?"

"I will tell you what I told your grandmother that night we made a deal for little Jennet's life: I am so much more than the likes of Tibb and Dandy, and thus I may bargain with whoever I choose."

"So you would avenge me of Anne Towneley?"

"In a manner of speaking, if that is your wish."

"Then I bid thee go; strike her down, since Dandy will not do it for me."

Fancie shook his head. "You are right in that we have no

pact. I cannot take such direct action, unless you would make a deal for her death. The price of life for your sister was your grandmother's eyesight. What will you offer me for the death of a foe, I wonder?"

James could feel his anger rising again. "Do you take me for a fool? You will not have my soul; I will find another way to have my revenge, and you can slink back to Chattox empty handed. No doubt she is the one putting you up to making these deals with our family!"

"Nay, I am here by choice. Old Demdike has taught you well, I see. But I did not really come here to deal, though I would be the fool not to make such an offer. Every soul has its price."

"Then how can you help me?"

"I came to tell you the easiest way to kill a person with magic, and in return you must agree to owe me a favour. Nothing more, nothing less – no sacrifice of any body parts required, soul or otherwise. Do you agree?"

"A favour? Why would you offer me aid at such a low price?"

"My reasons are not your concern. I will only make you this offer once, so think carefully, James Device. The knowledge you seek for a favour."

James frowned. He knew better than to trust spirits without question, especially one bound to a rival wise woman. But he also knew this was his best chance to get even with Anne Towneley, unless Dandy suddenly deigned to make an appearance.

"I am tempted," he admitted. "But I would know more of this favour before accepting your offer."

Clouds slid over the sun, revealing more of the demon to James's earthly sight. Fancie was smirking. "I may ask you to do something for me, or it could merely be a piece of information I have need of but cannot find out for myself. Even we spirits are not permitted to see everything. I cannot say for certain what I will ask of you until the time comes for me to call in this favour, but I can promise you that it will be a small thing compared to what you will gain from me. Once you have the knowledge I offer it is yours forever, to do with as you wish in your years upon this earth. It does not stop with Mistress Towneley – now that you have made your pact you will be able to use this magic time and again, as the need arises."

James was still hesitant. Perhaps it would be safer to ask his gran for advice after all. He didn't like the idea of owing Fancie anything, and how could he be sure the spirit's information was genuine? He would have no way of knowing if the curse would work until he actually tried it and either Anne died, or nothing happened, potentially leaving him worse off than he was now.

Fancie's smirk faded and his features took on a more serious set. "I can see you are a cunning man indeed to doubt me so. If you would walk away from this then I respect that. I only hope you find the help you need elsewhere. To let such injustices go unpunished affects us all, and if the likes of the Towneleys realise they can treat us so without fear of being spelled, well. I dread to think what that means for the future of any who would practise the craft."

James hesitated a moment longer. "I think I had best wait for Dandy to reappear."

"Very well," Fancie said with a dip of his head. "If only my mistress were capable of such restraint. I can only imagine your anger at being struck by a woman making false accusations against you and your family. It must have been humiliating with so many witnesses around – I fear

Chattox would have lost control and cursed them all. But I'm sure they will soon come to regret the jeers and mocking laughter."

The spirit began to walk away. James stared after him, but it was not Fancie's retreating back he was seeing.

As if at the bidding of the spirit's words, the altercation replayed itself yet again in James's mind. His rage rose up with the memory of Towneley's angry face and cruel tongue. Worse still was the thought of what might have happened after he'd left. It was easy to imagine the kitchen workers smirking and talking amongst themselves once their mistress had stalked off to some other part of her lair, and what must Maggie have thought? Would she still be interested in a man who could not stand up for himself? And then there'd been the muttering as he'd passed through Roughlee. It was all his anger needed to give it the strength to overcome his wariness.

"Wait!" he called after Fancie.

The spirit turned to face him again. "Yes?"

"I accept. The knowledge of how to kill Anne with magic in return for a favour."

Fancie grinned and bowed a second time. Then the spirit stalked back over to him and whispered in his ear. Anne Towneley's fate was sealed.

It wasn't until the next morning that James had the chance to act on the information Fancie had given him. The method he'd been told was so simple, he almost wished he'd waited to find out from someone he could trust. But his mam and gran were so guarded when it came to the dark arts, there was no guarantee they'd have shared it with him. And Dandy was still missing.

The clay he needed was easy enough to come by. He dug it up in the early hours by the light of the waning moon.

Lunar energy soaked into the grey lump until it resonated with a magic of its own, ensuring the success of the spell once it was cast. If spell was the right word for what he was about to do. There were no incantations needed to direct the curse like with the charms he'd been taught – he merely had to mould the clay into the likeness of Mistress Towneley and this would grant him power over her, or so Fancie had said. And so he set to work on making an image of his target, until he was forced to abandon it to go work in the fields. But the day was made easier by knowing he was doing something about Towneley's mistreatment of him, and the hours passed quickly.

That night, he took the clay and dried it by the fire as best he could without his mam seeing, then hid it in his room. It wasn't until the next day he was really able to start exacting his revenge.

A feeling of immense satisfaction settled over him when he began to crush the likeness of his enemy with his bare hands, wishing for her death as the clay crumbled beneath his fingers. Would it really work? That didn't matter to him right then. The mere idea of holding a life in his hands was intoxicating, and he intended to revel in it for as long as it lasted.

But James didn't just want Anne dead for what she'd done to him. He wanted her to suffer. And thus he only destroyed part of the image to begin with, so that her body would begin to weaken, but not yet die.

He had made the image large enough to allow him to prolong Anne's suffering for an entire week. It became a nightly ritual to grind a little more of the clay, crumbling it away bit by bit until only that last small piece remained. He crushed it with a feeling of such finality he imagined he had become Death himself. James felt drunk on that power.

"Dandy! Come on, Dandy. Go spy on Carr Hall for me. Tell me it worked!"

Still there was no answer.

"Fancie, then. Come tell me how the curse worked – tell me how Anne suffered and died."

The demon didn't answer either. James supposed he should have expected that. He considered borrowing his mam's tools to scry on Carr Hall, and quickly dismissed the idea. Scrying took more concentration than he had the patience for, and he was sure to hear news of Anne come morning.

All was quiet in the other rooms of the house. James crept into the kitchen and helped himself to a mug of ale, grinning all the while. Everything had changed. No one would cross him again.

The next day dawned brighter than usual.

"James, breakfast!"

James pulled on his shirt and strode into the kitchen, unable to keep the grin from playing on his lips.

His mam smiled and handed him a plate. "Good to see you looking happier, son."

"Oh yes." James puffed his chest out, beaming at her as he plucked his breakfast from the plate. "This is the last stale bread we'll have to make do with. Only the best food for us from now on – you'll see!"

His mam frowned. "What do you mean 'only the best food for us'?"

James grinned and pecked her on the cheek, then ducked out of the front door before she could ask him anything else.

There was a spring in his step as he made his way to Laund Farm, and an eagerness he couldn't quite hide. The gossip among the other villagers could no longer touch him. He kept his ears pricked for news of Anne's death, but the groups of neighbours he passed reacted the same as always – they quietened when he came within earshot and kept their mutterings too low to catch any words once he'd gone past.

Still, it was surely only a matter of time before someone talked about her death. His good mood remained as he set to work about the farm, but as the day wore on without a single mention of the hated woman, it began to darken. Had Fancie been tricking him all along?

By evening, James was back to being sullen and withdrawn. He returned from the farm to find all his mam had to offer him for dinner was the usual bland pottage. That only made him feel worse. He sat down and wrinkled his nose at the watery mix of herbs and vegetables, wishing they could afford at least a few chunks of meat to go in it. But how would that ever change if Anne Towneley still lived?

"Son, I wish you'd tell me what is the matter," his mam said, placing a gentle hand on his. She gave a slight squeeze. "Is it the other farm labourers? Are they picking on you for keeping to the old ways?"

James pulled his hand out from under hers. "I don't want to talk about it."

Hurt filled his mam's face, her eyes glistening with

tears. Jennet looked from him to their mam and back again. James sensed she was burning with questions but he shot her an angry look and she dropped her gaze to her own bowl of pottage. The atmosphere around the table was subdued then. It was as though his bad mood had leeched the happiness from his mother and sibling, sucking any further attempts at conversation from the room and leaving them in gloomy silence.

James began to shovel down his pottage as quickly as he could. He wanted nothing more than to slink back to his room, where he could be alone with his thoughts and his bitter frustration. But Jennet couldn't keep quiet for long. He still had half a bowlful of his meal left when she asked "Mam, what was wrong with Mrs Towneley today?"

James's heart leapt and his head snapped up, his eyes darting from his sister to his mother. His mam had stiffened. All traces of the upset James had caused her had turned to stone.

"What do you mean, lambkin?"

"She looked like a skeleton when I saw her in the kitchen. I think James did something."

Inwardly cursing, James looked back down at his half-empty bowl and resumed eating, hoping to avoid more of his mam's questions. It felt like her eyes were boring into the top of his head as she answered "Why would you think that?"

"Because he argued with Mrs Towneley last week and she hit him – Isobell says so. And I saw him playing with clay the morning after it happened."

"Clay?"

More silent curses went through James's head. Would his sister never learn when to keep her tongue still? He could feel himself turning red under the force of their mam's gaze.

Jennet nodded. "He shaped it like Mrs Towneley, before she looked like a skeleton."

"Oh, James, tell me you didn't."

"I did." He finally raised his head, meeting those mismatched eyes with defiance. His mam fixed him with a look of angry disappointment. "She had it coming after treating me like that."

"And what do you think you will have coming when Roger Nowell hears of this? Mistress Towneley suddenly falls ill after a quarrel between the two of you – he will make the connection."

"Well what would you and Gran have had me do after she started making accusations and then had the nerve to lay a hand on me? Would you have rather I let such a slight go unpunished?"

"We would have had you think with your head instead of that foolhardy heart of yours. I knew it was too soon for you to make the pact. Your temper will be the death of us all!"

"And where would we be if Pendle lost its fear of our magic? There is already precious little justice in the land, and respect for us is waning with the likes of Richard Baldwin in power now. They needed reminding of the consequences of mistreating one of the cunning folk, and I acted as I saw fit."

"And just what were you doing at Carr Hall in the first place? Anne made it quite clear she did not want you there after the incident at Samhain – your gran told me so. I would have hoped you'd have the sense to stay clear of the Towneleys after that!"

"She never paid me for that work at Samhain. It's not

right and you know it, Mam. The gentry need to know we will not stand for such injustices, or how will we ever win back their respect? They need to know our magic is as strong as ever, new religion or no."

"It's not right but it is the way of things. Keep on looking for trouble and they will hang you – no amount of fear is going to save you from the noose."

"If I hang then so be it. Anne is getting what she deserved and I would not take it back, even if I knew how. At least I will die a great magician!"

"There is no way to take it back," his mam said, defeated. "But how did you know to use the clay image to bewitch her?"

"Dandy told me," James lied. "He said if I wanted to kill her I had to completely destroy it, but I wanted her to suffer first so I crumbled it a bit at a time until there was only a small piece left, which I finished off yesterday."

"Then she will die tomorrow. It is important you keep your head down now – give Nowell no other reason to suspect you, and if we are lucky, there will be too little proof of witchcraft for them to send you to the assizes. And whatever you do, you must not go back to Carr Hall in the time it takes Henry to grieve for his wife."

"Yes, yes, I'm not stupid."

"Promise me, James." His mam took his hand again and squeezed, tighter than before. Her gaze softened and the glistening of tears was back. "Swear to me you will stay away until it is safe for our family to be seen round the estate, if such a time ever comes again."

"I promise, Mam," he said with a sigh, convinced she was worrying over nothing. The clay image was gone, and his familiar had not been around for anyone to see and connect to him. Henry could blame witchcraft for Anne's sudden sickness all he wanted, but there would be no proof, and arguing with someone was not a crime. They would not arrest him, much as they no doubt wanted to. He had given them no reason to.

But his promise was what his mother needed to hear and she seemed happier for it. James was able to finish his meal in peace and retreat to his room once he was done, feeling brighter again for knowing he had succeeded. He was confident his actions would win back respect for magic, which could only lead to easier times in the years to come. Maybe they would even hail him as the founder of the new age.

He smiled to himself as he lay back on his filthy mattress, imagining how his name would live on in the hearts and minds of cunning folk long after his mortal self had passed from living memory. He felt more contented than he had in years. Sleep was creeping over him, and just before he slipped into a restful slumber, he glimpsed Dandy padding over to the bed. The fearsome-looking dog settled next to him, the muscular form as solid as any mortal beast where it pressed against his side. James smiled again. All was right with the world.

NINETEEN

The passing bells tolled news of an imminent end. They echoed around Pendle Forest, solemnly emanating from St Mary's and dutifully carrying the message to all ears in the neighbourhood – even those as far as Wheathead. Anne Towneley would die soon. Her end was nigh.

In the social circles Richard was privy to, the news of her illness had been much quicker to reach his ears than those of James Device. It had been a long week. Only Fancie's advice to let events play out had kept him from visiting the Towneleys sooner, but now the time had come. He set out for Carr Hall in the grip of a dark thrill, one that quickened his heart and stirred flutters of excitement in his stomach. The wait was almost over. Justice for Rob would soon be had.

The bells were still going when Richard reached the path leading to the estate. He came to an impatient stop. It wouldn't do to approach Henry Towneley while the old bat was still breathing, so he hovered around the vicinity of the doomed woman's land, a crow circling carrion. No one questioned his presence in the area. He had plenty of duties to attend to in his professional capacity as steward of the Church, and was his true business there not of the greatest benefit to his fellow Christians? They would be thanking him when Demdike and her foul spawn were swinging from the gallows in the weeks to come.

Richard's face twisted into a wicked grin. By all accounts, it sounded like Anne should have died already, and no amount of money could save her from the vile spell James had cast. Her husband tried his best, of course. But none of the physicians he consulted with could find either the cause of the illness or a way to treat it.

Finally the death knell sounded.

"A blessing," John Duckworth said, his expression both sombre and sage. "None should have to endure that many days of suffering."

Richard dipped his head in mournful agreement, but inwardly his heart leapt. "The Church thanks you for your continued patronage, John. I must be off – I fear poor Henry is in need of company now."

A grim silence descended in the bells' wake. Richard hurried along the path from Laund Farm to Carr Hall, his coin purse slightly heavier than he'd left home with. He passed several labourers as he went. Their grim eyes followed him, dry and utterly devoid of grief. Few would shed tears over Anne's death. She had not been a particularly well-liked member of the community, even among the other gentry, and Richard had heard many express the belief she had brought it on herself by incurring a witch's wrath. Glee filled him now. No one doubted James had killed her. With Henry's testimony, Demdike and her family were sure to be found guilty, and they were certain to hang.

Richard hesitated as he reached the edge of the Towneley's estate. Henry was likely devastated by this latest turn of events, and Richard had his reputation to consider – and the damage it would do if he was seen to approach the grieving widower too quickly. Towneley should be allowed a little time to say his goodbyes.

Casting his eyes on the land around him, Richard's gaze settled on a large tree set a little way back from the path. There. He'd wait there for the right moment to enter the estate.

Richard seated himself at the back of the tree, out of sight of the path. The ground was hard and the trunk made for a poor support, but he leant against it anyway, closing his eyes and contenting himself with imagining the Demdike family's trial. Soon a whistling carried on the day's warm breeze.

Grunting, Richard opened his eyes and got to his feet. He peered around the tree to see the vicar approaching, strolling with a cheeriness at odds with Pendle's otherwise sombre pall. The sight filled Richard with a similar cheer.

"Thank you, Lord, thank you," he muttered to himself as he waited for John Town to near Carr Hall's gates. There was no doubt this was the Lord's work. Normally, the vicar would have stayed with the family from the moment he was called to Anne's deathbed, through her passing and right up until the final prayer for the deceased. But on this occasion, Town must have been called away briefly on some other business. Now he was returning, and it was exactly the opportunity Richard needed.

Richard circled back round onto the path. "John!"

The vicar turned with some surprise. "Richard? What brings you here?"

"I was in the area and heard the terrible news. I thought

I should offer my condolences to Henry and join him in prayer for his late wife."

"Really? I did not think you were that friendly with the Towneleys."

"You're right, we're not that friendly," Richard admitted. "But is it not our duty as Christians to aid and support our neighbours in times of need?"

"Indeed it is. You are a good man, Richard."

The miller smiled, glad to know the darkness that had taken hold of him had not become outwardly visible to his fellow men. If he could fool a vicar, he could surely hide the evil from anyone. Still, it would not do to become careless or overconfident. Town's former cheer turned to sympathy for the handful of mourners they passed along the path to the front of the hall, and Richard was careful to mirror him.

Within those grand walls, it was as quiet and gloomy as the inside of any tomb. Thick mourning cloths obscured the sun's light from filtering through the windows, and the dim glow of candles added an eerie quality to the Towneley's abode. The servants had already donned black clothes in respect for the death of their mistress. More dry eyes betrayed the absence of sorrow in their hearts, yet each of their faces wore a sombre expression, and they spoke in muted murmurs. The house was made all the more grim for it.

Incense hung thick and heavy on the air. Burners exhaled their perfumed smoke in a futile attempt to hide the sickly smell of decay already slithering through the nasal cavities of all those unfortunate enough to be in the hall. That foul stench entwined itself round the aromatic scents until it became something putrid, constricting the airways and making both miller and vicar gag.

Richard was no stranger to death – none of them were –

but he found himself uneasy in its unwholesome presence. A part of him wanted nothing more than to turn back then. He had to take a moment to remind himself of why he was there. The witches. This had to be their doing. And they **would** hang for it.

"Is something the matter, Richard?" Town placed a kindly hand on his shoulder. "There is no shame in turning back if this is all too much. Neither I nor the Lord will judge you."

Richard drew himself up and puffed out his chest. "It is nothing, Reverand. Let us continue."

He strode forward and into the next room. Displeasure filled him to see the mirrors had also been covered with black mourning cloths, in keeping with the old traditions. He suppressed the urge to tut and glanced at Town. The vicar remained his usual calm and patient self. There was no sign he shared in Richard's displeasure.

Richard almost commented on that lack of reaction. Purgatory was a misguided idea of the false Catholic faith, one the Holy Scriptures had disproven. Surely the vicar must feel some frustration to see members of his flock clinging to such silly superstitions?

It was not that Richard was ignorant of those superstitions. But to think a spirit could become trapped by its reflection was foolish. Anne's soul had already departed and gone to either Heaven or Hell. Really they shouldn't be praying for her now she'd passed, but the older families had been so resistant towards completely eradicating these Catholic rites that they'd had to allow some of the old funeral practices to continue. That wouldn't have stopped Richard saying something ordinarily, but he was mindful of the need to make Henry his ally. So he held his tongue.

They reached the room where Anne's earthly remains

lay awaiting burial, resting in an open coffin with that absolute stillness only the dead can achieve. Henry knelt beside her. Tears rolled down his cheeks in a steady stream, yet the sound of his sobbing was oddly quiet, as if the gloom had subdued even that.

The two men entered, bringing them in full view of the corpse. Shock brought them to a standstill. This was not the body of a woman who had died of natural causes. The face peering out from the ivory folds of her burial shroud was too rotten, the skin too blackened. It was no longer recognisable as the face of the woman she'd been in life. Her flesh was all but gone, her bones clearly visible beneath their necrotic membrane and her teeth bared where the lips had pulled back to give her the grin of the dead. Worse, her cheeks were coated in the crumbly white of grave wax, adding an extra level of the grotesque. It was as if she had been dead for a number of weeks or even months rather than hours.

A scrap of cloth lay beside the coffin to cover her face. It seemed Henry hadn't been able to bring himself to use it. Perhaps he felt hiding the rotting features – horrific as they were – carried too great a finality, signifying the last goodbye he could not yet bear to make. Richard almost felt a shred of empathy at that. Had he not felt similar pain when he'd had to say that same goodbye to Rob?

Henry turned his head and fixed them with eyes red from crying. Richard would have said he looked lost at first, his wife clearly his world throughout the years of their marriage, and that world now empty without her. But when their gazes met, Richard could feel the change in the newly turned widower. Something in the man hardened, and there was a hostility with which Henry regarded him, an enmity Richard would have to overcome.

"Baldwin. Come to ensure there is no secret Mass going on for her death?"

"No, I simply wish to offer my condolences to you at this difficult time."

Henry didn't seem to hear him. "Can you not leave us in peace just this once? Have you no compassion?"

"Come now, Henry, there is no need for that tone," Town said, alarmed by Henry's reaction. "We are all faithful to the Church here – there is no need to fight among ourselves."

"I do not think the Puritans among us would agree. Anne and I have done nothing but try our very best to embrace the new religion, and yet we are still hounded by those who doubt our conviction. And look where the new religion has got us. Here my Anne lies dead, killed by some evil the Lord could not protect her from."

"I am sorry for your loss." Richard's words sounded sincere, but that near shred of empathy had already withered beneath fresh impatience. He suppressed the smug smile flitting about his lips. What an accomplished actor he'd become. "And I honestly did not come here because I have any quarrel with you. It is the witches I am interested in."

"Now is not the time, Richard," Town hissed in his ear, but Richard could see he had Henry's attention.

"The witches? What have the witches got to do with this?"

Triumph flared. Richard felt it flash through his eyes, a brief hint at what lay beneath his sympathetic mask. It didn't matter. He had Henry now, he was sure of it.

"Evil did take Anne from you, evil conjured through their pact with the Devil. I think it is time we put a stop to such evil; time we brought these blasphemous heathens to justice for all the wicked crimes they have been committing and getting away with because of their magic. I am well aware of your late wife's argument with James Device. Can there be any doubt of his guilt in bewitching Anne to death?"

Henry frowned. "Well yes, they did argue. But Anne never mentioned to me that she suspected any kind of witchcraft at work, and I did not see James in our hall after the argument, nor any agents of the Devil. I had not thought to blame any of the Devices for this tragedy. How can you be so certain it was he?"

"How else do you explain the suddenness of her illness, the speed with which she deteriorated or the accelerated decay upon her body? What other explanation is there but witchcraft?"

Henry's eyes hardened again. "If this is the work of witches, then I will see each and every one of them hang for what they've done! I take it you mean to go to Roger with these suspicions?"

"Yes, but the law requires some form of proof to take them to trial. If you will come forward as a witness, I believe we can successfully bring them to justice for all the evil they have brought to this land. Without you, they will walk free, and Anne's murder will go unpunished."

"Then you can depend on me. I will tell Roger what I know of the incident in the kitchen and the illness that followed. Send for me when you are ready, but until then I would be left alone with my grief."

"Of course," Richard said, glad to be away from the corpse. He nodded to the vicar and hurried out of the building, heading straight for Read Hall.

"Richard." Nowell addressed him with a hint of impatience. "You are here to point the finger for Anne Towneley's sudden demise, yes?"

"We both know it was witchcraft," he answered, placing his hands on the desk and leaning over so he was at eye level with the JP. "Are you really about to let them get away with the murder of a member of one of the oldest and wealthiest families in Pendle?"

"I told you once before – I can do nothing unless you bring me proof of these accusations, regardless of whether I believe them or not," Roger replied, his voice level and his eyes impassive. Richard was not fooled. He sensed it was merely the calm before the storm.

"But we do have something to take to trial this time. We have a witness! Henry Towneley has agreed to come forward and he will testify in the assizes when called upon."

Richard watched the other man's entire countenance change from one of impatience and building anger to a jubilance which mirrored his own. After the witches had plagued them for so long, the mere thought of finally building a successful case against Demdike and her family was enough to bring a smile to each of their faces.

"And here I was, thinking you were about to waste my time again, Dick. But you have done well. Henry's testimony could change everything."

"Indeed. Do you want me to bring him to make his statement?"

"Not yet – he is in mourning after all. I think it is time

we brought James Device in for questioning first. Go to the constable to arrange his arrest."

Richard smirked, feeling things were going better this time round than he'd dared to hope. Vengeance for Rob was surely within his grasp. And the witches were so arrogant in their power over others that they wouldn't even see it coming.

CHAPTER
TWENTY

T rue to his word, James resisted the temptation to return to Carr Hall and went straight to Laund Farm on the morning of Anne Towneley's death. He even avoided confrontation with that self-righteous busybody Richard Baldwin when the miller turned up at the farm gates, ducking into the pig shed before Baldwin noticed him. James found he was content with simply knowing he'd brought Mistress Towneley to justice. There was no need to see his spell at work.

It was around noon when the death knell sounded. James waited for the echoes of the final toll to fade before he emerged from the shed, to find Baldwin hurrying away. The other labourers froze. James met their eyes with new confidence, and couldn't help smirking as they suddenly found jobs on the opposite end of Duckworth's land.

Change was definitely coming. On the plains of his imagination, James wandered the grand house and vast expanses of land he might one day own. It would take time though. Perhaps the first step would be something as small as an increase in his wages. No matter. Fear was a powerful ally. Whether in months or years, the rewards would come.

Dusk approached. He finished work for the day and set out on the road to Newchurch, tall and proud as he strode across the muddy track. Unbidden, his mother's words sounded within his memory:

"No amount of fear is going to save you from the noose."

But with no evidence of witchcraft, what could the JP do to him? The clay image he'd made was no more, and without it Nowell was powerless to act on any suspicions the villagers might have. James didn't fear the law.

The countryside felt unusually quiet as he drew closer to Newchurch. They had at least another two hours of daylight, and yet the people of Pendle seemed to have retreated behind closed doors already. He passed few on the road, and those that were about were careful not to look him in the eye. Had his reputation really grown this quickly?

St Mary's was only a stone's throw away when a low murmuring reached his ears. So that was where his neighbours were, seeking comfort in their god no doubt. Would they scatter and run when they saw him? He laughed at the thought. This promised to be the most fun he'd had all week.

James began to swagger again as he rounded the bend into Newchurch. His eyes fell on the gathered crowd, and his confidence crumbled to ash.

A force of around two dozen men stood outside the gates to St Mary's. The air around them was charged with the threat of violence, warning signs of its imminent arrival visible in the hardening of their eyes, the clenching of fists, and the raising of makeshift weapons. Several of them were armed with wooden mallets meant for bruising flesh and breaking bones. And most worrying of all, it appeared they were led by none other than Constable Hargrieves and that self-righteous arsworm, Richard Baldwin.

Fear turned from friend to foe. James froze, his heart pounding. They must have found evidence against him after all, for who else would they be out hunting in such numbers? It wasn't unusual for the constable to request assistance in the arrest of a dangerous criminal, but James had never seen so many before. They could only be there for him.

Uncertainty gripped him. His instinct was to run, but where to? There was no way he would reach the safety of his home or even Malkin Tower before the mob caught up with him, even if he could circle back round to either house. So who to trust?

One of the men locked eyes with him, and there was a cry of "There he is!"

That broke the spell. James's muscles fired back into life and he fled to more cries of "Get him!" and "Death to the witch!"

James flew across the bumpy road, stumbling on large rocks and dips in the mud but barely slowing. Standing and fighting didn't seem to be an option. It would only give Nowell more cause to hang him, so he pushed his body to its limits in a desperate attempt to stay ahead of his pursuers. If he could just reach Moss End Farm, the Bulcocks might hide him in return for the help his gran had given when their son was ill. It was his only chance.

The squelch of feet sounded unnaturally loud behind him. James pushed himself harder still. It would only take one of the mob to close the distance and wrestle him to the ground, then the rest of the men would be on him like a pack of rabid dogs. If he faltered, they would catch him for sure, and James didn't fancy his chances against the hate Baldwin had incited.

But he knew no magic that could keep him from tiring. His muscles began to burn and his legs to slow, and his breathing turned ragged. Too late, he realised he'd pushed himself too hard too soon. He was facing a losing battle to keep going all the way to the Bulcocks' farm at any real pace.

The feet were drumming over harder ground now, louder and louder by the second. They were gaining on him, and the farm was still about half a mile away. James gave a breathless groan of despair. How was he to hide at Moss End Farm if the men saw him enter?

Fear gave him one last burst of speed. It wasn't enough. James glanced behind him and whimpered. The mob were almost upon him.

He fixed his gaze back on the road ahead. It was no longer empty.

Red eyes blazed from a huge head wreathed in black, its fur possessing the same shadow quality as the hellhound familiars of his family. But this was no hellhound. Its form was bulkier, its nature wilder. And when the bear reared up on its hind legs, it appeared all the more impressive and terrifying.

Lips pulled back from a gaping maw, baring vicious fangs. James skidded before it and lost his footing, landing heavily on his side. There was a brief sting of raw flesh where a graze opened up. Then those terrible eyes locked on his, and the pain became lost in the sensation of cold terror.

The creature's gaze was filled with such malice, James knew it wouldn't just kill him like a real bear. No, his death would be slow and painful, and he attempted to mumble a quick protection spell before those huge teeth and claws came down on his flesh. Fear had him stumbling over his words and he kept having to start over.

He pulled himself up into a sitting position, his eyes still locked on the bear's when rough hands grabbed him from behind and dragged him upright. James screamed and wrenched an arm free, then brought it backwards. There was a cry of pain as his elbow connected with a man's face, and his would-be captor stumbled back. His other arm was still in the grip of a second man. He turned and sank his teeth into one of the fingers wrapped around his bicep. There was a second cry of pain, and the man's hold loosened. James kicked out and caught the man's shin, and the fingers slipped from his arm. He caught movement in the corner of his eye and pulled free, terrified it was the bear and desperate to flee. But the mob had encircled him. There was nowhere left to run.

"James Device, you are under arrest for the murder of Anne Towneley," Hargrieves said.

A new pair of hands wrapped around his arm and the shadow on the edge of his vision rushed forward, revealing itself to be Dandy. The bear had vanished.

His familiar lunged straight for the arm of the man restraining him, but James was no fool. "Dandy, no!"

Few of the men seemed to notice, but he felt Baldwin's eyes on him and glanced over. There was a look of puzzlement on the miller's face, which could only mean Dandy was still invisible to all those without the gift of spiritual sight. Then a fist connected with James's abdomen, driving all the air from his lungs. He was too winded to scream as the violence that had been building finally broke.

Dandy stopped short of his target and rounded on the man who'd hit his master, jaws wide and ready to clamp around soft flesh.

"No," James managed to wheeze, eyes firmly on his familiar.

The hellhound skidded to a stop and the snarl melted from his face. A look of canine confusion and perhaps even hurt took its place, that fierce gaze softening and turning as soulful as any mortal dog's. They hadn't been bonded long enough to fully understand each other, and James realised the spirit couldn't comprehend why he didn't want him to attack this time. After all, his familiar was only trying to help.

Dandy remained in a fighting stance as the next blow came, and the next, and countless more after that. James was soon forced back down to the ground, arms up to protect his head as best he could. His flesh bruised and ached, then the first of the makeshift weapons came down on his shin, and he screamed in agony as bone cracked and splintered. But Dandy stayed back, whining pitifully.

His familiar gave him one last reproachful look. Then the spirit vanished, leaving James alone and utterly at the mercy of both his captors and his pain. The last of the fight was driven from him. He closed his eyes and passed out.

The young cunning man swam in and out of consciousness as he was carried all the way to Read Hall, his arms thrown across the shoulders of the two men either side of him, his legs dragging uselessly behind. Every fibre of his being throbbed in protest at the damage wrought upon his physical self, his injuries too numerous to count. Yet the harm to his spirit was in some ways more severe. His ego felt as battered as his flesh, the incident at Carr Hall paling in comparison to this latest humiliation.

He was only half aware of the jeers from nearly everyone they passed, his one good eye fixed on Baldwin's back, who was marching so proudly at the front of the procession. His other eye rested in darkness beneath swollen lids.

A part of him wished he'd let Dandy wreak havoc on the mob, anger once again simmering within the broken shell they'd made of his body. But his familiar was nowhere to be seen, and he began to worry that, by denying the hellhound, he might have permanently driven him away. That upset James more than anything else.

He had not felt any guilt for bringing about the death of a woman who had wronged him, and he wasn't about to start then, but he was beginning to feel a sense of regret. If only he'd listened to the advice of his elders, he wouldn't have landed himself in this trouble, and if they really had found evidence of his magic then things could be set to get a whole lot worse. Yet in spite of that, the same hate he'd felt for Anne Towneley now directed itself at the man who was clearly behind all this. He swore to himself that he would find a way to get revenge on Baldwin as well, even if it was from beyond the grave.

The men dragged him into Nowell's study and threw him into the seat across from the JP. There was a smile on Nowell's lips but his gaze was cold and merciless. James fought to remain conscious, glaring through his good eye with all the defiance he could muster.

"Thank you, gentlemen," Nowell said, gesturing to the men who'd assisted with the arrest. "That will be all for now."

They bowed their heads and exited the study. Baldwin made no move to go with them.

Nowell raised an eyebrow. "You wish to play a bigger part in the King's justice, Dick?"

Baldwin nodded. "I can help you with the questioning. My ties to the Church may prove invaluable in gathering evidence."

"Very well. Hargrieves, you may also stay. This witch's body might be broken but who knows what curses might spring to his lips?"

Hargrieves gave a rough nod. "You can count on me, Justice. He so much as looks at you funny, and I'll beat him into painful slumber."

"Very good." Nowell's gaze settled on James again. "James Device, you stand accused of witchcraft. Do you deny it?"

The pain of James's injuries throbbed to new heights. He gritted his teeth and managed to hiss "Yes."

"So you do not practise the craft of your grandmother, who goes by the name Demdike and is also a known witch?"

It was becoming a struggle not to pass out again. James latched onto the word witch and his stubbornness that rose with it. "We are not witches."

"Then why is it that I hear reports of your family seducing good Christian folk into accepting magical solutions to their problems, and then bullying them into paying for your blasphemous acts?"

"We never bullied or hurt anyone."

"But you confess to practising magic?"

"We never did anything wrong."

"Master Device, we are all aware of the ungodly ways your family still uphold, even in this age of a new faith which leads us closer to God. We know you practise witch-craft, and we know you used it to bewitch one Anne Towneley to death. You would save us all a great deal of time if you would simply confess."

"Prove it," he grunted.

"Oh, we will," answered Nowell, his face triumphant. "You see, we have a witness who will testify when called upon."

James felt fresh fear stab through his aching body. The situation was even more serious than he'd first thought. Regardless of who the witness was, they would almost certainly believe the word of a fellow Christian over anyone they thought to be a witch.

"And," Nowell continued, "I believe there were numerous witnesses to the argument between you and Mistress Towneley, which occurred only three days before she fell ill and a mere week before her death. Surely you will not deny that?"

The fear pushed back the beckoning darkness and kept the pain at bay. James's mind cleared. "She accused me and my mam of stealing her turves, so I pointed out she still owed us payment for previous work done. We took the turves as part of that payment."

"And that must have made you angry. You could almost be forgiven for striking her down after she'd made such allegations."

"It did. But when she ordered me to go, it was she who lashed out," he answered, recognising the trap Nowell was trying to lure him into. "I turned to leave, and as I went forth through the kitchen door, she gave me a knock between the shoulders, even though I had offered her no violence and was simply doing as she'd bid. I could have struck her down with magic, 'tis true, but I restrained myself and have since kept away from Carr Hall where I am clearly not welcome."

"Then you must have done something after the incident to make Mistress Towneley sick and put her on her deathbed."

"No," James lied. "I stayed away from the Towneleys after the incident and have not been back since."

"Our witness tells us otherwise. Richard, I think it is time we talked to him now, if you would fetch him over here. Then perhaps Master Device may see fit to rethink his story and give us the truth."

James watched Baldwin almost trip on his way out of the room in his eagerness to do the JP's bidding, though he found no humour in it. He was too afraid of who this witness might be and what information they had for Nowell. What if they had seen him digging up the clay and knew how it could be used to make an image to gain power over a person? Or had they seen something in Anne Towneley's illness that could be used as evidence of witchcraft? It seemed there was but one solution to his predicament: the witness had to be stopped from testifying.

Dandy, I don't know if you can hear me, he thought. *I can't hear you with my mind like Gran does, only when you talk out loud. But if you can hear this, I need your help. I can't call out to you, or Nowell will know and use it against me. So please, hear my thoughts and come to me now. Help me leave this house a free man, safe from the noose. I know you were upset with me earlier, but I hope you can understand that killing any of the men would only have made matters worse. I couldn't accept your help then, but I need it now. I need you, Dandy, now more than ever. Honour our pact. Please, come help me.*

He put all his mental energy into those words, trying to make them as loud and clear as he could. Then there was nothing for it but to sit and wait.

Minutes ticked by with no sense of the spirit's presence. Nowell stared at him the whole while, as if the JP knew what he was up to. James could no longer meet that gaze, his good eye staring at the floor. Despair began to creep over him the longer the minutes stretched, but then there was a shifting of shadows on the edge of his vision, and sure enough, they coalesced into the shape of the black dog.

Dandy approached with caution, his ears pulled back and his tail wagging slightly between his legs. The uncertainty seemed at odds with the fearsome nature of the hellhound's race, but James was beginning to realise that spirit creatures had their own personalities, the same as any flesh and blood animal. It seemed to him then that Dandy was still young, just as he was. How that particular revelation came to him he couldn't say – it was just something he sensed through their bond.

"Yes, Master?" Dandy answered to James's ears only. The other two men in the room remained deaf to the spirit's voice.

It occurred to James that the sight of his familiar would only give Nowell more evidence to use against him. He couldn't ask Dandy to kill the witness, or it would look too suspicious, and they would no doubt link the second death to him. But he couldn't ask the spirit to simply frighten the man into silence, as they would also take that as proof of his guilt.

Fetch my gran if she hasn't heard of my arrest already. She'll know what to do.

The spirit dipped his head and vanished, leaving James alone with Nowell and Hargrieves once more. But the wait felt a little easier now, as did the pain, and his heart was lighter. There was still hope.

CHAPTER
TWENTY-ONE

I n a separate room, some two hours or so later, the key witness in his wife's murder sat down with the JP. Baldwin hovered beside them. A third pair of ears listened in, unseen and unheard, but present nevertheless.

"Ah, Henry. Thank you for coming forward at this difficult time," Nowell said. "Can I offer you a drink?"

"Perhaps a glass of your strongest wine, if I may," Towneley answered. "For my nerves. It is difficult indeed."

"Of course," Nowell replied, summoning a servant. "And for you, Richard?"

"I think I will join you in a glass."

"Very good. Then let us get down to business."

It was enough to make the blood boil. There James was in the other room, badly beaten and barely conscious, and here the gentry were acting perfectly civilised and enjoying a drink. The cunning man had not yet been proven guilty, and yet they hadn't even offered him water, let alone small beer or something stronger. All they'd offered him was suspicion and fear, despite the fact he was in no position to offer them any resistance.

"Now, tell us about the incident with James Device and the resulting tragedy that has befallen your family."

"Well, I wasn't there to see it but I know they argued. Anne was very upset to find that arrogant heathen invading our home. Especially after she'd already made it clear to him that he was not welcome the last time he came sniffing around."

"And when was that?"

"All Hallow's Eve – he was casting some kind of spell when Anne caught him in the act and confronted him. He claimed it was for our protection, but of course she told him we did not want it and demanded he leave our land. He was told he and his family were no longer welcome around Carr Hall.

"We did allow his mother to return and do some work for us over the winter, on the understanding that there would be no more witchcraft performed at our home. James was never invited back, however."

"And nothing untoward happened to you or Anne after that previous incident?"

"No, nothing unnatural occurred in those months, and James did keep his distance, except for a brief visit with his mother to take some of our turves. Neither Anne nor I witnessed the theft, but they were seen by several of our workers, and so Anne confronted him about it when she found him in the kitchen last week. From what she told me, he refused to apologise for stealing the turves and his attitude made her so angry she struck him as he was leaving to make sure he would not come back. Three days later she was taken ill."

The elderly man's voice cracked and tears filled his eyes. He raised the glass to his lips with shaking hands, took a large gulp, and set it back down again on the table by his chair. Baldwin fidgeted beside him, clearly impatient for Towneley to continue. If Nowell shared the miller's frustrations, he didn't show it.

"Take your time," the JP said, his face calm and sympathetic.

"Never have I seen anything like it in all my years on this earth, nor had any of the physicians we consulted. She was always so strong, my Anne, but this evil she succumbed to – it consumed her bit by bit, taking away a little more each day till she was naught but skin and bone. She could barely walk towards the end, and by the time the passing bell was tolling she had become completely bedridden. And her body, her beautiful body, started to rot as if she'd been dead awhile and already buried beneath the soil. The bewitchment took everything from her, even that pretty face I'd fallen in love with all those years ago."

Baldwin leant forward, unable to restrain himself any longer. "But what of the witchcraft that put her in such a state? Did you not see any strange creatures or foul beasts sent by the heathen to strike your wife down? Or perhaps she said something to indicate the Devil's hand in her illness, or even told you how James lay upon her?"

Nowell shot Baldwin a warning look, but the JP added "Any other details you can remember would help our case, so we can present the assizes with undeniable proof of Device's guilt."

"I am sorry, that is all I have to offer. I already told Dick that I saw nothing to give me cause to suspect witchcraft, and had not thought to blame the witch until he asked me whether I would be prepared to come forward as a witness."

"But you said you would testify!" Baldwin cried.

"I promised to tell our JP everything I know of the argument and Anne's illness, and so I have. I never agreed to invent further evidence simply to make your lives easier. Now if you will excuse me, I still have arrangements to make for the funeral."

"Of course," Nowell replied, shaking Towneley's hand and showing him out.

Baldwin stayed where he was, fists clenched and eyes ablaze with anger. As soon as he heard the JP returning, his gaze turned anxious, and as Nowell strode back into the room he asked "Is it enough?"

"To take to the assizes? No, Richard, it is not."

"What about the evidence I saw with my own eyes during the arrest. The witch was calling out to some spirit – I think he called it Dandy. I followed the direction his eyes were looking, but I could see no one besides the brave men who volunteered to assist with his arrest. Surely that must count for something?"

"Perhaps if one of the men is taken ill in the next day or two, as Anne was, but if no harm befalls them it is still not enough. Our King is very clear on the steps that must be taken in his Daemonologie book, and I intend to adhere to them, even if it means we may yet be forced to suffer the witches to live. I have far more fear for the wrath of a monarch than that of a witch. You should too."

"So we just let Device go, even though we all know him to be guilty of bewitching Mistress Towneley?"

"We may have to, but let us question him further. If he can be tricked into confessing that might just be enough."

Demdike returned to her own flawed body and the impenetrable fog of her sightless eyes, feeling the aches of her aged flesh all the more for her brief stay in Tibb's powerful form. She had begun to spend a great deal of time inside his head.

True to her word, Alizon had been acting as Demdike's eyes since Fancie had taken her sight from her. But it was Tibb Demdike relied on to show her all she was missing out on, from the faces of her loved ones to the happenings of the world around her. She was finding it harder to return to herself with each excursion into Tibb's skull.

A pair of hands helped her back up to her feet, her anchor to the mortal realm. For as tempting as leaving her infirmities behind might be, Demdike knew her family needed her to stay strong. Alizon was the perfect reminder of that.

She rarely ventured out without her eldest granddaughter's aid now, Fancie having not just taken her eyes, but also her freedom. Her body had begun to feel increasingly like a prison, yet it was one she must endure for a while longer. The safety of her family depended on it, as James had just proven by getting himself arrested.

Inform James of all we just heard.

Tibb didn't deign to answer but she trusted him to apprise her grandson of the situation and advise him while Alizon led her over there. She still did not know exactly what had happened in the time her familiar had been missing, but all that really mattered was the fact he'd eventually come back. If there was anything she needed to know then she felt certain he would tell her when he was ready. Until then she wouldn't push the issue, their bond remaining as strong as ever.

"Is it bad, Gran?" Alizon asked as they resumed the journey to Read Hall.

Demdike shook her head. "As long as your fool brother guards his tongue, they have no proof he killed Anne with magic. Tibb will let him know he has nothing to fear from the witness, which ought to keep him from falling foul of any traps Nowell tries to catch him in. The last thing we need is for him to be tricked into confessing."

They did not have much further to go, Demdike having chosen to stop briefly near Nowell's home so that she might witness the questioning of Henry Towneley for herself. She wanted to enter the building armed with as much knowledge of the proceedings as possible. Towneley must have already been well on his way back to his own home as they did not pass him on the path to Read Hall, his progress much quicker than theirs. Demdike hated walking without the aid of her sight. It was frustrating to have to keep to so slow and careful a pace.

There came a male voice as they approached the front door. "The master of the house is currently busy in his role as Justice of the Peace and is not receiving visitors."

"He will see me or there'll be far more deaths to investigate, starting with yours. That's my grandson he has in there."

She imagined the man paling at that. No answer was forthcoming, but he must have moved aside to let them pass, because Alizon guided her in.

"He's in the study," she told her granddaughter. "Third door on the right."

Demdike could sense Alizon's nervousness as they drew nearer to the JP. Like it or not, there was no denying he had a power of his own, and it was one thing to know that, but quite another to go head to head with it. Demdike was not afraid, however.

The door to the study swung open, the people within hidden to her. Only Tibb was visible through her clouded eyes.

As their gazes met, he granted her a vision of the scene she'd just walked in on. The look of shock and horror on Baldwin's face was enough to twist her wrinkled features into a grim smile. Nowell and Hargrieves looked angry, though the JP did a better job of concealing it.

"What is the meaning of this?" Baldwin snapped, recovering from the initial shock and joining his fellows in their anger.

"Now, Richard, that is not the way we receive guests in this house," Nowell said. "Is there something I can help you with, madam?"

"That's my grandson you have there. I've come to take him home."

"I am afraid your grandson has been arrested for murder, and we are not yet finished questioning him. If you would like to wait outside, I will have someone inform you when we are done."

Hagrieves growled "Do you want me to throw them out for you, Roger?"

"I am sure that will not be necessary, Constable. Our visitors would not want to give us cause to arrest them too."

"You have no reason to keep my grandson here and you know it, Roger Nowell," Demdike said, standing taller. Tibb showed her an image of Baldwin shrinking slightly from her shadow. She suppressed another grim smile, fixing the men with her sightless gaze and hoping it was making them squirm. "Master Towneley witnessed no actual witchcraft, and I believe James has already told you of the argument with Anne. I am not leaving here without him."

"And how could you possibly know that?"

"The how is not important. I know what little Henry Towneley had to give in his statement, and I know you have questioned James already. It is time he was back home now."

"A woman lies dead. We are simply trying to understand the cause of such tragedy, which by all accounts is not natural."

"Be that as it may, he has told you all he knows. If you want to arrest someone for witchcraft, you can arrest me. Otherwise, we are leaving."

"Are you confessing to being a witch?"

"I confess nothing. But if it means you will leave my family alone, then here I am."

She sensed one of the men moving towards her. Hargrieves, Demdike guessed. But she had no intention of being arrested that day.

Now, Tibb.

The spirit revealed himself for the briefest of moments before the candle flames died, ushering in the shadows at daylight's gate. To the men and even her granddaughter, his sudden appearance must have been frightening. His hellhound shape was impressive enough to strike fear in the hearts of mortals at the best of times, but for him to suddenly materialise without warning had to have been terrifying.

"Demon!" Baldwin screamed. She imagined he was pointing at the dark corner where they had just seen the apparition, invisible again now to all but her and James. The spirit's eyes were fixed on the miller and his hackles were raised, his fangs bared. Once again she could feel his eagerness to sink those wicked teeth into the fool's flesh, yet still he held back for her sake.

"The death of Anne Towneley is nothing," she continued. "I have been a wise woman for some sixty-odd years now. Imagine what misery I might have caused in that time for any who crossed me. So arrest me if you will, but be warned: justice will follow the innocent."

"And what does that mean?" Baldwin asked. His voice had risen several notes. "You just hinted at your own guilt!"

Tibb answered with a growl they could all hear. Nowell was defeated, and he knew it.

"Very well, take the boy. But you be warned: we will be waiting. If we find anything to link you to causing harm by witchcraft, even the Devil himself will not save you."

"I am glad we have an understanding. Come, James."

"I can't walk."

"Let me help with that," Hargrieves offered. "Grab his other arm, Dick."

Demdike could hear the two men dragging her grandson as Alizon led her back outside. His breath caught on teeth clenched in pain. Once they were through the front door, there came the sound of them dumping him on the ground. Both men laughed.

"You can crawl the rest of the way back for all we care," Hargrieves said. "Our business is done here, for now."

She heard the two men walk off, still laughing, while James moaned pitifully from somewhere at their feet. Her familiar had followed them out and he looked at her for permission. No doubt he was sensing her own desire to strike back against those who continually wronged them, just as her grandson had done to Anne Towneley. But she shook her head.

The time has not yet come, Tibb. Help James.

The spirit reared up on his hind legs and became the black-haired man once again. He knelt beside where James must be and took him into his arms, standing with his forearms outstretched in front of him. It was an odd sight to Demdike when she could only see the spirit and not her grandson. But she trusted that he was indeed carrying the boy as he appeared to be, and that he would be as gentle as he could about it.

"Back to your mam's, Alizon. She will need our help to tend to your brother's wounds."

"Will he recover from this?" her granddaughter asked in a voice filled with genuine concern.

"It will take time but yes, I believe he will make a full recovery with a bit of help from the spirits."

"I'm sorry, Gran," James said. "I just wanted to teach people a lesson so they won't treat us badly anymore. I didn't think they would arrest me."

"No, you did not think," she answered sternly. But the poor lad's voice was so weak, she couldn't stay angry at him. Her tone softened. "We will talk more of this later. Rest now."

They made the remainder of the journey in silence. Demdike could hear the relief in her daughter's voice when Elizabeth answered the door, though it soon turned to worry when she saw how badly James had been beaten.

Tibb took him straight to his room and laid him carefully on the bed, making him as comfortable as possible. The spirit didn't come back out after.

If she'd still had her sight, Demdike would have insisted on overseeing everything from the preparation of the poultices to the healing charms they would use to aid the knitting of James's flesh and bone. But as it was, she had to trust in her daughter's skills.

She was able to provide some help, yet many of the various tasks that would have once been easy proved impossible without being able to see what she was doing. In the end, she was forced to leave Alizon and Elizabeth to it, sitting in the kitchen while she waited for them to finish. Jennet watched for a while but soon grew bored and came to join her.

"Are we sinners, Granny?" her youngest granddaughter asked.

"What nonsense have they been filling your head with now, girl? I've told you before: men are fools. There is no god, not in the Christian sense. How could there be, when the care and nurture of life is for us women alone? The pain of childbirth is not for men to know, nor the joy of mother-hood. How could a male god create this world and every-thing in it all on his own? Listen carefully, and I will tell you it true now, so you can forget these silly notions of men. Forget what those fools preach and look to the natural world for all that you need, for there is only the Horned God and the Goddess."

"But why was James arrested if magic isn't bad?"

"Because your brother is also a fool, just not quite as big of one as the Christians who arrested him. Hush now and I will tell you of our God and Goddess, and the world of spirits."

And so she told the little girl all she had been taught by her mother and grandmother when she was young, until Jennet fell asleep in her lap. She heard Elizabeth enter the kitchen not long after, Alizon not far behind. Tibb was nowhere to be seen.

Her eldest granddaughter sat beside her, but Elizabeth insisted on carrying Jennet to bed before she did anything else.

"Is James resting?" Demdike asked.

"Yes," Elizabeth answered. "But I fear for him, Mam. Even with our combined skills at healing, they've made such a mess of his body. His face is so swollen I can barely recognise him."

"Have faith in the spirits; they will see him restored to health. And if he takes a turn for the worse or his wounds refuse to heal, then I will deal with demons again if I have to. But I do not think it will come to that. In any case, we will spend the night here so we can take it in turns to watch over him, and perhaps you can get some rest."

"Thank you, Mam."

Despite her confidence, Demdike sympathised with her daughter's worries. It would be a long night. She could only hope the spirits would see fit to lend James their healing energy, for she did not relish the thought of having to make another deal with the likes of Fancie. But only time would tell.

CHAPTER

TWENTY-TWO

Richard's laughter didn't last long. Fury took over as he bid the constable goodbye and returned to his usual evening haunt at the alehouse, unable to believe that the witches had once again been allowed to walk free. So much for Fancie's promises.

Fewer faces than usual turned to glance in his direction when he stepped into Widow Sawyers' dreary abode. Richard half hoped one of them would be Fancie, but a quick scan of the room brought only disappointment. He supposed he shouldn't be surprised. Something told him that if he was to have any further dealings with the heathen, it would be on the heathen's terms, and thus it would be Fancie who found him, not the other way around. Or he could try seeking him out in the home of Chattox he supposed, yet the mere thought of setting foot in there was a distasteful one. Bad enough that he had been given cause to treat with her consort, let alone to deal with the hag herself.

Quiet muttering filled the room, giving the same subdued air Richard had encountered in Carr Hall. He made his way over to Widow Sawyers. Her expression was especially grim that night, not even a ghost of a smile about her lips when their eyes met.

"Master Baldwin. I had not thought to see you this evening – should this not be a time for prayer over ale?"

Richard couldn't keep the scowl from his face. "I have said my prayers for the Towneleys, and to ask for the witches to be brought to justice. Now I require drink, if you would be so kind."

"Ah yes, nasty business with the Towneleys, and the arrest too, from what I hear." She broke eye contact while she filled his tankard, then looked up again. "But you mistake me if you believe that to be a judgement. I have no wish to be your enemy."

Richard resisted the urge to argue. "Forgive me, it has been a long day; and a frustrating one. Doubtless you have also heard James Device remains a free man?"

"I have, and believe me, I understand your frustrations. I have no love for that family. Not after they took my John from me."

"Then why do you not go to the Justice of the Peace? If enough of us came forward as witnesses, Roger would have just cause to question the lot of them. We could build a strong case!"

Widow Sawyers grimaced and dropped her gaze. "Because people are frightened, Master Baldwin. John argued with Squinting Lizzie and rightfully accused her of having her bastard child with that man Seller, and they bewitched him to death, and now Mistress Towneley has been struck down after arguing with Squinting Lizzie's son. What will they do to us if we try to have them arrested?"

Richard gave an angry snort and turned away from her. It was only then he realised the room had fallen silent. He glared at Sawyers' other patrons. They quickly returned to their muttered conversations, but he wasn't fooled. His eyes narrowed.

"Best tread carefully now, Master Baldwin," Widow Sawyers called from behind. "You and all the others who had a hand in James Device's arrest."

Richard paused at those words, but he didn't turn around. With another scowl, he took a seat at the nearest table, then proceeded to drink himself into his nightly stupor.

Months passed with no sight or sound of Fancie. The hags still plagued his nights and many of his days though. Fresh fury filled Richard at the sight of James strolling down the path to Laund Farm, bold as ever and all but recovered from the beating they'd given him. The young witch hadn't even been left with a limp which would have at least been some punishment for his heinous crimes. Every breath the vile family took vexed Richard, but what more could he do other than pray for them to finally be brought to justice?

Winter came again and still the witches walked free. Richard kept his ears open for rumours of any unnatural happenings that might indicate magic – anything more he could present to Nowell to strengthen what little they already had on Demdike's wretched clan – but all seemed quiet. They were taking greater care to hide any evidence that they'd been practising their craft just to spite him, no doubt. Then they had the nerve to come begging at his gate one cold December morning, and something inside him snapped.

"Get off my ground, whores and witches!" he screamed, storming over to confront them. "I will burn the one of you and hang the other!"

He glared into the clouded eyes of the hated old woman, prepared to physically throw her and her wretched granddaughter off his land if he had to. There was no room in his heart for fear. Not when his anger blazed stronger than a furnace. But then those blind eyes met his own and his anger evaporated. A chill deeper than winter's bite took its place, and he knew with complete certainty that in that moment she saw him, impossible though it was.

"I care not for thee; hang thyself," Demdike answered, bold as ever and standing as tall as her age allowed. "Come, Alizon. We will find no justice here."

They turned away. Richard's anger blazed back into being the moment those horrid eyes pointed elsewhere, and it was as if his fear were a distant dream.

"You speak of justice?" he screamed. "You, who commit murder and yet still walk free?"

Neither woman looked back. That only infuriated him more. He didn't even know what business they had coming to his land – surely they hadn't really expected him to show them charity after everything they'd done? Or... had their intent been far more malicious than merely begging for scraps? He remembered the words of Widow Sawyers the evening of Anne Towneley's death.

"Best tread carefully now, Master Baldwin. You and all the others who had a hand in James Device's arrest."

Had that been the hag's true purpose? To seek revenge for her grandson? He went cold again at the thought.

Richard turned his gaze skyward. "Please, Lord, I am your humble servant, now and forever. Please, protect me from these agents of the Devil. Protect my family."

No heavenly signs answered him. If anything, he thought he saw the sky darken, the grey clouds as bleak and gloomy as a house in mourning. Despair gripped him then. Had the Lord abandoned them? Were the good people of Pendle to forever suffer at the witches' mercy?

A familiar voice sounded from behind, dripping with cruel amusement. "Do you really think it will be so easy as a prayer to your god?"

Richard jumped and spun around. His gaze fixed on the very man he'd been wanting to talk to. "You! I followed your advice before and look where it's got me. The witches are still breathing and they trouble me now more than ever."

Fancie smiled, but it seemed to Richard there was nothing genuine in it. The heathen's eyes seemed to glitter with the same cruel amusement heard in his voice. "I came to you in good faith, bringing knowledge I had gleaned from gazing into the future. It is no fault of mine you did not act on it accordingly."

"Do not speak to me of faith. I am sure you had your own selfish reasons for giving me that information, and what little good it did me. I waited a week after the argument and went to Henry as you instructed. You assured me he was the key, and yet it was still not enough."

"And he was. If you had only convinced him he might have seen something to prove Device's guilt without question, or persuaded him to put aside his morals – just this once – and exaggerate what he had actually witnessed, the entire Demdike clan would already be rotting in the ground." Fancie's expression turned sombre. "But alas, you did not. And so we must suffer them to live."

"Then why did you not make that clear when last we spoke?"

"I did not think I needed to."

Richard clenched his jaw. "Enough riddles, Fancie. I am sure you did not come back to me after all these months simply to point out my failings. Why are you here?"

Fancie's smile returned, sly and mocking. "I will give you another insight into the future; a second chance to make history. There will not be a third. Choose your move carefully when the time comes."

Richard considered those words, his dislike for the heathen wrestling his desperation to put an end to Demdike and her foul brood. Was this all a game to Fancie? There was no denying the heathen could see the future, for how else could he have known there would be an incident between Device and Towneley a day before it happened? But did Fancie really want to help him find evidence to take to Nowell, or was the heathen merely enjoying watching them thwarted at every turn?

"Should you succeed this time," Fancie continued, "your name will live on through the ages. As will Roger Nowell's, and all those who have a part to play in ridding Pendle of the blight of Demdike and her bloodline. But if you fail, there will be no trial and their witchcraft will prevail."

Defeated, Richard felt his shoulders slump and his anger recede once more. There was too much at stake to simply dismiss Fancie's words. "Go on."

"This incident will not take place until the March of 1612. It will potentially be Alizon who is the family's undoing this time, but unlike the unfortunate Anne Towneley, this victim will survive. If you can persuade both he and his son to make a statement which leaves no doubt as to the nature of his affliction and who is responsible, there will be nothing the Demdike clan can do to escape the King's justice. But as I told you before, the witnesses are the key."

"And who are these witnesses?"

"You will know them when the time comes."

Something about those words gave Richard the assurance he needed. "Very well." He straightened, new determination surging in his veins. "I will not fail again. My soul cannot take any more of the torment brought by the witches. I will do whatever it takes to end their evil."

"Then I wish you luck, Richard Baldwin. But be warned – take no action until this incident has occurred. No matter how tempting it may be or what evidence you think you might have for Nowell, you will not succeed any sooner and you risk setting fate on a new path. Is that clear enough for you?"

"I shall bide my time, fear not."

"We shall see. Farewell, my friend."

Fancie gave a nod and started to walk away. Richard watched him go. His determination faltered, his doubts returning. The rivalry between Chattox and Demdike was well known – it could well be that Chattox was sending her companion to help those in a position to take Demdike and her family to trial. There was something about the heathen though, something in that mocking voice and smile, and those cruel eyes. Richard watched him vanish long before he'd reached the horizon and felt the hairs raise on the back of his neck. Fancie wasn't to be trusted, that much was clear. But there was too much at stake to simply ignore the heathen's warning.

Richard went back inside the house. A stack of official papers awaited his signature, and it would not do to leave them any longer.

"Is there trouble, Dick?" his wife called from the kitchen. "I thought I heard you shouting."

His anger was quick to flare up at the reminder of the unwanted visitors.

"Whores and witches," he repeated, shutting the door behind him. "I caught them at our gate just now. The audacity of it! But fear thee not, my wife; I drove them off before they could cause anything unnatural."

"Not the witches again," Jenneta said, striding through from the kitchen to join him in the lobby. "Honestly, Richard – I do not know why you let a blind old woman trouble you so. I expect they were after payment for the work Elizabeth did for me last month."

"Work? You invited Squinting Lizzie onto our land and offered her payment, in return for what? Some blasphemous act against God? And you thought to keep it from me, knowing I would never allow them or their magic into our home?"

"There was washing to be done and she has a little girl to feed. Do you really expect me to turn a desperate mother away?"

"Foolish woman!" he spat, his anger reaching breaking point and seizing control of his hand. The slap to his wife's cheek was so forceful it left a mark, as if the heat of his fury were so intense it had burnt her. "That girl is the product of incest, born of devilry and as vile as any one of them. Her innocent guise is a trick sent to test us. I care not what they think they have earned; they will not receive a single penny from us, nor our table scraps. Let them starve!"

Jenneta raised a hand to her face. There were tears in her eyes, and yet her voice retained its strength. It was a quality he had loved in her once, before his foul curse had corrupted their holy matrimony and destroyed those tender feelings with its corrosive poison.

"The only devil I see is you, husband. Your sins are far greater than the witches' will ever be."

He could not believe his ears. How dare his wife speak to him so? She turned away before he could respond and retreated to the grounds outside.

Richard's anger gained in such power that words failed him then. After a moment of standing there seething, hands balled into fists and teeth grinding together, he forced himself to walk into the parlour and retrieve the papers. Gradually, his mind began to turn back to the conversation with Fancie while he worked. The heathen's warning troubled him, and he wondered if Fancie had foreseen something which would bring the temptation the heathen had spoken of. But even if Fancie had seen fit to tell him exactly what was coming, it would have done him no good. Fate's die had been cast.

TWENTY-THREE

F our days had passed since the argument with Baldwin. Demdike could not blame her daughter for being reluctant to go and collect payment for the work she'd done herself, nor did she think any less of her for seeking work there in the first place. Crop yields that year had been disappointing. Famine was becoming an even greater enemy than the previous winter, and they had to take on work wherever they could. But she knew when to admit defeat. It was not worth fighting with the Baldwins over a few mouthfuls of food, and so they'd gone back to Elizabeth empty handed.

Night had already fallen when the knock at the door came. Her granddaughter answered it, but Demdike did not need the use of anyone's eyes to recognise the voice of their visitor.

"Jenneta," she said, feeling her way over. "Does your husband know you are here?"

"He does not. I come of my own accord to beg you: undo this bewitchment you have placed on my poor girl."

"Bewitchment?"

"She became feverish this morning and has not risen from her bed all day, not even to eat."

Tibb? Is this your doing?

No, Mistress. You forbade me to take revenge, though I still think Baldwin is deserving of our justice.

Inwardly, Demdike gave a heavy sigh. She could only imagine the pain her next words were about to cause. "Then she could indeed be spelled, but I fear your journey here has been in vain."

Jenneta's voice remained strong. "I will pay what we owe and more if you will undo the evil wrought upon her soul."

Admiration filled Demdike at the other woman's strength. She reached to where she guessed Jenneta's shoulder was, and moved her hand upwards until it found its target. Squeezing, her voice turned kinder. "I cannot, lass, for it is not of my making."

"You swear it? My husband is convinced otherwise, and I know the two of you argued a few days ago."

"I swear it. We only came seeking what my daughter is owed for the work she did, nothing more. I was angry to be turned away, I'll admit, but I would never curse an innocent child."

"Then I ask you as a mother to take pity on our plight and do what you can for my little girl. Please, it was wrong of my husband to treat you so, but I would ask that you find it in your heart to do this and quick, while he is out of the house. He would rather watch Ellena die than accept the help of pagans. But men do not understand a mother's pain. I would see her live no matter the cost."

Let the girl die, Tibb advised. *It is no more than the family deserves.*

His children are blameless in this, Tibb. It is no fault of theirs that we are met with such unfairness from their father. Perhaps an act of kindness is precisely what is needed to change the family's view of magic and the cunning folk. 'Tis too late for Dick, I fear, but his children might grow up more sympathetic to our ways if we can save the girl.

She could sense his disapproval as aloud she said "I will do what I can. Go on ahead while I gather my tools, and prepare a pot of boiling water for my arrival. Ellena will need herbs to bring down her fever."

"Thank you." There came the sound of footsteps, indicating Jenneta was hurrying back down the path.

"My tools, Alizon." Demdike turned in the direction she sensed her granddaughter to be.

"Is this a good idea, Gran?" There was the light touch of Alizon's dutiful hand wrapping around Demdike's arm, and a gentle pull towards their stores. "It's not even a week since Baldwin was threatening to burn one of us and hang the other. What if he comes home and catches us working the craft!"

Demdike smiled, one that was mostly affection and only part amusement. "'Tis good to hear you exercising caution, lass, but you needn't worry. Baldwin can threaten us all he wants. Taking the law into his own hands is still murder, and he knows it. He won't get himself arrested just to see us burn and hang."

Tibb showed Demdike a brief vision of Alizon's face. There were more doubts and fears than her young years called for, and Demdike almost changed her mind about letting Tibb deal with Richard Baldwin then.

She patted her granddaughter's hand. "Just help me gather the right tools for healing and lead me to the Baldwins' home. You needn't go in with me."

Alizon gave an impatient snort. "Obviously. I'm not going to leave you wandering Pendle on your own!"

Demdike fought to hide another smile. "I did not mean to imply otherwise."

Armed with the same tools for healing as she'd taken to cure the Bulcocks' son only a year earlier, Demdike followed Alizon's lead to the Baldwins' home. Even without her sight, she could feel the misery surrounding that cursed mill, a misery made no better for Jenneta's welcoming demeanour when they reached the door to their home.

"Come in. The water's ready for making the tea."

Demdike nodded in Jenneta's direction and turned to her granddaughter. "Thank you, Alizon, I can manage from here. I need you to go to your mam's now, in case our rivals attempt the same as before, when I was last called on as healer. You know of which I speak."

"Yes, Gran," she answered obediently enough, but she still sounded worried.

"Good. I will meet you there." Demdike patted her granddaughter's hand again and lowered her voice. "All will be well, lass. Don't you worry about me, and don't fear for your own life either. I have every faith in the combined protection you, your mam and James can conjure."

"But how will you get back without one of us to lead you?"

"Don't you worry about that either."

The guiding hand slipped away. Demdike listened to the girl's retreating footsteps for a moment.

Tibb, I need you to warn my daughter and grandson of this

latest turn of events, and their familiars. Instruct them to lay fresh charms about the house for their protection, lest this goes the same way as with the Bulcocks.

As you wish.

Jenneta gave a little cough. "Shall we?"

The poor woman had been waiting with forced patience, but her voice betrayed her. Demdike couldn't blame the woman. Fathers loved their children in their own way, but it was naught compared to the bond a mother shared with her babies. She gave Jenneta an apologetic smile, one mother to another.

"Lead me to the pot. We'll begin by making the tea."

Jenneta's hand was surprisingly gentle, yet there was an urgency to the pull of it that Alizon had never shown. Demdike didn't comment as she followed the other woman to the boiling water she'd asked for.

Mixing the herbs into a tea was easy enough, even without her sight. One of the other Baldwin children carried it up so their mother could lead her to their sickly sibling. She was taken to the child's bedside, where she bid them leave her to work her magic, just as she had when treating John Bulcock.

Closing her eyes, Demdike took several deep, steadying breaths and allowed her mind to clear. Soon there was nothing but the sound of the little girl lying on the bed in front of her. The laboured breathing and wordless whimpers sounded every bit like John's had, and then Jennet's after Chattox had made her wicked trade. Pity threatened to take hold, but Demdike pushed it away. Her mind still clear, she opened her eyes to the strange sight of Ellena's outline floating in the mists of her blindness. Or rather, the outline of her aura.

This aura was orange rather than red, but it was just

as washed-out as John's had been. How grave her case was would be hard to tell without some means of seeing the child's earthly symptoms for herself, though she could be certain of one thing – just like with John, this illness was entirely natural. There was no evidence of anything more sinister at work, neither from spirits nor curses.

Tibb appeared to her before she'd even had chance to call him. Through his eyes, she perceived the girl's pale form, all slick with sweat and shivering beneath the bed covers, trapped in the same kind of troubled sleep Demdike had witnessed in John and Jennet.

Her heart heavy, Demdike repeated the same healing rites she'd performed for the Bulcock boy while the herbal tea cooled. Jenneta looked in on them briefly, Tibb providing another vision to show the worried mother. Demdike noted the paling of the younger woman's face and the widening of her eyes, and through Tibb's ears she caught the words "What world is this when good Christians must turn to Devil worshippers for aid? May God forgive me."

Demdike pretended she hadn't heard. Jenneta retreated without any further comment, which Demdike took as a blessing to continue the rite, her chant growing steadily louder as she handed Tibb the chervil to throw in the fire downstairs. But this time the spell's target awoke before it was completed.

"Mam?" Ellena asked, her voice weak and cracked with thirst. The girl's eyes fixed on Demdike, and widened just like her mam's had. "What's going on? Where's my mam?"

Demdike forced herself to keep chanting, even though her maternal instinct was to break off to soothe the girl. That proved to be a mistake. Ellena screamed and cried for her mother until Jenneta came running in, interrupting the final part of the spell.

"What have you done to her?" the miller's wife demanded, cradling her daughter in her arms. "I asked you to heal her, not scare the poor child out of her wits!"

"And so I am trying to do, but I'm afraid the spell is not yet done, and now we must start over."

"No, no more spells! This was wrong. I should never have asked you to come here and perform these ungodly acts. Take your payment for the washing and go."

Demdike felt something hard bounce off her bosom. Tibb guided her to where it had landed on the floor, revealing it to be a crusty loaf of bread.

"Your daughter is very sick," she said, bending to pick up the generous offering. "She might die without the proper healing rites. If I could just finish the ritual I was working–"

"Out! Get out before my husband returns and unleashes his wrath on us all. Out I tell you!"

"Ellena could die if I leave now," Demdike repeated, though she had to admit to herself that the girl's death was a very real possibility, even if they allowed her to finish the rite. Her magic had not been enough to defeat the sickness that began with John Bulcock and transferred to little Jennet, so why would this third case be any different? But her words only increased the child's hysterics and incensed the mother further.

"If that is the Lord's will, then so be it. Out!"

There was no sense in arguing any further, so Demdike felt her way out of the room and back down the stairs. Jenneta made no move to follow her. Presumably, she was too busy cuddling her daughter and attempting to calm her to worry about what a blind old woman might do on her way out. Demdike hoped Ellena would at least be given the herbal tea. Whatever her feelings towards the adult Baldwins, she still bore no ill will for the innocent children.

"I do not understand why you concern yourself with the health of your enemy's progeny," Tibb said as he continued to guide her. "Jenneta Baldwin might have paid what you were owed and then some, but I do not like the manner in which she paid you. It was disrespectful."

"We do not get to choose our family, Tibb. The girl has done us no wrong, and it is no fault of hers that she was born to such despicable parents. Besides, Jenneta was merely acting out of fear for that which she does not understand. I do not think she is as bad as Richard, nor do I think she is beyond reasoning with, unlike her husband."

"And I think you are too forgiving. I would still seek revenge against them on your behalf, if you would but allow it."

"Perhaps you are right, Tibb, but if the girl dies, is that not revenge enough for now? The Baldwins will be heartbroken if they lose her, a pain any of us mortals are all too familiar with."

"Granny!" a familiar young voice called, moments before a thin pair of arms wrapped themselves around Demdike's waist and a small body pressed against her own.

"Jennet? What are you doing out here at this time of night? Does your mam know you are out?"

"Ball said you would be ready to come home before Alizon even got back to us, so I came to help."

"I believe your daughter is out looking for her," Tibb offered. "James and Alizon as well."

"Curses, Jennet, how many times must I tell you 'tis dangerous to be out at night? Now your brother and sister are in danger, and your mother as well."

"I'm sorry, Granny," the little girl sobbed, sounding sincere. In her mind's eye, Demdike could see the tears in her granddaughter's eyes, without the need for a vision from Tibb. "I just wanted to help."

"Well, now that you are here, I would be grateful of your guidance. But you do not come out after dark again until you are older, understand?"

Jennet brightened instantly. "Yes, Granny."

Demdike was grateful for someone to guide her besides Tibb, she had to admit. Navigating any great distance with only the visions he granted her was hard, and she was prone to stumbling on the uneven ground. If she was really struggling he could make himself more solid and lead her like Alizon did, or even carry her as he had James that night at Read Hall. But she knew it cost him a great deal of energy to perform such feats, and she did not like to ask it of him unless she really had to. She would rather he saved his strength for any more fights they might find themselves in.

There were no more fights that night, however – not even with Richard Baldwin. Their paths did not cross on the way back from Wheathead, and they reached Elizabeth's house unchallenged.

Jennet was full of the chatter of small children along the way.

"I miss going to Carr Hall," the little girl said. "Maggie in the kitchens was always kind to me, and the Towneleys' home is so big. I'd give anything to live in a house like that."

Demdike laughed. "Aye, child, 'tis a grand house indeed. But not for the likes of us, I fear."

"Why not, Granny? Why can't we have a big house and lots of servants to do all our cooking and cleaning?"

"We haven't the money, lambkin, and our family never

will. Honest work will never be rewarded the same as noble blood. You will understand, some day."

Her daughter and other two grandchildren were already back inside the Device household when they got there, no doubt notified of Jennet's whereabouts by their familiars. Elizabeth came rushing to the door.

"Jennet!"

"Mam!" Jennet protested. "Get off – I don't want cuddles right now!"

Tibb provided another brief vision of the scene. Jennet wriggled in her mother's arms while Alizon and James sat at the table, both uncertain.

"What happened, Gran?" Alizon asked. "Did Master Baldwin return home? Did he try to hurt you?"

Demdike shook her head and felt her way over to the table. "Not quite, lass. Best we stay here tonight though. The hour is late."

The pitter-patter of little feet announced Jennet's escape from her mother's arms and her arrival at the table. She climbed into Demdike's lap.

Affection swept over Demdike in a warm wave. Elizabeth's footsteps sounded a moment later, much heavier and also heading for the table. The poor girl had never been graced with light feet.

"Here you are, Elizabeth." Demdike handed over the loaf of bread. "Courtesy of the Baldwins."

"I thought you said they wouldn't pay me for doing the washing for them!"

"It seems Jenneta is much more reasonable than her husband. But I would not go back there again, no matter how desperate you may find yourself. I was not permitted to heal their daughter in the end, and I fear the child is already shadowed by the Reaper. He will come for her soon enough."

Elizabeth seemed to grow very still at that. "Are you sure, Mam? Might Chattox not intervene again?"

"Nay, we need not fear another attack from Chattox now." Demdike grimaced. "Ellena awoke before I could finish my healing rite, and screamed so loud you'd have thought I was trying to kill her. Jenneta Baldwin will not be seeking out any more magical cures after this misunderstanding, especially not if Richard gets wind of me being invited into his home. At least she gave the payment you were owed before she ordered me to leave."

"Thank you, Mam." Elizabeth sounded placated, though Demdike suspected her daughter would be lying awake worrying for much of the night. "Would you like some?"

"Yes please, my love. I have not yet eaten this evening."

Elizabeth tore the loaf into chunks and handed them round the table. Demdike smiled as she accepted her share, thinking that they might not have much, but at least they had their health. And for that she was grateful.

PART THREE - 1611

TWENTY-FOUR

A mused, Fancie watched a young human pulling the legs off a beetle she'd found in the field she was meant to be working. The insect kicked with its two remaining good legs, writhing in delicious pain. A moment later, the child had ripped those off as well. She dropped it on the soil and watched it land on its back, to die a long, slow death as it rocked helplessly from side to side in the bright spring sun.

Even more amusing, fate's current path would see the child suffer a similar fate. Fancie could see the most likely course her life would take, and at the end of it lay an adolescent girl only a few years older, twitching in a spreading pool of her own blood. What a delightful prospect. Fancie focused on that moment, and the present faded away, becoming the potential future on a lonely road between Roughlee and Barrowford.

The wheels of an upturned cart still spun at the base of the tree it had collided with. One of them was bloody. Fancie went back a few moments to just before the crash, watching as the horse and cart approached. A stray dog came running towards it, snapping at the horse's legs and barking excitedly. The horse bolted and its harness came loose. It raced toward the girl as she spotted her friend across the road and started running to him.

Pounding hooves brought the girl to a stop. The horse galloped past, free of its harness now. The cart wasn't far behind. Still frozen in shock, the girl turned to see it barrelling toward her with mounting horror.

"Run, girl!" the driver screamed. "Run!"

He was able to leap and save himself, but it was too late for the girl. The left wheel went over her leg with a satisfying snap. Bone pierced skin. Blood welled around it, spilling over the sides of the wound and soaking into the earth below.

Grinning, Fancie looked into her pain-filled eyes. The passage of time was a curious thing. To the child he could see in the present, the seconds were probably dragging slow and tedious, and tormenting the beetle had been nothing more than a way of trying to make them pass quicker. But to her victim, and now to her dying, future self, it had become just one long moment of unending pain. Doubtless death would come as a blessing, but the wait for that blessing might feel like an eternity.

What a limiting experience time to them was. Even the cunning folk were only granted glimpses into events happening beyond the confines of their earthly bodies. They could never truly experience anything but the moment they were living in. A moment that with each passing second moved on, so that the future became the present and the present the past, a memory that would eventually fade and inevitably die out with any who experienced it. To a mortal, this girl would soon die and they would never again see anything but her spirit. For beings like Fancie, the concept of time was not so restrictive.

He could visit any point in history, be a part of almost anything as it unfolded in the present, or gaze millennia ahead if he so chose. But the future would never be set in stone. Fate would never be a fixed thing like the past, for it would forever twist and turn in new directions determined by all those with a part to play. Fancie could look into a possible future and see things yet to come, but it was all too easy for those on Earth to completely alter the course of destiny. And in the passing of a moment, a whole new future could arise. That was why he concerned himself with the affairs of men, to steer events towards a future of his liking.

The months following his second conversation with Baldwin had passed in what humans might have called the blink of an eye, no more than a few grains of sand in the endless desert of time he was free to wander as he chose. There was nothing of consequence in the winter months, and it was not until just after this next turn of the seasons, at the time Christians called Lent, that he had begun to take an interest in the people of Pendle once again.

Fancie lingered a few moments longer in the girl's possible future, watching the driver run over to her and kneel helplessly by her side. He chose to show himself to her then. Perhaps she should even be treated to a glimpse of his true face? Yes, he could drop his human mask for her.

Terror crept into the dying girl's face. The driver barely even noticed, oblivious to Fancie's presence and too intent on stemming the bleeding. He had the sense to rip off a strip of his shirt and tie it round her leg, too late. Her wide eyes stilled a moment later, and she was gone.

Satisfied, Fancie returned to the spring of 1611. The child

grew bored of her no-legged victim and returned to her work. Fancie also moved on. She had no more to offer him.

The green of the field became the dusty brown of the land around John Duckworth's house. James Device strode across it, bold and full of purpose. His humiliation at the hands of the mob was already forgotten. Fancie's mouth twitched into another malicious smile. The boy's arrogance was exactly what he needed.

Duckworth opened the door before James could knock, his expression grim. Fancie didn't need to look any further to know the yeoman had seen James coming. James must have come to the same conclusion. There was only a brief flitter of surprise in those youthful features.

"John. I've come for the shirt that was promised."

Something flickered in Duckworth's eyes. Not fear, delightful as that would have been. This was more like acceptance of the troubles Duckworth knew his words could well cause him. Acceptance of the consequences of incurring a witch's wrath. "That was two weeks ago. Things have changed."

"What could possibly have changed? You promised me your old shirt in return for healing your prized bull. The bull is now healthy, and you owe me a shirt."

Duckworth shook his head. "I will give you a cut of meat instead."

"You know as well as I that is not equal payment to what was agreed. I want the shirt."

"Look, the whole community has been under suspicion ever since you bewitched Anne Towneley. I'm not saying the old bat didn't deserve it, but now the JP is out for blood and he's questioning anyone suspected of hiring the cunning folk, like we're as much to blame for any witchcraft as you! I don't think he was happy to see you go free. You might think you escaped this time, but it is not over yet – he's still investigating anything that seems suspicious. You and your family would do well to keep your heads down from now on, till this all blows over."

"But why does that prevent you from giving me the shirt? It was what we agreed on, and I'm not leaving without it."

"Jesus, use that brain of yours, lad! If Nowell hears about you walking around in my old shirt, he will haul us both in for questioning. He's no fool – he knows I wouldn't part with anything of such worth for the usual farm work. Take the meat; it's less risky for both of us."

James's temper flared. Fancie could sense it in the same way a beast detects the blood of its prey, and his smile widened. The boy's dark impulses burned as strongly as ever, but there was currently no Dandy to help him act on them.

"Very well, give me the meat. But I will not forget this, John. I will take what I am owed, whether it be in a few weeks or a few years from now. Nowell will not be in power forever."

"No, for all we know there's worse ahead. Wait here and I'll fetch your payment."

Duckworth disappeared inside his house, returning with a generous share of meat a moment later. "Here, take this."

James accepted it with another angry glare. Fancie watched the darkness swirling at the centre of his being. Duckworth might have gone back on his promise, but James had not been treated particularly unfairly on this occasion. The boy seemed to recognise that. His temper remained, simmering away beneath the surface. But Fancie sensed it was directed at people like Nowell and life in general now, rather than at Duckworth. No matter. The boy would be harder to sway this time, but not impossible.

"Thank you," James growled, and turned on his heel. The labourers still working the land glanced at him as he strode back the way he had come, with more anger than the purpose he'd had before. James ignored them and they soon returned to their work. Fancie followed.

Once they were out of Laund Farm and a little way along the path, Fancie came up just behind his intended pawn.

"Master Device," he said, stepping into sight.

James came to a stop and rolled his eyes skyward – Fancie could sense that too. The boy turned to face him, eyes narrowed with suspicion and distrust. "What do you want now, Fancie?"

"Now, James, is that any way to greet a friend? I simply come to offer you more advice."

Fresh anger flashed in James's eyes. "You are no friend of mine, and I will hear no more of your advice. Not after where our last conversation got me."

"Allies then. Was the information I gave you not to your liking? Did it not achieve your heart's desire? It seems to me as though it did, given that you are still standing here and what remains of Mistress Towneley is rotting beneath hallowed ground."

"Yes, the clay image worked as you said it would, but it also got me arrested! I could have been hanged if Henry Towneley had told Nowell anything more condemning than the fact we argued just before she was taken ill. And now times are becoming even more dangerous from what Duckworth just said. I should never have listened to you!"

"Yet here we are. You were not hanged, and Nowell is still lacking the evidence he needs to take any of you to trial. Imagine if Anne Towneley had lived. The cunning folk would have lost a great deal of the respect people have for you all, my mistress included. And how would you have survived the winter on the pay for manual work alone, without the added rewards the craft brings?"

"So what would you have me do now? Kill Nowell? Duckworth is right, his successor could be even worse. Or would you have me bewitch a member of his family, and potentially land myself in more trouble than I'm already in?"

"Of course not. Such a move would be unwise, as you said yourself. But did Duckworth not just deny you what is rightfully yours? It seems to me that he lacks the appropriate amount of appreciation for all you have done for him. It was not just his prized bull that you saved by curing the animal's sickness – the entire herd would have succumbed to the disease, had it not been for your daring and skill as a cunning man. Should such a feat not be rewarded more handsomely?"

James hesitated. His darkness hissed its approval at the ideas taking root in his head, but something was holding him back, some of that annoying sense of morality humans were so restricted by. Fancie could see it struggling to make itself felt through the darkness, a tendril of light piercing the shadow beneath James's flesh.

"I can't kill him," James finally said. "It's not his fault he can't honour our bargain. He only does what he thinks is right, and he has been nothing but kind to me over the years. I cannot blame him for denying me the shirt when it is really Nowell who stands in my way."

"Oh but you can," Fancie coaxed. "You know how easy

it is now, and just think of what it will do for your reputation."

James straightened with new conviction. "I won't do it. Gran was right, better to stay clear of the dark arts – the price is too high. I have no intention of giving Nowell any more reasons to arrest me."

"Then you leave me no choice but to call on that favour. I want you to kill Duckworth for me."

James frowned. "Why? You are far more powerful than I am; what do you need me for?"

"The why is not important. You owe me a favour, and this is what I ask."

"And if I refuse?"

"I did not think you were the type to go back on a promise, or have you as little honour as Duckworth? Whether out of fear or not, he is still breaking his word. But you are a man I can trust to honour a bargain, are you not?" Fancie took a step closer, allowing his true demonic nature to bleed through the illusion of his human eyes. Red filled them once more. "And besides, you would not want to disappoint me, James. I am greater than both you and Dandy combined. Do not look to him to protect you."

James gave a cry of alarm and stepped back. Fancie advanced, giving the boy a taste of the cruelty at his heart. The boy started to shake. Fancie took one final step, then he allowed his eyes to regain their human guise. His smile turned perfectly friendly. "Kill Duckworth and you need never see me again, if that is your wish. Or deny me and suffer the consequences. The choice is yours."

Again James hesitated, wrestling with his conscience. That darker side to human nature burned all the stronger in him for being allowed to murder, and now it yearned to kill again. Even stronger was his fear of what Fancie would do to him if he said no – all of which Fancie could sense. He had the cunning man in a bind James could not wriggle out of, and the boy knew it as well as he.

"I need some time to think."

"Do not take too long, Master Device. You have a week. If Duckworth is not dead by then, I will be back for some other form of payment for the information I gave you, and you can expect worse than a guilty conscience. Good day."

Fancie faded back into that place just beyond the earthly realm, like one of the great sea predators sinking beneath the surface of the waves. There he remained hidden from his prey once again, though James was no less distinct to him. Fancie watched the young man turn away and continue down the path for a moment, then stepped through the shadows to his mistress's cottage, knowing she would want to hear of how their plan was progressing.

Nightfall found James back beneath the waning moon, digging for the clay he needed to commit another murder with magic. A crude likeness of Duckworth began to emerge in the boy's hands, ready to be dried by the fire the next evening. Fancie expected the cunning man to crumble the effigy straight away, but four days passed without any harm coming to the intended victim. The time limit he'd imposed was almost upon them, and despite the fear he'd planted in the boy's heart, still James showed a reluctance to act.

Fancie kept a close eye on his puppet through the

daylight hours. James seemed to be avoiding Laund Farm out of guilt for what he was supposed to do, but he carried the clay image around with him. He kept pulling it out of his pocket to study his handiwork whenever he was certain no one was watching. Then he would return it after a few moments of fighting his inner battle. His morality was stronger than Fancie had anticipated. No matter. Fancie was certain James's darker desires and sense of self-preservation would prevail.

On the sixth and final night in which James had the chance to act, he surprised Fancie again by leaving the safety of his mother's house in favour of sitting beneath the starlit sky. The way the boy gazed up at the beauty of those burning embers glinting from so very far away, it was as if he had come to make his peace with the world and say his final farewell to all that he had enjoyed in his time on the earth. But it seemed his mind was not quite made up, for his eyes returned to the effigy in his hands.

Fancie watched with that patience mortals lacked, savouring the turmoil his puppet was in. He noted how James turned the clay over and over in his strong fingers, but did not yet apply the pressure needed to reduce it to dust. It would be so easy a motion on the young man's part, and yet it remained so hard to carry out.

Eventually fear and darkness won out, seizing control of the boy's muscles and forcing them to squeeze tight. The clay exploded, dozens of little pieces falling between his fingers like the sands of time. The last one fell to the ground, heralding the end for Duckworth. His body was soon to waste away, his fate already sealed, and no manner of magical protection could stay the Reaper's scythe. Fancie allowed himself another brief smile. Destiny had taken its course, and none could stop it then.

Chattox was not as pleased with the news as a human accomplice might have expected. For her familiar spirit, the lack of gratitude came as no surprise.

"I grow tired of your games, Fancie. When will my rivals go to the gallows as promised?"

"Patience, my love. Soon they will be working their charms in a gaol, seeking help that will not come."

"You said that last year when you tricked young Master Device into killing Towneley. Yet still they walk free and very much alive!"

"A minor hindrance, I assure you. Baldwin was not as persuasive as hoped in his dealings with the one potential witness Nowell could have used in the assizes, but I am certain he will perform better when given his second chance."

"I still do not understand why you left it up to that idiot in the first place."

"Because he is in a better position than we are for such things. As skilled as I am at manipulation, there is no getting around the suspicion and distrust most of the community hold for one such as I. They might not know I am more than the man I appear to be, but they are certainly aware of my partnership with you. No amount of whispering in Henry Towneley's ear would have brought him on our side. Baldwin, on the other hand, is uniquely positioned to meet all of our needs. He is desperate enough to listen to my promises of revenge for his dearly departed lover, and he has the ear of the people we will use to bring about Demdike's demise."

Chattox cackled then. "A pity for him that Demdike is not the cause of all his unhappiness. Christian fools; they know nothing of our world."

"Indeed."

"And if he fails us again? You also promised me Tibb had been dealt with, and look how that turned out. He came back to his mistress, powerful as ever."

"I drove him off for as long as was needed. It allowed us to weaken Demdike, did it not?"

"But still she lives!"

"Patience. I will see to it that destiny remains on course this time."

"You better, or we are through, pact or no pact."

He gave a mock bow and faded from her sight, leaving her to simmer. But Fancie had no intention of giving up his pact with her anytime soon, for the old hag still had her uses. He remained close, watching her as much as their enemies and continuing to bide his time.

More weeks passed. Summer came, though the weather growing ever warmer and the days longer did nothing to improve Chattox's mood. Fancie sensed she blamed him for all her misfortunes, from the days spent in hunger because she could not find work, to the ongoing tensions with the Moore family and the Nutters of Greenhead. Even her beloved daughters, Anne and Bessie, could not lift her spirits.

He kept out of even her inner eye and leeched off her emotions, bolstering his own energy for all that lay ahead.

It went some way to nourishing him, but like most spirits who chose to make the pact with one of the cunning folk, he needed more. He needed that crimson river at the heart of all life.

Feeding on her blood was only a part of their deal, the main cost of his aid being her soul – one she had gladly paid all those years ago. It was a higher price than most spirits demanded of their humans. Fancie was well aware of that, but he had so much more to offer than the lowlier creatures most cunning folk made a pact with. And there were always those willing to pay so high a price.

Yet when he came to Chattox that night, she was so frustrated with her lot in life and his apparent inability to deal with it that she would not speak to him. Fancie's own rage flared up then. His form swelled with that anger, so that muscles bulged beneath black fur, teeth lengthened into fangs thicker than the old woman's arms, and nails grew into wicked claws, like hooks for seizing prey. He remained standing on his hind legs, towering above Chattox with his jaws agape. But still she would not speak to him, even when he crashed down to all fours in a fierce display of brawny strength.

This ursine shape was his preferred animal guise. Taking the form of a hellhound had its uses, but he favoured the greater might of the bear and its untameable nature, so savage and wild and uncontrollable by man.

Chattox had seen him in this shape many a time, and his show of physical power no longer impressed her. He grabbed her leg in his great maw and dragged her to the ground, drawing the blood he craved. But he didn't lap it up immediately, instead standing over her and fixing her with his bloodshot gaze. She needed reminding of his real power, the real nature of the force she had chosen to ally herself with. So he revealed to her his true face for the first time in all their years bound together, the same face he had treated the dying girl to in a future that may or may not come to pass. Chattox screamed.

TWENTY-FIVE

Childish laughter carried on the warm summer breeze. It was the rare sound of innocent joy, known only to those young enough to have not yet been touched by the darkness of the world around them. Jennet had been lucky to have lived the first years of her life free of Death's shadow, her childhood untainted by the loss of any loved ones. Alizon could not help but feel a little jealous of that. Such pure happiness had been denied to her when Chattox had seen fit to take her father. A part of her envied that joy still found in her younger half-sister, and a part of her found it extremely annoying.

"Jennet, slow down!" she shouted. "Stop getting too far ahead!"

"Come catch us, Alizon!" the little girl shouted back, her form disappearing into the trees. Isobell Bulcock followed her in, oblivious to the dangers lurking in the forest's gloom.

Alizon cursed and started to run. She was already beginning to resent having to care for her grandmother in her blindness, and now she'd been left babysitting her little sister while both her mam and her grandmother were off doing Goddess knew what. James never had to look after Jennet, so why did she have to? It was so unfair, and now the idiot girls were just asking to get them all into trouble. She'd had enough.

"Jennet, get back here this instant!"

"You have to catch us first," her sister taunted.

Alizon's skirts flapped about her legs as she struggled to close the distance, thinking she would drag the girls all the way back home by their ears when she caught them. But as she reached the treeline she began to slow, wary of what awaited within. There were stories of wolves still haunting the countryside, and worse, far worse. Any wise woman worth her while knew of those magical places which formed a gateway between worlds – places where the spirits of the land could cross more freely and the fae were able to work their mischief.

"Jennet!" she hissed, not daring to shout too loud now. "It's not safe. Come back and we'll find somewhere else to play."

Either the girls did not hear or it was part of the game not to answer, but no childish voices called back to her. Instead, there came a sinister whispering from between the trees. The ferns growing around the trunks began to sway, even though the air had grown still and uncomfortably hot. An involuntary shiver ran through Alizon. Yet, reluctant as she was to pass beneath those ancient boughs, she knew she could not leave Jennet and Isobell at the mercy of the creatures lurking in the shadows. So she took her first step into the forest gloom.

A dozen or so seconds trickled by while she stood there, straining her senses for any further signs of danger. The land continued to whisper around her, and she could hear a rustling from somewhere off to her right. But no movement accompanied the sound; nothing to indicate the presence of any natural animals foraging in the undergrowth. That only added to her sense of unease.

Alizon forced herself onwards, lifting her legs high to avoid the sting of the nettles which grabbed at her skirt and sought the tender skin of her lower legs.

"Jennet!" she called again, still keeping her voice low. "This isn't funny – get back here this instant!"

Still the girls would not answer, giving her no option but to continue deeper into the woods. Her fear of what she might encounter was outweighed only by her fear of what would happen if she returned home without her charge for the afternoon. Alizon had seen James endure their grandmother's wrath after the Towneley incident. She was loath to find herself the subject of any similar displeasure.

The snap of a broken twig sounded. Heart racing, she spun round and could have sworn she'd caught a glimpse of something large and muscular just on the edge of her vision, yet when she scanned her surroundings the forest remained as seemingly empty as ever. Alizon found that more unnerving than if she'd been confronted with some great beast. Her adversary was not of the mortal world, of that she was certain. But it must have wanted her to know it was there. Such creatures did not suffer the same bouts of clumsiness as those of flesh and blood.

A sudden scream pierced the eerie muttering, silencing the disembodied voices for the first time since she'd reached the trees. The shrill sound came to an abrupt stop. An unnatural quiet followed in its wake. No birdsong started up in the branches overhead, nor did the crickets begin their chorus in the vegetation on the forest floor.

Only the flies buzzed in her ears as they continued to harass her, but even that seemed muted.

Certain it had been one of the girls, Alizon broke into another run. She crashed through the undergrowth with complete disregard for her own safety now.

The trees grew denser the deeper she went, the clumps of vegetation on the floor sparser, but not before her legs had begun to sting where the plants scratched and whipped across her skin. She barely noticed the pain with the fear for her sister driving her on, and she never once slowed.

Alizon flew up the hill, tripping more than once on the roots where they wove in and out of the soil like the sea serpents of legend. Somehow she managed to keep her feet. She had often thought the pattern the roots had formed looked like a natural staircase, and she climbed it now, all the way up to the clearing at its top and the great stump at its centre where an ancient tree once stood. It wasn't her first visit to that place with its otherworldly feel. But she'd never had to venture there alone before. In the past, there had always been her mam or gran to protect her from the spirits she was sure dwelt within that cursed glade. Now she had to wonder if the thing she'd sensed had wanted to lure her there all along.

Her gaze fell to the body at the base of the stump. Its small form lay perfectly still, bathed in the bright sunlight shining through the trees with false cheeriness. The little girl's dress seemed surprisingly clean after running through the woods, her skin so pale it was as if all the colour had drained out of her. Her head faced away, but Alizon knew with a terrible certainty she would find the eyes staring the unblinking, sightless stare of the dead. The last thing she wanted to do was look at that face. She was going to have to, though. It was the only way she'd know which of the girls the body belonged to.

"Please, not Jennet," she whispered as she crept over to the child's corpse. Her hairs raised with a cold the sunlight couldn't touch. It was more than just the fear of what she was about to see. Alizon felt like she was being watched, probably by the very thing that had taken the girl and ripped her young soul from the mortal world. Was it the same creature Alizon had heard following her through the forest?

There came a final surge of dread when she knelt beside the body. It quickly turned to relief to find it was not her sister after all, but her sister's friend, Isobell. That relief was short-lived at the thought of delivering the sad news to Henry Bulcock. Tears filled her eyes with the mental images of what this tragedy would do to the family. And then there was John, Isobell's cousin and Henry's nephew. Their families had always been on good terms, but would they ever forgive her for failing to protect little Isobell from this evil? Would John ever speak to her again? Would he ever look at her with any warmth or kindness in those handsome blue eyes, or would they turn hard and cold with hatred? John, who currently held her heart in his muscular hands, and who could now crush it in revenge for her failure that day.

Not that he had ever shown her any interest in anything more than friendship. That didn't seem to matter to her heart, though. She'd continued to dream the dream of youth discovering the giddy rush of such emotions for the first time, and now those dreams may well be shattered, courtesy of whatever had taken Isobell from them.

Alizon's eyes filled with fury as she looked up from the dead face. Fresh shock doused it a second later. Shock, and rising fear.

A pair of eyes stared back at her from the edge of the clearing, set in a hulking form hidden in just enough shadow to keep its shape concealed. The twin fires were enough to put her in mind of Tibb or Ball. It might even be a hellhound sent by one of their rivals. Could it be Fancie, sent by Chattox to drag her and the two girls into early graves, just as he had with her father?

The clearing had one final horror to reveal. A ghastly apparition appeared beside the hellhound, a thing vaguely resembling a man, yet horribly disfigured, as if twisted by the evil of its own nature. She thought there was something familiar about those deformed features, but she couldn't place where she might have seen them before. And it was not a face anyone would soon forget. Not with those eyes nearly as mismatched as her mother's, the left made almost impossibly wide by the flesh not just sagging but hanging so loosely that it looked like it was about to slide away from his skull. The right appeared to squint in comparison.

The spectre lurched towards her. Its left leg dragged behind it, and its skin looked in danger of sloughing off with every awkward step it took. An arm reached out. Yet despite the terror and revulsion at the mere thought of its touch, she found she couldn't move.

A second scream broke the thing's spell and spurred her back into action. There was no more time for her fears of what might be, or her sorrows – she had to find her little sister before the spirit beast and the deformed thing could strike Jennet down as well. Or at least she had to try. She leapt to her feet and sprinted back down the hill, her legs pounding the earth until they built such momentum that she found she couldn't have stopped, even if she'd wanted to.

There came a third scream as she ran, but something

about it didn't seem right then. It took a fourth cry for her to realise these were not the vocalisations of abject terror she'd heard from within the clearing. No, these were the wordless expressions of silly excitement only young children can make. She felt her temper rising again in response.

How could Jennet be so stupid as to think this was all a game? Clearly her sister was unaware of the grim fate her friend had suffered, or she would surely be crying tears of her own by now, but was she really that blind to the fact her friend had gone missing and the danger they were in?

Alizon raced towards the noises of a child at play. She stopped only when her sister was finally back in her sights, and paused for a moment to catch her breath. Her chest heaved as she stood there, scanning between the trees for any further sign of the beast stalking them. A second figure did run into view, but it was not the spirit. Confusion took over.

"Alizon!" Jennet shouted. "You still have to catch us."

Isobell came to a stop beside Jennet, very much alive and looking as healthy as ever. Alizon stared. What was going on? Had she just had her first vision? But how could it have been? Her inner eye hadn't opened yet, and everything had seemed so real. And yet, this Isobell seemed equally as real, and Jennet could clearly see her as well.

"Come on, Alizon!" Isobell said. "Chase us; chase us!"

The childish ignorance brought her temper back to the fore.

"Enough games," she snapped, storming over to grab each of them by the arm. "You know it's not safe to play in the forest, you stupid girls! Do you want to die out here? Because the grave is where you will both end up if you don't come home with me this instant."

Both girls burst into tears, quaking before her fury. She only grew angrier at that.

"We do not have time for this. You're coming home with me until Gran gets back."

"We're sorry, Alizon," Jennet sobbed, but before any of them could say anything else, a growl rumbled through the trees just ahead.

It was as if her fury had been given form. The blazing red eyes were back, burning in their sockets just above a muzzle which must have been shaped by the Horned One himself, filled with teeth made for rending the flesh of prey. Those fangs were bared in a feral snarl, the hellhound's entire being primed for violence and bloodshed. Alizon's anger gave way to fear once more, especially when one of the girls screamed in terror. Just like she'd heard from within the clearing. That seemed to confirm the worst – that the sight of Isobell's corpse had indeed been a vision of what would come to pass.

Alizon pulled the two children into a run, practically dragging them behind her as they were forced to flee at speeds almost greater than their little legs could carry them. Vegetation rushed by in a blur, slapping their legs and catching at their skirts. Alizon took little notice, pushing them until they could run no more. Even then, she wouldn't allow them to stop, forcing them further at a fast walk.

She didn't dare look behind to see if the thing was running after them, too intent on navigating her way back out of the forest and to Malkin Tower. Of course, if the beast had come to kill them, it didn't even need to hunt them down like a flesh and blood animal. With every step they took, Alizon half expected it to appear on the path ahead or, even worse, for it to pounce out of nowhere and rip into their vulnerable skin with those vicious teeth. Such thoughts were far more terrifying than the mental image she had of it giving chase.

The one thing she didn't expect was to reach her grandmother's cottage without any of them coming to harm.

"Thank the Goddess," she muttered, dragging the girls to the door. "And the Horned One, and any other spirits watching over us."

Alizon let go of Isobell just long enough to let them in and ushered the two girls inside.

"Not a word of this to anyone," she said, once they were safe behind the charms woven into the very walls of their home, "or we will all be in trouble. Understand?"

The girls nodded.

"Isobell, you had better stay here a while until we can be sure the danger has passed. Go play with Jennet in the bedroom."

The two girls did as they were told. Alizon watched them retreat behind Jennet's bedroom door, then set to work making a charm to protect Isobell once it was time for her to return to her father's house. After all, she couldn't have the cousin of her future husband dropping dead. Not when she had the power to do something about it. She might even be rewarded with a kiss.

Alizon scowled at the prospect of looking after Jennet a second day running. She and her gran had barely been through the morning routine of a quick wash and a nibble at the scraps in their kitchen before her mam was back with her little sister in tow.

"Thank you, Alizon," her grandmother said. "Your mam and I have more business to attend to. We will be back before nightfall."

"But why do I have to look after Jennet? Is it not James's turn today?"

"James already got himself into trouble once and is likely watched by Nowell's puppets day and night. Jennet is safer with you."

"Well why can't she go with you two?"

"'Tis not safe for her to be around us at the moment either."

Alizon opened her mouth to argue again.

"Just do as you're told," her mam snapped. "Jennet, you behave for your sister. We will be back later."

"Yes, Mam," the younger girl answered. Jennet waited until she and Alizon were alone before asking "Can we go and play in the forest again?"

"No! Why would you want to go back after yesterday? We could have been killed!"

"But we're both fine. I want to go see the dog again."

"You were terrified of the dog."

"I was not; it was Isobell who screamed. I want to go back and you're too slow to stop me."

With that, Jennet ran for the door. The little girl had barely reached for the handle when the knock came from the other side.

Wariness seized Alizon, even though she knew Malkin Tower was probably the safest place in the whole of Pendle. It seemed early for visitors, and that alone made her suspicious of their caller. What if the forest spirit had returned, and was seeking a way inside to seize the prey who had escaped its clutches? If it was powerful enough, it might breach her grandmother's protective charms, and then they would be cornered and vulnerable, with no familiar spirits of their own to defend them from the onslaught.

"Alizon Device!" a familiar voice roared through the wood, beating his fist so hard against it that she thought he might break it down in his anger. "Open this door!"

Still she hesitated, unsure if it could be another trick. What could Henry Bulcock possibly want with her?

"I know you are in there!" he bellowed. "Open the door, now!"

She decided a spirit in the guise of Henry was more likely to try tempting them out with promises of all their young hearts desired, rather than approach them in so threatening a manner. Taking a deep breath, she did as he demanded. But it was going to take much more than that to appease the wild-eyed man standing before her. Something had got him worked up to the point of violence, and she was careful to place herself between him and Jennet as she answered "What can I do for you?"

"You will come to my house and remove this curse you have placed on my daughter. I know it was you, so don't you dare deny it. Isobell has told me all about the black dog and how angry you were just moments before it appeared, and then I find this around her neck." He brandished the little wooden charm she'd made. "I will not lose her to the same foul bewitchment your brother brought on Anne Towneley!"

Alizon felt herself go cold again. She had been so convinced the spirit creature had come to attack her and the children that she'd never considered the possibility it might have taken an interest in her. Perhaps it was even intending to offer her a pact when the time came. But she'd never meant to curse anyone, as angry as she'd felt at the time. Could she have brought a sickness upon the Bulcock girl without meaning to? From what she knew of spirits, it was entirely possible – the hellhound could have picked up on her fury and interpreted it as a desire to bring harm upon Isobell for running off. But if the child was indeed bewitched, how did Henry expect her to remove it? She had never been taught how to unbewitch anyone. And without the aid of a familiar she was at a loss as to how to do what Henry wanted.

"Isobell's sick?" Jennet gasped. "You have to help her, Alizon! You can't let her die. She's my friend."

"Of course I will do what I can to help. Jennet, stay here. I can't concentrate on curing Isobell if I'm worrying about you."

For once, her sister did as she was told, and Alizon was able to follow Henry down the path without her younger shadow. She did not know what she would do when they reached his house, but she was going to have to try to do something. Otherwise, she may well find herself dragged before Roger Nowell as James had been. She just hoped the herbal remedies and healing spells she knew would be enough.

Henry Bulcock lived a fair way from his brother at Moss End Farm, and the walk to his house was a long one. She wondered if their path might take them to wherever her gran was helping her mam out with what must have been some intricate spell, or why else would they be working together? Perhaps then she could ask them for help. She just needed to think carefully about how she asked for their aid so as to avoid getting herself into any more trouble.

Her mind raced as she tried to come up with a plan while they walked, almost blind to all else around her until there came a flash of movement on the edge of her vision. Had the black dog returned to cause more mischief? Alizon spun round, certain she'd seen something large out of the corner of her eye. There was nothing there.

"Come on, girl, my daughter has no time for stopping!" Henry grabbed her arm and dragged her down the path.

Those rough hands gripped her flesh tight enough to cause pain, and her face reddened with humiliation. Her temper threatened to boil over again, yet she was afraid to let her anger take over after what had already happened to the man's daughter in the spirit's presence. She was terrified of causing more harm to the family if she let herself lose control a second time, especially if the hellhound was indeed back. How would she ever win John's heart if she had cursed both his cousin and his uncle? He might even turn on her and take her to Nowell himself. The mere thought of it brought tears to her eyes as she imagined trying to explain to him how it had been accidental. But in his own anger and grief, John probably wouldn't want to hear it, and it could be him dragging her by the arm before long. She couldn't let that happen, no matter how she hated being treated so.

"Master Bulcock," James called out from a nearby field. "I trust all is well betwixt you and my sister?"

Alizon had never been so happy to see her brother as she was then. If she could just persuade him to come with them, they would at least have Dandy to call on for help.

"You stay out of this, James Device!" Henry snarled. His eyes grew wilder still, as if the dog had possessed him and turned him into something feral. "Your family has done enough damage round here, but Alizon is about to make it right, for my daughter at least."

"And what is it you think my sister has done?"

"She called on some vile spirit after losing her temper with my Isobell yesterday, and bade it strike her down with the most wicked of enchantments, just as we all know you did to Mistress Towneley. Well I will not lose my daughter the same way! Your family has always pretended to be friends with my own, so now you can prove it by undoing this evil before it is too late, or I swear you will rue the day you ever crossed the Bulcocks."

Alizon fixed her tear-filled gaze on her brother. "I didn't mean to, James, I swear!" A silent plea entered her eyes.

"You will be quiet," Henry growled, slapping her cheek with his other hand before turning his attention back to James. "And you stay back. We are leaving."

"Then perhaps I should come with you. I have more experience than my sister, and I know more about bewitchments since it is like you said – I placed one on Mistress Towneley. I can help."

Alizon could have kissed him. It took a moment for Henry to make his mind up, but eventually he growled "Very well."

James climbed over the dry stone wall and fell into step beside them. The worried father seemed to rein in some of his anger after that, possibly for fear of what the siblings might do now that he had them both in tow. He even released Alizon's arm. She rubbed the temporary brands. Her cheek stung where Henry had struck her, and she could see his hand imprinted in white upon the skin of her limb. It was slow to fade, even with her efforts to rub it better.

They were silent for the rest of the journey. Henry wasted no time in showing them up to Isobell's room when they reached the house.

"See what your foul magic has done to my poor girl? None of us are leaving this room until you cure her, unless you'd prefer to involve the JP."

"We will do what we can for her," James assured him.

"But it will go better if you allow us to work our healing charms without interruption. The best you can do for your daughter is to boil water for making a medicinal tea. We will call for you if we have need of anything else."

"And leave you two alone to summon more spirits and make Isobell worse? What kind of fool do you take me for?"

"Then you had best say your goodbyes. Magic requires concentration. We can't save her if you are up here breaking that concentration."

"Very well. But if she dies in your care, then you had best prepare your defence for the assizes. For I will not rest till you both hang."

"We will do all we can," James repeated, his voice level. But Alizon caught the flash of anger in his eyes.

Henry glared at the two of them for a moment longer. She couldn't hold his gaze, too guilty in her belief she was to blame for Isobell's condition, and too afraid of being taken to Nowell if James couldn't undo it. It came as a relief when the older man left the room.

"Do you want to tell me what really happened?" James asked in a low voice, the moment the door closed behind them.

"Oh, James, I never meant to hurt anyone!" she began. "You know I hate having to look after Jennet, but she just wanted to play, and she was quick to find Isobell. Then they had me chasing them and they went running into the forest near Roughlee, even though I told them it wasn't safe! Of course they wouldn't listen, so I lost my temper and shouted a bit when I caught up to them. Then the next thing I know, her father's claiming I bewitched her and demanding I come over here to remove the curse, even though I know not how."

"And that is all that happened? What of the spirit he talked about?"

"No, that's not all," she admitted. "There was something out there with us."

She told him everything, from the whispering in the trees to the vision of Isobell's death, and the encounter with the black dog and the gruesome spectre. James was quiet while she recounted the previous day's events. He took his time to answer after she'd finished, as though deep in thought. She fidgeted with the hem of her dress while she waited.

At last he spoke. "Gran did say I might have met my familiar already before making the pact. It's possible this hellhound spirit could be trying to build a bond with you, ready for when you make your own. I don't think Isobell is bewitched, though. She looks to have fallen victim to the same illness our Jennet had, and John Bulcock before her. And one of Baldwin's girls, too, from what I hear. All we can do is try the same healing magic Gran used for those three and pray it works. Ellena Baldwin is not dead yet, so there might be some hope for Isobell."

"It has to work. She can't die, James, or you heard Henry – he will go to Nowell like he promised; I know he will. If you hadn't been so stupid as to kill Anne, he might not even have suspected witchcraft!"

"So now this is my fault? Be warned, sister. I came to help because we are bound by blood, and I would not see our family mistreated by all the god-fearing folk who think they are better than us. But I can easily walk away and leave you to deal with your own problems."

"You would not dare."

"Try me."

She was almost certain he was bluffing, but years of

arguing had taught her that his temper was every bit as fierce as her own, if not more so. Towneley's grave stood as testament to how far that temper could go. There was just enough doubt to make her back down and mumble an apology.

"You stay up here and do what you can for Isobell," he said. "Let me deal with Henry."

"Me? You're the one with a familiar already. Can you not call on Dandy to heal her?"

"If it were that simple, don't you think Gran would have had Tibb heal Ellena? Hellhounds can do a lot of things, but healing is not one of them. You know the same healing rites as I. Perform them on Isobell now while I speak with Henry – he is more likely to listen to me in his anger than the one he blames for his child's sickness. Perhaps he can be reasoned with."

Misery settled over Alizon as James left the room. Her brother had been her only hope.

She glanced at Isobell, so frail on the bed. The little girl had been completely transformed from the happy child she'd been the day before. This Isobell looked closer to the image of her corpse than the Isobell in the forest, when she'd been so full of laughter and joy. As annoying as the girls could be, Alizon didn't want to see her die. Nor did she want to die herself – the thought of going to trial terrified her. But could Henry really be reasoned with?

She had to know what was being said between the two men. Their voices carried from the room below, muffled at first, until Alizon crept over to the door and pressed her ear to the wood.

"Well? How goes it up there?" Bulcock demanded. "Have you removed the curse yet?"

"I am afraid it is not that simple, Henry. Your daughter

has not been bewitched, by my sister or any other. We will do all we can to cure whatever ails her, but we can make no promises as to her recovery."

"Do not lie to me, James. If this isn't your sister's doing then why did my daughter come running home with tales of black dogs and a charmed pendant, and not a day later shows every sign of being bewitched?"

"You are not thinking clearly, Henry. What reason would Alizon have to bewitch your Isobell? Yes, she has a temper, but our families have always been on good terms, and you should know us well enough by now to realise we would never hurt an innocent child. Why would she risk creating bad blood between us after all these years? And why risk being arrested, as I was, over nothing more than a bit of childish disobedience?"

"There are plenty of witches who have killed for less. We all know the stories round these parts."

"But not our family. As we keep telling people, we are cunning folk, not witches."

"And yet you killed Anne Towneley. Nowell might not have been able to gather enough evidence to send you to trial, but the whole of Pendle knows it was you."

There was a pause, in which Alizon imagined her brother struggling to control his temper. When he spoke again, he sounded different, like there was a darkness in him taking over.

"Yes, I killed Anne. She deserved it for treating me so unfairly and denying our family payment for all the good work I did for her during Samhain. But you would never give me reason to bewitch either you or yours to death, would you, Henry?"

"Are you threatening me?"

"Of course not. Let us just say that if I ever hear tell of

Nowell being given any false accusations against my sister, I will send a curse so terrible it will make your daughter's illness look like naught but a mild cold in comparison. But if you leave the JP out of this, then the goodwill between our families can continue, and you will never have anything to fear from me, Alizon or even our gran. You remember who our gran is, don't you, Henry? And if you are afeared of all I am capable of, you can be sure it is but a fraction of what Old Demdike can do."

Silence fell. The sound of footsteps on the stairs followed shortly after, and Alizon quickly withdrew and set about working the healing spells on Isobell, like she was supposed to be doing. James came in a moment later and she smiled at him with fresh confidence. They might not be able to save the little girl, but it looked like she no longer had to fear being hanged for something she hadn't done. All would be well.

TWENTY-SIX

T wo figures made their way through the half light of dusk. No doubt they would have appeared a fearsome pair to any they passed, and it was easy to imagine folk keeping their heads down and avoiding the gaze of the two women. Demdike was sure her clouded orbs, coupled with her daughter's mismatched eyes, must have seemed nothing but sinister. Yet in reality, they merely wanted to return to the safety of their homes without any trouble. There had been enough of that already, and she was well aware of her daughter's fears that there was worse to come.

"I worry about him, Mam," Elizabeth said. "I lie awake all night wondering what mistake he might make next, and how long it will be before Nowell has him arrested again. I worry his temper will be his undoing, and that we will not be able to save him the next time."

"Let me do the worrying, my girl. Events have been getting out of hand these last two years, but it is time to take fate back into our own hands. It begins now. Why else would I ask you to assist me in this?"

"But will it not complicate matters more? And how can you know this will work? How can you know it will divert suspicion from our family, and not give them something else to point the finger at James for? I worry he will lose control again, and that this will only throw more fuel on the fire next time he is questioned."

"Fear not, love. The lad has some brains in that scalp of his, even if he does not always see fit to use them. He knows how lucky he was to get away with murder, and what a fool thing it was, too. After the fear the whole incident put in him, I think he will be more careful in the future."

"I wish I could believe that, Mam. But I know what they whisper in the alehouses. He had a quarrel with Duckworth over an old shirt he was promised, and a week later Duckworth was found dead and decaying, just as Anne Towneley was. Do you really believe Duckworth's sudden passing was no more than a coincidence?"

"Aye, lass, the same mutterings have reached my own ears, and I know well of the rumours flying round. I will talk to James about it if you wish, but I cannot believe he would be so stupid as to kill with magic a second time. For all we know, Duckworth fell prey to a demon and met his end that way."

"I tried asking Ball, but something is preventing him from seeing what truly happened, and James will not speak to me. I worry someone will come forward with evidence against him, whether he is truly guilty or not. We both know most of the folk round here are not as noble as Henry Towneley, and they are not above making things up if they believe they have something to gain from it."

"Well, there was some good to come out of James's fool move last year. He has restored the fear in us that most have, which should be enough to keep the majority of tongues from wagging in front of Nowell, save those we want to. My plan will work, and I will see to it that the right evidence reaches the JP. His sights will be set on a different prize to our James. And besides, I have been gleaning as much as I can of the future through scrying, so we will have some advance warning if the worst should happen. I am sure our familiars will forewarn us as well."

"We were given no warning the last time. What makes you think the next will be any different?"

"Because our guards are up now, and we will be ready for whatever the future may hold." They reached the door to Malkin Tower. "You worry too much, my girl. Go home and try to rest. I will see us through any hardships that lie ahead, as I have always done since the day you were born. No harm will come to you or the grandchildren for as long as I live, I swear it."

There came the creak of the door opening and footsteps running to greet them. A small body threw herself at Demdike's waist. Demdike smiled and patted Jennet's head.

"Run along with you now, lass. Night is fast approaching – time we were all safe behind closed doors. Be good for your mam, and I will teach you another charm." She hugged the little girl.

Jennet squealed with delight. "When?"

"Soon, lambkin. Go with your mam now."

Elizabeth hugged her goodnight, then Demdike allowed Alizon to guide her inside, to her place by the fire.

Tibb appeared, a lone figure in the mist of her blindness. His canine features looked as fierce as ever, though she sensed there was also a great deal of worry behind those burning eyes.

"You would do well to ask Alizon about the events of the past two days," he advised.

Demdike raised an eyebrow, but didn't question him.

"I thank you, lass," she said to her granddaughter, "and I am sorry to be a burden. But I do appreciate all you do for me with the loss of my sight."

"Don't be silly, Gran, you are no burden."

"You are a poor liar, girl, but I thank you for saying so all the same." Demdike paused, then did exactly as Tibb had suggested. "I take it all has been well in my absence?"

Alizon was somewhat slow to reply, and Demdike imagined her granddaughter stiffening in surprise at the question, which was all the answer she needed.

"Of course, Gran."

"Now, lass, what did I just say about you being a poor liar. Are you sure there is nothing you wish to tell me?"

Alizon hesitated again, but Demdike didn't have to wait long for the girl's next answer. She could hear the tears in Alizon's voice, even if she couldn't see them.

"Oh, Gran, I didn't mean for anyone to get hurt, not like James and his stupid clay figures. We were out with Henry Bulcock's girl and she and Jennet ran off to play in the forest. I told them to come back but they wouldn't listen, and I had no choice but to go in after them. There I saw a vision of Isobell lying dead but from what I couldn't tell, and a spirit appeared to me. I ran to find the girls and we fled back here, but then Henry came round this morning demanding I unbewitch his daughter. James helped and he thinks it's no more than a natural sickness, but the more I think back over the strange happenings in the forest yesterday, the more I worry it was my doing after all."

"Tell me everything, in as much detail as you can remember."

Demdike's eyes fixed on Tibb while the girl gave a more vivid account of her experiences, her brow creasing with the same concerns she sensed from him.

"I was hoping to find you on the way to the Bulcocks' home," Alizon said as she reached the end of her tale. "But James did a good job of convincing him I wasn't to blame for his daughter's illness, and we did all we could without resorting to black magic."

"Yes, you did well."

Her granddaughter seemed to brighten. "What have you and Mam been up to this week anyway?"

"Naught for you to worry about, lass," Demdike answered, though her thoughts strayed back along the dark route she'd chosen, and had now committed herself to. She'd taken the first few steps over the last two days. There was no turning back now.

Despite all the warnings she'd been given, Demdike had long since decided it was the only way to strike down the corrupt and the unjust without risking any of them escaping her vengeance, and thus securing a safer future for her family. So she'd asked Elizabeth to lead her out to the farms round the Higham area first of all – Chattox's territory. There she'd started to work her mischief, spoiling ale and setting Tibb on herds of cattle until entire fields of cows and sheep began to drop dead. Then she'd moved on to other areas in the Forest of Pendle, such as Fence and Roughlee, stirring the rising tensions between herself and her neighbours for when the time came to make her move. She did not relish the carnage in the same way her familiar did, but it was a necessary evil. And better a few livestock than the children of those she sought revenge on, whatever Tibb might think of the matter. But she would keep her grandchildren as far from that sinister path as possible, not wanting to risk dragging them into the blackness with her when the time came. She'd only involved Elizabeth because she really needed someone of flesh and blood to guide her over long distances, and she could trust her daughter to follow her instructions and keep a clear head.

"You should be more concerned with this hellhound spirit who seems to have taken an interest in you," Demdike continued.

"Why, do you think he means us harm?"

She was quiet again while she considered her next move. The creature might have latched onto her grand-daughter but it didn't appear to be by the girl's side right then. Unless it was powerful enough to hide from them, which was an even more troubling thought than the prospect of a mere unknown hellhound.

"I can think of only one way to find out. Boil some water for me please, then bring me whatever herbs we have left."

"Why, what do you have in mind?"

"I will enter the spirit realm and go in search of him, to learn what I can of his true nature and intentions."

"I thought you could do that without the aid of herbs?"

"I can, but entering such a trance takes time and concentration. The aid of herbs is much quicker."

Alizon did as she was asked without further questions. Most of the plants they kept in stock were for healing, but it didn't hurt to keep a stash of other useful herbs whenever they could be dried to preserve them longer, ready for when they were needed. They still had some dried henbane leaves, which were easy enough to identify from the smell.

Demdike instructed her granddaughter to mix a small dose into a tea, once the water began to boil, and fill a tankard with the concoction. Then she drank long and deep of the brew, closed her eyes... and opened them on a large grassy plain beneath a twilit sky, as clearly visible as the moors around Pendle had once been. It was a similar effect to leaving her body to travel with Tibb, except she was now wandering the astral planes as a spirit herself, giving her the freedom to go where she pleased, rather than settling for being a passenger.

Yet it was not without its risks, and it would only last as long as the immediate effects of the henbane in her system. She knew she would probably have been safer in Tibb's head, but she thought the spirit they were searching for was more likely to talk to her if she came alone. That didn't stop Tibb from guiding her for as long as he could though.

Demdike followed him across the grassland, fully alert for the first hint of danger. There was everything to fear in a shadow passing overhead, the rustle of something in the vegetation, and the splash of a creature breaking the surface of a nearby lake. All those stories the people of Earth passed down from generation to generation had their roots in the spiritual. These lands were the home of the fantastical, from the fairy creatures of folklore to the great fire-breathing dragons of legend. And there she was, nothing but a human woman far from home. Her soul was just an insignificant speck in the vastness of the universe, her energy burning far less brightly than the mythological beasts in all their might and otherworldly glory.

Tibb led her across the grassy sea for what must have been miles. Spirits similar to the great bear and mighty lion she'd encountered on the night of her pact stalked nearby. Most of them paid her little interest. Once or twice Demdike thought she'd caught a glimpse of something rarer – the upper torso of a woman on the body of a horse or the head and forequarters of a fierce eagle fused with the hindquarters of a lion – but such spirits proved more elusive and they vanished before she could get a good look.

A lake glittered in the soft, purple light. The deceptive calm of the water's surface split around the coils of something huge and scaly, and Demdike's curiosity got the better of her. She paused to watch, mesmerised by the enchanting shimmer of greens and blues flowing through its skin.

The wet touch of Tibb's nose against her palm broke the spell. "Come, Mistress. This is not a place to tarry."

No sooner had he spoken than a malicious cackle sounded from behind. Tibb sprang forward, planting himself between Demdike and the cackler with a threatening growl. Demdike turned to find a short creature no taller than Jennet. Fiery-red eyes glittered with villainous mischief above a long, pointed nose and sharp, crooked teeth. Skinny fingers ending in talons grasped a pike stained with old blood. But what really drew Demdike's eye was the blood-soaked cap on his head, still dripping with the life fluid of his last victim. She sought the silver pentagram pendant of her ancestors and found her neck bare. It didn't exist here.

Hackles raised and his great fangs bared, Tibb took a step closer to the creature. The redcap's eyes flicked from Tibb to Demdike, lingering for a moment on her throat with undisguised longing. Another warning growl rumbled up from Tibb's throat and out between those deadly teeth, and his aggressive bark boomed across the astral plane. The redcap grimaced and backed away. Demdike sighed with relief. They waited for the spirit to turn and flee, then resumed their journey.

Finally a cliff face loomed in the distance. Demdike followed Tibb to where the wall of rock breached the lush green of the plains, and through a crack in its surface which widened into a tunnel sloping down into the depths. There they would find the creature who had latched on to Alizon, or so Tibb seemed to think.

Deep beneath the surface of the world they went, into the blackest pits of what Christians would have called Hell. There should have been no visibility in that utter absence of light, but her spirit self did not possess the same limitations as her flesh. She could see the stony walls around her and the shape of her familiar padding along in front. And she could feel the hostile eyes of things worse than redcaps, tracking their progress.

They reached a large chamber with three more tunnels leading out of it. Tibb came to a stop and indicated the middle passage with his forepaw. "In there. He is the one who appeared to Alizon yesterday."

Cold fear stabbed through Demdike's gut. They had come to the place where the darkest spirits dwelt, and she was under no illusion as to what she might encounter lurking in the blackness. Was Alizon's spirit truly a hellhound, or had evil taken the guise of a black dog to trick their family into trusting it? There was only one way to find out. She took a deep breath to steady her nerves and stepped forward.

Tibb kept back, lest the creature took him to be a rival and fled before they could talk to it. But Demdike knew he was keeping watch, his body coiled and waiting to spring into action at the first sign of trouble. That gave her the strength to go on, even though her instincts were screaming to run from this cursed place.

She had almost reached the mouth of the passage when something appeared in the one next to it. There was the impression of bulkiness, yet the creature remained oddly indistinct, as though its form was partly cloaked from view. Only its eyes were visible. Glowing eyes glittering with malice greater than any redcap's. Eyes she had seen once before, blazing with promises of pain and misery for all those unfortunate enough to be fixed by their gaze.

The old wise woman began to back away, but with every step she took, the thing advanced. It was coming for her, and she knew it would be impossible to outrun it.

Their gazes locked. More cold fear went through her, fear that her soul would be sucked into the twin points of blackness in an otherwise sea of crimson, and she realised she had faced this thing more than just once. It was only the second time she'd seen those eyes glow, but there was no mistaking them.

"Tibb, run!" she screamed, and shut her eyes tight, willing herself back into her body. When she opened them, her sight was gone.

Her other senses registered the warmth of the fire beside her and the hardness of the stool she was sitting on. She was back in Malkin Tower, safe once again.

Alizon's voice was full of worry. "What happened? Did you find the hellhound?"

"Not quite. Something found us," Demdike answered. "I fear danger lies ahead."

"When isn't there danger," her granddaughter scoffed. "Maybe it's a sign I should make the pact now, for my own protection."

"No! I should have listened to your mother when she said James was not ready and saved us all a great deal of trouble. The last thing we need is a second spirit tied to the rashness of youth."

"But, Gran, if the spirit is already trying to work with me then would it not be better to bond with him and gain enough control to keep him from causing unwanted mischief?"

Demdike shook her head. "Not yet, lass. You go back to your love charms for young Master Bulcock, and let me worry about this new spirit."

"How do you know about my feelings for John?" Alizon asked. Demdike imagined the girl's cheeks reddening, twin roses of her affection.

"Because I was your age once, and I remember what it was to fall in love. Trust me, you are better off waiting to bind yourself to a familiar spirit until there is less suspicion surrounding our family. Your time as a wise woman will come but until then, enjoy your youth while it lasts."

She knew it was not what her granddaughter wanted to hear, but she feared the mischief the girl might cause if she was allowed to bond with the spirit. James and Dandy were proving enough of a handful without adding Alizon and the unknown hellhound to their troubles as well. But most of all Demdike feared that thing which had surely been waiting for her in the darkness. The same thing which had invaded the very room she had just fled to, not two years ago. He who was now bound to Chattox. There was no forgetting those eyes. Fancie, master of lies and sculptor of fates. And the demon she had denied the pact.

CHAPTER
TWENTY-SEVEN

P ale as the frost-touched ground she lay there on the bed. Withered hands grasped the drink her mother forced on her, limbs all but wasted away. Several months she'd languished in her sickness, all the energy of her youth sapped from her small body by the evil of the witch's curse. Long gone were the days when she would join her sisters at play. Weakness confined her to her bed now.

Richard lingered by the doorway, watching helplessly as Jenneta mopped their daughter's brow. He had prayed and prayed for Ellena's deliverance from Demdike's vile spell. All in vain. No matter how fervently he beseeched God's help, it simply was not enough to bring her out from under Death's shadow and back into the light. It was a miracle she still clung to life at all, and for as long as she still drew breath, there was hope. But that hope was fading fast, her condition clearly in decline. She was barely eating or drinking now, and she had already taken on the appearance of a corpse, waking so rarely that his wife had to keep checking for a heartbeat.

Jenneta felt his eyes on them and turned to glare, as if this was all **his** fault. Anger swept aside the worry and sadness. How dare she lay the blame at his feet? She was the one who invited Squinting Lizzie into their home. What had she expected him to do, pay the hags for their 'honest' work? As if anything they did could truly be called honest! That they would curse an innocent little girl only strengthened his belief in denying them anything. Let them starve for their sins and return to their dark lord's fiery domain where they belonged, and leave the Christians of Pendle in peace.

Ellena gave a weak cry, writhing in the Devil's grasp. Jenneta's attention returned to their daughter in an instant. Richard pushed the anger back down, for his daughter's sake. The feeling of helplessness returned as Ellena whimpered and shuddered in his wife's arms. Finally he could take it no longer. He strode outside and turned his eyes to the heavens.

The days had grown as short and gloomy as Richard's mood in the run up to another Christmas which promised little joy. But never before had those grey skies felt as empty as they did then.

"Please, Lord, I beg of you. Please lend my daughter your strength – let her fight this evil curse the witches have placed her under, and return to health."

There came the splash of an icy raindrop landing on his cheek. More followed, quickly turning into a light drizzle which only served to make the land gloomier. It was the only answer Richard was given, and his heart felt all the heavier for it. Had the Lord forsaken him?

Soon the passing bells were tolling once again. Ellena's breathing rattled through what little was left on bones framed by paper thin skin. Finally, one cold December morning, she breathed her last.

Richard felt surprisingly numb as he stood over her body. He noted how there was a strange beauty to her in death, despite the skeletal frame she'd been reduced to – unlike the cadaver he'd beheld at Carr Hall. A small mercy, but one he was grateful for. The nightmarish visage Anne Towneley had presented would have been too much to perceive in his beloved daughter.

His family may have ceased to bring him any joy, but there was a part of Richard that still cared for his children. Seeing Ellena's battle with the Devil finally at an end was perhaps a blessing. Maybe this was even God's way of answering his prayers. Yes. His faith may have wavered as Ellena's battle raged on, but now the look of serenity on her face was all the confirmation he needed. After nearly a year of suffering, his little girl had risen up to God's Kingdom and found peace. He had to believe that, or what hope was there for any of them? The witches would not take that from him.

Yet it was hard to keep his head above the darkness in the days following his daughter's death, especially when it came at such a bleak time of year. The ground was so hard that it took an entire team of labourers to dig the grave, the land feeling as devoid of life as the dead resting beneath it. There was a certain feeling of rightness about that – Richard had always felt that death seemed out of place in the spring and summer months, when the countryside was rich with God's beautiful creations and the world was bright with the warm summer sun. But even though it might be considered the right season for a funeral, with no sun shining like a beacon of hope through the dullness of the clouds, it only made the time of mourning more difficult.

The funeral ceremony came on the blackest of nights, the sky utterly devoid of any sign of light – even the faint twinkling of stars. Ellena was buried at Colne rather than St Mary's, for Richard would not allow his girl to rest in any church where the witches were known to go, and he would certainly not allow her remains to be dug up for use in their Devil worship. From Wheathead there was little difference in the distance between the two, the mourners facing a long walk upon the winding country roads either way.

Richard led the procession with his wife and surviving children, walking behind the cart carrying Ellena's coffin to the slow, steady pace of grief. They bore their own lights which seemed to do little to beat back the darkness engulfing them, even with the added torches of more than a yeoman should have been able to afford. But with his rise in social status as a result of his work with the Church, Richard was granted a greater show of wealth than he actually owned. It had been his request to his friends among the gentry, in a display of defiance against the witches. He wanted Demdike to know their Puritan faith would remain the light against her blackness, and so it was that hundreds of flames lined the procession as they made their way to the burial site.

The party reached St Bartholomew's and lined the pews within. They shivered through the ceremony, the old building offering no more warmth than the frozen grounds where Ellena was to be buried. Then it was back into the night to gather around the graveside and say their last goodbyes.

Finally they faced the long walk back to the house, where at least there was wine waiting in the parlour. Richard could not wait to get his hands on a bottle. He wanted nothing more than to drink away his sorrows until he passed into the blissful oblivion of deep, alcohol-induced sleep.

Several of their neighbours joined them for the wake. Some men might have found that to be a comfort, but to the miller it was more of an annoyance. He just wanted to drink in peace.

"Our condolences, Dick," John Nutter said, his face solemn.

Nutter's wife gave a polite nod. "Where is Jenetta?" Agnes scanned the crowded parlour, her gaze settling on the forlorn figure weeping in the corner. "If you'll excuse me. She needs someone with the understanding of a mother's pain."

Richard grunted and raised his glass to his lips.

"We'll be praying for your family later." John gripped Richard's shoulder and gave a firm squeeze. "To help you stay strong in the days to come."

Richard forced a smile. "My family thanks you. Now, if you'll excuse me..."

He turned away, only to find Constable Hargrieves approaching with a bottle of ale. "My deepest sympathies, Dick. This might not help in the fight against the witches, but perhaps it will bring you some comfort in the long nights to come. Don't you worry though. We'll catch the hags at their craft one of these days, I'm sure of it."

"Thank you, Henry. You are most kind."

Hargrieves waved that away. "Least I can do."

"You are kind to think of me nonetheless. If you would excuse me, I would rather be alone for a while..."

"Nonsense. What kind of Christians would we be to leave you alone at a time like this? Come, let us pour another glass of wine and drink to your little girl."

Hargrieves threw an arm around Richard's shoulders and steered him over to a group made up of many of the same men who'd helped with James Device's arrest. A few of their neighbours eyed them as they passed, and Richard had the sense they too wanted to approach him, but were wary of the constable. Then he was surrounded by so many of the well-wishers that he began to feel trapped.

"Really, you are all very kind to think of me and my family, but you must excuse me – I need some air." Richard pushed his way through the crowd before any of them could argue, and over to the door. An entire bottle of wine went with him.

The bitter chill of the air outside helped clear Richard's mind, but it left him open to a fresh assault of all his sorrows. When the tears started to prick his eyes, there was little he could do to hold them back. And so he wept, not just for the loss of his little Ellena, but also for the happiness he had once known with his family and everything else the witches had taken from him. He wept for his soul and the sins Demdike had forced on him, and the loss of control over his own lust. And most of all, he wept for his Rob, the one source of goodness he'd found in the evil of his blasphemous affections.

In that moment, he felt he would have given what was left of his soul for one more night with the man he'd loved, even with his conviction not to deal with the Devil or any of his agents. But no bargains were offered to him, and his only solace remained the bottle in his hand.

Richard raised the wine to his lips and tilted his head back, pouring it down his throat in great gulps until only a few drops remained. Those last few beads of liquid refused to trickle out from their glass container and into his mouth, and he tossed it aside in frustration. His tolerance for alcohol had reached an extent where the wine had yet to exert its influence on him. He thirsted for more.

The miller considered going back inside for another bottle, but the raised voices of those who couldn't hold their liquor were enough to deter him. The alehouse beckoned once again, and he was no more able to resist its allures that night than on any other. All he needed was the lantern he kept hidden outside for such occasions. Once it was lit, he was on his way.

There was no fear as he made his way down the road of the damned. He felt certain there was nothing worse the witches could do to him, short of bringing about his own demise. Let them. He no longer feared the grave, for God would surely forgive him the sins caused by witchcraft and allow him to take his rightful place in Heaven. In many ways it would be a release from the evil they'd already brought upon him, just as it had been for Ellena. There had even been times when he'd considered freeing himself in that one final act of sin, though he was not quite there yet. Perhaps it was the only way his story could end at this point, but he was determined not to reach that ending without completing such aspects of the Lord's work as had fallen to him first. It was his duty to lead his flock through the darkness of the witches' devilry and ultimately defeat that darkness by assisting Nowell in sending the wretches to the gallows. And if he was going to survive long enough to succeed in this great quest he'd been given, he was going to need more ale to see him through it.

But Richard never reached the alehouse that night. He was not far off when his eyes picked out a shape moving towards him.

"Who goes there?" he called out, gripping his lantern tight. He'd use it as a makeshift weapon if he had to.

The stranger stepped within the dim halo of light, revealing himself not to be a stranger at all but Henry Mytton of Roughlee. Richard breathed a sigh of relief and relaxed his grip.

"Dick Baldwin? What brings you out here on this cold winter night? Should you not be at your daughter's wake?"

"It was too much to bear, so I thought I would seek a drink in solitude. But I could ask the same of you. What are you doing out here?"

"I've had my fill of the alehouse and now I'm returning home to my wife. You might find the Widow Sawyers reluctant to serve you at so late an hour, but I've some ale left in my tankard, which you are welcome to if you want to walk with me awhile. Lord knows you need it more than I."

Richard glanced down the road, thinking he could probably try for some sympathy from Widow Sawyers. Surely she would understand his need for ale to help him sleep. But there was something about Mytton and his kindness which made him accept the man's offer, and it did not hurt that the farmer was not unattractive. He could almost imagine it was Rob come back to him, with a little help from the alcohol.

"I thank you, kind sir," he said, accepting the tankard and taking a swig. "This is good ale."

"Aye, from Widow Sawyers' strongest batch. It ought to

steady your nerves and dull your mind, ready for a good long sleep I expect."

Mixed with the wine already in his system, it didn't take long for that drunken feeling to creep over Richard as they made their way back towards their homes. It soon became a struggle to walk on the treacherous track winter had reduced the road to. Several times he stumbled, and he nearly lost his footing entirely when he tripped on a particularly large stone jutting out from the mud. They were forced to come to a brief stop while he fought to stay upright, Mytton throwing his arm around him with a cry of "Steady there, Dick!"

His mind cloudy from the ale and already lost in the memories of the times he'd spent with Rob, Richard could only interpret the feel of the other man's arm around him as a show of affection. It was a sensation he'd not experienced in the two years since his lover's death.

A warmth crept into his cold heart, transferring itself into a movement in his neck which had him leaning into Mytton for a kiss.

Mytton gave a cry of surprise and pushed him away, his eyes alight with anger and his face twisted with disgust. "Richard, what the hell are you doing?"

The miller could not keep the hurt from his drunken features. "I only want to feel the warmth of another man beside me, it's been so long. I thought we had a connection just now."

"God, the rumours about you are true. Get away from me, you vile aberration!"

Hearing those words opened up another wound in the heart which had been so briefly resurrected, only to shrivel and die once more beneath the cruelty of his affliction. Richard felt a sense of revulsion for himself then, every bit as strong as Mytton's reaction to his unnatural attraction, and more self-pity that he should be cursed with such unwanted feelings. Above all, he felt a fresh wave of hatred for the witches. There was also fear. It took a moment for the mention of rumours to cut through the drunken haze, but once it had sunk in he felt panic rising in his gut.

"What rumours?"

"Jack Robinson saw you with Rob one night. None of us wanted to believe it, especially not from such a Godly man as yourself, or so we thought you were. But here you are trying to kiss me when all I was doing was trying to keep you from falling! You make me sick, Dick Baldwin. Your wife shall hear of this; she deserves to know she is living with a monster filled with this filthy, unnatural aching in his loins. How can you take any pleasure from such acts against God?"

"Please, Henry, 'tis not my fault," he pleaded, grabbing Mytton by the arm. "I was not always like this! It is clearly the Devil's work, inflicted on me by none other than his servant, Demdike."

"Don't touch me!" Mytton shrieked, shaking him off and turning away.

Panic had completely taken over now. If Mytton was allowed to tell his story to another living soul, it would be over for Richard. Everyone in the Forest of Pendle would know his dirty secret, and he would be shunned by the community and stripped of his rank in the Church. He may never be allowed to walk on hallowed ground again, and would probably be denied a burial at St Bartholomew's when his time came. His life was about to come crashing down, and he would be left little more than a phantom among its ruins.

Without thinking, he placed the lantern on the ground

beside him and dropped to his knees. Desperate hands grasped the stone he'd tripped on and wrenched it free of the dirt with a loud sucking sound, as if the mud didn't want to surrender its treasure, the land not wanting a part in the greater sin he was about to commit. But Richard had become a vessel for the panic possessing him, capable only of reacting to a bad situation about to spiral even further out of control. There was no room in his panic-stricken mind for thought, only action. And so he rose to his feet like an avenging angel, jaw set with fierce determination and eyes fixed on the back of Mytton's head. He clutched the stone so hard beneath his fingers that a sharp edge found its way into the soft flesh of his palm, releasing a warm trickle of blood. There was no pain in his current state.

A primal roar burst forth from his mouth, out of place in the civilised world he had always strived so hard to help maintain and keep in order. Richard lunged after Mytton and brought the stone down on his skull with a sickening crack. The farmer cried out and fell to his knees, a stream of dark fluid running down his face from the grisly spring Richard had created in his scalp. That fountain of the man's lifeblood appeared almost black in the dim glow from the nearby lantern. Yet it was leaking far too slowly for Richard's liking, so he struck again, before Mytton had chance to pick himself up.

More bone crunched beneath the natural weapon and his victim collapsed to the ground beside him, still and apparently lifeless. Richard was taking no chances. He hit the other man a third time, and Mytton's head caved in with a great splash of blood and slimy slivers of brain. There was no doubt then that the farmer had just taken his secret to the grave, his tongue stayed by death. Richard sank to the ground beside him, shock replacing the panic.

"What have I done?" he whispered into the night, looking down at the stone in his hand, so slick with blood now. Blood – it was everywhere. His face was splattered with gore, his shirt ruined with it. Who knew a man could leak so much from so relatively small a wound? The murder weapon glistened with the dark fluid in the candlelight, the blood of his victim mixed with his own blood from the cut in his palm, forever linking them in this terrible act. He had broken the most sacred of commandments. Truly he was one of the damned, Hell bound without a doubt and so far beyond redemption that he might as well accept his fate and turn himself in, confess to his crimes against both man and God, and let the assizes condemn him to Gallows Hill. No amount of praying could save him now. He would swing alongside his sworn enemies, no better than they in the end.

No. He couldn't just give up, not now. The witches had to be stopped and if not by him, then who would be left to stand against them? Fancie had trusted him alone with the knowledge gleaned of events to come; had tasked him with the necessary action to steer those events in the right direction to bring about the Demdike family's demise. He had to believe there was a reason for that. After all, it was well known that the Lord works in mysterious ways. Perhaps this was His will, even if it came through an agent of the Devil. Could it be that he had been chosen as God's instrument to stand against the wicked forces which had held Pendle under siege for so long? And if that were true, Richard had a duty not just to his fellow men, but to God as well. Only he could carry out this divine task; only he had the power to succeed where others had failed.

Richard rose with new purpose. It would not do to be found beside his victim. He was going to have to burn his gore-stained clothes to avoid suspicion – his first task once he was back at the mill. The bloody stone he took with him, nestled in his fingers as far as the road leading out of Roughlee and on to Wheathead, at which point he threw it into the stream running by the muddy track. It landed with a plop, to be cleaned by the waters washing over it and lost amongst the many pebbles lining the shallow watercourse, unlikely to be found and linked to Mytton's murder. All that remained was to pin the death on the witches – an easy task once he succeeded in gathering some real evidence against the heathens and their blasphemous ways. He just had to endure until the day came in 1612 which would bring the opportunity to build a solid case against them, just as Fancie had promised. Then they would hang for his crime, along with their actual sins. He would make certain of it.

PART FOUR - 1612

Cold winds battered Malkin Tower, tugging at the linen on the bedroom window and threatening to rip it from Alizon's grasp. She gripped it tight, watching the rain pelt the earth with a sense of awe. Never had she felt so close to her deity. Here was a sure sign of the Goddess's strength, greater than ever in spite of the Puritans' attempts to banish all knowledge of her from the land. Alizon liked to think she too would be able to show them the same powerful defiance, some day. If only her mam and gran would let her make the pact! She was doing everything she could to prove how ready she was, but still it hadn't been enough. Alizon sighed. It was beginning to feel like she'd never have a familiar of her own.

She let the linen fall back across the window and began to ready herself for the long day ahead. John's charming smile took shape in her mind's eye as she washed and dressed. A silly grin spread across her face. Those blue eyes twinkled invitingly and she found herself in the home they were going to start together, laughing and drinking and falling into his loving embrace. Did he long for the same?

There were times she thought he was beginning to notice her beauty, times when she felt there was something more than friendship between them. Maybe he just needed a little nudge into finally making a claim for her heart. Perhaps a love charm?

"Alizon," her gran called from the kitchen, "be a dear and prepare my tools for scrying before you go out today, please."

She sighed, the daydream shattering in an instant. The wind changed direction and tore at the linen barely hanging on to the window now, and the rain found its way into the room, bouncing off the floor with new ferocity. Spring seemed even more distant than her dreams. Had the Goddess decided it was time to cleanse the land of the Puritans for good? Alizon hoped so. Why else would the weather be so unsettled for March?

Hunger rumbled through her belly. She turned from the window and made her way into the kitchen and over to the tools of their craft. "I don't know why you bother, Gran. It's been months since I had my vision and so far none of it has come to pass."

"It does no harm to keep trying," her gran answered from her place by the fire. "There is no telling when I may be granted a glimpse at something meaningful."

Alizon snorted. "What little the spirits permit you to see only brings more questions."

"And what else is there for me to do in this bad weather? I may as well continue hunting for answers while you are out hunting for work. And speaking of, where are you off to today?"

Alizon passed over the tools her gran had asked for, gently pressing them into the outstretched hands. "I've not been to Trawden in some time – thought I'd do a bit of begging round there."

"Aye, very good, lass. Be off with you then." Her gran smiled, closing her fingers around the sheep's blade-bone and the oil to cover it with. Alizon still found it incredible her gran could scry anything at all after going blind, even with the use of the Sight. She smiled back and wondered if her gran could sense it, but then the lines on her gran's face smoothed and the old woman's expression grew serious again. "But be careful!"

Alizon's smile widened at that. She patted her gran's arm and moved over to the door, undeterred by the blast of cold air as she opened it. "Aren't I always?"

She closed the door behind her before her grandmother could respond. The fear of that day in the forest had long since faded. Why keep worrying needlessly? There'd been no more trouble for any of them since. Isobell still lived, the hellhound had not returned, and the Puritans hadn't been to arrest anyone for witchcraft since her brother had killed Anne Towneley. All was as it should be.

The journey was hard going. With every step she took, Alizon's feet sank deep into the mud, as if the ground were trying to suck her in. She imagined the earth only allowed her to pull each foot free with great reluctance, the squelching sound it made as she battled against the elements its cries of protest. But she was Alizon Device, wise woman and grand-daughter of Demdike. She wouldn't be defeated so easily.

Then there was the wind. It blew with such force that it soon became a struggle to breathe, and she had to fight to keep moving forward. But it was the rain that had her shivering uncontrollably. Alizon felt as though she would not need to wash again for weeks, the heavens were doing that thorough a job of it for her. She had barely taken her first few steps before her clothes grew sodden and became uncomfortably plastered to her skin.

Such heavy rain also hampered her ability to see. There was a stinging in her eyes which could not be blinked or wiped away, both her hands and her clothes too wet to use. And for each drop expelled by her rapidly blinking eyelids, there were already several more ready to take its place.

Navigating the road leading first to Colne, and then to Trawden, was fast beginning to feel like more effort than it was worth. Her stomach disagreed. It gurgled its demands for food, serving as a whip to spur her onward.

Alizon kept her head down as she walked. A few people passed her, but she barely noticed them, intent only on reaching her destination and gathering as much as she could from the families better off than hers. She made it to Colne and paused to catch her breath beneath one of the buildings' overhanging upper floors. Maybe she should try her luck round here instead? It was still a fair walk to Trawden, and there was no guarantee she'd find more food there than in the market town.

"You looking for work, love?" a rough voice breathed in her ear.

Alizon jumped and turned to find a filthy old man stinking of ale and worse. Wicked brown eyes looked her up and down, lingering on her bosom with open hunger.

"I can feed you if you'll show me a good time," he leered, revealing several crooked teeth and as many gaps.

Alizon might have been afraid if he'd caught her on a street with no witnesses, but they weren't the only ones braving the storm. She straightened and fixed him with her best glare. "I will do no such thing. I am a wise woman, not a whore, and you would do well to keep your distance or I will curse you with a rot that makes your cock shrivel up and fall off!"

She strode away as best she could in the current conditions. The man's eyes seemed to follow her, and she had to fight the urge to turn and check he wasn't following.

"Don't show weakness," she muttered to herself. "Don't encourage them."

It came as a relief when she turned safely onto Colne Field Lane. Alizon bowed her head and continued her battle to reach Trawden.

Colne wasn't that far behind when the mud sucked especially hard at her boot, and she had to wrench herself free to take her next step. She almost lost her balance then, and stumbled forward. A shoulder bumped against hers.

"Watch where you're going," another man's voice growled.

Alizon struggled to clear her eyes. "Sorry, I didn't see you there."

She peered through the downpour to see the man continuing on in the opposite direction, obviously looking to do business in the market town she'd just been through. A pack hung from his back, bulging with all kinds of valuable trinkets. Alizon's heart leapt.

"Wait! Are you not the pedlar, Master Law?"

He paused, facing her with a questioning look on his haggard features. Fit as he undoubtedly was, the storm seemed to be taking its toll on a man of his age. There was a weariness in his voice, as if the wind and the rain were wearing him down, like a rock weathered from too many years of exposure. "I am."

Alizon smiled. "Then I would like some of your pins, if you happen to have any in your pack today."

"Some of my pins?" he sneered. "You have not the

money for something of such worth. I won't waste my time opening my pack for the likes of you."

Law turned away again, and something in Alizon snapped. Who was he to deny her perfectly reasonable request? Pins were the perfect tool for working love charms – her best chance at steering John's heart in the right direction. And this old fool was refusing to sell to her because he thought himself better than her? Well, he would soon realise his mistake.

"And do you know who I am?"

The pedlar did not stop this time, calling over his shoulder "I care not for the identity of some beggar girl. The weather is too foul for these silly games so I'll be on my way, and do not try to stop me again."

Alizon's temper blazed higher still, and she chose her threat with even greater care than the last one. The words poured out with more passion than any she'd spoken before, and in that moment it no longer mattered she hadn't yet been allowed to make the pact. She felt the power of her family's bloodline giving her a strength greater than any this idiot would ever know.

"I am granddaughter of the greatest wise woman in these parts in over a hundred years, and you will heed my words or suffer for all time. Walk away from me now and I will lay a curse on you so terrible, you will pray for the end to come. But death will be no release and your soul will never know peace. So I swear to you, on the power of the Horned One himself."

Law did stop at that and turned to her a second time. Defiance burned in his eyes. "A witch you may be, but my soul is no offering for Satan. And so I swear this to you: strike me down and my son will not rest until your corpse swings in the wind with all the other black-hearted hags of these parts. You are not having any of my pins, and if you have any sense you will let me continue on unharmed, or suffer the consequences. Good day!"

He resumed his struggle toward Colne, but Alizon could tell she'd unnerved him, deep down beneath those brave words he'd uttered. She was about to shout out to him again when a large black shape came running through the downpour, just ahead of Law's retreating figure. Anger turned to horror when the pedlar appeared to stumble. After all those months, had the hellhound returned to cause more mischief?

Law cursed and shouted something inaudible at the animal, but when he tried to continue onward his legs seemed to collapse from under him. He fell face down into the mud.

The beast stopped and circled the stricken man, sniffing him with interest. Then it looked up and met Alizon's gaze. Shock took hold. These were not the eyes of a hellhound, utterly devoid of Hellfire. The only thing unusual about them was the way they did not match, one a pale blue that seemed to glow even in the dim light, and the other as brown as the earth beneath their feet. Besides, this dog was female, while the hellhound from the forest had definitely been male.

Alizon might as well have sunk into the mud then, her legs rooted by the shock clouding her mind. Had she bewitched someone else without meaning to? But how? The dog was just a dog, not a powerful spirit come to strike down her foes. It was so underfed that its legs looked like sticks, and its ribs were visible beneath its short black coat, even at that slight distance. So how could this be her doing if the hellhound had not returned after all? Unless... That strength she'd just felt – had that been real magic?

Her gran might be able to answer those questions, but the old woman was all the way back at Malkin Tower. Alizon was on her own, and if the situation wasn't handled correctly she knew it could have serious repercussions, especially if Law believed she had bewitched him. In the end, that was all that really mattered – what he believed and what he might accuse her of. And if she was somehow to blame, she felt she should at least try to make it right. It wasn't like she'd actually wanted to hurt him. She might even be rewarded with the pins she needed.

Alizon started back down the road towards his prone form. The dog cowered submissively, wagging its tail uncertainly. Law began to stir before she reached him. He picked himself up without any apparent difficulty, but he seemed shaken. There was panic in his eyes when he looked round and saw her walking over. Then the dog brushed its nose against his hand and he jumped and gave a cry of alarm.

"Stay back!" he shrieked, backing away. His eyes darted between Alizon and the dog in a clear effort to keep both in his line of sight.

"Let me help you," Alizon said.

"Back, I tell you!"

She came to a stop and eyed the man uncertainly, unsure of what to do next. "Master Law, are you well? That looked to be quite a fall."

He didn't answer. Wide eyes stared out from a muddy face and dirt stained his clothes, giving him a wild look. It was as if his panic had transformed him into something primal – a hunted animal caught between fight and flight. Alizon knew then there was nothing more she could do but let him flee. She watched helplessly as he staggered towards Colne with all the haste the current conditions allowed. No doubt he hoped to find help from his fellow Christians there.

The dog made no move to follow him either. It turned its unusual eyes on her a second time which she might have found unnerving, if she hadn't grown up around the mismatched gaze of her own mother.

There was no hint of aggression in the animal or desperation that might lead it to attack, despite the intense hunger it must be suffering. No, there appeared to be nothing other than a silent plea for help in those odd eyes, and she felt only pity in return.

"Come on then, let us go begging and see what food we can find to share. But I can't give you it all – my gran's counting on me to fetch her some as well."

She knew a normal dog couldn't possibly have understood her words, but the creature acted like it had, wagging its tail in response and padding dutifully at her side as she resumed her own journey towards Trawden. They had only gone a few paces when she came to a stop again. Events replayed in her mind and her doubts grew.

Alizon looked back at the pedlar. He was still struggling on ahead, with more than just the weather it seemed. Something had caused him to fall, bewitchment or no. If he was given the chance to tell anyone of their argument, there would be plenty ready to point the finger at her, which could only bring more trouble. What if it was wrong of her to let him go? She tried to convince herself all would be well, but her doubts insisted otherwise. Alizon bit her lip. What if he collapsed a second time? She started after him.

Law did not go far. Alizon almost called out to him as his hand reached for the door to The Greyhound, but something stayed her tongue. It would probably only give him another scare, and what if that made things worse? So she waited for him to go inside. Only then did she walk right up to the inn.

First she peered in through the window. There was no sign of Law there. Following him in seemed risky, but she had to know what had become of him. There was nothing for it. She took a deep breath, squelched over to the door, and reached for the handle with a shaking hand. The dog looked up at her and wagged its tail uncertainly. Alizon's determination strengthened. She opened the door.

A quick scan of the room and her eyes fell on the pedlar, lying on a bench up against the left wall. He seemed to be in pain and unable to move, both his left arm and leg hanging off the makeshift bed and trailing uselessly on the floor. His eyes were closed and she took courage from that, resolving to go over to him and attempt a healing charm while he rested. That way, they could avoid any further misunderstandings which might get her arrested.

Her new companion had other ideas. The tantalising smell of food wafted out to them the moment she opened the door, too great a temptation for the dog to ignore. The animal rushed into the inn before she could stop it and grabbed a chunk of mutton from the nearest plate, to cries of protest from the men inside. She cursed and called out to the bitch, but it ignored her and ran over to the very man she had intended to check on. And the moment that cold, wet nose touched his skin, his eyes snapped open and widened with the same look of panic as before.

"No!" she shouted again and patted her legs. "Come, girl!"

Meat still clamped in its jaws, the dog finally did as it was told. Law's gaze was on the two of them and she suddenly realised what a terrifying sight she must have presented to him then, framed in the doorway against the backdrop of the storm with the strange-looking, skeletal bitch by her side. Alizon could see the fear taking hold of him, and she realised any attempt at helping him was now futile. What's more, there were plenty of familiar faces inside – people who knew all about her family and their magic. Defeated, Alizon stepped back out into the rain. The door swung shut behind her, but not before a wave of suspicious murmuring rolled out.

The morning's events haunted her on the rest of her journey to Trawden, but a fruitful day of begging helped steer her thoughts to happier things. She ate well and still had a good portion to take back to her grandmother, even after sharing some of the pickings with her new canine friend.

Alizon's return to Malkin Tower that evening felt like a triumphant one with her basket so full of goodies. But her joy at the day's success was short-lived when she walked in to find her gran waiting. Those sightless eyes fixed on her with that uncanny ability her gran had of seeming to look at a person through the blindness, and the old woman uttered two short sentences which sent a chill through Alizon's flesh.

"Oh, lass. What have you done?"

CHAPTER
TWENTY-NINE

Through Tibb's eyes, she had seen it all. The argument over the pins, the appearance of the dog now nuzzling at her hands, and the collapse of Law, followed by the incident in The Greyhound Inn. And it was the incident in the inn that troubled Demdike the most. For she had looked on after Alizon had left and heard the people of Colne whispering into Law's ear and muttering over their tankards. Scrying had proved fruitless once again but her familiar had come with more of his warnings and now she had seen for herself, and she was afraid.

"What do you mean, Gran?" Alizon asked, the fear contagious and causing her granddaughter's voice to shake.

"It was a mistake to go to the inn, child. Law is now paranoid of the hold he has been assured you have over him, and if he didn't believe you had bewitched him before, he most certainly does now. This is not the last we have seen of him."

"I was only trying to help him," the girl sobbed. "I didn't mean for any of this to happen, Gran, I swear!"

"I know, lass. Hush now, the damage is already done. Tomorrow I will travel to Colne and see what can be done to give him back his strength, before he gets it into his head to go to Nowell."

"No, it's too dangerous for you out there in this weather! We can ask Mam and James to go with me."

She shook her head. "The pedlar's condition continues to deteriorate even as we speak. I will go to him. But enough of this for tonight. My stomach has not ceased its gurgled demands for food all day long – let us enjoy our evening pottage and forget John Law till the morrow."

And so they did. But when morning came, it brought fresh troubles. The winds had whipped into a greater frenzy through the night and brought even worse conditions for travelling, especially for one of her advanced years. That alone might not have been enough to deter Demdike from visiting the pedlar herself, but she awoke weak with fever and barely able to leave the bed, never mind the cottage.

"I am here, Mistress," Tibb said, appearing by the bedside. "And there is still much you need to see, for the worst is yet to come."

"What could be worse than the scaremongering from the men who already witnessed Alizon at the inn yesterday?"

"News of the incident has reached Baldwin's ears. He too intends to pay Law a visit and now battles the weather, even as we speak. I told you we should have dealt with him when we had the chance."

"You may be right, Tibb," she answered wearily. "But we did not, and here we are. Take me to the inn, so I might hear what Baldwin has to say."

"I warn you now, it is nothing good. You know he has

been whispering in Nowell's ear for the past three years and 'tis only lack of evidence which has stayed the hand of the Justice. Our enemies move against us, and their next move rests on the words of that man. He goes to convince Law to testify, just as he did with Towneley."

"Killing Baldwin now will only create more trouble, so what would you have me do?"

"Prepare for the worst. Come, see for yourself."

She left her body for his and he took her directly to the inn, where Law now lay bedridden in one of the rooms upstairs. The pedlar did not look well at all. One half of his face drooped slightly, the muscles seemingly unresponsive, and his lips appeared to be mouthing something in a fashion similar to Chattox. But only wordless sounds passed across his tongue. His limbs still looked to be limp and useless and the half expression he bore on the other side of his face spoke of nothing but pain and terror. There was no doubt as to the level of torment he had been trapped in.

Baldwin did not take long to appear at the inn. Either he had to have been staying in the area on some official business, or news had travelled fast enough to reach his ears the previous night and he'd risen early. He wasted no time in going straight to Law's room.

"John," he said, walking in and closing the door.

Law looked at Baldwin and his mouth continued to move, but the words continued to elude him.

Maybe it is not as bad as you thought, Demdike said. *If Law cannot speak then how can he give evidence against our Alizon? Nowell still lacks what he needs to drag us before the assizes.*

Baldwin is a desperate man, Tibb answered. *Do not under-*

estimate him. We both know he is not above falsifying the evidence they need. All it takes is a quick statement claiming Law confided in him before he was robbed of his speech, and they will come for Alizon as they did James. And do not forget the son. He will be sent for in due course, leaving Baldwin free to whisper in his ear as well. Your fates are now tied to the Law family. The future has come to a fork in the road, and which route it takes all depends on the men here in this room, along with Law Junior.

"You poor man," Baldwin said with false sympathy. "I hear you had a run-in with Alizon Device yesterday. Did she do this to you?"

Law tried again to speak, and failed.

"My apologies, I can see you need your rest. I will pray to God and ask that He might see fit to restore your strength, or at least your speech, so we may take action against the evil of the witches. If Alizon has bewitched you we must send word to my friend Roger Nowell, the Justice of the Peace in these parts. I will see to it that the witches are brought to justice for you, my friend, and that your family may never have to live in fear of them again. But rest now. I shall be back to check on you later."

I have seen enough, Tibb, she said as Baldwin left the room. *I think we both know this man is the victim of a curse, but not one of Alizon's making. And I think we can both guess who is responsible.*

The events around his bewitching are clouded to me, but yes, I believe your rival and her familiar are to blame. What would you have me do?

I think our best hope is to remove the curse, or failing that, we will have to be more convincing in our efforts to persuade the Laws that our Alizon is innocent of this crime. But I have seen enough for now. I need to return to my own body and recover my strength. Keep watching for me, Tibb, and let me know of anything else that happens.

Your time for revenge is running out, he warned. *We should strike soon, or our enemies will win and you will hang.*

But he did as she asked, staying with Law while she concentrated on recovering from her sickness. Alizon was waiting for her when she returned to her own body.

"Is it bad, Gran?" her granddaughter asked, holding another cup of herbal tea to Demdike's cracked lips.

"I won't lie to you, lass," she answered, taking a sip and grimacing at the bitter taste of it. "The pedlar is gravely ill and the finger is being pointed our way. But do not lose hope yet. With luck, this sickness will pass overnight, then I will journey to Colne and put this right."

The next morning they found the weather to be much more settled, though the same could not be said of Demdike's illness. She still felt weak and feverish, confining her to the bedroom for a second day running. By the third day she began to regain her strength, but it was already too late to cure the pedlar before his son was contacted.

Abraham Law received a letter detailing his father's condition, and by then it was only a matter of time before he made the journey over from Halifax. Events had been set in motion, and Law was watched day and night by all those in Nowell's pocket. The best Demdike could do was to continue to watch the events unfold and prepare for Abraham's arrival. She tried to remain optimistic that he would be more willing to listen to her than men like Baldwin and Hargrieves, but the more conversations she overhead between the gentry, the more she began to despair. Nowell had no shortage of influential allies. There was one in particular who seemed to have been in talks with him over the 'witch problem' for the past few months, and she cursed herself for not seeing it sooner.

"I am as keen to see the witches executed as you are," Sir Thomas Gerard said. "But what makes you think this time will be any different?"

"Alizon Device was seen to have followed Law into the inn by an entire roomful of people, and his condition has only deteriorated since," Nowell answered. "We finally have the evidence we've been waiting for, Sir Thomas. Even if Law Senior cannot testify himself, we have no shortage of witnesses this time, and I am sure we can rely on his son to press charges."

"Let us hope so, for both our sakes. Lord knows I could do with gaining fresh favour with the King after that nasty business with the gunpowder plot tarnished my family's good name. I wrote to Abraham as you asked, so I would expect him to arrive at Colne soon."

"Successfully trying and executing a group of witches will be beneficial for us all. My family's name could also stand to be polished after the recent accusations against my son, but there is a good chance those allegations will be forgotten in the midst of the excitement we are about to stir up. The witches have been causing a great deal of unrest in our communities for far too long now. Folk will come forward when they realise we have the power to combat their magic. You will see, soon enough."

Demdike almost had Tibb strike the men down there and then upon hearing those words, consequences be damned. There they were discussing how a witchcraft case could help them climb higher up the social ladder, with not a care for the lives they would have to take along the way! Was her Alizon nothing to these people? Her innocent granddaughter who had never so much as given anyone a cold through the craft, let alone something as serious as Law's condition. But she had to remind herself there was a reason she had not acted sooner, and she had to keep her faith that her plan could work.

Even more worrying than the gentry was the visitor who stopped by The Greyhound Inn the night before Law's son arrived. The pedlar's true tormentor appeared at his bedside and once again Demdike knew fear. There was no hiding their presence from Fancie.

Tibb was quick to take a defensive stance, fangs bared in a warning snarl as he eyed their rival. But Fancie merely laughed.

"We both know you cannot defeat me alone, Tibb. Spare yourself the pain – let me carry out my business here and you may both leave unharmed."

Tibb growled but made no move to attack the other spirit. Demdike could feel his need to protect both herself and her kin, and the frustration at knowing Fancie was right – whatever the demon was up to, there was nothing they could do to stop him without the aid of Ball and Dandy. And even with that ability the spirits had to simply appear anywhere they wished, by the time they'd called for the other two hellhounds it was going to be too late. The damage would already be done.

Fancie was completely ignoring them now, his focus upon the pedlar as he bent over him and whispered into his ear.

"Easy now, Master Law," the demon said. "Be free to speak your fears to Abraham when he visits tomorrow, and be sure to tell him how you have been tormented with

Alizon Device ever since your ill-fated meeting last week, and how your pains continue. But remember nothing of me, the strange man by your bedside who relieves some of your symptoms so that your tormentor might be brought to justice."

"You varlet!" Demdike snarled through Tibb's jaws. He happily surrendered the use of his tongue so that she might voice her anger, though they both knew attempting to reason with the demon would ultimately achieve nothing. "Was it not enough you killed my daughter's husband? Or forced me to give up my sight to save Jennet? Alizon is innocent in all this. Must she pay for my mistakes? Has Chattox really become so consumed by hate that she would harm those I love just to take revenge upon me?"

"She has wanted you all dead for some time now, though that is not my only reason for meddling on this occasion. This is bigger than the petty rivalry of mortals, if only you were not so blinded by your own struggles to see it."

Demdike would have frowned if she had been in her own body. She had sought to see beyond the 'petty rivalry' they were entangled in, but her attempts to scry the future had shown her little of real consequence. If the demon was telling the truth, why had she not been able to glean even a hint of what was to come?

"What game are you playing, Fancie?"

"You will see."

And with that, the demon vanished, leaving them to watch as fate took another step down the path leading to the gallows. Law screamed, and there came the sounds of boots thundering up the stairs. Baldwin burst through the door with two other men at his side, as if they were expecting to find Alizon somehow returned without them noticing and working more black magic on her 'victim'.

"John?" Baldwin said. "What is it?"

Law locked eyes with Baldwin and his jaws worked soundlessly for a moment. Finally he managed "I thought someone was just here with me." The words were slow at leaving his lips and seemed to cost him a great deal of effort to form. On his good hand, the fingers grasped at the bedsheets and clutched as though to distract himself from the agony of his curse.

"You can speak! Our prayers have been answered."

"No," Law rasped, both sides of his face creased in pain now. "I still languish under the witch's spell. Day after day I hear you talk to me of the power of Alizon Device and her family and I fear now your suspicions were correct."

Triumph flashed in Baldwin's eyes. "There is no doubt about it. Will you come with me to the Justice?"

"I am too weak. My son... I must speak with my son and find a way to return to Halifax, away from these witches."

"Your son has been sent for and will be here any day now, I am sure. What if I ask Roger to come visit you here; will you speak to him then?"

"Let me speak to my son first."

"As you wish." Baldwin did an admiral job of keeping his voice neutral, but Demdike could see the frustration burning beneath the false calm he struggled to maintain.

This is not good, Tibb. How am I to relieve this man of the torment Chattox and Fancie have placed him in now? He will likely tell his son of his fears the moment the lad gets here, and I doubt Abraham will want any of us near him once he has heard his father's side of the story.

All is not lost yet, Tibb answered. *Look.*

Her familiar gazed ahead at that dangerous path fate

was currently set on, and together they watched a brief vision of a man she did not recognise, but who she assumed was Law Junior. The vision began with him on the road to Colne, quickly changing into the image of him standing over his father, and finally altering to a scene in more familiar surroundings as he knocked on the door of Malkin Tower and confronted Alizon. Demdike felt a surge of hope. The son was open to their help after all.

What of Fancie's riddles? Do you know of what he alluded to just now?

I know no more than you, Tibb said. *Much of the future remains clouded to me now, and that which I have seen is not very illuminating. But I can tell you that Abraham will arrive tomorrow.*

The vision gave way to the inside of her home, and a moment later the world was hidden behind the milky shroud Fancie had placed over her eyes. Demdike spent the rest of the night gathering her tools, ready for the visit to Colne the next day, but she was back in the inn with Tibb long before Abraham was due to come knocking at their door.

Baldwin was there to greet the cloth-dyer from Halifax the moment he entered The Greyhound, brandishing the letter he'd been sent and demanding to be taken to his father without delay.

"You must be Abraham. My name is Richard Baldwin, miller of Wheathead and steward of the Church. Allow me to show you up to your father's room, but be warned: a terrible evil is upon him which may cause quite a shock. You should prepare yourself for the horror of his sickness."

"Yes, yes, the letter was quite informative. I would see him with my own eyes now."

"Of course. But there is something else you should know – we fear this is the work of witches. By the grace of God your father has been allowed his speech back, but their hold on him is still strong. He was unfortunate to cross paths with the granddaughter of the blackest of hags in these parts – Old Demdike of Malkin Tower. Perhaps you have heard of her?"

Abraham came to a stop and eyed the other man as if he was trying to decide whether to believe him. "And why would a Lancashire witch curse my father? They have no quarrel with our family."

"I am sure your father will tell you the particulars, but ask any man who was in The Greyhound on that fateful day and they will confirm Alizon Device was here."

"Then let us not waste any more time. Take me to him and let me hear his side of the story, so we may learn the truth of these fanciful tales."

Baldwin did as Abraham asked, closing the door behind him on his way out to give the illusion of privacy. But with Tibb's senses Demdike saw and heard all. The miller's heart pounded with excitement from the other side of the wood. He was also eavesdropping.

"Father! Is it true what they say? Are you bewitched?"

Law reached up with his good hand and grasped his son's shirt. "My body feels as though it is pricked with knives, elsons and sickles, son. 'Tis the same hurt which was done at Colne Field after meeting with a young beggar." Law grimaced and fell back, his expression settling into regret. "She demanded some of my pins, and when I told her no she threatened me with her curses, and oh how I wish now that I had listened and given her what she wanted, my son. But I did not want to waste time opening my pack for items she clearly had not the money for, and so

I carried on until a strange dog ran out in front of me and I fell down lame."

"Who is this girl? If this has been done to you through witchcraft then it can be undone, and I will not rest until she is found and has removed this curse."

"Alizon Device."

"The same name I hear from the man who brought me up to you. You are sure?"

"The men round these parts say she is Alizon Device, known witch practised in the blackest of magic."

"Then she will come here at once and relieve you of this great pain she has placed you in, even if I have to drag her all the way myself. Rest now, Father, and find some peace in knowing this will all be over soon."

"Please hurry. Ever since that meeting I have been troubled day and night with this Alizon Device, suffering in my waking hours and yet unable to sleep. For every time I close my eyes she is there, and she does lie upon me when I would rest and recover my strength, until my pains grow stronger and I awake screaming in great distress."

"She will be with us before the day is through, I swear it."

Demdike watched the man stride from the room, confronting Baldwin on his way out and demanding to know where he might find her granddaughter. She waited until she was sure he was on his way, then returned to her own body once more.

"What news now, Gran?" Alizon asked, her voice full of anxiety.

"Abraham Law is on his way. Fear not, lass. He is desperate to find a cure for his father, and I will do whatever it takes to give him one."

Alizon went quiet, but Demdike heard a small whimper

escape her granddaughter's lips. She reached out to pat the girl's hand, wishing there was more she could do to reassure Alizon all would be well.

It felt like a long wait for the knock at the door. Alizon jumped up to answer it. Demdike began to feel her way over as well, but age and blindness slowed her.

"Alizon Device?" came Abraham's voice.

"Yes. Can I help you?"

"You bewitched my father. I ask you now to come with me and unbewitch him, so I can take him home to Halifax where he can recover from this ordeal without further fear of your wicked ways."

Demdike finally reached the door. "We will of course help your father, but my granddaughter is young and inexperienced. You would do well to take me in her stead for I have seen similar curses in my many years and I know how to remove it."

"No," Abraham said, in a voice that indicated the subject was not open to debate. "Your granddaughter did this, and now she will undo it."

"Then at least let me come and help her undo it."

"No! I will not have you causing more harm while he lies there helpless and suffering, you who I have just been told are known as Old Demdike, most wicked of witches in Lancashire! Stay back, demon woman, or I will be forced to call on the authorities."

Despair engulfed her. *What can we do, Tibb? You and I both know Alizon has not the power to drive out Fancie's curse upon the pedlar. How do we avoid another trip to Read Hall?*

There is nothing to be done, Tibb answered. *Let her go with the man and be seen to try helping him – it may help her case if the Laws do go to Nowell.*

"Very well," she said aloud, with a sigh of resignation. "But if you change your mind, you know where to find me."

"But, Gran, I don't—" Alizon started to protest.

"Go on, lass, take the basket I prepared last night and perform the healing rites I have taught you. All will be well, fear not."

"No more delays," Abraham growled. "My father has suffered long enough – come!"

Doubt filled Alizon as she walked with Abraham to Colne, despite her grandmother's parting words. She was reminded of the previous incident with Isobell, except this time there was no James to come to her rescue.

They reached The Greyhound and Abraham led the way inside. Her heart pounded as she stepped in after him, afraid of what she would find there. From what little her gran had told her, Law Senior's condition had been worsening with each passing day. How was she to cure him when the workings of black magic remained a mystery?

The main drinking room was full of men. She felt their eyes on her as she followed Abraham up the stairs, her own gaze fixed firmly on the stone beneath her feet. A group of them trailed after her, and her unease grew.

More followed, lining the stairs and the corridor between rooms. Yet more had already taken up position in the bedroom the pedlar had been given, crowding round his bed in their excitement to see what would happen when she was confronted with her supposed crime.

"Out of the way!" Abraham snarled, pushing his way through. "Make space for the witch so she can rid my father of her evil."

The crowd parted and Alizon raised her eyes to the bed. Never before had she seen a face so twisted in pain. One hand clutched at the blanket he was wrapped in, while the other lay stiff and useless across his chest. Their gazes met, and she looked into eyes filled with torment. She fell to her knees, all hope lost.

"Forgive me, Master Law, but I know not how to cure you," she cried.

"Do not lie to us, girl!" Abraham said. "You bewitched my father after he denied you the pins you begged of him, and now you will unbewitch him! It is no secret you are a witch; do not think you can trick us into believing otherwise."

"My family are all cunning folk, yes, but it is as my gran said – this is beyond my skill to heal. Please, I beg your forgiveness, but there is nothing I can do!"

"Then go," the pedlar answered her with such weariness, she found herself wishing with all her heart that there was something she could do for him.

"I am sorry," she whispered.

"You are forgiven. Go." He closed his eyes as if in acceptance of his grim fate.

Alizon got back to her feet, wanting nothing more than to flee the scene before she could be blamed for anything else. But it was more than that. Male eyes continued to gaze with lustful hunger. She knew all too well what they were capable of when they gathered in such numbers. She knew what evils were often done to a woman on her own, defenceless against such a mob. And she knew that, far from the pleasurable experience it was supposed to be with the man she had chosen, it would bring nothing but pain and a deep shame, such as no woman should ever have to feel. So she kept her head down and tried not to make eye contact, and began to make her way out of the room.

"Do not think this is over, Alizon Device!" Abraham called after her. "If you will not undo this vile curse then you will pay for your crimes, one way or another! This does not end here."

She sobbed and ran for the stairs, her fear growing when she heard Baldwin speak up. The miller did not bother to keep his voice down, and she could clearly hear him as he said "Perhaps it is time we went to the JP? I promise you he will take the allegations against the girl very seriously, and you will have the full support of the law in this matter. I understand the fear of what the witches might do in retaliation for giving evidence against one of their own. But rest assured, there is little they can do to you once in gaol, where there are no tools for working their wicked magic."

"Very well, Richard," Abraham answered. "I will come with you to press charges against the witch, and pray that the fear of the noose will change her mind about removing this curse."

Anything else was lost in the thundering of Alizon's own heartbeat and the great sobs racking her body as she reached the bottom of the stairs. But at least none of the men had tried to grab her. It was perhaps only a small mercy, yet one she was inherently grateful for nevertheless.

The next day, she had barely had chance to complete her morning routine when another knocking came at the door. Alizon felt a fresh pang of fear. She looked over at her gran, but the old woman was struggling to rise from her stool, as though the aches of her years were especially bad that day. Swallowing, Alizon crept over to the door and reached for the handle with a shaking hand. There came more knocking before she had the chance to open it, loud and angry and accompanied by the rumble of voices. Her heart thundered in her chest, and she hesitated, almost paralysed with fear now. A third round of knocking came, with such force the door shook. She shrank back.

"We know you're in there!" the voice of Constable Hargrieves yelled. "This is your last chance – open the door or we're going to have to break it down."

"Do as he says, Alizon," her gran said.

She glanced back, more terrified than she had been in the inn. Her gran was still several steps away from the door, and there was a tremble to the wizened limbs Alizon hadn't noticed before. Time looked to finally be taking its toll. Alizon suddenly felt very small and insignificant then. If the great Demdike could be made so frail and old, what hope was there for any of them?

Her gran's voice grew sharper. "Do it, Alizon. Open the door."

An involuntary whimper escaped Alizon's lips, but she did as her gran bid her. She opened the door to a sea of angry faces with Hargrieves at its head – a mob similar to the one which had come for her brother two years previously. Her vision swam and her legs began to wobble, and she had to cling to the door to keep her balance.

"Alizon Device, you are to come to Read Hall for questioning," Hagrieves growled. "If you resist, we will take you by force."

Her gran's warm presence could finally be felt behind her. "Go with them, lass." A gnarled hand grasped her shoulder. Was she imagining it, or was that familiar grip weaker than usual? "I promise you all will be well."

Alizon didn't dare look away from the mob. "But I was not the one to bewitch Master Law, I swear it!"

"We have no other choice, Alizon," her gran whispered in her ear. "I want you to go with them and blame me for everything."

"No!" she cried, turning to her gran in horror. "Then they will arrest you as well!"

"Trust me, lass. Tell them I am to blame for everything that has happened, and tell them of my pact with Tibb."

"No more talking!" Hargrieves barked. "The girl is coming with us and an old crone like you can do nothing to stop it, witch or no."

Rough hands grabbed at Alizon and pulled her outside. She looked back at her gran one last time, fresh tears rolling down her cheeks. Anger flashed in her grandmother's eyes, anger and a great reluctance to stand back and let events take their course. Was there defeat there or was that just Alizon's fear talking? No, they were defeated, Alizon felt sure of it then. How could she give up her gran to save herself? The old woman would never survive gaol. Alizon couldn't do that to her, no matter how irritating looking after her had become.

The door closed and Alizon's terror grew. The sheer hopelessness at how impossible her situation was filled her – one she'd been so unfairly dragged into. Law had forgiven her, so why was she being arrested? Her gran had confirmed it – she hadn't done anything wrong!

Jeers and catcalls rang out as the mob marched her to Read Hall. Any fear or respect the people of Pendle had once shown vanished at the sight of her helplessness in the constable's firm grasp. She was soon trembling before the Justice of the Peace, eyes red from crying and arms bruised where the men's fingers had dug into her flesh. But Nowell seemed oblivious to her fears and sorrows, or perhaps he simply did not care.

"Alizon Device," he said. "You are accused–"

"It wasn't me!" she cried.

"A room full of people saw you at the inn where the pedlar sought rest from the pain you had brought upon him. I have already heard from his son and I will speak to the man himself when he is well enough to talk with me. So you can see that the evidence is stacking against you. But if you co-operate with me now, then I promise we will show you more mercy than you have given them. So, will you confess to the bewitching of John Law?"

"I never did anything to harm Master Law, even after he refused to sell me any pins, and I have nothing to confess. Perhaps you should be talking to Old Chattox and her family – she murdered my father! And I have seen them making clay images to harm others. Maybe that's how she bewitched Master Law."

"And why would Chattox bewitch the pedlar? It was you who he argued with."

"You will have to ask her that. I don't pretend to know the minds of witches. My family are cunning folk devoted to the white arts of healing and divination, nothing more."

"Indeed? Then we have a problem, Alizon Device. You see, this is not the story given to me by Abraham Law after he took you to his father yesterday and you failed to heal the poor man. He tells me that not only is his father convinced you are the source of his torment, but you were also seen to fall to your knees and confess to your crime, and then ask forgiveness."

"No! I went with Abraham to see if I could do anything for his father, but the curse placed upon him is beyond my skill to heal. So I begged forgiveness. I never confessed to being the one to place the curse on him, for it was not my doing."

The JP fixed her with a piercing stare. She was given the feeling he was examining her very soul, and she was forced to look away.

Her gaze roamed over the grand furniture and the ornate rug beneath her feet, so very different from the simplicities of her gran's humble home. How could he ever understand the struggles of her family when they lived worlds apart?

"What about the strange animal you were seen with," he said, his eyes still boring into her own. "Perhaps you can tell me about your familiar spirit and how he might have been the one to work the black magic on your behalf?"

She kept her gaze on the rug, studying its patterns and intricacies. Nowell must be fishing for anything incriminating, she decided. Alizon wondered if anyone had even told him about the bitch she had come to adopt on the road to Trawden. Or was he simply going by the limited knowledge of familiar spirits gleaned from other witchcraft cases he had read or heard about?

"I have no familiar," she answered. "And I have nothing more to say."

"Then you leave me no choice but to have you searched for the witch's mark, so we might get to the truth of this matter and bring justice to the Laws; little comfort though that may be after the terrible spell you have placed upon

Law Senior. This is your last chance to confess and save yourself the ordeal I am forced to put you through."

"I have nothing to confess," she insisted, trying to stay strong but feeling fresh dread at what was coming next. She'd heard the stories of what Christians did to suspected witches.

"Very well," Nowell said, then raised his voice to summon two of his men into the study, both of whom had been a part of the mob. Alizon couldn't help but flinch. They strode in and grabbed her a second time, holding her firm.

First Nowell pulled at her hair, searching between the strands for the mark he was convinced he would find on her body, the one which would prove her guilt without a doubt. She froze at his cruel touch and desperately tried to imagine this was her John, finally showing her the love and physical affection she craved from him. They were back at Moss End Farm, hiding away from the world in the barn used for storage.

A cry tore from her lips when a particularly painful tug brought her back to the inside of Nowell's study. Evidently the JP had found nothing incriminating hidden beneath her hair, because his hands moved round to trace the smooth skin of her face and neck.

He gripped her chin and forced her to tilt her head backwards and then to either side. Again Alizon tried to retreat to the barn. Her lips were pressed to John's with the passion of their desire, manifesting in the way he tore at her dress in his desperation to explore the flesh beneath.

Material ripped and her bare breasts spilled out. *It's **John**,* she told herself. *It's just John showing his true feelings for me.*

But John would never have squeezed with such

violence. The pressure proved too much. It broke the fragile fantasy as though it were no more than a thin layer of ice, and the loving face of the yeoman's son turned into the harsh features of this so called 'Justice' once more.

That was not all the pain broke. Alizon's chest felt tight, her stomach a vile ball of nausea and her body suffering from the shakes. But she was no longer frozen.

"No!" she screamed, kicking and wriggling in a desperate bid to free herself. Yet no matter how hard she fought, there was no escaping the humiliation they were subjecting her to. The men's grip only strengthened around her arms, too powerful for her to break out of.

Nowell became a monster far worse than any malevolent spirit then. His hands ripped through more of her clothes with all the ease of a beast's claws. Soon the rest of her flesh was exposed and her modesty lay in tatters. But simply looking over her naked body was not a degrading enough punishment for the depravity of the men she found herself up against. Nowell continued to grab and grope, hunting for any marks that might have been hidden in the crease of her skin or a cluster of body hair.

When he reached her groin, she felt him deliberately brushing his fingers against the smooth flesh between her legs as his hand roamed back and forth, dancing to the music of her pleas for him to stop. Mocking laughter was all she received from the men holding her. Somehow that made her ordeal all the worse and brought more tears streaming down her cheeks. And it was then, through the watery veil blurring her vision, that she saw the hellhound once again.

He announced his presence with a thunderous growl, his form made huge by the hackles raised on his back. Fury blazed in his fiery eyes, wild and savage. The men seemed weak and unimportant in comparison, their fragile human bodies vulnerable to those vicious teeth and the crushing force of his jaws. He who was vengeance given shape, this spirit who had already chosen her before she had even attempted to seek out a familiar and make the pact, and who now fought for her when no others would.

Alizon looked at the hellhound with confusion. She felt like a dense fog had settled over her mind, making thoughts hard to form and even harder to grasp. Somewhere within that fog a voice was screaming danger. But why? He looked to be on her side.

The voice was so persistent that she found herself attempting to call the spirit off with a terrified scream of "No!"

It was too late. The hellhound was already mid leap.

He landed beside one of the men holding her and clamped his maw around a leg, his fangs shredding the flesh with bestial rage. And yet none of the men reacted to the sudden appearance of the spirit. It was as if he was only visible to her with the aid of her inner eye, even though she had not yet been allowed to complete the rite which should have been required to open it. Only when those wicked fangs sank into the man's flesh, and a shriek of pain tore from his throat, did Nowell and the other man fall back with cries of alarm.

The injured man fell to the floor, his leg apparently now useless. Blood welled from the horrific wound and spilled all over the limb, soaking through his trousers and pooling on the floor beneath.

Alizon's gaze locked with the creature's and she shook her head. The hellhound whined like any mortal dog after being reprimanded, then he was simply gone. Her third eye seemed to have closed again: the man's leg was no longer a bloody mess to her earthly sight, though it seemed no less painful and every bit as lame as a moment before.

"Was this your doing?" Nowell demanded, indicating the injured man.

She turned her gaze from where the hellhound had been standing to the wicked man in front of her. His words had been clear enough, but she couldn't seem to make sense of them then. Her eyes were wide with shock, her mind clouded by it. She could only stand and stare as the tears continued to flow down her cheeks.

"Has your own curse struck you mute? Answer me, girl!"

Curse? Her gran was the only one in their family who knew about curses. Her gran, who she'd been told to blame everything on...

Perhaps it was because her thoughts were all muddled that she uttered her next words. Or maybe that same part of her to recognise the fresh danger the hellhound brought had now accepted it was her only chance at escape. But having her gran's blessing made it no less difficult to incriminate her own family. It felt nothing less than a betrayal of one she loved, and if she'd been thinking clearly, she would never have spoken the words at all. But she was not, and so she said "It was my gran."

"Your gran?" Nowell answered in disbelief, sitting himself back down at his desk and picking up his quill.

"Yes."

She shifted uncomfortably as he stared at her, but not from being naked. Alizon was too dazed now to bother attempting to cover herself up. It was the intensity of those eyes, searching her skull for her innermost thoughts. She truly believed he could read her mind then. There was no hiding from this monster, an idea which filled her with a new bout of fear.

"Tell me about your gran," Nowell prompted.

The words came flooding out.

"They call her Old Demdike, but her real name is Elizabeth Southerns. She's the only one in our family who knows about curses and black magic."

"So this," he said, indicating the injured man still lying on the floor, "is your gran's doing?"

"Yes. She's been advising to let a familiar appear to me. She said if I let him suck at a part of my body, he would see to it that I had everything I wanted and could do anything I wished. But I told her no, I did not want to make a deal with any spirit, and so she has been sending her own familiar in the form of a thing like unto a black dog. That is what injured this man's leg and attacked Master Law after he sturdily refused me the pins I asked for."

Alizon could not say where these words came from. Was it a fanciful tale taking shape in her own imagination, or was something else guiding her tongue? She did not know, but once she'd started, she couldn't stop.

"So now you are telling me your gran is to blame for bewitching the pedlar?"

"Yes. And the cow at Bullhole, after she'd gone blind. She promised to heal it and had me lead her there about ten o'clock that night. I left her for about half an hour, yet what she did in that time I cannot tell. But the next morning I heard the cow was dead, and I think it was Gran who bewitched it to death."

"I see. And are there any other crimes committed by your family that you would like to report?"

"Only that of the falling out with Richard Baldwin of Wheathead and the bewitching of his child, about two years ago now. It was four or five days after the argument when she asked me to lead her to their land. We left her for about an hour before my sister fetched her back in. The next morning, I heard one of Baldwin's daughters had fallen sick, and I then heard that she languished for about a year and died."

"And you believe that was your gran's revenge against Baldwin?"

"Just after the falling out, I heard her say that she would pray for Baldwin still and loud, and I then heard her curse Baldwin several times."

Nowell rubbed his temples. "And what of these claims against Anne Whittle, alias Old Chattox. You say she murdered your father?"

Alizon frowned, struggling with the change of subject.

"You accused Anne Whittle of witchcraft," Nowell said. "You mentioned the murder of your father and causing harm with clay images."

"Yes. My father was afraid of Old Chattox, so he made a deal to pay her a measure of meal every year if she would do him and his goods no harm, until he died eleven years ago. And he said to me on his deathbed that Chattox had bewitched him to death because he did not pay the meal that last year."

"I see. And who else do you think she has cursed?"

Again the words began to flow. The mist over her mind was clearing somewhat and thinking grew a little easier.

"Hugh Moore, after he accused her of cursing his cattle. He languished for about half a year before he died, and I heard he accused Chattox on his deathbed, just as my dad did.

"Then there was Anthony Nutter's daughter. I was visiting when Chattox came to call. She saw us laughing and said we laughed at her, and she said 'I will be meet with the one of you', and my friend became sick the next day and died three weeks after that.

"And one more death I know her to have caused: a child of John Moore. And during the time of his languishing, I saw Chattox sitting in her own garden with a picture of clay in her apron, which she hid when she saw me passing by. And when I told my mam this story, she thought that it was the picture of John Moore's child and the reason for his illness.

"And so I tell you, sir, that she is a murderer and a witch, and is far more deserving of your justice than any other in these parts."

"That is for the assize judges to decide, but I thank you for giving me this evidence. Had you started to talk sooner, we might have avoided all that unpleasantness," he said, again gesturing towards the hellhound's victim, who was still on the floor, clutching his leg and groaning in pain.

"May I go now?"

"I think not. Master Robinson, take Miss Device to her temporary lodging and find her some fresh clothes. Then do something about that fool writhing round on my floor, will you? Take him to a physician if he won't stop his moaning."

"Yes, Roger," Robinson answered, grabbing Alizon by the arm once again. She flinched at his touch, but submitted when he began to drag her out of the study.

She was pushed into a small room with little more than a bed inside. There came the sound of the door being locked behind her and retreating footsteps, and Alizon collapsed to the bed, alone with her fears and her doubts. Shivers racked her naked flesh. She drew the blankets around her body and covered herself as best she could, until Robinson returned with more clothes.

Only when she heard the sound of his footsteps fading did she feel able to trade the safety of the blankets for the new garments. Dressing made her feel no better, however. Her shame was too fresh, her skin crawling with the memory of those awful, groping fingers. She tried to think about anything but the events of the morning, yet always her mind returned to the search for the witch's mark. It made her feel dirty. She started to think she would confess to bewitching Law if it meant she could go home and bathe in the river. But she knew Nowell would never agree to that.

Her gran's promise that all would be well was beginning to feel less and less likely. They would arrest her grandmother next and question her about the evidence she'd just given them, Alizon was certain of it. But if her gran thought to save her from the assizes by taking the blame for everything, it looked like the old woman had underestimated the JP in that respect. Perhaps Nowell simply hadn't believed her story, or maybe he felt there was still sufficient evidence to take her to trial. Either way, her chances of escape were beginning to seem increasingly slim.

THIRTY-ONE

Demdike did not have to wait long before she too was arrested and brought to Read Hall. It was only a matter of hours before the constable was back at her door.

"Elizabeth Southerns, alias Old Demdike, you are under arrest for suspected witchcraft," Hargrieves said.

"Constable," she answered. "I've been expecting you."

He was quiet for a moment, as though she'd unnerved him. There was a touch of fear to his voice when he addressed the men he'd brought to assist with taking her to the JP.

"Take no risks with this one! Grab her before she can start casting any curses."

She felt strong fingers wrap around her wrists.

"Unhand me, Master Robinson, or I *will* curse you."

"How does she know it's me?" Robinson asked. He sounded on the verge of panic.

The pressure on her limb receded, and she continued "I will come willingly."

They didn't try to grab her again as she stepped outside

and shut the door behind her. Tibb was by her side, guiding her as best he could without physically manifesting. It was going to be a much longer walk without Alizon to lead her, but better that than allow the men to drag her along.

She faced a similar reaction from her neighbours to the one her granddaughter had received earlier. It saddened her to hear voices like the Nutters of Bullhole crying "How could you, Demdike? We believed in you and your family and now you've proved yourself no better than Old Chattox!"

Others simply shouted "Witch!" but a few yelled "Foul hag! Burn in Hell!" and similar harsh words.

Some threw dirt as she passed, but a warning growl from Tibb soon put a stop to that. It seemed the bewitching of an innocent pedlar was the last they would tolerate. Demdike recognised all the warning signs. People she'd grown up with were developing a thirst for blood, and nothing short of her family dangling from a gibbet would satisfy it. Yet, in spite of their cruel words and actions, she held her head high and guarded her own tongue.

Demdike didn't need sight to tell her when they'd reached Read Hall. The same male servant she'd encountered on her last visit was there to greet them once again. But that was not all. There was an air of anticipation about the place that day – Nowell believed he had already won.

"Another witch," Hargrieves growled to the servant.

"Aye, I know this one well. Only two years have passed since she last darkened this door, though I believe today is under happier circumstances. For the master, anyway."

Demdike could hear the smirk in the servant's voice. Her desire for vengeance reared up. It was with great effort she wrestled it back down.

"In the study," the servant said, showing them through.

"Ah, Constable," Nowell addressed Hargrieves. "I think we had best proceed with the search for the witch's mark before we begin questioning, if you would be so kind as to help."

"Robinson," Hargrieves barked.

"Oh no, I'm not laying another hand on her," Robinson said.

"Search me. I will not fight you," Demdike promised. "But nor will I tell you anything until I have seen my Alizon. If you would see fit to release her, then I will happily give you a full confession to the bewitching of Master Law, and more."

She might as well have been a dog standing before its human masters. Not one of them spoke to her. A set of hands did take hold of her, though. Had Nowell not been so sure of himself and his victory over her family, they probably wouldn't have dared. But she was true to her word and remained standing tall and proud as they subjected her to the same humiliation as her granddaughter.

Demdike made no sounds of protest as she was groped and prodded. Instead she concentrated on her connection with her familiar, and keeping their combined need to retaliate in check. *Not yet, Tibb. Not just yet.*

Nowell began ripping into her dress when a gasp sounded from Robinson. "The stories are true! 'Tis the mark of the Devil!"

"Indeed," the JP answered. "Can I rely on you to fetch the daughter for me, or are you afraid of her, too?"

Demdike reeled backwards as though he'd slapped her. *Elizabeth is here?*

"I'll go." Robinson sounded sullen now.

James as well, Tibb answered. *They were brought in even before you were. I believe Nowell hoped to be able to use them* *as witnesses, but so far your daughter has refused to say anything. He hopes the sight of your ripped clothing will provoke a response from her now. She has been spared that particular torment, however, because of the belief that her disfigurement **is** her witch's mark. James has yet to be questioned.*

Demdike stared at her familiar in shock. The last thing she'd been expecting was the arrest of her daughter and grandson. *What of Jennet?*

I know not of Jennet's whereabouts. Something clouds her from my vision.

That worried her, but she wasn't allowed much time to dwell on it.

"Elizabeth Southerns, do you understand the seriousness of the allegations made against you, by your own granddaughter, no less?" Nowell asked, addressing her at last. "And now we have found further evidence of your involvement with the Devil in the form of this mark his agents have left on your flesh. This is your chance to give me your side of the story and prove your innocence, if that is what you would have me believe."

"I have already told you, Roger Nowell, I will not give you anything until you have shown me Alizon and given your word that she will be released in return for my full confession."

"Madam, I am not sure you do realise the gravity of your situation. That is not how this works. You have no power here and you do not get to make demands; you will answer my questions or I will be forced to hold you indefinitely, along with the rest of your wretched family."

She turned her eyes on the JP but said nothing.

"I will find a way to make you talk, Southerns," Nowell continued, showing no sense of unease at being fixed with her sightless gaze. "Let us see what your daughter has to say to your witch's mark."

Elizabeth was also silent as they marched her in, but Demdike heard her gasp a moment later.

"Elizabeth Device, see the actions I am forced to take when you refuse to co-operate. Here we have proof of your mother's profession as a witch, unless you care to give me some other explanation for this mark upon her skin? A relic of the time she went stark mad for eight weeks after a spirit had visited, perhaps?"

"That was only fourteen years ago! She has had the mark on her side for over forty!"

Demdike closed her eyes, instantly recognising the mistake for what it was. She knew what her daughter meant to say – that the mark had been there for as long as Elizabeth had lived and was not something which had suddenly appeared in the course of Demdike's dealings with spirits. But the old wise woman also knew how Nowell would interpret that statement for the assizes, even if he knew how it was meant as well.

Had it only been fourteen years since the incident they were referring to? It seemed longer. And in that time, it had become the thing of legend amongst the locals, even though she barely remembered the bout of madness herself. No doubt it would come up again over the course of Nowell's interrogations, and she made a mental note to include it in her confession when the time came.

"So you admit your mother has been a witch for at least your forty years on this earth? And perhaps you would like to tell us about the familiar spirit she allowed to suckle on her left side, where this mark appeared?"

The room went silent. Demdike could picture her daughter's mouth hanging open as she stared at the JP, stunned that he had twisted her statement to make it incriminating, rather than the proof of innocence she'd intended it to be. And once that realisation had sunk in, she imagined Elizabeth's lips to have tightened with her unwillingness to speak another word. Nowell attempted to tease more from them to add to his evidence, but her daughter stayed strong and held her tongue.

How long the Justice persisted in his attempts to question them she could not say, but eventually he ordered for them both to be taken away. It would be James's turn next. They were led a short way through the JP's home until they reached a room which her daughter was pushed into. She heard the men lock the door, then she received similar treatment in a separate room a little further down the hall.

Tibb, I need to see what's going on out there.

Of course, he answered, dutiful as ever.

And so she crossed back into the hellhound's skull, and he took her to see first her granddaughter, and then Elizabeth, before returning to Nowell's study. It angered her to see the state Alizon was in, bruised and dishevelled and weeping on the bed, but she had to believe her family would still walk away from this – the alternative was simply too much to bear.

James had not yet been searched for a witch's mark, and having escaped the JP once before, he did not seem particularly concerned to find himself back in for questioning. Demdike could only hope there was some sense left in that arrogant scalp of his – enough to keep him from saying anything stupid, at least. She doubted Nowell had any evidence against her grandson or her daughter, as long as they weren't tricked into confessing.

The JP began with the events surrounding Anne Towneley's death, but her grandson answered much the same as he had two years ago. With Tibb's senses, she could see Nowell had been expecting as much, and he was quick to move on to the real line of questioning.

"Master Device, do you know why you have been arrested again?" the JP asked.

"No," James admitted. "And if you have no further proof against me, then I ask to be allowed to return to work."

"It is in fact because of your sister that I had the constable bring you back here. You see, there have been some very serious accusations made against her and I am simply trying to get to the truth of the matter so justice can be served, as is my duty as Justice of the Peace."

James snorted. "Justice. What justice is there for those of us you wrongly brand witch, when in fact we are on the same side? The cunning folk have always been against witchcraft and could even assist you in hunting down the real witches in these parts, if only you would listen to us. But no, you hear what you want to hear and would rather believe the word of 'good' Christians over our own. What is this blame you now lay at my sister's feet?"

"I am sure you have heard of the incident with John Law by now. His son has been to me with the accusations from his father's own mouth – horrific tales of an innocent traveller struck down by your sister's wicked spell, and left in torment ever since. If your sister is truly innocent in this, perhaps you can tell me why he is so convinced it is she who has bewitched him?"

Demdike felt her grandson's horror as that sunk in. *Move closer, Tibb, so he can see us. Let our presence here give him strength.*

The boy glanced across, his eyes widening in surprise at the sight of them. Relief swept it aside a moment later, and he looked back at Nowell with renewed courage. "My sister has not spoken to me of that incident, but I am sure it was a simple misunderstanding, same as my argument with Mistress Towneley."

"But this is not the first time your sister has lost her temper and struck an innocent down, is it, James? What of the incident with Henry Bulcock and his child – can you tell me anything about that?"

"That was not her doing!"

"Then tell me your version of events."

"It was about Saint Peter's Day last when Henry Bulcock came to my grandmother's house and said that Alizon had bewitched a child of his. He wanted her to go to his home and unbewitch the girl. Master Bulcock had my sister in a mighty fearsome grip and when I saw him dragging her along and the pain and distress he was causing her, I offered to go with them to help. When we got there, she did all she could for the child and assured him of how mistaken he was to blame her for the girl's sickness, which was of natural causes. I do not know if his daughter survived, for I have not had any dealings with the Bulcock family since, but I have not heard tell of the child's death."

Tibb moved around the desk so they could look at what Nowell was writing. Fury filled Demdike to see the JP was not just twisting their statements but had gone a step further, putting entirely different words in her grandson's mouth: 'About Saint Peter's Day last one Henry Bulcock came to the house of Elizabeth Southerns, grandmother to this examinate (James) and said that the said Alizon Device had bewitched a child of his, and desired that she would go with him to his house: which she accordingly did: and thereupon she, the said Alizon, fell down on her knees, and asked the said Bulcock forgiveness, and confessed to him she had bewitched the said child, as this examinate heard his said sister confess unto him this examinate.'

James, not another word! He is using everything we say against us, even that which should be proof of our innocence!

Her grandson's eyes widened again, darkening with the anger rising up with his fear. His hands balled into fists and he clenched his jaw, and for a moment Demdike thought Dandy would manifest and make matters worse.

"Perhaps we should talk about your grandmother. What can you tell me of the familiar she has often been seen with – this thing like unto a black dog?"

James balled his hands tighter and stared stubbornly at the floor, his anger in check. Demdike breathed a sigh of relief. But if dodging the law were as easy as holding their tongues, no witchcraft case would ever have made it to the assizes. She knew they could not hold out forever, and she was going to have to do something if she wanted to see any of her family freed.

Two long days passed in much the same way. Nowell kept the pressure on, interrogating each of them in turn and using their statements against them. Only their ability to communicate through their familiar spirits saved them from falling foul of the JP's traps. Try as he might to trick them into believing members of the family were betraying one another, they were able to see through it.

Demdike feared for Alizon though. Every time she visited her granddaughter in Tibb's body, it was to find the girl in as poor a condition as the first morning of their arrests.

She felt helpless, watching Alizon hug herself and stare at the wall with a haunted, faraway look in her eyes. Tibb had manifested in an attempt to console the girl but Alizon barely seemed to recognise him, and she did not seem to hear the words of comfort they brought.

Most of all, Demdike feared for Jennet. None of their hellhounds were able to locate the girl, and she could not help but worry something evil had befallen her youngest granddaughter. At such a tender age, Jennet was the most vulnerable of them all.

Their familiars alone were not enough to keep Alizon and James from being coerced into answering more of the JP's questions, however, particularly regarding the Chattox clan. Her grandchildren were all too willing to give evidence against the woman who had murdered their father. The one thing they did keep quiet about was Jennet's sickness, lest it lead to the JP finding out about Demdike's deal with Fancie.

But Nowell's attempts to get them to co-operate could only go so far and by the end of the second day he must have realised it would yield no further results, because on the third day he decided to try a new approach.

Demdike had finally slipped into a troubled sleep some-where in the early hours, only to receive a rude awakening not long after dawn when the sound of the door to the room she was being kept in slammed open. She was pulled to her feet and dragged back through the hall, but they were not taking her to the study this time. The caress of a light breeze filled with early morning chill told her she was outside, and she soon guessed she was being moved to another location.

"You can release me now," she said. "I won't run, and I can find my own way as I did from my home to Read Hall."

The men charged with escorting her found great mirth

in that. Any fear they'd had in her curses had been driven out by Nowell's apparent power over her. The fact he'd been able to hold nearly her entire family for two whole days could not be overlooked, and his men were emboldened by it.

The walk was long and arduous in the men's charge. Alizon's guidance had always been slow and gentle, but the men were only concerned with getting Demdike to their destination as quickly as possible. Even with Tibb giving what help he could, it was still a poor substitute for her own eyesight and she stumbled often. Somehow she managed to keep her feet for most of the journey, falling just once.

She cursed as she went down hard, bruising both knees. Laughter encircled her. Still the men did not release her from their grip, and it was only their hold on either arm which saved her from going down on her hands as well. She received no sympathy. They hoisted her back up and pushed onwards, until eventually they reached Ashlar House, home to one of Nowell's many allies.

The JP was already waiting for her inside, and the reason for the change of building soon became clear.

"That's her!" a voice cried, unmistakable as that of her rival, Old Chattox. "She and her devil, Tibb, are the real reason for all these deaths! Truly it is they who have the innocent blood on their hands, for it is they who led me into the darkness of witchcraft and had me make a pact with my own devil, Fancie."

"Anne, you fool," Demdike hissed. "Do you not see what the Justice is doing? He brings me here knowing we will likely argue, and give him more evidence to use against us in the process."

"Ladies," Nowell interrupted. "I think it is clear you are

both guilty of causing harm through witchcraft, for which the punishment is death. I have already given you both numerous chances to co-operate, in return for mercy at the assizes. Am I to understand that of the two of you, Elizabeth Southerns has been a witch the longest, and you are, in fact, her disciple, Anne Whittle?"

"That's right," Chattox answered.

What would you advise now, Tibb?

Nowell has already sent for more witnesses to strengthen his evidence against the two of you, Tibb answered. *If you are to confess, I think it has to be now, before this is allowed to go any further. My vision is still clouded and I cannot promise it will save Alizon as hoped, but I believe your family's situation will only grow more dire if you do not take control of the situation soon. The time for waiting has passed. The time to act is upon us.*

"Enough!" she thundered, her voice filled with such strength that both her enemies appeared to have been struck dumb. "I wish to confess."

Nowell took a moment to recover. "Then by all means, confess."

"Not in front of her. If you want my full confession you shall have it, but not in the hearing of my rival."

"Very well," he replied.

Chattox only laughed at that, even as Demdike heard her being led away. No doubt she thought she had won and expected to be celebrating with Fancie that very evening. But Demdike knew better, and she shook her head at her rival's foolishness. Chattox was too blinded by hate to see what was coming.

"You have your privacy. I am waiting, Southerns."

So she told the Justice everything he wanted to hear, from how she came to be a witch to the argument with Richard Baldwin. She invented a story about how she met

Tibb twenty years ago near a stonepit on her way home from begging and how he offered her anything she desired in return for her soul, which she gave freely.

"He would appear to me sundry times about daylight's gate over the space of the next six years, asking what I would have or do but I answered nay, nothing, for I wanted nothing yet. And so he came to me one Sabbath day in the morning while I slumbered with young Alizon on my knee. In the likeness of a black dog, he was. And he sucked the blood under my left arm, for I was dressed in naught but my smock, when I awakened and called on Jesus to save my child, but had not the power to ask Christ to save myself. The dog then vanished, leaving me almost stark mad for the space of eight weeks."

"I thought your family worshipped the heathen gods of our pagan forefathers, before they were shown the light of Christ?"

"I have worshipped the Goddess and the Horned One but when I felt my granddaughter was threatened, it was to Christ I turned," she insisted, knowing the idea that a witch would ask Jesus to protect an innocent child from the devil she had welcomed in was too attractive for him to dismiss. "But it was Tibb I called on when Richard Baldwin wronged our family by denying us the pay he owed for work my daughter did and throwing us off his land."

And so she related to him the tale of how Baldwin had called them whores and witches and threatened to burn the one of them and hang the other.

"Tibb appeared to me around the next hedge and said 'Revenge thee of him.' To which I bid him revenge thee either of him or his family, and he then vanished from my sight and I have not seen him since."

"And what is the significance of these clay images I keep hearing about?" Nowell asked.

"The speediest way to take a man's life away by witch-craft is to make a picture of clay, like unto the shape of the person you mean to kill, and dry it thoroughly. And when you would have them to be ill in any one place more than another, then take a thorn or pin and prick it in that part of the picture you would so have to be ill, and when you would have any part of the body to consume away, then take that part of the picture and burn it. And when you would have the whole body to consume away, then take the remnant of the picture and burn it, and so the body shall die. But it only works for those who have a familiar spirit."

"I see. Your grandchildren both claim to have seen Anne Whittle making such pictures, along with her daughter, Anne Redferne, her daughter's husband, Thomas Redferne, and their daughter, Marie Redferne. Would you care to shed some more light on these accusations? These are your rivals, after all."

"Yes, I have seen them making clay images. 'Twas about half a year before Robert Nutter of Greenhead died – I went to the house of Thomas Redferne, about midsummer, and there I saw the four of them outside their home with clay pictures as I passed by. Tibb appeared to me then, this time as a black cat, and told me to turn back and do as they do. I asked him what they were doing and he answered they were making three pictures, and so I asked him whose pictures they were. And the spirit told me they were the pictures of Christopher and Robert Nutter of Greenhead, and Robert's wife."

She added a little more to the story about how Tibb had been angry when she'd refused to go back and help, doing her best to give Nowell what he wanted so that he had every reason to arrest her and let the rest of her family go. She also told him of the mischief she'd started to cause the previous year, spoiling ale and having Tibb kill cattle, though she made no mention of her daughter being with her. She even admitted to cursing Baldwin out on the moors nearly three years ago, ensuring the JP had more than enough evidence to take her to the assizes.

"Thank you, you have been most helpful today. I am afraid you will have to be held a while longer, in case any further questions arise, but we are done for now. I will question Anne Whittle next."

She was led away and thrown into one of the vaulted cellars while Chattox took her place. It was far less comfortable than the rooms in Read Hall. A strong smell of damp hung heavy in her nostrils and the air was much cooler on her skin. There she was forced to wait for their fates to be decided as the JP continued building his case against them, still kept apart from the rest of her family who remained at Nowell's home. Nor did she have any further contact with her rival for the rest of the day, and the next day after that. It was not until her second night in Ashlar House had passed, sleepless and uneasy, that she was moved again, this time to a cart, the purpose of which she could guess even without Tibb's help.

Chattox was also brought out. Her rival cursed and threatened them all with the most terrible spells she could think of as they dragged her over and threw her in the back beside Demdike. None of the men were struck down in the time it took to bind her and load her onto their ride to Lancaster. Chattox's performance only drew more laughter.

The two old women had it easy compared to Anne Redferne, however. The younger woman was tethered to the cart by rope and made to walk along behind them with tears streaking down her pale face and pleas for mercy upon her lips. Chattox was incensed by that, and despite their differences, Demdike could not help but feel a measure of sympathy for the woman who, in that moment, was simply a mother trying to do all she could to protect her daughter.

"You vile rantallion!" Chattox screeched, struggling against her fetters like a mad dog twisting and turning at the end of its chain. "You promised her freedom in return for my full confession!"

"Nay, hag, I promised mercy, and so you shall have it. I will see that the judges look at your case with merciful eyes."

"Lies! Where is your justice now, Roger Nowell? You who accuse us of sin and mischief, when you are no better yourself. Your god will punish you for this! He will cast you out and you will burn in the fires of your Christian Hell for all eternity, and we will be there to aid the demons in your suffering. And oh, what delight that shall bring."

Nowell did not reply. He walked alongside them as they began the miserable journey to prison where they would await trial at the assizes, and through Tibb Demdike saw the smugness in his eyes and the sense of triumph in his form. The JP carried himself with such pride that she almost wished Chattox's curses had delivered the promised torments. But Demdike's mood was not one of utter despair or bitter sorrow. For she was, in fact, right where she had wanted to be, though she had not intended to be in such company when the end came, nor had she intended for it to come at a time other than her choosing. The mischief she had started to cause was supposed to pave the way for this moment, not the pedlar's bewitchment.

Demdike had hoped to delay a while longer, knowing

the price she would ultimately pay to strike down all those who continued to wrong the cunning folk. She would have preferred to have been arrested closer to the assizes as well, to avoid the long months she now faced in prison. The next trials to be held at Lancaster were not till August, and they had only reached the beginning of April.

"This is your fault," Chattox said, turning her anger on Demdike. "Had your family not invented such fanciful tales about my own, we would not be here right now."

"No, Anne. Do you not see what has truly happened here? Fancie has taken us for fools."

"More lies! Fancie is loyal to me – we have a pact!"

"Did he not promise you my entire family's executions if you worked together to bewitch Master Law? I know it was the two of you who placed the curse on the pedlar; Tibb and I saw Fancie with our own eyes as he gave the man his speech back. Yet it looks as though he failed to mention that you would be joining us."

"Fancie would not betray me. He will find a way to save the two of us, you shall see. We will come out of this unscathed, even as your wretched family swings in the wind upon Gallows Hill."

Demdike shook her head. How could the woman not see the truth of Fancie's actions? The demon had been working against them all, she was sure of it. A spirit of his power simply would not have let Chattox and her daughter be arrested in the first place, if he truly was loyal to them. But there was no sense in arguing when her rival refused to listen to what she had to say.

They had not been on the road long when the cart came to a halt. Demdike frowned, trying to fathom why they would be stopping so early on in the journey. It was a long way to Lancaster and no doubt Nowell and his allies would be anxious to see them thrown in the dungeon as soon as possible.

Tibb showed her another vision of the events unfolding around her, and she saw that they were back at Read Hall. The door to the JP's grand home opened and out came three figures; one bound and seemingly broken, her entire countenance appearing dejected and forlorn; the other two clearly Nowell's men, conducting their business as harshly as ever.

Horror gripped Demdike when the figures approached the cart, and the fourth prisoner was tied to it so that she would have to walk alongside Anne Redferne. But the girl made no attempt to struggle throughout. All the fight seemed to have left her, she who had always been so full of life and the fierce spirit that burned at the heart of their family. And now that fire had been doused, there appeared to be only an empty shell, condemned to the very fate Demdike had tried to spare her from. She, her beloved granddaughter.

THIRTY-TWO

J ames lay in his room in Read Hall, staring at the ceiling and dreaming of all the things he'd like to do to Nowell and his men. He was not overly worried about the future. Surely it was only a matter of time before the JP was forced to admit he still lacked sufficient proof to send them to the assizes. And when that moment came, the evidence James had given against their rivals should appease him. Until then, there was nothing to do but wait.

So he waited. It was made easier by the company of not just Dandy, but also Tibb and Ball. Without them, there would have been nothing to break up the tedious passage of time in his makeshift prison, other than the turning of the key in the lock.

For his poor sister, and perhaps even his mam as well, it must have been an ominous sound. But James remained confident. They had not given him a beating this time and Nowell had no new evidence against him. Enduring another interrogation was probably the worst that was about to happen.

The door opened. One of Nowell's servants stood framed in the entrance. There was a sour look on his face, as though the words he'd been ordered to speak had left a bad taste in his mouth. "You are free to go."

"About time," James muttered under his breath. It had been five days already.

He followed the servant out into the corridor.

"James!" his mam cried, rushing over to give him a hug.

"Not now, Mam." His face reddened as he gave her a gentle push backwards.

"Oh, James, I was starting to think the Justice would keep us locked away in his rooms forever! My heart could not bear the thought of never seeing you and Alizon again, save through the eyes of Ball."

"Mam!" There was a warning to his tone now. Was she trying to get them thrown back into their cages?

"Touching as this is, my master would like you gone from his hall. Come."

"Are Mam and Alizon outside?" his mother asked.

The servant continued walking towards the door without any acknowledgement he'd heard the question. She gave James a pleading look, as though she expected him to make everything all right.

"I'm sure they're fine, Mam," he said, placing a hand around her shoulders and steering her outside.

After being locked inside for days on end, the cool spring breeze was a welcome sensation on their skin. Even his mam seemed to forget her worries in the simple delight of their freedom. They took a moment to stand and enjoy the sun on their faces, while the birds flew overhead and the trees swayed in jubilation at their release. But the joy of it was short-lived.

The sound of the cart making its way out of the grounds

carried on that pleasant breeze. They turned toward it, and their eyes fell on the four prisoners being transported towards their grim fates.

"No!" his mam cried, running after them and screaming Alizon's name. She didn't get far before she tripped on the uneven ground and fell to her hands and knees, still crying and shouting after his gran and sister.

James ran after her and crouched beside his mother, hugging her as she wept. But Alizon never once looked back. Nor did his gran attempt to shout any words of wisdom or encouragement over the growing distance between them. Their family had just been torn apart, and nothing would ever be the same again.

They returned home to find Jennet waiting. The little girl ran down the path to meet them, flinging her arms around their mam who returned the hug with obvious relief, glad to find that her youngest was at least safe.

"What's wrong, Mam?" Jennet asked as they broke apart and resumed the rest of the walk to their home.

Their mother was still too upset to answer, so James replied "Alizon and Gran have been sent to Lancaster, where they are to be imprisoned in the castle."

"But we never did anything wrong."

"No we didn't, and we'll find a way to free them both before any harm comes to them. Mam, we need to gather what food and money we can spare and some fresh clothes and bedding. I will go to visit Gran and Alizon and see that their gaoler is treating them right."

His mam took a deep, shaky breath and wiped away the

worst of her tears. Pride shone through. "We should both go."

"No, Mam. Nowell kept us locked in his home for five days. Jennet needs you now, and a visit to the prison will only cause you more upset. Let me go, and when I return we will see what can be done to spare them the trial at the next assizes in August."

"Then I shall send word to all our friends and allies, and we will arrange a meeting at your gran's house. Malkin Tower is better suited to it than our own home."

James nodded and clasped her hands in his own. "We will find a way to free them both, Mam, don't worry."

Fresh tears welled up, but she was smiling now. "Thank you, son." She squeezed his hands until he gently pulled away.

They entered the house and set about preparing a pack full of supplies to take to the prison, including various tools of the craft.

"And where have you been these past few days, lambkin?" his mam asked Jennet as she went through their stores.

"Just with Isobell. Her father has been looking after me." Jennet's face was the usual picture of youthful innocence, but there was something about the way she said it, something which made James feel she was not being entirely honest with them. He frowned. What reason would she have to lie?

His mam didn't seem to notice.

"This is the best we have." She handed him a bundle of food – already going stale. He would have to trade his magic for fresher bread, cheese and onions, and whatever else he could lay his hands on.

"Thank you." His pack now full, he tied it and set off in

the footsteps of the prisoners. Jennet's deceit was soon forgotten.

"Be careful, James," his mam called after him as he started back down the road. "Make sure you come back to me safe and in one piece – I do not think my heart could bear to lose you as well."

He turned and gave her a wave and his most reassuring smile. "I will, Mam. I'll be back to take part in the gathering at Malkin Tower."

"See that you are. It will take place Friday next, when the Puritans are busy with their Good Friday customs."

She retreated back inside, probably to worry about them all, and consult Ball for advice and any glimpses of what was to come. Arranging the meeting ought to be easy enough, and James had no doubt she would get word to everyone who needed to be there, either through Ball or by using more mundane methods. His thoughts turned to the long road ahead. There were around thirty miles to cover between Pendle and Lancaster – too much for one day. He was going to have to rest overnight somewhere to make sure he didn't use all his strength on the road. There was no time to waste.

Through the countryside he walked, passing fields he'd worked and animals he'd healed. Neighbours regarded him with fresh suspicion, but he paid them little mind, keeping his eyes fixed on the road ahead and his legs moving as fast as they could go. Soon he was crossing the moors in the shadow of Pendle Hill.

Like the back of a giant beast it loomed, crouched in wait for its unsuspecting prey. The Puritans were right to be wary. This was not the land of their new god, but the realm of the ancient Goddess and the Horned One. The hill was surely their guardian. And he imagined it protected him as well, for once he'd reached the wildness of the moors, he had little to fear from any who would accuse him of further witchcraft. That didn't mean the path was any less dangerous, though. He kept his wits about him and remained wary of any strange noises or flashes of movement, calling Dandy to his side in readiness for dealing with any unwanted company.

James was lucky not to encounter any highwaymen or worse. He reached the Forest of Bowland before he was forced to stop for the night, roughly halfway to Lancaster.

Darkness had already begun its advance across the land when he came to the local inn. Candlelight glowed invitingly in the windows, and the cheerful hum of voices filtered through the door. James opened it to find a busy drinking room. No one paid him any attention as he stepped inside, and he was able to wind his way over to the innkeeper without incident.

"Good eve–" the innkeeper began. He was interrupted by a fit of coughing. James had to wait several minutes before the man was able to continue. "What can I do for you?"

"I'd like a room, please."

"We only have one room left and it doesn't come cheap."

James cursed himself as the man's gaze roamed over his grimy clothes and skin. Why had he not had the sense to wash before rushing out? People might have been more trusting if he had.

Giving his most winning smile, James raised his voice to make himself heard over the rowdy chatter and the innkeeper's coughing, and bartered "'Tis true I have little coin, but if you would provide me with food and lodgings for the night, I will relieve you of that nasty cough."

"Ha! The physician could not cure me of this cough. What makes you think you can succeed where a learned man could not?"

"I am no physician, but I have skill as a healer. How long has it troubled you?"

"Must be months since I recovered from the sickness that first brought it, yet still it refuses to go."

"That sounds terrible." James's smile turned sympathetic. "What if it stays with you now till the day you die? Would you not like to be rid of it?"

"Of course I'd like to be rid of it!" The man coughed again. James stood tall as those eyes looked him up and down a second time. "Very well, if you can cure me, then I will give you a proper meal and a bed. Looks like you could use one."

"Thank you, kind sir. Wait here – I shall not be long."

He wound his way back outside and into the long grass growing on either side of the road. In the half light of dusk, he searched for a suitable insect among the blades of green, a sacrifice for the healing magic. The movement of a hairy caterpillar caught his eye.

James smiled. Perfect.

Keeping his eye on his prize, he loosed his pack and retrieved a pouch. Then he scooped up the caterpillar and transferred it to the pouch, reciting a quick charm as he fastened it tight. He returned to the innkeeper a moment later.

"Wear this around your neck, but do not open it. There's a caterpillar inside. As it withers and dies, so shall your cough fade as though it had never been."

"Why a caterpillar?" the man asked him.

"To symbolise the unpleasant tickly sensation of the cough."

"And how am I to know this will work, and I've not just been tricked into giving away a free meal and a bed?"

"I give you my oath. I will pass back this way in about two days' time, and if the cough has not improved or disappeared entirely then I swear to you I will find some other means to pay what I owe. Agreed?"

The man considered for a moment, then offered him his hand to shake. "Agreed."

After a comfortable night in the inn, James rose early and resumed his journey. It was around noon when he arrived at Lancaster. He'd already found a few people in need of his services and had raised a little extra money and food for their cause, and so he made his way straight to the castle.

His sister and gran were being held in the Well Tower, down in the darkness of the dungeons where all the unfortunate prisoners wallowed in a state of despair and hopelessness, just beyond the reach of the sun. James could smell the stink of sweat and worse the moment he entered the prison, and anger filled him to find his family chained in such horrific conditions. But more worrying was the way Alizon still refused to look up when he called to her through the bars of the door, and even his gran's strength seemed to be waning.

"You, gaoler!" James rounded on Thomas Covel, the man responsible for overseeing the prisoners' 'care' while they awaited trial. "Do you know this is Alizon Device and the great Demdike? Do you know what they have been imprisoned for?"

"Watch your tone, boy. I know them right enough — they be the witches brought in earlier today."

"Then you know the profession of our family and all that we are capable of," James said. "I am grandson of Old Demdike and brother to Alizon, and I make you this promise: if they are not treated with the respect they deserve then I will curse you and all your family, until your entire bloodline writhes in a hell of your own making."

"That kind of threat might work in whatever backwards village you come from, but we do not fear your witchcraft here," Covel spat. "They will get the same treatment as any other wretch down there, determined by how much you can pay."

"You'll get your coin, but first I have fresh clothes and bedding for them, if you will permit me to go in."

"You do so at your own risk. There's worse than witches in there."

Covel unlocked the door so that James could make his way into the cramped cell. James paused by the entrance and turned to the gaoler again. "Will you not lend me your lantern?"

Covel stared at him, then his face split into a cruel smile and a mocking laugh slid from his lips. "What do you think this is, a charity? Show me your coin or deal with the darkness."

The anger boiled higher. Dandy growled from James's side, and for a brief moment their minds touched, and James was filled with the desire to taste Covel's flesh.

Oblivious to the danger, Covel's laughter subsided into a sneer. "Surely you're not afraid, witch?"

Let me bite this one for you, Master. I know you want to strike him down as much as I.

Surprise cut through the anger, and James looked down at his familiar with wide eyes. *Dandy?*

The hellhound didn't take his eyes from Covel, his fangs bared and his hackles raised. *Yes, Master. Let me show him the power of the cunning folk.*

James grimaced. *It will only make matters worse. Perhaps you can help guide me to Gran and Alizon instead?*

As you wish. Dandy entered the dungeon, waiting just beyond the doorway.

James turned his gaze on the gaoler again. The man's expression had settled back into a mocking grin. "Your ignorance will be the death of you."

Covel sniggered at that and closed the door behind them as James followed Dandy inside. James tried reaching for the mental link their shared anger had just given them, but it was as though that brief contact had never been. He gave a disappointed sigh and reached with his hand instead. Smooth fur brushed against it. Dandy took a careful step forward and James went with him, and together they were able to make their way through the dungeon.

Desperate hands grasped at the cunning man as he waded through the filthy bodies. James was able to shake most of them off. There was just one that latched onto his trouser leg and refused to let go, even as James pulled and slapped blindly at the unseen fingers. Dandy lunged and there was a scream of agony, then the hand fell away and James was free. The hellhound returned to his side and they continued further into the room, until finally Dandy came to a stop.

They are in front of you.

The dark brush of Dandy's mind returned, and with it a vision of the dungeon as the hellhound saw it. To him, the room might as well have been flooded with daylight. The hunched forms of James's family were clear to see, and beside them the hated figures of Chattox and her daughter. James might have scowled at the sight of their rivals, if his family hadn't looked so pitiful.

"Gran? Alizon?"

Still Alizon would not look at him, but his gran stirred. "James?"

"Yes. I've brought you fresh clothes and bedding, and all the food I could gather."

A nearby prisoner raised his head at that and turned in their direction. James ignored him and offered a lump of fresh bread to his sister, but she whimpered and flinched away from his outstretched hand. His heart sank.

"I'll take those, lad," his gran said, holding her hands out.

"There should be plenty to keep you going for the next few days at least. I even saved a bit of the meat from my meal last night – I thought you would need it more than I."

Chains rattled. More prisoners were beginning to take notice of fresh food in their midst, including Anne Redferne. Chattox also glanced in his direction, her lips moving soundlessly, but then her gaze strayed to Dandy and she quickly looked away again.

"If anyone so much as thinks of stealing my family's rations, they will be the next to scream."

Dandy growled, and the other prisoners shrank back. Alizon also recoiled, but their gran smiled with pride. "Thank you, James. I will see Alizon has her share, when she is ready. She just needs time after the ordeal Nowell put her through."

"I hope you're right, Gran. It pains me to see you so. But do not lose hope – Mam is arranging a gathering of cunning folk and our allies for next Friday, and we will combine our powers to free you both."

"Do not worry about me – just see that Alizon is spared the fate awaiting on Gallows Hill."

"We will do all that we can," he promised.

"Time's up!" Covel called from the doorway. "Come on out, or I'll lock you in there too."

James was reluctant to leave them, but he had little choice. Even with their familiars by their sides, there was no way they could escape the prison in full view of all the guards – not when Alizon and his gran would have to break free of their fetters first. And even if they could somehow pull that off before the guards stopped them, the two women were in no condition to run. So he turned and strode back out of the cell, casting a brief, final glance at his rivals as he did so. Much as Chattox had given their family every reason to hate her and her daughter, he felt slightly guilty for his role in their imprisonment. No one deserved the horror of that dungeon, not even his worst enemies, and he made a silent vow to do all he could to free them as well. Perhaps they could even put old feuds aside and forge an alliance, at least for as long as men like Nowell remained a threat.

"Here, take this," he said to Covel once the gaoler had locked the door, thrusting a handful of coins into his hand. "See that they have their chains removed and are fed properly. I will return tomorrow, and you will learn to fear us if I find no signs of improvement by then."

"Pay me well and they'll be looked after well enough, you have my word."

James scowled but didn't bother to argue. How could this man be so frustratingly resistant to his threats of magical retaliation?

He left the horror of the prison and emerged from the darkness of the Well Tower into bright sunlight. A crowd had gathered outside. He only had to glance across at the pillory to see why.

Pleading eyes looked back at him. James imagined the convicted woman was no more guilty of her supposed crime than Alizon and his gran of theirs, but at least she had been shown mercy. She would be publicly humiliated as the crowd pelted her with dirt and rotting fruit, or at worst they would throw stones. But it was unlikely she would be unfortunate enough to meet her end there, for the mood of the crowd did not feel particularly violent. She was not another innocent for the Reaper.

James turned away and went in search of another room for the night.

Lancaster was no larger a town than Colne, despite the castle towering over the other buildings. He wandered along Market Street to find it all but deserted. That didn't trouble him. Most of the people he might otherwise have passed were probably back at the pillory. There was nothing about the quiet to make him uneasy.

The stink of raw fish was strong as he approached Moor Lane, wafting across from the fish market two streets over. His stomach rumbled a reminder he had not eaten since arriving in the town. It was tempting to spend what little he had on another meal, but he resisted and continued on to The Red Lion Inn.

James entered the gloomy drinking room to find it empty but for the innkeeper.

"Here for the execution tomorrow?" the man said by way of greeting.

"Execution?"

"Joseph Baily, sentenced to death at the March assizes for sending a threatening letter."

James stared. "He'll hang for sending a letter?"

The innkeeper shrugged. "They don't call this The Hanging Town for nothing. I always assumed the assizes in these parts were especially strict compared with other places, but word is they like handing out executions because it's good for trade. Brings more people into town than market day!"

Despair engulfed James then. What chance did his sister and gran have if this was the sort of opposition they faced? Combined with the case Nowell was building against them and the hatred of witches, it was almost certain they would be sent to Gallows Hill.

"I'm not here to watch the hanging, but I do have need of lodgings for the night."

"You're in luck, young sir. There's not many arrived here yet, but come evening this room will be full, you'll see. I still have two beds to offer, along with supper and breakfast."

"Then I'll take one. Would you accept my services as a cunning man in payment?"

"No. Show me a sixpence or be on your way. And don't be causing any trouble or I'll send for the constable, then we might watch you hang this summer."

James grumbled to himself but paid the man nevertheless. He did his best to hide his frustrations as he took to the streets again, where he would use his skills to raise more money and food. People were less likely to trade with him if he wore a frown.

It was hard going – the people of Lancaster were less open to magical solutions to their problems than in the Forest of Pendle. They were too willing to place their faith in the physicians, with their cures that failed as often as they worked in James's experience – and their Christ of course. Most would not be swayed into trying his magic, and he had to resort to begging for the rest of the day.

He wandered the streets of the town until nightfall. When he returned to The Red Lion Inn, it was to find it crowded, just as the innkeeper had said.

His sixpence bought him a share of the food at the host's table, then he retreated to his room. He had no desire to sit listening to the talk about the hanging the next day.

James rose early again. He spent more time begging before returning to the prison, aware that he would not get a chance for another visit until after the meeting at Malkin Tower. It was harder to leave Alizon and his gran that second day, especially when they looked so vulnerable amidst the caged beasts of all shapes and sizes, from the men eyeing his sister in the dim light from Covel's lantern, their eyes burning with a hunger for more than food, to the starving children. These young wretches were desperate enough to steal from their elders, even after the threats he'd made the day before, and a blind old woman was the perfect prey.

Had it not been for the promises the meeting offered, James might have stayed in Lancaster. But he felt the gathering of cunning folk was their best hope at freeing the four wise women, so he tore himself away from the pitiful sight of Alizon hugging her knees and crying silent tears. And his gran, so strong and proud for as long as he'd known her, sitting slumped with her back against the wall, trembling in the frailty of her years. To see his gran suffering was the most unnerving. If the terrible conditions of the dungeon were so dire as to beat her down, what chance did any of them stand against the power of the law? He wondered if either of his two family members would ever fully recover from this dreadful experience, even after they'd won back their freedom. Or was it already too late to save them?

Such dark thoughts circled his mind as he started back on the road to Pendle, like a murder of crows swooping and harassing him as he walked. They attacked with beaks made up of the sharp images of his gran and sister's suffering, and talons of his family's fate if he could not free them soon. He doubted the wise women would survive one month in that disease-ridden dungeon, let alone the four to pass before their trial. Their lives were riding on the friends and family his mam was calling to Malkin Tower, and he felt the weight of responsibility as he set out for that momentous event.

James's route took him back past The Red Lion. He reached a stream of people trickling out of the town and over to Gallows Hill, and soon found himself swept up by that stream. At its head was the cart transporting the unfortunate Joseph Baily, sitting atop his own coffin. James could not see much of the man through the crowd, but from what little he glimpsed, he had to wonder what manner of threat Baily had made for them to take his letter so seriously. A less threatening man he had never seen.

He'd had no intention of witnessing the hanging. And yet, once he was part of the crowd heading to the gallows he found he couldn't turn away. He'd become linked with this man's fate. Something was drawing him to watch, and he could not return home until he'd seen Baily's end. So he followed in the wake of the cart, across the moors and up Gallows Hill.

The sky was overcast that day. Between the dull clouds and man's own cruelty, the beauty of the land felt sullied. James could not wait to be back to his own Pendle Hill then, but still his feet would not obey him.

Baily kept his head down as they tied the noose around his neck, and he remained silent. Dejected and forlorn, he appeared to have long since accepted his fate. He made no attempt to fight as he stood there on the back of the cart, waiting for the end.

The cart rolled forward and Baily twisted at the end of his rope. His legs jerked with the instinct to find purchase and take the pressure off his neck, and his eyes bulged with terror as though he could see the Reaper drawing nearer. His face turned an alarming shade, darkening and taking on a blueish tint. But more horrific was the reaction of the crowd – the way they cheered and mocked as though this were no more than a play or some other harmless form of entertainment.

Only when Baily went limp and utterly lifeless could James finally turn away. Around him the crowd began to offer the executioner money for everything from the hanged man's clothes to the rope and parts of his body. They put James in mind of dogs fighting over scraps.

He resumed the journey home with new determination. That would not be the fate of Alizon and his gran. He would make sure of it.

CHAPTER
THIRTY-THREE

J ames stopped to rest at the same inn in Bowland. The innkeeper's cough had cleared up as promised and the man was so happy that he allowed him another room and more food, in return for casting a few quick charms of protection about the place.

The cunning man arrived back in Pendle around mid-afternoon.

"James! Thank the Goddess you're back," his mam cried, pulling him into a relieved embrace. "How are they?"

He did not have to ask who the 'they' in that question were. But he couldn't bear to tell her just how bad the situation was, so he said "They are well looked after, Mam, especially now I've paid the gaoler a generous amount for food and drink while we work to free them. Their spirits are as high as can be hoped in such a place, and they are each in good health."

She was too desperate to hear that things were not as bad as she'd feared to see through his lie, and she hugged him again, smiling with the comfort his words brought her.

Words which only added to his own burden and the pressure he felt to free his gran and sister from that foetid cage.

All his hopes now rested on the gathering of friends and allies; another day that dawned grey and overcast. Mist shrouded the land, leaving none in doubt that their chosen date had again been touched by the hand of fate. James almost felt suffocated by the responsibility hanging over him then. But he knew he had to find the strength to lead the proceedings at the coming gathering, for his mam was in no fit state. And his first task was to obtain a living animal.

His mother had been preparing for the meeting all week, collecting any debts she was owed and giving all the magical favours she could in return for extra food for their guests. But they still needed a supply of the most powerful of ingredients to empower their magic and imbue it with greater force than whatever energy the spirits they called on granted them, and so his path took him to Barley, and the farm of Christopher Sawyers. He sought out the yeoman and reminded him of work he'd done earlier that year, and the payment still owed.

"I need one of your sheep, and I will accept nothing less," James said.

"A whole sheep for a week's labour and a few charms? I think not, Master Device. What about the trouble just being seen with you could cause? We all know Nowell's out for blood. He'll drag anyone seen to be associating with suspected witches to his hall, guilty or no."

"I would remind you that we can do far worse than the Justice. I need a living sheep to take back with me, and I'm not leaving here without it."

Sawyers closed his eyes as if silently asking some greater power to give him strength. He opened them again with a sigh. "If I let you have one of my animals, you will owe me six more weeks of work with no further pay. Agreed?"

"Agreed. And I get to pick the animal myself."

"Very well. But I best not hear tell of my sheep being used for some foul spell, or I will go to Nowell myself and tell him of this agreement. Understood?"

"Understood."

He left Sawyers muttering to himself and shaking his head, probably questioning the wisdom of doing business with cunning folk in light of the recent arrests. James turned his mind to more important matters. He did not have time for the yeoman's doubts.

A large ram caught his eye. It was a fine animal, filled with all the life's blood their magic called for, and with enough meat on the bones to feed their guests and leave them with plenty to salt for their stores. Satisfied with his choice, he tied a length of rope about its neck and led it to Malkin Tower with a little help from Dandy. The hell-hound's snapping jaws were the perfect kind of persuasion to keep the animal moving.

Once at his gran's house, James secured the sheep outside and helped his mam prepare the rest of the feast for the gathering. Then there was nothing to do but wait. It was nearly noon when their guests began to arrive, seventeen in total. But there were two more who'd been invited.

"I don't see my aunt or uncle," James said, scanning the assembled friends and allies one more time in case he'd missed them coming in.

"They have not come," his mam confirmed, unable to keep the disappointment from her voice. "I had hoped Christopher would be here to lend whatever aid he can in freeing your gran. He is still our blood, and she is still the woman who brought him into this world and raised him as best she knew how. But perhaps that is no longer enough."

A spark of anger leapt into the forefront of James's mind. He forced it down, addressing all those who had answered his mother's call as calmly as he could manage and with as much warmth as he could muster.

"Friends," he began, "I thank you all for coming to visit in these dangerous times. No doubt you have already heard news of the arrest of not only my sister and my gran, but also Chattox and her daughter, if not from my mam, then from one of our other neighbours. We have called this meeting today to discuss what can be done about freeing our family and fellow cunning folk, and we beg your help in this grave matter."

"And just what do you have in mind, young James?" asked one of the few men in attendance, Master Jackes of Thorneyholme.

"I don't know," he admitted. "But we have to do something. Even as we speak, the four of them are locked in the terrible dungeon beneath the Well Tower of Lancaster Castle. The rats and lice keep them company, and worse."

"Any move we make against Nowell is going to be dangerous," Katherine Hewitt pointed out. She was a wise woman herself, from Colne, and no stranger to the blame often laid at their feet. "No matter what path we take, attempting to free the four of them could just as easily end in our own arrests, and earn us a place at the gallows right alongside them."

James balled his hands into fists, fighting to keep his calm. The meeting was not off to as good a start as he'd hoped, and he could see his mam was unlikely to be any help in persuading them to pledge their assistance. She had always been shy because of her unfortunate disfigurement and often struggled in social settings, especially when large groups of people were involved. That day was no different. She had seated herself in a corner of the room and had her head down, her fingers twisting the material of her dress.

Jennet could not be relied on either. His half-sister was far too young to speak on the family's behalf. It was all up to him.

"Yes, it is dangerous," he agreed. But before he could continue, the door began to creak open and he froze. What if the constable had not been at the Good Friday services after all? What if he'd been watching them for any suspicious activity? What if he was about to burst in and make more arrests, even though they had not yet done anything illegal?

James tensed. Dandy was by his side, materialising for all to see. The door opened wider, and a man's face appeared.

They relaxed. It was not Hargrieves after all, but his aunt and uncle. New hope rose in him when he realised his only other surviving family had not abandoned them as they'd feared, but were simply late to the gathering. And he felt some of the responsibility lift from his shoulders. He was sure he could rely on his uncle to share the burden.

"Did I miss anything good?" Uncle Christopher asked, a hint of mischief playing across his features and glinting in his eye. The man might have chosen to distance himself from the family and their craft over the last decade or so, but there was no running from the blood of Old Demdike flowing through their veins. Even with a different father, James could see the familial likeness between his mam and uncle. And there was something of his gran's strength in his uncle's bearing, even if he was not quite the same force of nature as she.

"Not yet," James answered as Dandy faded back out of physical sight. "Perhaps you have some idea of how we can save Gran and Alizon from going to trial, Uncle?"

"If Nowell wants a fight, we'll give him one. I say we go to Read Hall right now and show him the true power of the cunning folk."

"'Tis too dangerous," Hewitt repeated. "We will all hang if we use the dark arts they accuse us of."

"Who said anything about killing people?" Uncle Christopher said. "Burn the evidence and scare the witnesses into silence, and the JP has nothing. Mam and Alizon will be found not guilty, and we can put this unfortunate business behind us. Nowell won't be able to do a thing about it, so long as we are careful not to give him any more reasons to arrest us."

James shook his head. "They would still have to survive in the dungeon for the four months to the trial. You should have seen the conditions down there, Uncle. 'Tis no place for our elders."

"Then what do you propose, Master Device?" Grace Hay asked.

"We need to get them out of prison at the first possible opportunity. I say we kill the gaoler and free them."

"Oh aye, and why not blow up the castle while we're at it?" Hewitt snorted. "Listen to your head for once, and not that fool heart."

"Are the majority of us here not cunning folk?" Uncle Christopher asked, seemingly including himself as one of their number, much to James's surprise. "We have the power of the spirit world on our side. What use are the guards' swords against hellhounds and other creatures of spirit?"

"That still puts not only ourselves, but also our familiars in unnecessary danger," Hewitt argued. "For all we know, the gaol has magical protection as well as its earthly defences."

An idea came to James then, and his voice filled with excitement. "Alizon never made the pact, but it seemed as though a familiar had chosen her already about a year ago, when she saw a hellhound she had not met before while they were out in the forest. Jennet saw him too."

"He was bigger than Ball or Dandy with scary eyes and teeth," the little girl confirmed. "But I wasn't afraid of him!"

"Could we invoke the spirit and send him to join with Tibb and maybe even Chattox and her daughter's familiars? And if any are willing to send their own spirits to lend their aid, surely that would be enough to enable the four of them to escape."

"And what then, go on the run? I am liking your ideas less and less, James Device," Hewitt said.

"It is dangerous," Jane Bulcock agreed, with her son beside her. Christopher Bulcock was nowhere to be seen. James supposed he'd had business elsewhere. "But Demdike has helped us many times over the years, including when John here was sick. And when she couldn't cure him, Chattox stepped in and took over, and look at him now, fit as a fiddle. We Bulcocks may not be cunning folk, but we have called on practitioners of the art many times over the years. You have always been there for us when we have needed you, and we have not forgotten. We will give you whatever aid you need in your efforts to free the four wise women so wrongly labelled as witches."

James nodded his thanks, keeping quiet about the fact that Chattox had only cured John as a means to strike at their own family. It was not the time to remind their friends of the bad blood between their two clans.

"I do not mean to say I will not help," Hewitt said. "I just think we need to be smart about whatever it is we agree to do."

"I will agree to risk my life for your family," another of the women spoke up. James recognised her as a wise woman of Gisburne from across the county border, in Yorkshire. "On one condition."

"Name it," he said.

"A man by the name of Thomas Lister and his brother, Leonard, wish me dead for nothing more than falling in love with his father, such as that can be considered a crime. They tried accusing me of witchcraft once and failed, the evidence they'd falsified too weak to stand up in the York assizes. I was released just four days ago, and I am here today because I would not see the same happen to my sister wise women. But I also came to ask for your help. If I risk my life to save the four in Lancaster Castle, I ask that you aid me with my problem. I do not want to be back in the assizes, accused of more crimes I never committed. But I fear that will be the outcome if something is not done soon."

"Then you have it," James answered. "But we have yet to agree on a plan and time is of the essence. I suggest we attempt to summon the hellhound that's bonded with Alizon, and if we're successful, we can start by asking him if he will help."

"Good luck invoking a spirit without its name," Hewitt said. "Maybe your gran could achieve such a feat, but not one of your years."

"We shall see," he replied, his voice turning cold. He'd had enough of her naysaying.

"It is not impossible with so many of us here to help,

just incredibly difficult," the Gisburne woman said. "A sacrifice would help."

"And a sacrifice we shall have."

He went outside and untied the ram, leading it in for the ritual. Then he grabbed a dish to catch the blood he was about to spill and his gran's ceremonial knife.

The ritual itself was simple, but reaching out to the correct spirit without a name to call on was not without its challenges, or its risks. Dandy and Ball, and any of the others' familiar spirits who chose to help him, would make his task that bit easier. Yet there were no guarantees of success, or who they would summon at the end of the ritual.

James reminded himself that his gran and sister's lives hung in the balance, took a deep breath to steady his nerves and slid the blade into the animal's flesh, then started to chant as a torrent of blood burst forth. The others joined in, all but his little sister, who had not seen enough of death to be unaffected by the slaughter she'd just witnessed. Her eyes widened and her mouth opened in horror. Their mam pulled her into a comforting embrace, smiling gratefully at James over Jennet's head. He nodded without breaking his chant. Energy poured into the rite through the ram's blood, and the power each of the cunning folk gave built around James, raising the hairs on his skin and creating a tingling throughout his body.

"A spirit we summon,
A spirit we call,
A life we offer,
An answer we seek.

Dark in nature,
Hellhound by race,
Bound to Alizon,
Your help we plead.

No pact yet made,
Bonded no less,
Bound to Device,
Your help we plead.

Accept our offering,
Feast on this blood,
Appear to us now,
Answer our plea."

As they chanted, James formed an image in his head of the place in the forest where Alizon claimed to have first seen the spirit. He imagined his sister there, making the mental picture of her as clear as he could. For the words were not enough, but intent was everything, in any spell. They had a far greater chance of summoning the hellhound they wanted if their intentions were made clear, and not confused by emotion or stray thought, and so James focused all the concentration he had on holding that image.

But before the ritual could be completed, there came a knock at the door, and his concentration was broken. Fear gripped him. He glanced at his mam. She shook her head in affirmation that they had not been expecting anyone else, her mismatched eyes wide and fixing on the door. To his paranoid brain, that could only mean one thing. The constable had indeed found them, and worse, he was about to catch them right in the act of performing the same forbidden acts his gran and sister stood accused of. Dandy was back beside him, responding to his fear with savage fury.

Uncle Christopher was the first to recover from that initial shock, striding to the door with all the bravery of his mother, James's gran, and cracking it open just enough to see who waited on the other side. But the damage to the ritual was already done. James felt the power waning, the tingling in and around his flesh slipping away until there was only the usual feeling of the still air on his skin. Defeat and disappointment took its place, though there was one consolation. When his uncle opened the door wider, he could see it was in fact friend rather than foe again. Dandy calmed instantly.

Alice Nutter looked as shocked as the rest of them, clearly unaware of the meeting they'd called and unprepared for the sight of James standing over the ram with the bowl to its throat. The animal's blood was still pumping out, and the whites of its eyes showed as the Reaper beckoned. Uncle Christopher ushered her in, quickly glancing around outside before closing the door.

"Alice," James said, releasing the dying ram and placing the knife and the bowl of blood on the table. "What brings you to our door in such troubled times?"

"I am sorry to intrude, but I did not know who else to turn to. A sickness is spreading among our farm, threatening the lives of every animal we own. If we lose them all, you know as well as I it will ruin us. So I come to beg your help, even with the danger Nowell poses in this witch hunt he has begun. I understand if your family is too caught up in its own problems to save our cattle, but if you do this then I give you my word that you will have all my family's resources on your side. We will do anything we can to prove your innocence and we will pay the gaoler's fees to bring your gran and your sister every possible comfort while we work to free them. This I swear on my honour as both a Nutter and a Whitaker of Huncoat."

James looked again to his mam for confirmation, and this time she nodded her approval. "We will do everything we can to cure your cattle, as soon as we are finished here. Please, join us for this feast Mam and I have prepared. You are all welcome to our food while we think on how best to help free those already imprisoned in Lancaster Castle, and then perhaps we can agree on a plan."

He was about to start preparing a share of the mutton to cook for their guests when Dandy returned to his protective stance and gave another display of aggression for all to witness.

"What is it, Dandy?"

The hellhound's eyes remained fixed on something James couldn't see, his lips pulled back in a vicious snarl and his ears flattened against his skull – a sign of fear.

Other familiar spirits were beginning to react in a similar manner. Dread crept over James. It looked like the summoning had been successful after all.

An unnatural shadow spread across the room. All eyes were fixed on it now, their faces set in grim determination. Even Alice Nutter, whose experience with the craft was limited to the protection charms they worked for her at Samhain, stood resolute. They would fight this threat together, just as they would fight Nowell and anyone else who made themselves an enemy.

It was James's uncle who first took up the chant. The rest of the cunning folk were quick to join in, and together they thundered:

Dark presence, we banish thee,
By wind, fire, rock and tree,
Leave–

The shadow lunged at Grace Hay and the chant died with her screams. It moved in a blur of blackness, too fast to distinguish its shape. Grace's familiar rushed to her defence. His form swelled from an ordinary-looking black cat to one of the great feline beasts of stories from far off lands, and he leapt at her attacker in a clash of tooth and claw. Seconds later, the creature fell to the floor with an animal scream of agony, unmoving and fading from their sight as if he'd never been. James did not know if the spirit's life had just been extinguished, or if the creature had simply returned to his own realm to recover and lick his wounds, as Tibb had been forced to do when he'd been attacked that Samhain of 1609. But he did not want to risk Dandy's life to find out, and he feared for his familiar as much as he did himself and his flesh and blood family.

"Everybody out!" he bellowed, grabbing the bowl of blood and running for the door.

The gathered friends and allies needed no second prompting, fleeing outside before the spirit could do any more harm. James slammed the door shut as soon as the last one ran out and dipped his fingers in the blood, splashing it across the wood in the shape of a cross. Then he chanted:

"Spirit unwelcome,
Spirit be gone,
Never to pass,
Beyond this cross,
By my will be done,
And power of blood,
Return to your realm,
There to roam free,
Or from this house,
You shall never leave!"

As banishing spells went, it was not the most reliable, but at least the creature they'd summoned would be trapped inside the walls of his gran's home, unable to do anyone else harm if it refused to leave the earthly realm. So long as no one was foolish enough to attempt to venture back inside, of course. And any who did dare intrude on the empty cottage deserved every torment the spirit could inflict, as far as he was concerned.

Most of the cunning folk and their friends had already fled down the path, putting as much distance between themselves and the cottage as possible. But a few had stayed to watch him work the charm, from a safe distance. Among them was the wise woman of Gisburne.

"Well done, Master Device," she said. "Since Malkin Tower is no longer safe, I would like to offer my own house for any future meetings."

"I think that would be unwise while the Listers are looking for any excuse to have you hanged as a witch, but I thank you for the offer all the same."

"Then I suggest we meet at Romley Moor in the meantime, if the need arises."

He nodded and what remained of the gathering

dispersed. His mam and little Jennet were beside him as they made their way home in near silence. Even his sister was quiet, obviously shaken by the day's events, and he was sure his mother must share the same sense of despair he had now fallen into. The meeting had not gone as planned and they were no closer to freeing his gran and Alizon, despite the support they'd been promised. But they'd sworn to help the Nutters of Roughlee with their sick cattle, and so they were forced to turn their attention to the task at hand, stopping at the house only briefly to collect their tools. Duty called. Any plans to save their family would have to wait.

With their combined efforts, James and his mam saved most of the cattle and thus secured the help of the Nutter family in the coming battle against Nowell. James felt that was at least one small victory they'd achieved that day, and he began feeling a little better. It wasn't to last.

Just days after the meeting, James was out begging and looking for work from any who would still talk to them, intending to return to Lancaster with a pack not just full but bulging. He was on his way to pay Alice Nutter's estate another visit, when he encountered Constable Hargrieves once again.

Nowell's dog looked to be hunting for someone. His eyes scanned his surroundings as he walked through Roughlee, his head turning this way and that. James tried to slip away, but it was too late. Their gazes locked and the constable's nostrils flared, a bloodhound catching the scent of his prey.

Hargrieves started towards him, a mixture of triumph and malice in the hated man's eyes. James stood his ground. He doubted they'd suddenly found fresh evidence of his guilt since his last arrest. There was no reason to panic.

"Device," Hagrieves growled. "There has been word of a great assembly of witches at your grandmother's house. I want you to come with me and remove any curses Old Demdike laid about the place."

James felt the colour draining from his skin. "Take me back in for questioning if you must, but do not make me go back there, I beg thee. 'Tis no longer safe."

"Do you think me simple, you insolent wretch? Doubtless you would say anything to escape casting further suspicion on your vile family."

"I am telling you the truth! A great evil has been unleashed in my gran's absence. Please, don't make me do this." James started backing away.

"Oh no, you're not running from me this time, boy," Hagrieves said, grabbing the cunning man's wrist. James fought to pull free but Hagrieves was too strong for him. Panic took over. He raised his other fist to strike that mean, hateful face, and Hagrieves wrenched his arm so hard he thought it would come out of its socket. With a cry of pain, he stumbled forward, and Hagrieves started dragging him back to Malkin Tower.

"You fool, you will be the death of us!" James continued to protest. He kept on struggling against Hargrieves' grip all the way to the front door. The cross he'd made had faded from bright red to a dull brown, but he could still feel the power of the spell across the threshold. Why couldn't Hargrieves see the folly in breaking that magical barrier?

"I will hear no more of your excuses," the constable

said. "I am under instruction to search the house by the Justice himself and you will assist, or we will add it as evidence of your guilt. Now, open this door!"

James saw no option but to do as the constable ordered then, flinching as the door swung inwards. He expected the spirit to come rushing out the moment his spell broke. All was quiet. The only thing to assault them was the stench of death and decay coming from within. James almost lost his nerve at that foul smell, but the same fear did not grip Hargrieves, ignorant as he was to what horrors might await inside the cottage. James felt a hand on his shoulder. He was pushed through the doorway, and the constable followed close behind.

The stink of rotting flesh came from the ram's carcass, as was to be expected. Dead eyes, unnaturally wide without the lids that should have at least partly concealed them, fixed James with their eerie stare, and bloody jaws grinned with grim amusement. Most of the meat had been eaten from the skull. Only a few gory strips remained, hanging uselessly across the bone.

Its tongue was surprisingly still attached. A fly crawled across the muscle to enjoy the scraps of the unwholesome meal left by the spirit creature. Another of the insects landed on one of those staring eyes and rubbed its legs together as if in anticipation of the feast it was about to enjoy. Yet more buzzed around the left side of the empty ribcage, where the flesh had been completely torn away.

"What evil practice is this?" Hargrieves said.

"Not ours. I told you it is not safe in here. We have to go, now!"

"You think you can escape that easily? The Justice ordered this place searched, so I will search. What other evidence of your foul witchcraft are you trying to hide here, I wonder?"

James kept as close to the door as he was able while the constable hunted for more evidence, ready to bolt at the first sign of another attack. Most of the tools they owned were not against the law, but he knew Nowell could charge them with digging up human remains if they found any of the old bones they used. Fortunately he'd had the foresight to hide such things before the Good Friday meeting. What was left of the sacrifice he'd made looked to be the only damning piece of evidence Hargrieves would find, and he was relieved when the man finished his search and began to head for the door.

The constable came to a sudden stop, staring at a patch of disturbed earth beneath his boot. "What's this?"

James did his best to look nonchalant, but inwardly his heart sank. "Gran had a bitch in here for a while. The dog must have buried something before it ran off – we've not seen the animal since she and my sister were so wrongfully arrested."

"Then you won't mind showing me whatever's down there."

"I'm sure it's nothing. We really should be going before anything bad happens, or do you want to risk being eaten by whatever fed on that poor ram? A dark spirit has invaded and I am telling you once again, the house is no longer safe!"

"Nice try. We can leave as soon as you show me what the dog buried."

James cursed and knelt over the patch of earth, uncovering the four human teeth he'd hoped to hide and a lump of clay. But that was not all he'd wanted to keep Nowell's men from seizing. They were dangerously close to the old bones his gran had so often relied on, and he could see no way to keep the constable from taking them.

An unearthly cry sounded from behind and he felt fresh terror strike his heart. Springing to his feet, he fled his gran's home before Hargrieves could stop him.

James turned round only once he was outside. The constable was close behind. And just beyond the constable, there rose a ghastly vision sure to haunt their sleep for many nights to come.

The spirit had lingered on the earthly plane. It possessed the rotting sheep bones, standing up on its hind legs and starting towards them with untold menace. The two dead eyes rolled in their sockets, fixing James with a malevolent gaze.

He slammed the door shut before the thing could attack, quickly intoning the same spell to trap the spirit inside as he'd used after the meeting. But deep down he feared it would not work a second time without fresh blood to daub across the threshold. He wasn't even sure it would hold the creature now it had found a physical form, the corpse it had been allowed to inhabit taking much less energy to use than manifesting as a spirit. But he wasn't staying long enough to find out.

The constable seemed similarly shaken after the encounter, though it did not last. Nowell demanded James be brought back in for questioning, and Hagrieves did as he was ordered, obedient as ever.

This time James was taken to Ashlar House. Nowell awaited, tall and foreboding in his chair. But there was a second man sitting beside him, eyeing James with distaste. The young cunning man recognised him as another Justice of the Peace, Nicholas Bannister.

James could not think why Nowell would need his fellow JP's aid, but he suddenly felt less confident facing two of them. And now the Justices had that much more leverage to use against him, he soon found himself telling them much of what they wanted to hear, starting with the discovery of the teeth and the lump of clay.

"The teeth came from a burial at St Mary's twelve years ago – Old Chattox picked up three skulls of people who had been buried and then cast out of the grave, and took eight teeth. She kept four for herself but gave the other four to my gran, who has kept them buried in the earth at her home ever since."

"They were cast out of the grave – that is awfully convenient for Anne Whittle and your gran, do you not think?" Nowell said.

James shrugged. "That is what happened. No grave robbery was committed, and unless the law has changed, it is not illegal to lay claim to any old bones that happen to be lying around."

"And what of the clay?"

"It is the picture of Anthony Nutter's daughter, friend to my sister and victim of Chattox, buried there in an attempt to unbewitch her. But we were too late – she died to Chattox's curse."

"So you say. Perhaps it is, in fact, the withered image of John Law, buried by your sister so we would not find it."

"No! She had nothing to do with his condition, I swear to you."

"I might be more inclined to believe that if you

confessed to the crimes your family are guilty of. Starting with Anne Towneley's murder."

James was beginning to feel more and more like a cornered animal. There was nowhere left to run and no more eluding the questions Nowell threw at him, unless he was willing to let his family take the blame for his crimes. So he told the JP of how a spirit convinced him to seek revenge against Mistress Towneley, keeping to the same lie he had told his family and stating that it was Dandy who told him how to kill her by magic.

He suspected the black bitch Alizon had so briefly adopted would have been mentioned somewhere in the statements concerning Law. Maybe he could take the blame for the bewitching of the pedlar if he told Nowell of his black dog familiar, and at least save his sister from the noose. The Justice also teased Duckworth's murder from him, but when it came to the meeting at his gran's house, he tried to protect all those who'd been there for as long as he was able.

"Mam and I did plan a great feast. I took one of Christopher Sawyers' rams and slaughtered it the night before to use as the main dish," he said. "There was more than our family could eat in one day so we salted the rest."

It seemed the constable hadn't told the JP about the gruesome appearance of the ram's remains or the encounter with the dark spirit, because Nowell never asked him about it. He could only guess as to why Hargrieves had kept that information from his master. Perhaps the constable feared the Justice would want to see the spirit for himself, which would mean having to face it again and potentially freeing it to come after him in his own home. Or maybe it was something else entirely.

"James Device, we have witnesses who claim to have

seen several of your fellow witches visiting your grand-mother's home on Good Friday," Bannister said. "We need names."

"If you have witnesses, why do you need the names from me?"

"Oh we know who was at your grandmother's house," Nowell said. "We would just like you to confirm it for us."

"He lies," Dandy growled, appearing beside James. "Say nothing."

"Mam did call a meeting on Good Friday," James admitted. "But it was not to perform any witchcraft. We discussed what might be done to help Gran and Alizon after you so wrongfully sent them off to Lancaster Castle. That is all."

Bannister looked disappointed, but Nowell did not seem troubled by his response. "There was nothing wrongful about it. Your grandmother confessed, and the evidence against your sister was most telling. The case against them is strong. However, I might be persuaded to show mercy during their trial in exchange for your confession as to what really happened on Good Friday."

"Do not trust him," Dandy said.

James glanced at his familiar. He didn't trust either of the JPs after the way Nowell had twisted his statements before, but if there was a chance he could save his family from the gallows, how could he not take it?

"Very well," he answered, while Dandy growled his displeasure. "It is as I said. We met to see what could be done for Gran and Alizon. I tried to summon a spirit to help them escape the prison, but the ritual failed and something evil came through. We ran before it could attack any of us, and I drew a red cross on the door to Malkin Tower and said a charm to lock it inside. The only magic performed was my own."

"That is a good start," Nowell said. "But there is more to this story, I think. Perhaps your mother will be more open with me."

James was led down to the same vaulted cellars where his gran had been held. It wasn't long before he faced further questioning.

"Tell us again about this Good Friday meeting," Nowell said.

"I already told you everything there is to tell," James insisted.

"This spirit you tried to summon. I think you were trying to find a specific one – the black dog who serves your sister perhaps? The one we know to have struck Law down lame?"

James stared. How did Nowell know that?

"No," he said, recovering. "My sister has no familiar. Even if she did, I would need to know the creature's name. But she was not at the meeting to ask, since she now rots in prison."

Dandy was back by his side. "Be careful, Master. They write 'First cause for meeting was for the naming of Alizon Device's spirit, but they did not name him because she was not there.' You cannot trust them."

"And what of this plot to murder Thomas Covel?" Nowell asked.

James stared again. It was as if Nowell had a familiar of his own, feeding him this information. Surely his mam had not told the JP all this?

"I believe you spoke of killing him and freeing your family, then blowing up the prison," Nowell continued.

James's temper flared. "No! Mouldheels's wife joked of

blowing up the prison, but we never made any serious threats!"

"So Katherine Hewitt was at the meeting?"

James cursed, realising his mistake.

"And who else was there?" Bannister asked.

In the end, there was nothing James could do to keep all his friends and allies from being arrested. The JPs pressed him until he had no choice but to give up some of the names, so he chose those who he felt would be harder for Nowell to arrest due to their good standing in the community, such as Alice Nutter. It would not save any of them. He would be returning to Lancaster soon, but not with the bulging pack of supplies he'd wanted to take. And most of 'the great assembly of witches' would join him. The Well Tower's dungeon had a claim on them, and there was no wriggling out of it.

THIRTY-FOUR

Hell. Christians spoke of it as fire and brimstone, wrought by god to punish the fallen angels and those who sin, while the cunning folk understood it as a spiritual plane where dark spirits lurked – all those with demonic origins, including hellhounds. But Demdike was coming to understand that neither had been right. For she now knew Hell to be of man's own making, and the Well Tower was but one of many forms it could take.

Her torments were many. There was the ache deep in her aged bones, which came of sitting on a hard earthen floor with only the rigid stone wall at her back to provide support. There was the raw skin of her wrists and ankles from the chains which chafed day and night, despite the money James had paid the gaoler to remove them. There was the uncomfortable heat of the still dungeon air, thick with the stench of sweating, disease-ridden bodies and various other bodily excretions – a constant stink her nose had eventually grown numb to. And of course there was the hunger in their bellies. For even with the money James had raised to make them as comfortable as possible, the little food they were given was still not enough to satisfy those constant pangs in their guts. But perhaps worst of all was not the loss of their freedom, but the dignity they'd had stripped away, and the lack of privacy in that overcrowded prison.

The tickle of something crawling across her skin had become such a regular occurrence that she no longer bothered to attempt to swipe away the creature, whether it be spider or louse. Her clothes had turned to a source of unrelenting discomfort, sticking wetly to her skin. She tried not to think about what filth clung to them. Then there was the pounding in her head, like the beat of a thousand hammers striking again and again at the soft matter inside her skull. It was a pain so severe that it brought with it an acute feeling of nausea. And within the first day or so, her body had begun to tremble uncontrollably as a chill took root deep within her core.

A brush of fur against her hand indicated the return of one of the many rats they shared the dungeon with. Its company was preferable to the other prisoners in that festering room. Starvation turned even the most civilised of people to animals, every scrap of food they were thrown fought over more fiercely by the prisoners than the vermin. If it hadn't been for Tibb to protect them, Demdike and Alizon probably wouldn't have eaten at all. She dreaded to think what would have become of the girl without the hellhound to keep the men at bay. It was not long before her own feelings of hunger were lost in the new torment of her gradually-sickening body, and she worried only for Alizon, who needed the nourishment to stay strong.

Demdike had lost all sense of time. Without the feel of the sun on her skin to give a sense of day and night, it was just one long, continual period of never-ending suffering. If she had to guess, she would have said they'd been down there for weeks already, but it could well have been a much shorter period, like a fortnight or even less.

However long it had been, it was evidently not enough time for Alizon to recover from the horrors she'd been subjected to ever since their arrest. The girl's ordeal had rendered her mute, and she seemed to have as pitiful an appetite as Demdike's. The old wise woman tried to encourage her granddaughter to eat every crumb of bread they were given, but Chattox and Anne Redferne claimed most of it – that which wasn't wrestled from their grasp by the younger, more able-bodied prisoners.

Sleeping was near impossible and at first Demdike assumed her headache was born from the lack of the rest her body craved. But as the days passed and the sweat beaded on her skin, her body swinging from a feeling of intense, unbearable heat to a cold that left her teeth chattering, she realised she was suffering from a fever. Soon she was experiencing coughing fits and her nausea turned to vomiting, which only added to the unsavoury mixture coating the straw beneath them. Then a new discomfort manifested in the form of an angry patch of skin on her bosom. It had probably started as a small bite where the legions of lice had begun their assault on her flesh, but once it grew into a rash, it became so itchy that no amount of scratching could relieve it. Time continued to pass and still it refused to ease off, adding to her misery.

Despite her body's weakness, she knew she had to stay strong for her granddaughter, or the girl would never survive the wait to the assizes. Demdike forced herself to eat and drink when she could and rested as much as she was able. She **would** recover to see Alizon safe through their trial. She had to. Her granddaughter needed her.

There was not much to break up the long hours of torment. Chattox was taken out of the dungeon a few times, only to be returned to the foetid chamber a while later. Demdike assumed it was because Nowell was not satisfied with the statements she'd already given, and had put Thomas Covel up to questioning her further. But that was only a guess. Her rival never spoke of what went on outside the prison, and Demdike never asked. Otherwise it was just one long period of suffering, until the day when she heard the unexpected call of "Demdike, you have another visitor."

She turned her sightless eyes towards the door and perceived the image of the last man she'd expected to see – none other than Richard Baldwin. The vision of him standing knee deep in sinners had to have come from Tibb, though her familiar said nothing as the miller came closer.

"Demdike."

"Baldwin. Come to gloat?"

"I had to see with my own eyes. Pendle has suffered your devilry for long enough, but now Christ prevails, at long last. You will hang and I will raise a toast to victory, even as your bodies swing over Gallows Hill."

"Do not celebrate just yet. Hope remains for as long as life still flows through these old veins."

"But for how much longer? You are sick and getting worse by the day, not better. You know as well as I your end is not far now. And I have news of your daughter and grandson – they are already rotting down here with you, in one of the other cells in this accursed tower. I can think of no better home for you wretches than this ungodly place."

"No!"

"Yes. They are still adjusting to the same terrible conditions, even as we speak."

"You lie, Baldwin. You just want to make me suffer even more. You lie!"

"You call me a liar now?" he hissed. "You, the blackest of hags ever to walk these lands? Well I have more news for you. Nowell is trying to pin every last suspicious death on your witchcraft, including Henry Mytton of Roughlee. You and that ugly daughter of yours were seen round his farm in the months leading up to his death, and I shall personally see to it that the two of you are blamed for his murder. And you will hang for my sin."

Alizon stirred for the first time in what might have been days. "Gran, who are you talking to?" she croaked, her voice small and uncertain.

The image of Baldwin vanished and there was nothing but darkness once more. Demdike frowned, confused. Had her granddaughter not seen the miller, perhaps because she was sleeping? Had he fled after confessing to committing murder? But surely Alizon must have seen something of him as he left the room, or was she too far gone to recognise a familiar face, even if it had been an unwelcome one?

Chattox cackled. "Your gran is delirious, girl. Can you not see the sickness creeping through her body and corrupting her mind?"

"You be quiet!" Alizon said. "Do not think we don't know what you do when the gaoler takes you to another room – spinning more tales about us no doubt."

"No more than your family have done to me and my girl," Chattox grumbled.

"She is right, lass, I am sick. But I thought I saw Richard Baldwin here with us. Is it true what he says? Have your

437

mam and James been brought into this hell now, to suffer with the rest of us?"

"Hush, Gran; take no notice of any of them. You just concentrate on getting better."

There was a pause, then Chattox said "I might be persuaded to summon Fancie if you can give me something worth my while in return."

"Fancie?" Demdike frowned. "He has betrayed us all, do you not see that yet?"

"He would never! Fancie is loyal to me and he will deliver me from the hangman's noose, you shall see."

"Ignore them, Gran," Alizon insisted. "Rest now."

But Demdike had to know. *Is it true, Tibb? Are Elizabeth and James now prisoners as well?*

Yes, Mistress, he answered. *It is as the vision said. They are in the next dungeon, along with most of the others who answered Elizabeth's call to meet at your home; even Alice Nutter, who was simply in the wrong place at the wrong time. The Gisburne woman is not among them, however. She was arrested, but she is awaiting the assizes in York, alone and without hope. As for your youngest grandchild, I cannot tell.*

The old woman closed her eyes, almost ready to admit defeat. Nowell had gained the upper hand, and she was losing the will to fight. Her limbs ached with a weariness such as she had never known before, and she was tired, so tired. All she wanted was to rest, and to leave her earthly struggles behind her; to find peace. Was it really too much to ask?

But life was not quite done with Old Demdike yet, and so she endured a while longer. At least her sickness had given Alizon something to concentrate on. No doubt the girl had been reliving the JP's hunt for a witch mark on her body over and over. Now Alizon had finally been brought out of that internal punishment, she would not let her gran go without a fight.

The girl poured drink into Demdike's mouth when it was given to them and encouraged her to eat, just as Demdike had done while her granddaughter had been trapped in the horror of recent events. Yet there was nothing Alizon could do to relieve the itching, which had now spread from her chest to her limbs and back, nor the agonies of her flesh, relentless in their painful assault. The throbbing never ceased.

Another vision came to Demdike in her final days on the earth. But this time it was someone she wanted to see, and she felt tears prick her eyes at the sight of him.

"Christopher, my son," she said. "It has been so long."

"Mam. I trust you have already heard about Elizabeth and James?"

"Yes, Tibb tells me the Justice rounded up everyone who came together to talk of freeing us. Are you not with them?"

Her bastard son shook his head. "My connections through marriage kept me safe from the constable. I want you to know we are doing everything we can to build a defence for you all, but so far we have had little luck disproving the evidence Nowell has gathered. And I doubt he will let us act as witnesses unless we are against you. He is not interested in those who wish to speak of your innocence."

"I did not think you would come. I thought you would keep your head down while this battle raged, after you chose to walk out on us that day."

"What else could I do, Mam? I had my own family to protect, and John Device's death felt like a bad omen. It was a sign of the dangers of being involved in magic and I had to get out, for the sake of my wife and children. But of course I had to come back to see you one last time. And if you really believed I would turn my back on our family in our greatest hour of need, you do not know me at all. That is not the man you raised me to be, so here I am."

"I wish I could believe that. Is any of this true, or do you simply tell a dying woman what she wishes to hear?"

"Ask Tibb for the truth of it," he answered, and with that he was gone. She was back in the Well Tower, cradled in her granddaughter's arms.

"No! Christopher! Come back to me, son, come back," she cried.

"Please, Gran, don't cry," Alizon said. "We will see Uncle Christopher again soon, I promise. After the trial we can visit him but you have to rest now and recover your strength, or we will never make it back to Pendle."

Her granddaughter's words sounded distant through the ringing that had started in her ears, and that which she could hear she struggled to understand. "Where's Jennet? I would like to look on her pretty face one last time. Where is she?"

"She's not here, Gran," Alizon sobbed. "Please, you need to rest."

"Save your tears, lass," Chattox advised. "She's dying, and no amount of help from the spirit world can save her without the right herbs and tools to work our healing magic."

"That's not true!" Alizon shouted, her fiery temper bursting into life once more. "She's not dying; you just want to believe she is because you hate us so much."

"She is dying, and if you cannot see it then you are more of a fool than the men who had us brought here. You've only to look at those black and crooked fingers and the pus oozing from all those blisters on her skin."

Demdike suddenly found herself being given a moment of clarity, a return to reality and a realisation of what was being said and who was with her.

"Anne," she said, using Chattox's real name again. "I fear you are right, and so I would ask something of you now."

"If you've decided you want Fancie's help, it is too late. Even he cannot save you now."

"No, Fancie cannot be trusted, whether you wish to see it or not. But if you would grant a woman her dying wish then it is simply this: I ask only that you look out for Alizon now, or she will be alone down here and even more vulnerable in her grief. Promise me, Anne."

"Please, Gran, don't talk like that!"

"And why should I help my rivals?" Chattox asked.

"For the friendship we once had," Demdike answered.

"That was a long time ago, Elizabeth Southerns."

"Yes, and I accept full responsibility for ruining that friendship. I should never have let you persuade me to teach you the craft or guide you through the pact. Had it not been for Fancie, our lives may have taken very different paths."

"But you did, and then you left me with only my demon for guidance because you were too afraid of his power and too disapproving of the dark arts he instructed me in."

"Please, Anne. This is a time when the cunning folk should be united against our common enemy, not fighting among ourselves. It is time to cure the bad blood between us and allow old wounds to heal, by working together."

"She's right, Mam," Chattox's daughter said. "We stand more chance of living through this if we join together."

"Fine, I will take care of your brat after you pass. Now get on with it and leave the rest of us in peace."

"No, you are not dying, Gran! You can't; we need you."

"Alizon, you have to be strong now. Be strong for your mother and James, and little Jennet when you are reunited with her. Ah, Jennet, our baby girl. How I would love to hold you one last time."

Demdike's mind settled on a picture of her youngest granddaughter and she slipped into a kind of bliss. Her eyes began to droop, finally closing shut for the last time, and the thoughts and images in her head faded until there was only darkness. From somewhere beyond she could still hear Alizon, but there was also something in front of her, a patch of light with a figure standing at its centre.

Somehow she knew who the figure was, even though she was too far off to see anything of his features. She started towards him with Tibb appearing by her side, her heart singing with joy at the prospect of being reunited.

"Gran? Gran! Please, wake up. Please, Gran, come back to us; save us from the gallows."

Demdike paused, caught between the darkness of her fading mortality and the light of the spirit realm. But the figure was starting to come into focus, and she could see it was indeed the man she longed to be with again, waiting for her as she'd known he would.

"Wake up, Gran, please! We need you to save us. Please wake up."

Alizon's voice was growing ever more distant, while the man Demdike loved was almost within touching distance. She ran towards him, no longer slowed by the limitations of her mortal flesh. One last, contented breath sighed through her body as she threw her arms around his muscular form. And thus ended the mortal life of the great Demdike, a smile upon her lips as she beheld her Tom, the last person she would ever see...

Well, not quite the last. For the Reaper had finally come for her, and he still remembered their last meeting.

"It is time," he said.

"Aye, and a promise is a promise. But I wish I could have lasted long enough to see the trials. What will become of my family without me?"

"That is not your concern. Or will you make me fight for you after all?"

"No. There would be no sense in fighting, and I do not wish to anger Death himself; not when my daughter and grandchildren are at risk of falling prey to the same sickness I succumbed to. But I would like to know their fates before I go with you."

"Then look," he said, pointing a bony finger back down at the mortal plane. Her gaze was drawn to the castle, and the events to come.

Demdike forgot her desire to find peace and reunite with her husband then, feeling only a desperate need to return to her earthly body and save her family. It was no use. Even Tibb could not protect her from the Reaper's unstoppable force. Once Death had her in his grip, there was no running from him. He offered her his skeletal hand, which she took with great reluctance. Demdike turned her back on the living, and she wept.

THIRTY-FIVE

Alizon's cries rang through the Well Tower. James heard her beg for help that would not come, and scream that their gran would not wake. His mam was quick to add her own screams and his voice was not far behind, like wolves sounding their mournful chorus for a lost pack member. Their familiars were beside them, declaring their own grief with actual howls.

"Quiet in there!" Covel yelled, banging on the cell doors. He must have been able to hear the hellhounds baying, clearly unnerved by it. James felt a grim pleasure in that. The gaoler had made a point of being especially cruel to him after the threats he'd made on his last visit. No doubt Covel thought he needed to make clear who had all the power now, in case James got any more rebellious ideas. But all he'd really succeeded in was fuelling the fires of the cunning man's anger, and James's thoughts were already on how best to get revenge. If he was to die soon anyway, he might as well let Dandy strike his enemies down. And Covel seemed like a good place to start.

Their family were barely given a chance to mourn the

loss of the great wise woman who to many had been 'Old Demdike', but to James had only ever been Gran. All they wanted was to be left alone with their grief, but Covel paid no mind to their emotional needs. His intrusion came without a shred of empathy.

"On your feet," he ordered, beating James with a stick to force him to comply.

Dandy was looking to him for permission to attack this latest perpetrator of injustice, and he mouthed "Soon."

"None of that!" Covel said, beating him again. "Keep quiet or I'll have your tongues. Your curses have no place here, you hear me?"

James was seething as the gaoler and a few of the guards led him and his mam into separate chambers.

It was a small room with little in the way of furniture, save for a table. His eyes fell on the instruments laid out on its wooden surface.

"No," he breathed, face paling. There was something wicked about the way those tools gleamed in the candle-light, like the glitter of malice in a demon's eyes. The parts of the metal clean enough to gleam, that was. Many of those sharp edges and points had been dulled by the blood of long-dead prey.

"I'll not tell you again. Quiet until you're questioned!"

James struggled against the guards as they stripped him of his clothes and forced him into shackles hanging from the ceiling, so that his arms were restrained above his head and his feet barely touched the ground. There he was forced to stand, on the very tips of his toes, for as long as Covel saw fit.

Dandy prepared to attack, but the moment the hell-hound crossed into the torture chamber, he vanished, leaving James alone with his captors. The spirit had been banished to his own realm, and that scared James more than the instruments of torture.

But the pain began long before the gaoler so much as lifted one of those cruel devices. The position he was placed in put a strain on his calves and feet from the moment the iron rings closed around his wrists, and he knew it would only worsen the longer he was left like that.

"Where are your curses and your hellhounds now, witch?" Covel sneered. "Here you are at my mercy and I see no devils or black dogs come to your rescue. After all those threats, I see a prisoner with no more power than any other, or surely you would have struck me down already."

James was determined not to give him the satisfaction of a reaction to those words. He kept his eyes fixed on a section of wall beyond the gaoler's head, his mouth firmly shut.

"I am sure you can guess why we are here," Covel continued. "My good friend Roger Nowell would like you to confirm some more of the evidence he has found against your mother and your fellow witches who so foolishly agreed to meet on Good Friday. You can save yourself a lot of pain if you choose to co-operate – I am sure you must be very uncomfortable, stood there like that."

Still James refused to look the man in the eye, let alone speak to him. But his temper flared up again when the gaoler laughed.

"I was hoping as much. I will leave you here to think things over, and perhaps you will be feeling more talkative upon my return. But until then, know that I will be taking a great pleasure in your suffering, after all that insolent tongue said to me last month."

Covel locked the door behind him, and James's torture began.

A dull ache throbbed through James's lower legs, the muscles screaming in protest at the unnatural position they'd been suspended in. His wrists hung limply in their shackles, a sharp pain stabbing down his stretched arms and into his shoulders, and now progressing into his back. But perhaps worse than the protests of his flesh was the empty chair placed at the other end of the room. It looked so inviting as it stood there just out of reach.

Worse still was the thought of what his mother might be enduring. Was she similarly strung up to suffer for hours on end? Was she growing so desperate for it to stop that she was considering giving Covel what he wanted? Or had the gaoler decided to start extracting confessions from his mother already, with the aid of the same wicked tools James had been left to look over and contemplate? Imagining what Covel might be doing to her brought tears to his eyes which had nothing to do with the torments on his own body.

It felt like days had passed. There was nothing for him to do but stand there on the balls of his feet, waiting for the gaoler's return and fearing for his mam. He began to wonder if he'd been forgotten. Was he to perish in this solitary chamber, alone and suffering right up until the merciful release of death? No, that could not be his fate. He was too important a prisoner to simply forget.

Sure enough, the moment came when he heard the click of the lock, signalling Covel's return. The door began to open, like a portent of doom.

"And how are you doing in here, James?" Covel said, walking over to look him in the eye.

"Never better," he managed through gritted teeth. The involuntary trembling of his limbs betrayed the agony he endured, but his anger would not let him show any other weakness in front of the man he wished he'd let Dandy kill when he'd had the chance.

"Really? You look most unwell to me. Surely you are ready to take the weight off your legs by now. Your mother has already confessed to the murders of John and James Sawyers, no doubt in an attempt to save your wretched soul. She claims the clay image found at Malkin Tower was in fact a picture of John Sawyers, who her familiar helped her bewitch. Tell me what you know of Sawyers' death, and I will remove your shackles and allow you to sit in this chair and rest awhile."

"Happy here, thank you," he grunted.

"As you wish. Everyone has a breaking point, and look at what fun we could have finding yours," the gaoler said, indicating the table laden with its devices for inflicting more pain.

James returned his gaze to the far wall and held his tongue.

Covel selected a knife from the table top. The point made its way into the edge of James's vision as the filthy length of metal was pressed lightly against the corner of his eye. He couldn't keep himself from flinching at its touch, panic rising at the threat to his sight.

"I imagine your eyes aren't much use to you down in the darkness of these dungeons. Your grandmother certainly managed well enough, and by all accounts she was blinder than a bat in the end, so I am sure you won't be too upset to lose these handsome eyeballs."

Still James refused to talk, though the thought of blindness terrified him.

"You might be wondering why the Justice isn't here to question you himself," Covel continued, tracing the blade down from his eye and across his cheek. "But as the use of torture isn't entirely in keeping with English law, he wishes to avoid the embarrassment of any legal implications that might otherwise come back to him, as I'm sure you can imagine. I'd sooner avoid that kind of trouble myself, so I'll leave your face for now."

The gaoler withdrew the knife, but James barely had the chance to breathe a sigh of relief before it sliced into his side, leaving a trail of crimson in its wake. Fresh pain flashed through the cut. Yet still he would not betray his own mother, even when Covel repeated his question and opened up a second wound on James's side. This one the gaoler took his time with, slowly dragging the blade through James's flesh.

"How about a list of names of everyone at your grandmother's house on Good Friday? We already have most of them, so you might as well confirm it for him and spare yourself some of this unpleasantness."

James endured several more cuts before Covel decided to move on to a different instrument. This time the gaoler picked up a thumbscrew, standing on his own tiptoes to secure the device to both thumbs.

"The names, Device."

James's resolve did not waver as the metal gripped his digits. He told himself that the first twist of that cruel screw was not so bad. But for each question he did not answer, Covel gave the screw another twist, until the crush of the metal had him screaming and making more threats.

"Curse me, will you? Go on then, witch. If you think you

have any power left in you, strike me down here and now, right where I stand."

He glared at Covel through the haze of agony. But his strength was crumbling, and his anger could only carry him so far.

"That's what I thought," the gaoler said, giving the screw another twist and raising another cry of pain. James's head slumped against his chest, his body shaking uncontrollably. "You will talk, witch."

He was given only a brief reprieve before Covel started twisting the screw round and round, so that the pressure kept on building and his screams were unending. Yet still he would not beg for it to stop or give up any of the information the gaoler demanded of him. But his bones could only take so much before they gave way to the metal. He felt them shatter in an explosion of agony. And he passed out.

James awoke to the sensation of the gaoler's hand slapping his face. He did not know if it was only moments later or hours, but he was plunged back into the agony of his flesh the moment he regained consciousness.

"We can put a stop to this as soon as you are ready, Device. Just tell me about how your mother killed John Sawyers, and the role her familiar played by bidding her to make the picture of clay," Covel said, holding up a turcas. The craftsmanship of evil, James almost lost his nerve at the sight of that wicked point designed to burrow under his nail. He reminded himself of who he was protecting and pressed his lips together, turning his head to the side and staring at the floor. The gaoler was not about to give up, however. Covel knelt to use the instrument on James's big toe as he continued "Or we can start with the Good Friday meeting, if you'd prefer."

"Go to Hell," James rasped.

His screams filled the chamber once more as the point dug into tender flesh. The nail split around the iron barb in a stream of blood, the two halves creating a valley of gore with a crimson river at its centre. Next came the grip of the pincers at the edge of first one half of the nail, then the other, slowly prising it away from its bed of raw tissue until the entire area was one big lake of red. The pain was so intense, James almost passed out a second time. It would have been a blessing.

The gaoler rose, giving him a moment to tremble and cry as his toe throbbed in harmony with the rest of his wounds. And yet still he did not talk. Instead he thought of Maggie working in the kitchens at Carr Hall. Maggie, with her pretty face and ample bosom, and eyes that he imagined would twinkle even in the midst of the dungeon horrors. For a brief moment he thought he could see her standing there, just out of reach. But the dungeon was no place for a fair maid such as she, and the vision faded. He was alone with Covel once more.

The gaoler knelt to pry off a second nail, and only when the point began its laborious journey into his other big toe did he crack. The last thing he wanted was to give Nowell more evidence to use against those he loved, but everyone has a limit. The words sprang to his tongue without him even realising what he was saying.

"Stop! Please, no more. I confess, I confess!"

A triumphant grin spread across the gaoler's ugly features as he noted down everything Nowell had asked for. James invented an account of the bewitching of John

Sawyers, even though his death had been entirely natural, and told of how Ball had come to his mam and urged her to do it. Then he gave the list of names of all those who had been at the meeting at Malkin Tower and confirmed all that Covel asked of him about the various crimes of the attendants. Many fates were sealed in the torture chamber that day, and James was powerless to stop it.

"Very good," Covel said, reaching for something else from the table.

James's eyes widened. "No! You promised, no more in return for my co-operation."

"Yes, I did. But Nowell also told me of your plot to murder me and blow up this castle. I think there is more I can bleed from you before I take you back to your prison."

The gaoler gripped a simple needle between his fingers this time. Once again he knelt to work on James's tortured feet, driving the nail into the soft, unprotected flesh of his toe where the nail had been removed. And once again, the cunning man screamed. The pain was too much, and this time he did slip back into unconsciousness, and temporary relief.

James felt like he was floating in that darkness, far from the agonies of his physical self, when suddenly he was back in Pendle, up on the hill. His body was whole and free from pain as he took in the beauty of the land he'd lived and worked on all his life. The people below were like ants from so great a height, going about their business without a care for the beings dwelling above them. But he was not alone.

"You," he growled, his anger returning. "This is all your

fault. If it hadn't been for you, I would never have killed anyone, and none of us would have got into trouble."

"Perhaps you are right, Master Device," Fancie answered. "And perhaps not. This path was always one fate might take, with or without my guidance. I merely gave you all a little push in the right direction."

"Why?"

"All will become clear, soon enough."

"And why have you come to me again now? I granted you your favour. Our business is finished."

"Why else would I be here, but to offer you another deal in return for your soul?"

"Then you have come here in vain, for my answer is still no."

"Think carefully, cunning man. The trial will not go well for you with all the evidence Nowell and his associates have taken and falsified as they've seen fit. Everything you have told them will be used against you, regardless of whether it was meant to prove your innocence or not. This is your last chance. I could strike where Dandy has failed. I could give you the vengeance you are so desperate for against all those who have taken part in the injustices you have suffered, not least Nowell and Covel, the gaoler who inflicts such torments even as we speak. We could wield such power, you and I, that your accomplishments will shadow even the work of your gran in her long life as a wise woman. All you need give me in return is your soul."

"I told you once before and I tell you again now: my soul is not for trade. I will find another way to take my revenge upon all those who wrong me."

James felt a new strength burning in him as he spoke those words. Dandy reappeared by his side, larger than before and humming with power. Fancie's form began to shift into something more demonic, but before he could reveal his true face the hellhound bounded forward and lunged at the malevolent spirit. The two creatures crashed to the floor, and James was just given the impression of something large and winged fighting his familiar when the hellhound wrapped his jaws around the thing's head and bit down with enough force to crush Fancie's skull.

There came an inhuman cry and a flash of blinding light. Then James was back in his own body, and the spirits were gone.

"Well, Device?" Covel asked him as he blinked and came back to the chamber. "Is there anything else you would like to confess?"

The gaoler still gripped the needle in his fingers. James eyed it wearily as he said "Just one last thing."

He did not know if that last encounter with Fancie had been real or merely a product of his imagination. But in that moment, it didn't really matter. It brought him a sense of pride, knowing he'd at least stood up to one evil and won, even if he had no hope of doing the same when he was taken to trial in August. And so he told the gaoler a version of everything that had just happened. Why he confessed to the spiritual encounter he could not say, other than it gave him a feeling of victory which he felt compelled to share, even if it was only with this cruel man who had taken such liberties with his flesh.

But everything he had shared did not finish with Covel. It had to be given in front of a Justice of the Peace in another formal examination, and at the prison that was a

Justice known as Anderton, more local to Lancaster than Nowell. The Mayor of Lancaster was also present.

Covel squeezed James's broken thumbs just before taking him into the room where the two powerful men waited, hissing threats in his ear of what would happen if he did not co-operate. The damaged bones moved inside their fleshy sacks, putting pressure on more nerves.

Yet the experience with Fancie gave James a newfound strength, just as it had in that spiritual place where it had happened, real or imaginary, and he would no longer be bullied. He retracted everything he'd told Covel, save for that encounter with the dark spirit when he was asked once again to give up his soul. But he kept to his story that it was Dandy who had appeared to him each time, and he made out it had happened just before his arrest.

"This demon said he was above your Christ, and therefore I must give him my soul. In return, I would have the power to revenge myself of anyone I dislike," he began. And though he didn't know it, in words that echoed his gran's in her dealings with the very same demon, he continued "But I told him my soul is my own, and not for the likes of demons. And such was the strength of my conviction, the spirit gave a fearful cry and vanished in a great flash of fire which was all around me, and he has not troubled me since."

"Is that all?" the Mayor asked him.

"It is," James confirmed.

"Very well. Covel, take him back to his prison, then we will have words."

A grim smile played on James's lips as they returned him to the same overcrowded room he'd started out in, where he could at least sit and rest his damaged flesh. The Mayor and the JP had not seemed pleased to have been called into the castle simply to take a statement about a fanciful story involving his defeat of a dark spirit. No doubt it would be humiliating for Covel, who would have assured them the trip would be worth their while. It was but another small victory, yet James relished it all the same.

THIRTY-SIX

Footsteps echoed through the dungeon, accompanied by the jingle of keys, loud and ominous. Covel approached. Alizon recognised his footfalls, heavier than any of the guards, despite his slim build.

"Ah, what a happy day this is," the gaoler said in a loud voice.

Alizon hugged herself. A pitiful, dejected figure once again, she struggled beneath the crushing weight of her grief. Whatever game Covel was playing, she wanted no part in it. He put her in mind of a fox or a weasel. A wily creature who knew he wasn't the biggest hunter around, waiting for the opportune moment to strike when prey were at their weakest. Like her poor brother. She didn't need to see James to guess what Covel had done to him. The groans of pain told the story well enough.

"I have news for you witches," the gaoler continued. "News of your fellow hag from Gisburne."

His words held little meaning. Even if she'd been at the Good Friday meeting her mam had called, they would still have fallen into the sorrow gaping inside of her. Despair defined her now. She felt as lifeless as the wrinkled body the guards had prised from her arms and taken she knew not where. It was unlikely her gran would be given a proper burial, but she hoped the body had at least been treated with some respect.

"And it is the most joyous of tidings," Covel said. "For she has been found guilty in the York assizes and was hanged this very day! Tried by the same judges who will preside over your own trial in the weeks to come, no less. Does that not gladden your hearts? Soon this will all be over and you will join the Gisburne hag in Hell. Yes, a happy day indeed."

Alizon felt no anger at his taunting. She heard a sob from the other prison where her mam, James and all those arrested for being at the Good Friday meeting endured. But no tears fell for her own grim fate. Not that day.

Her thoughts were with her gran. Loneliness reigned in her heart, loneliness and guilt at resenting the burden her grandmother had become after going blind. She would have given her own sight just to have the old woman back beside her. Gran had always known what to do. Without her guidance, Alizon was lost.

"But that is not all," Covel said. "Never have I seen such excitement building around a trial, and oh, if you could hear the same rumours which have reached mine own ears."

Chattox had at least been as good as her word, honouring Gran's dying wish and attempting to give Alizon what little comfort she could. It had brought the adolescent girl some solace to hear Chattox talk of the days when she and Demdike had been friends, and even stories of times when they'd been at odds cheered Alizon a little. There was a surprising amount of reverence in her former rival's voice whenever she recounted such tales, even when speaking of the times Demdike had bested her and Fancie. If not for Chattox, Alizon felt she too would have perished in the dungeon.

She half expected Chattox to speak up then, either to tell the gaoler to be quiet or to threaten him with more curses. But the old woman was as quiet as she was, and Anne Redferne had none of her mother's bravery or spiteful temper. There were none left to defend them against the cruelty of monsters like Covel – a different breed of monster to Nowell, but a monster nevertheless.

"Who would have thought such wretches would attract the attention of an associate clerk all the way from London?" Covel said. "I believe he has been tasked with writing an account of your case, with an eye towards reaching the ear of the King. Do you know what this means?"

Alizon did know what it meant. Their deaths were merely a means to further the careers of the men overseeing their trials. She should have felt the same fury as her gran had upon realising that, but the fire in her spirit had completely burnt out, dying with the old woman. The motives behind the gentry's quest to create the most sensational witchcraft case Lancaster had ever known meant as little to her then as it did to the creatures that crawled through the castle walls.

"I'll leave you hags to ponder it. Perhaps I'll even treat you to a little extra food later in celebration of these momentous events." The gaoler laughed and walked away.

"Oh, Gran," Alizon whispered. "Why did you have to leave me?"

Finally the day came when Alizon would face Nowell and other supposedly 'great men' one last time. She already knew the outcome. It was to the gallows she would go.

The walk through the castle felt much longer than it actually was, each step made heavy with the weight of what she imagined to be history in the making. But it was only as they approached the room where the assizes were held, and she heard the noise of the Christians eager for her blood, that her fear returned. Chattox and Anne Redferne were beside her. Their company made no difference – Alizon still felt an acute sense of loneliness as the court-room loomed ever nearer.

She tried to think of her gran as she'd been before the sickness had taken hold, strong in the face of the injustices brought against them. And as she took her first step into that room of judgement, she thought she heard a voice breathing words of comfort.

"Courage now, lass; you may all yet walk free. But if it is at the gallows your fates lie, then let us walk tall and proud. Let not your fear show; do not give them the satisfaction."

Alizon glanced at Chattox and her daughter but neither showed any indication of either hearing those words or having spoken them, and the guards gave no reaction either. Confused, she thought again of her gran. It had sounded just like something Gran would say, and perhaps it had been spoken with Old Demdike's voice, but had it truly been her grandmother or was she merely telling herself what she wanted to believe? Was it possible her gran hadn't left her after all? She had to wonder if the old woman's spirit walked right there with her, by her side in death even as she would have been in life.

In the end, it did not matter if the voice was only in Alizon's mind; those words brought new strength. She raised her head high and held it there amidst the jeers and insults as she took her place before judges and jury. Chattox seemed to notice the change in her but she made no comment, fixing her gaze back on the men who took it upon themselves to decide their fate. Chief among them was Nowell and two judges, Sir Edward Bromley and Sir James Altham. Alizon also glimpsed Richard Baldwin's face in the crowd of spectators, and she found herself bitterly wishing one of her family had bewitched him to death. If any man in Lancashire deserved it, then it was he.

"Ladies and gentlemen, we begin today's proceedings with the cases of Anne Whittle, alias Old Chattox, and her daughter, Anne Redferne," Sir Bromley began. "Thomas Potts, the indictments if you please."

Potts puffed himself up before he read out the charges. Another man filled with self-importance and silly ideas of power, as her gran would have put it.

"Anne Whittle, alias Old Chattox, you stand accused of murder by witchcraft of one Robert Nutter of Greenhead. How do you plead?"

"Not guilty," Chattox answered.

"Then this trial for your life shall be put to God and country. Anne Redferne, you are accused of the same. How do you plead?"

"Not guilty," Anne answered in a small voice, her head bowed with the fear she too must have been feeling, and her eyes fixed on the ground.

"Sir Roger Nowell, let us hear the evidence you have collected against the accused," Sir Altham said.

Nowell proceeded to read all the statements he had taken, including those from James and her mam, and Alizon herself, and presented his witnesses. She glanced at Chattox and her daughter as the damning evidence she'd given was heard by the court, feeling ashamed of how she'd been so ready to condemn them both to the foul dungeon and the noose awaiting at Gallows Hill. But Chattox was surprisingly quiet on the matter, and her daughter merely sobbed and maintained her innocence.

By the time Nowell had reached the end of the statements, Chattox's eyes were closed and she'd hung her head in defeat. There was a pause, then she admitted "Yes, I am a witch. I sold my soul to a demon who commanded me to call him Fancie, just as I told the Justice when he first questioned me in Fence." Her eyes opened and Alizon saw new fire there. The old wise woman drew herself up to her full height and held her head high. "It was I who called upon Fancie and bade him kill Robert Nutter in revenge for him attempting to take his pleasure of my daughter, which she denied him, being a married woman free of your Christian sin of adultery. He died about a quarter of a year later, and I repeat this confession now free from guilt. Deserved it, he did."

An uproar began at those words. Clearly it did not matter to anyone present that Robert Nutter had been in the wrong. All they wanted was to see the witch hang for her black magic.

The judges had to shout to make themselves heard as the trial against Chattox and her daughter was brought to a close. The jury would not deliver their verdict straight away but Bromley left them in little doubt as to how he expected that verdict to go. Alizon had heard tell of how juries could be punished for an outcome that displeased the judge. How were any of them to find justice when the system was so biased?

"I wish you were here in the flesh, Gran," she whispered. "If any could sway them, it would be you."

Then it was her turn.

"Alizon Device, you stand accused of the bewitchment of John Law, causing his body to be wasted and consumed," Potts intoned. But before he could ask her for her plea of guilty or not guilty, the door to the courtroom opened and Nowell's ally and fellow JP, Sir Thomas Gerrard, appeared. With him was the very man whose curse she had been blamed for, somewhat recovered from when she'd last seen him insofar as his paralysis went, but still unable to walk unaided. Abraham had to help him into the room.

Mobility was the least of Law Senior's problems. His face had become horribly disfigured and terrible to look upon. There was little wonder it had terrified Alizon so in the forest.

The sudden appearance of the pedlar and his son caused the shock among the crowd it was intended to. Almost unrecognisable as the man he had once been, the left side of his face had started to slough away from his skull and his left leg dragged just as it had in her vision. Clearly it had been a glimpse of the future she'd witnessed, not that it had done her much good. She only had one small glimmer of hope in that the vision had not given her an insight into what the consequences might be from the fateful meeting with Law. There'd been no apparitions of her own lifeless body swinging on Gallows Hill, no images of the courtroom she now stood in or premonitions of the verdict she would soon be handed. Perhaps her fate was not yet set in stone after all.

Abraham helped his father to the front of the room,

where he was sat as comfortably as his current condition allowed. But the outcry his ghastly appearance caused would not die down.

"Please, I'm innocent!" she shouted, but her words were lost in the din. "It was Gran's familiar who attacked the pedlar after he refused to open his pack and sell me the pins I wanted. I have no black dog of my own. It was Tibb!"

Covel grabbed her and dragged her closer to the judges. Still they struggled to hear each other. When Nowell ordered her to confirm her statement from Read Hall, she shouted as loud as she could "Everything I told you about the black dog is true!"

But the smug smile Nowell gave her told a very different story. She felt certain then her words had been twisted and were being used against her, and she burst into terrified tears.

"Please, Gran, I need you!"

The men ignored her pleas. Potts continued his scribbling, taking detailed notes of the proceedings. She realised he must be the clerk they'd ordered to write a record of the trials, and she could only guess at how he was distorting the truth.

Nowell went on to read Law's statement. The uproar finally began to die down, and Nowell's words were allowed to ring out, clear and damning. "About the eighteenth of March last, I went with my pack of wares through Colne Field, where unluckily I met with Alizon Device who demanded of me some pins. But I would give her none. She then seemed to be very angry, and when I had walked past her, I fell down lame.

"I struggled to an inn in Colne, and as I lay there in great pain, not able to stir either hand or foot, I saw a great black dog standing over me with fiery eyes, great teeth and a terrible countenance. It looked me in the face, and immediately after came in the said Alizon Device. She did not stay long but looked on me, and went away.

"And ever since, I have been tormented both day and night with the said Alizon Device, still lame and in great pain."

Nowell paused for effect, letting the court digest Law's words.

"Master Law, can you confirm this statement?" the JP asked.

The pedlar responded with a cry not to Nowell, but to Alizon as he fixed her with that terrible left eye staring unblinkingly from out of the sagging flesh. "This you know to be too true!"

"No!" she shouted back at him. "This is not my doing."

The crowd roared their disbelief at that. Nowell had to hold up a hand for silence and the spectators quietened, but he still had to raise his voice to make himself heard.

"And now, considering this fact of witchcraft is more eminent and apparent than the rest of the cases," Nowell said, "I humbly pray the favour of the Court that I might also read the examination of Abraham Law."

"Then let us hear it, sir," Sir Altham answered.

Nowell obliged. "Upon Saturday twenty-first of March, I was sent for, by a letter that came from my father, who lay in Colne speechless and lamed on his left side, save for his eye. And when I came to my father, he had recovered his speech well enough to complain that he was pricked with knives, elsons and sickles, and that the same hurt was done unto him at Colne Field, after Alizon Device had asked to buy some pins from him. And though she had no money to pay for them, he gave her the pins she desired. And I heard my father say that his pain was done unto him by the said Alizon Device, by witchcraft.

"He then said Alizon Device did lie upon him and trouble him. And seeing my father so tormented with the said Alizon and with one other old woman, whom my father did not know as it seemed, I searched after Alizon, and having found her, brought her to my father who, in the hearing of myself and various others, did charge her to have bewitched him. She then fell to her knees and confessed and asked my father forgiveness, whereupon he accordingly did forgive her."

Again, Nowell paused for effect. Alizon could only stare in shock at the twisted story. First Law Senior's statement had been made to sound as if she had tried to take the pins from him and he had refused her, and then Law Junior's had suggested he'd given her what she'd wanted out of charity and she'd cursed him anyway! How could any of these people believe something so wicked of her? There were many familiar faces among the spectators and not one called out against the accusations being made. She had grown up among them and worked with her grandmother to help bring magical solutions to all their problems. And yet all they could see was the evil witch Nowell was painting her as. It broke her heart anew.

"Master Law, can you now confirm this statement for the court?"

"I do confirm this to be a true and accurate account of the unfortunate events this past March," Abraham said.

A list of Law's afflictions were then given, detailing all Alizon had supposedly done to him. But her tears and protests turned to a bitter laugh at their next question, though the irony seemed lost on the court.

"Can you undo the wicked enchantment upon this poor

pedlar and restore him to his former strength and health?" Sir Bromley asked.

"No," she answered. "But if my grandmother had lived, she could and would have helped him out of that great misery. If only you hadn't thrown her in prison before she was given the chance."

And she continued to laugh at that, until the door to the courtroom slammed open, banging against the wall with a sound as loud as thunder, as befit the dramatic entrance the figure behind it created – one which caused an even greater shock than John Law's had. Silence trailed in its wake.

The court stared at the woman standing there. Into the silence she spoke four simple words which had a far greater effect than anything that had gone before. Words Alizon imagined filled most of the room with dread. For this was the essence of legends, a tale that would undoubtedly be told for many years to come.

Four simple words which caused many of the spectators claiming to be Protestants to relapse into their Catholic ways, crossing themselves and mouthing prayers to their god. Others fainted. But not Alizon. She looked on at the impressive figure now striding into the courtroom, and felt the muscles of her face pulling into her first genuine smile since arriving at the castle.

Four simple words, and they were as thus: "But I did live!"

There was no denying the truth of them. Her gran had returned.

THIRTY-SEVEN

Demdike made her way over to her granddaughter, glaring at the court with open defiance. The milky shroud Fancie had placed over her eyes had now cleared. She could see once more.

"How is this possible?" Nowell said. "We received word that you died. Covel himself removed your corpse from the dungeon you were imprisoned in!"

"Aye, he moved my body. But did any of you come to oversee my burial?"

The men did not reply to that, still floundering in their disbelief.

"No, you did not," she answered for them. "And if you had, you would have found my body had already gone. For I am not dead."

"How is this possible?" Nowell asked again.

"Perhaps Death has a greater sense of justice than any of you gathered here. The how is not important. I live, and I have seen enough of this farce – I am here to see that my family receives a fair trial, not this sorry state of affairs."

"I am afraid you are too late, madam," Sir Bromley said.

"Your granddaughter's case has already been heard, and a verdict will soon be reached."

"I did not pass through the veil and back to be told I am too late. The assizes have heard evidence from witnesses John and Abraham Law. Now they will hear my evidence."

She paused to eye each of the men in turn, daring them to so much as try to deny her the chance to defend her granddaughter. Had she been anyone else and had her entrance seemed any less impossible, she would probably have been thrown back in prison to await her own trial. But such was the power of her unexpected appearance in the court that day that none dared challenge her.

"Most here know me as Old Demdike, healer and great wise woman of Pendle," she began. "But I am also mother to two handsome children, including the one so cruelly named Squinting Lizzie by her neighbours, but who is more beautiful than any here in this room, in her own way. And I am grandmother to three grandchildren who have always done me proud, including Alizon, who so bravely stands before you now. Alizon, this young girl who you call witch. And I ask you, does she look like the evil hag you are so eager to brand her as?"

"Evil takes the form of beauty to deceive us. Her pretty face is no proof of her innocence. Now if you have quite finished—"

"I have not. My family are cunning folk, yes, but they are not in the business of cursing innocents. This black dog in Law's statement was not a creature of spirit but in fact a flesh and blood animal that so happened to follow Alizon into the inn when she went inside to check on him. There were men there who could confirm this, if given the chance."

"I have already spoken to all the witnesses willing to

come forward," Nowell said. "And the evidence found in the course of my investigation has already been presented."

"Then allow me to present new evidence. You see, my granddaughter never accepted a familiar. But it is no secret that I am in league with a spirit known as Tibb. Look upon him now, and see where the blame truly lies."

Her faithful hellhound manifested with a low growl, hackles raised and fangs bared. The room filled with screams and cries of alarm, and many spectators began to fight their way outside, away from the demonic beast.

"Come, Alizon," she whispered in her granddaughter's ear, leading her back to where Chattox and her daughter awaited their verdict.

"An impressive performance," Chattox murmured. "But I too would like to know how you are back."

"Later. We have not the time for it now."

The jury did not take long to reach their verdict, and it was not what Demdike had hoped to hear. Only Anne Redferne had been found not guilty.

"Anne Whittle, alias Old Chattox, and Alizon Device, you may step forward again," Sir Bromley said. "You have both been found guilty of harm by witchcraft, and are to be sentenced accordingly. Have you anything more to say to this court?"

"I have more to say, and it is this," Demdike replied, while her granddaughter shed fresh tears. "Let history record the injustices visited on these poor women here today, and many others besides. Let it record the corruption at the heart of the assizes and how innocent blood was spilled to gain power over other men, not by the accused, but by those who bent the law to their will. And let it record that I could have had Tibb kill you all right here where you stand, and yet I did not, because I chose to show mercy. All I ask now is for these two to be shown mercy in return."

"History will record what we write of it," Potts answered, his pen still poised over his parchment. There was a slight tremble to his hand that betrayed the fear behind those brave words, and his face had turned a similar shade to the paper he'd been writing on.

"Perhaps," she said. "But the land has a way of remembering old injustices wrought upon it, still heard in the screaming of the wind and the thundering of the storm centuries later. Record what you will of our lives and deeds. A day will come when the truth will out and our bloodlines will know true justice."

"Do you threaten us, madam?" Sir Bromley asked.

"Nay, I merely state a truth – which is more than can be said for any of you in this court of lies. Go on, pass your sentence."

"Then the court doth order you to be taken back to prison, and thence to the place of execution, and that you be hanged by the neck until you are dead. And may the Lord have mercy upon your souls," Sir Bromley said.

Alizon let out a cry of anguish, all the colour draining from her skin. Demdike wrapped her arms around her granddaughter. "Have faith, lass," she whispered in the girl's ear, gently stroking her hair as she had when Alizon was young. "I will see you safe back to Pendle."

"How, Gran?" her granddaughter sobbed. "You heard them. We are to be hanged, just as you always feared."

"They have not won yet. Have faith."

Alizon did not look convinced as Covel marched over. He paused while Bromley asked again if they would remove the curse from the stricken pedlar, to which Demdike answered "If you had seen fit to spare my granddaughter's life then I would have been all too willing to return Master Law to his former health. But instead you chose to condemn her for a crime she did not commit, and so I see no reason why I should heal this man, even if he is as equally undeserving of his fate as she. I will not help any who had a part to play in today's great injustice."

She turned away, allowing herself to be taken back to the dungeon with the other prisoners – including Anne Redfern. Alizon continued to weep on the long walk down the stairs into the darkness of the Well Tower. The staircase was too narrow for them to walk together, but Demdike kept a supportive hand on her granddaughter's shoulder, determined not to leave Alizon's side again until she had fulfilled her promise and delivered the girl from the hangman and back to safety.

They reached the bottom and she drew Alizon into another hug, pausing as they passed the prison where her daughter and grandson were being held. With Tibb's help, she was able to pick them out in the gloom, checking to see how they fared. Elizabeth must have felt her gaze because she looked up and her expression turned to shock.

"Mam?" she said. "How is this possible?"

"Keep moving," Covel snarled from behind, pushing her back towards her own prison before she could answer.

Demdike could barely contain her anger as she stepped back into the foetid room. The toll the gaoler's questioning had taken on Elizabeth and James was plain to see, not just in the crooked thumbs on her grandson's hand or the cut on her daughter's cheek where she'd been hit, but in the dullness of their eyes and the look on their faces that said they'd all but given up. She sat seething in conditions no less repulsive than when she'd last been in there. But the horror of her surroundings no longer had any power over her. Demdike's spirit could not be dampened, nor could her strength be taken from her then. For fate was about to take the path she had always intended, and even Death would not stop her this time.

Her mind wandered to that place on the other side of the veil. She was back in the moment where she'd been about to go with the Reaper. Those cold fingers closed around her own hand, and she heard a voice call out from behind.

"Wait!"

Demdike turned to find Fancie there.

Death fixed the spirit with his unique glare. "You have no power here, demon. You meddle in the lives of others, but you are no architect of fate. You cannot stop the natural order I am bound to."

The corner of Fancie's mouth twitched, his eyes glinting with cruel amusement. "Perhaps, but do not mistake me for powerless. I wish to make a deal with Mistress Southerns, and bargaining a soul in itself has power, as you well know. What happens next is up to Elizabeth."

Demdike raised an eyebrow. "And what makes you think I will give you my soul this time, Fancie?"

"Because I can give you more life, to do with as you wish."

Hope leapt in her spiritual heart. She pushed aside the thrill of excitement, mind racing as she gave his offer careful thought.

"In return for something so precious as my soul, I also want you to guarantee the lives of all those wrongly accused of witchcraft. Promise me, for my soul, you will protect them when I make my move. You will keep them from harm when I bring fire and fury upon the corrupt and the power hungry."

"You have my word."

"And I want my body whole and undamaged when I return to it, and my eyesight restored."

"It shall be done."

"Then my soul is yours. But first, answer me this: why has it always been so important to you? What has all this been about?"

"There is a reason I came to offer you the pact all those years ago. You will learn, but only when it is time to keep your end of the bargain."

And with that he vanished. She sensed that Death was not happy to have been cheated, but the Reaper was forced to release his grip, and a moment later her eyes opened to darkness, her nostrils filling with the stench of decay. A thin material covered her body and a crushing weight pressed down on every inch of her flesh. She tried to breathe and found she couldn't. Terror took over.

Instinctively she reached out to Tibb. He sent her a vision of human shapes wrapped in their shrouds and buried in the earth, and the terrible realisation of her resurrection hit her like a slap in the face.

The soil pinned her arms to her sides, making it impossible to dig for the second chance at life that awaited above, and she could not draw in the breath to do so much as scream. Fancie had tricked her, and she had just sacrificed her soul for naught.

Or perhaps not. She strained against the dirt with all the strength she could muster, and gradually the weight lifted. Sounds of canine panting filled her ears and spots of light appeared in the blackness, and air found its way through the fabric clinging to her mouth and nose. Never had it tasted so sweet. Tibb snorted and redoubled his efforts. The spots of light grew larger and Demdike glimpsed the paws digging and widening the hole he'd made.

Moments later, the pressure lifted from her limbs, and she found she could fight her way free of the burial shroud she had been wrapped in. The air tasted even sweeter now. It caressed her face in a pleasant, mild breeze, the warmth of the sun a welcome sensation on her skin after the dark of the dungeon, and then the grave.

Demdike blinked in the brightness of the sun and squinted at the shape lying next to her. True to his word, Fancie had lifted the mist of her blindness. She blinked again, and the corpse came into focus.

This one was most definitely dead and staying that way, its body rigid and pale, eyes wide and staring sightlessly at the world its spirit had left behind. Demdike turned her gaze skyward. Ravens circled overhead, cawing as she sat up and beheld more cadavers awaiting burial. But there were no people to witness her resurrection, which she suspected was also Fancie's doing.

Tibb whined and nuzzled her cheek, his tail wagging. "Come, Mistress. Our moment is now."

Excitement gripped her again. "The trials – they have not yet ended?"

Tibb shook his head. "Evidence against Chattox and her daughter is being given as we speak. They will call Alizon forward next."

That spurred Demdike into action. She pulled herself to her feet, pleased to find her body to be as healthy as could be expected for a woman of her years. There wasn't even any stiffness in her muscles from the time spent lying in the earth with the other dead. It was a fair walk back to the castle, but to Demdike it was the shortest she'd had in months. Renewed confidence coursed through her veins, and she made her way to the courtroom as strong and proud as ever.

It was not until the next day that Covel returned to take any of them back to the assizes. The door creaked open, many of the prisoners visibly flinching at the sound, and he stood there like a demon himself, eyes filled with malice and hate.

"You," he said, pointing at Anne Redferne and starting forward. "On your feet. You're coming with me."

But Demdike was the first to rise. "All four of us will come."

"Your parlour tricks have no power here, witch," he laughed. "I do not know how you tricked us over your own death, but I will not be fooled into fearing your magic. The daughter of Chattox is to be tried a second time, and the rest of you will wait down here until your execution. You do not even get the courtesy of a trial, Old Demdike."

He said her name with so much scorn that something inside her snapped.

"I think not." Tibb materialised with another fearsome growl. "The four of us will go up to court, and you can wait down here until your execution. It begins now."

The gaoler's face burned red with anger, but when he tried to speak, no sound escaped his throat. Blood began to collect at the base of his tongue, pooling in his mouth and spilling out between his lips, his teeth staining red. It also leaked down his gullet. Covel's eyes widened and he began to cough, so violently that he was struggling to breathe.

His tongue broke free of the muscles and ligaments anchoring it in place. Another cough sent it flying. The muscle landed at Demdike's feet, twitching with the words Covel could no longer speak. More blood pooled around it.

The man's eyes grew even wider as he fell to his knees, still coughing uncontrollably and dropping his lantern. One hand clutched at his throat. The other reached for Demdike as though begging for mercy.

Tibb bounded forward, latching onto the arm with crushing force. Something snapped, and Covel managed a gargled, wordless cry. Tibb didn't let go, savaging the limb until it was reduced to gory rags hanging from broken bones. Then he drew back, a piece of the gaoler's meat clutched in his jaws. He swallowed it with a growl of satisfaction.

Covel continued to cough and choke, his arm still outstretched but the hand hanging limp and useless at the end of it now. Demdike gave him a cold, dark smile. She could bid Tibb to finish the job, and put the gaoler out of his misery. She could let Covel die there and then. But she was done with mercy, and she wanted him to suffer for all that he had put her family through.

"Fancie," she called. "It seems only fair you should have a share of the revenge now, too."

The shadows around Covel shifted and the four wise women were given the brief impression of bat-like wings wrapping around the doomed gaoler. Then their chains snapped open and Demdike led them calmly away.

She paused in the doorway and glanced back. Covel could still be heard coughing and gurgling but the light from his dropped lantern couldn't touch him now. Darkness smothered him from head to toe, and there came the crack of another bone breaking.

Demdike reached through the new connection she'd been granted from her deal. *Do not kill him, Fancie. Have your fun, but do not kill him yet.*

His mind brushed hers, far darker than Tibb's and alight with a malevolent pleasure that went far beyond the savage joy of her beloved hellhound. There was approval there too. His chuckle slid into her mind, and the words *I knew I had chosen well.*

She strode over to the prison where her daughter and grandson were being held, only to find they had already been taken up to the courtroom, along with the rest of the accused. The time for revenge was drawing nearer. Demdike turned her earthly sight to the stairs out of the Well Tower and started toward them, pausing when she realised the other three weren't following.

"Our business down here is done. Come."

Alizon and Anne Redferne had gone equally pale, their eyes wide and staring. Chattox's face was harder to read. There was a look in her eyes Demdike couldn't decipher. Contempt? Jealousy? Respect?

"Come!" The word left her lips harsher than she'd intended, and regret immediately pushed through her darker emotions when the two younger women flinched. Chattox looked like she wasn't going to react, but then she walked forward, steering Anne with her. Alizon's eyes darted between the dungeon they'd been imprisoned in and Demdike, like a cornered animal trying to decide which danger she feared the most. Covel screamed again, and Alizon whimpered and scurried after Chattox. Shame seized Demdike. How could she have scared her grand-daughter so?

There is no shame in revenge, Fancie said. His mind brushed hers again, and he showed her the torments Covel had inflicted on her grandson. Her gaze hardened. The vision changed from the inside of the torture chamber to the very dungeon they were leaving behind, and Fancie let her watch as he continued to break Covel's bones and wreak more havoc than any living body should have the strength to endure – at least in the hands of a mortal torturer. Only once they were ready did they let the man know the release of death, in the swarm of rats flowing from every crack and crevice in the cell, and the horde of lice crawling across his skin. And the dozens of hands of angry prisoners eager for their own share of revenge. Fancie showed her how they pulled at Covel's damaged flesh and tore muscle from bone, bone from socket, and organs from their meaty nest. And finally, beneath tooth and hand, Thomas Covel died.

Chattox's voice sounded from the step behind as they climbed out of the Well Tower. "I see you have taken Fancie from me now as well."

Demdike stiffened for a moment, then forced herself to keep moving upwards.

"I assume it was he who brought you back from the dead?" Chattox continued.

"He did."

"So you finally gave in to the darkness you have been fighting against your entire life," Chattox cackled. "Your soul belongs to him now, same as mine."

"Yes. It was the only way."

"I trust you have a plan?"

"I do. You have already heard a little of the meeting my daughter called just after we four were first imprisoned. James spoke of it while he was here visiting as a free man."

"What of it?"

"In the written statements Nowell has produced, he has made it sound like James confessed to plotting to murder Covel and blow up the castle, and that it was discussed at that meeting. So I say if they want a second gunpowder plot, let us give them one. Let us bring these old stone walls crashing down."

"That's it? That's your great plan, for which you returned from the grave to carry out? Why not just curse them and be done with it, instead of killing us all with your reckless display of power? Fancie is just as capable of killing our enemies as he is of tearing down the building."

"I did intend to use a curse, but it seems some ancient power protects these walls – I saw it from the other side of the veil. Waning perhaps, since Tibb has been able to manifest in both the court and the dungeon, but strong enough to banish Dandy when he tried to protect James from the torture Covel was about to put him through. I'll not risk the same happening to the rest of our familiars, nor my curse failing."

"That did not stop you with the gaoler just now."

"I let my anger get the better of me," Demdike admitted. "But Fancie assures me the castle can be brought down if he and Tibb attack it where the power is weakest, so that is what they will do to avenge us of the rest."

"There is still the problem of us dying in there with all the rest of them."

"You think I would throw my soul away for the low price of sacrificing all those I love? I think you know me better than that, Anne Whittle. Fancie has promised me all who have been named witches will leave the assizes alive and unmarred."

"You seem to be placing a lot of trust in the spirit you were so sure had betrayed us all when last we spoke."

"He will honour his word in this. I still do not know why, but my soul is a prize he has had his eyes on ever since I made my pact with Tibb, when I was but a girl. He will not risk losing it by breaking our deal."

Chattox seemed satisfied by that and they fell quiet as they neared the courtroom. They entered to the same reception Demdike had received the previous day. But the silence did not last long.

"What is the meaning of this?" Sir Bromley asked. "Where is Thomas Covel?"

"Dead," Demdike answered. "And any guard who attempts to remove us from this court shall suffer the same fate."

Most of the room looked at her with a mixture of fear and uncertainty, unsure whether to believe her, yet too afraid of what would happen if she was telling the truth. Only those about to be tried looked happy to see her, and one or two actually seemed to regain a sense of hope. She did not approach any of them yet. Her attention remained on the judges as she fixed them with her gaze, daring either of the men to defy her.

For a tense few moments, Sir Bromley simply glared back. Then he looked away to address the rest of the court, seemingly deciding his wisest move was to continue on as if nothing had happened. "Let us proceed with the trial of Elizabeth Device. Master Potts, the indictments please."

"Elizabeth Device, daughter of Old Demdike and mother to both Alizon and James Device, you are indicted with the murders of the brothers John and James Sawyers of Barley, committed by witchcraft, and the same of one

Henry Mytton of Roughlee, the latter committed with the help of your mother and Alice Nutter. How do you plead?"

"Not guilty," Elizabeth answered in a quiet voice, quailing before so many pairs of eyes.

"So you deny confessing to numerous counts of witch-craft when questioned last April?" Justice Bannister asked.

"Yes," Elizabeth replied, a little more forcefully.

The trial continued in much the same way as Chattox's and Anne Redferne's the previous day, but it was only as Bannister read the statements taken at Ashlar House that Demdike realised Nowell was missing.

"Something is wrong," she murmured in a low voice, so only the other prisoners could hear. "Where is Nowell?"

"Fled from the castle if he knows what is good for him," Chattox said. "What does it matter? If he is not here when the walls collapse, we will make a clay image and take revenge of him that way. He cannot escape our magic."

"It is not his escape which concerns me. We will make our move soon – be ready."

"For what? It sounds like our familiars will be doing all the work."

"You know as well as I they cannot meddle in the affairs of mortals without a mortal to work through, not for some-thing as big as this. And Fancie remains as much your familiar as he has become mine. I will start the chant; you need simply add your voice and your will."

"Then I shall join with you this one last time. But the moment we have had our revenge, we shall be rivals once more, understood?"

"Understood," Demdike said, a touch of sadness in her voice then. She would have been willing to forgive Chattox for all the pain she had caused their family and start anew, but she supposed she should have known that could never be. Even when they'd still been friends, the woman had known how to hold a grudge.

Bannister continued "And you further said and confessed that you, along with Alice Nutter and your own mother, joined together and did bewitch the said Henry Mytton to death. Do you now deny confessing to that?"

"Yes," Elizabeth replied.

"So you are now saying you had no part in his death?" Sir Bromley asked.

"Our family are cunning folk devoted to the white arts of healing and divination. We are innocent of these crimes."

"And yet we have just heard that Mytton died in suspicious circumstances and his body was found in the area of Roughlee where he lived, and where your friend and accomplice, Alice Nutter, also lives," Sir Bromley said. "So why would you confess to being involved when first questioned, only to deny it now?"

"I was trying to spare my children by taking the blame upon myself."

"Do you mean to say it was in fact your children who were responsible for his murder?"

"No! I knew they were also being wrongly accused of crimes we are all innocent of, and so I hoped to save them by claiming it was I who bewitched these men to death."

"Justice Bannister, continue. I trust you have more evidence of this woman's guilt?"

"Indeed," Bannister answered, turning his eyes to the door at the far end of the room.

Demdike followed his gaze to see the door opening and Nowell appearing at last. She waited a moment to see if Sir Gerard was with him, wanting to be sure they would all die within the castle, regardless of what Chattox had said. If she could crush them all beneath the stones she would gladly go to her death again, knowing justice had finally been served and the land would become a little safer for her daughter and grandchildren, at least for a time.

Nowell turned to someone and she prepared to start her incantation. This was it. A kind of excitement filled her as she concentrated on the spell she was about to work.

The excitement died the instant she saw who Nowell had with him. Her blood turned to ice, and the words she was about to speak shrivelled and died on her tongue.

She felt like all the power had faded from her being as she watched the figure following the JP into the courtroom, the key to Nowell's master plan. Yet this was no victim like the pedlar. This was no frightened Christian wanting to help condemn them all to the gallows and thus put an end to their magic once and for all. No. This was but a little girl, out of place in a court of law. And not just any little girl. This was her youngest granddaughter, the beloved child who had been the light in the darkness of recent years. This was Jennet.

"What are you waiting for?" Chattox hissed. "There is Nowell. Let us call on Fancie to tear this place down and be done with it."

"It's over," Demdike said, defeated. "That's my youngest granddaughter he has with him."

"What of it? I thought you made a deal with Fancie to keep us all safe."

"The agreement was for the protection of all here who have been wrongly accused of witchcraft. But Jennet was never arrested, or she would have been thrown in the dungeon to rot with the rest of us. Do you not see? Nowell has brought her in as a witness."

Even as she voiced the thought, her mind rebelled against it. How could Jennet betray them like this? Then she remembered what her granddaughter had said on the way back from the Baldwins' home. 'I'd give anything to live in a house like that.'

Was that all it had taken? A few promises from Nowell, perhaps even a taste of the life of luxury the little girl craved, and she'd turned on them all? No. The JP had clearly manipulated her into giving evidence against them, but Demdike had to believe there was more to it than that. Jennet loved them; she wouldn't just forget that for the chance at a life in Read Hall. She *loved* them. Didn't she?

"I should have chosen my words with greater care." Demdike bowed her head, realising she had condemned them all with her folly. Her shoulders slumped with the weight of her failure, and her gaze fell to the floor. "It is too late now. I'll not pay for my revenge with her young life."

Elizabeth could only stare at little Jennet with her mismatched eyes. Demdike was not sure whether it had occurred to her daughter why her youngest was in there with them, but she suspected not. If only there was some spell she could recite to spare her daughter the pain that was about to come.

"Your Lordships, I present to you my first witness, Jennet Device, daughter of the accused," Nowell said. "Jennet, in your statement dated twenty-seventh April you said you had seen a spirit in the likeness of a brown dog come to visit your mother in your own home, who she called Ball, and that this spirit would ask your mother what she would have him do. And you confessed that your mother answered she would have Ball help her kill John Sawyers of Barley, and with his help Sawyers was killed by witchcraft. And since that day, your mother has continued in the practice of witchcraft. Is that correct?"

"Yes," Jennet answered.

"No!" Elizabeth screamed.

Demdike closed her eyes, unsure which was worse – the ache in her heart caused by Jennet's damning confirmation or watching the reality of the situation cut through the numbness of her daughter's shock.

"Jennet, not another word," Elizabeth said, her voice

trembling with anguish and her legs developing a visible shake, "or I will set Ball on you next!"

Jennet merely glanced at her mam with eyes dry and utterly devoid of sadness or guilt. Nowell didn't even react. His gaze remained on his star witness as he continued "And you confessed further that your mother called for Ball, who appeared as before and asked what she would have him do, and she said to him that she would have him kill James Sawyers of Barlow, brother to the said John Sawyers, to which Ball answered he would, and about three weeks after, James Sawyers died. Is that correct?"

"Yes."

Anger seized Elizabeth at that. It burst from her throat in a wordless cry and she pointed a shaking finger at Nowell, new strength in her accusing eyes. "You! You will suffer for this. You will endure torments far beyond any of John Law's."

There was a collective intake of breaths. Demdike gave a sad smile. It might have eased some of her daughter's pain if Ball could have manifested and sunk his fangs into Nowell, but she could sense the castle's mystical defences keeping him at bay. Even Tibb was struggling to appear in the courtroom now, and Fancie did not deign to answer her call. They were on their own.

A brief flicker of worry passed through Nowell's eyes. Fresh triumph replaced it when nothing happened, and he turned his attention back to Jennet with a smile of contempt. Elizabeth screamed again and started forward. The guards caught her in seconds. She writhed in their grip, working herself into such a rage that she had to be dragged from the courtroom, screaming all the while. Her cries could still be heard even after she was taken from the room, echoing down the corridor outside.

"Curse you for this, Nowell! Curse you all for bringing her into this!"

The court descended into a similar uproar to the one caused by Law Senior's appearance the previous day. Another guard had to bring a table for Jennet to stand on, so that she could still be seen and heard. The little girl seemed shaken by Elizabeth's outburst, though it did not stop her confirming damning statement after damning statement. Tears rolled down Demdike's cheeks as she watched. Her granddaughter didn't even look at her. Her beloved little Jennet, who she had to believe had been tricked into testifying against them. The alternative was just too terrible.

Elizabeth was no calmer when they brought her back in to hear the evidence James had given against her. There should have been similar rage coursing through Demdike's veins when she heard how Nowell had added everything Covel had extracted under torture to James's statements from April, after James had refused to confirm it all before a JP. But those fires had become mere embers in the gloom cast by Nowell's victory, and the hurt at Jennet's betrayal.

Her daughter continued to deny all she'd been made to confess. It would do her no good. In her anger, the poor girl looked as wild and dangerous as their familiars, with her one eye lower than the other and the filth of the dungeon staining her clothes and coating her skin.

James's trial came next, and it broke Demdike's heart anew to see the damage done to him by Covel. The lad could no longer stand unsupported and he was so weak he seemed only vaguely aware of where he was and what was going on. Like his mother, he was able to deny some of the charges. But as the evidence against him mounted, he seemed to lose what little will to fight had been left to him, and he gave up any attempt to defend himself. He might even have been deemed simple by those who hadn't known him before the dungeon. The gaoler had left but a shadow of the man he used to be.

Chattox fixed Demdike with her spiteful gaze. "Are you really going to just stand there and listen to these lies?"

"What's the use in arguing any further, Anne? We are defeated."

Chattox snorted. "I never thought I'd see the day you would just give up."

"I know when I am beaten."

After James, Alice Nutter was indicted with the murder of Henry Mytton, and evidence was also given of her part in the Good Friday meeting, where she had apparently helped in the plot to kill Covel and blow up Lancaster Castle. The Justices were quick to point out how none of her children had come to defend her and yet, standing there alone and seemingly abandoned with the same unwholesome stains from the dungeon as the rest of them, she somehow managed to retain an air of dignity about her.

Alice also pleaded not guilty. She could have attempted to direct the blame elsewhere, but she remained loyal to the last, even when Jennet was asked to identify her as one of those present at the Malkin Tower meeting.

"Now, Jennet," Nowell said. "I want you to look carefully at this line of prisoners. Do you recognise anybody?"

Jennet smiled at Alice and ran to take her by the hand. "This is our good friend Alice Nutter. She sat with us for our Good Friday feast, next to my Uncle Christopher."

The evidence against poor Alice was weak at best, and lacking when compared to all that Nowell had managed to accumulate for Demdike's daughter and grandchildren, yet the jury found this to be enough to declare her guilty. Alice remained noble and dignified to the end, standing tall and proud even as she was condemned to die alongside the real cunning folk at Gallows Hill. Demdike admired that, and felt a fresh wave of defeat. How could she have failed them all like this?

And so the trials continued until guilty verdicts were reached for ten of the eleven tried over those two days. Anne Redferne could not escape a second time, despite the heart-wrenching pleas from her mother.

"No!" Chattox cried. She fell to her knees, tears streaming down her cheeks. "I beg of ye, hang me for my crimes, but spare my daughter. She is innocent!"

Her pleas fell on deaf ears. Chattox's gaze hardened, and she picked herself up, rage flashing in her eyes. "Then you will all die. Fancie!"

Nothing happened. Curses sprang to Chattox's lips, but they were lost in the uneasy muttering from the crowd, and the mocking laughter from the likes of Baldwin when nothing continued to happen. Eventually Chattox fell into mournful silence. Demdike suspected her rival had finally accepted that she, too, was beaten.

Nor could John and Jane Bulcock escape, guilty of no more than being friends to the cunning folk in their hour of need. Christopher Bulcock shouted in protest, and was quickly seized by the guards, as Elizabeth had been. His was the only friendly face among the spectators Demdike could see.

Her anger did spark back into being then, given fresh life at the sight of all the pain and anguish the gentry had caused.

"You ought to be ashamed of yourself, Roger Nowell," she shouted above the jeers of the spectators, striding over to him in her fury. "Using our own little girl against us like that. Did you make it clear to her she would lose almost her entire family if she did as you asked? Or did you offer her the same false promises of mercy as the rest of us?"

Nowell's lips lifted into a cold smile. "I cannot claim the credit for the Lord's work. God delivered her to us, and what Justice would I be if I ignored the evidence given by an innocent child merely wishing to tell the truth?"

"Truth? Ten innocent people will hang because of the distorted version of events you ensured the assizes would be presented with, that is the truth. And what of me? Will you let me rot in that prison until I am presumed dead a second time, or is it true what Covel told me before he died – am I to hang alongside my friends and family, without the formality of a trial?"

"You will hang on the strength of your own confession made in open court, as well as the statements taken when you were examined at Ashlar House. I suggest you spend the last of your hours searching for redemption and praying for more mercy than you showed all those you bewitched, if such a thing is possible for one with as black a soul as you."

Two prison guards came to drag her away. It brought her some small sense of satisfaction to see their reluctance to touch her, no doubt fearing she would do the same to them as she had to Covel, or worse. They began to lead her away.

Potts leant over to Sir Bromley and she just caught the words "How do you want me to write this in my account?"

"Let it be said she died in prison, Master Potts," Bromley answered, his eyes fixed on her as he did so. "And let all but the confessions she made to Justice Nowell die with her."

"The land will remember!" she cried over her shoulder.

"Record what you will, but my words and my deeds will not die so easily. My legacy will live on!"

None of the men bothered to answer, probably dismissing her claims as the fanciful tales of a doomed old woman seeking some sense in her death. She was taken back to the dungeon to await her execution, along with the rest of the condemned prisoners. It made her blood boil to think of the gentry and yeomen like Baldwin congratulating themselves and celebrating over wine and ale, and maybe even enjoying a feast. They were no doubt spending the night in luxury, while she and the ten others must endure their final night on the earth in Hell. And what of Jennet? Neither Tibb nor Fancie would answer her calls. Was the little girl being rewarded for her treachery with a place at Nowell's table? Had he promised to take her in, starting with that very first day they'd all been arrested for the bewitching of Law? Was that where she'd been all this time they'd been in prison? It was entirely possible. And yet, still she could not believe Jennet had traded their lives for wealth. The little girl must have been tricked. She must not have understood what the consequences of her evidence would be. It was the only explanation that made any sense.

Those last hours in the prison were some of the longest of Demdike's life. Sleep was impossible for everyone but James, exhausted as his body was after all he had suffered during his time in the castle. Most of the prisoners were silent. Some wept. Alizon cried not just for herself and her family, but also for John Bulcock. Demdike held her eldest granddaughter close and tried to whisper what words of comfort she could, but there was nothing she could really say to ease the girl's pain. All she could do was share in it.

"On your feet!" one of the guards commanded.

None of them gave any indication they'd heard or understood, save for Alizon's whimper.

"I said, on your feet!" the guard repeated, striding through the filth. Covel's blood still stained the hands of many of the prisoners, but the dark force which had driven them to such violence was no more. They made no move to attack the guard as he passed.

Demdike looked the man in the eye only when his fingers wrapped around her collar. There was a flicker of fear there, but it wasn't enough to keep him from dragging her into a standing position. Nor did it stop the other five guards from following his example. Two more entered their prison to help with Alizon, Chattox and Anne Redferne, barely flinching when Demdike turned her gaze on them.

Covel's gruesome demise had created a temporary power over these men. But for every passing moment in which they continued to breathe, a little more of that power faded. It would take another curse to restore their fear and perhaps allow the prisoners to escape. Demdike knew that was their last remaining hope, yet her calls for Tibb and Fancie continued to go unanswered. There was little choice other than to obey the guards and follow them into a secret passage.

Sombre was the mood as they walked the length of that ancient tunnel. It stretched long and dark, with only the guards' lanterns to guide their way. In a just world, there might have been light at its end. Demdike smiled bitterly at the thought. It came as no surprise that there was only a cellar murky with the grim fate awaiting them, inevitable now and inescapable.

They were led up to the drinking room of the very inn James had lodged at during his first stay in Lancaster. Bright sunlight streamed through the windows. It couldn't quite vanquish the gloom of their surroundings, but it still caused them to squint after the weeks spent in near complete blackness.

"Welcome back, cunning man." The innkeeper gave her grandson a devilish grin. "Here for the executions this time, I see."

"Just pour them their last drinks," the lead guard said.

"With pleasure. Many prisoners have I served on their way to the gallows, but never an entire coven of witches. This will make us famous, so it will."

The 'witches' crowded round one of the large tables. The guards stayed at a respectful distance, and the rest of the room was empty.

"Will it hurt, Gran?" Alizon asked. Her eyes were red from crying but there was a last glimmer of hope shining in those tears.

"Yes, tell us what we can expect," Chattox said. "You alone have crossed the veil. Need we be afeared of what is to come?"

Demdike felt the weight of their gazes as all but James looked across at her.

"No," she answered to both questions. "It will be quick, and you will all find peace afterwards. Drink now. Let us find a final dose of courage in our cups."

Chattox shook her head as if to say she did not believe her, but she took a large gulp of ale and held her tongue.

"I cannot," Elizabeth said, pushing her tankard away.

Demdike passed the extra measure to Alizon, then

helped James sip his ale. His went down the slowest, though none were in a rush to reach the bottom of their tankards.

"Time to go," the lead guard said. "Drink up."

Where are you, Tibb? Our time is running out.

Demdike looked for her familiar but she could not sense him, as though he'd been driven away again. Sadness welled up inside. After a lifetime together, had he abandoned her at the last?

Nowell was waiting outside, smug beside the cart they were to ride to their deaths. It was but a short ride across the moors and up to Gallows Hill. Above them the sky was the rich blue of a beautiful summer's day, the glare of the sun warm but not unbearably so. A gentle breeze helped keep the heat at bay. And yet the sweat beaded on the skin of the other ten prisoners. Despite the comforting lies Demdike had told in the inn, fear and anxiety ruled her fellow cunning folk and their friends.

As they drew closer to the gallows, the clear air filled with a ghoulish excitement. A large crowd had gathered to see the eleven witches hanged, possibly the largest Lancaster had ever seen.

The wooden frame towered over them with a menace that should have had no place amidst the beauty of their Goddess. Its timber radiated malice, as though the structure had absorbed all the evil of both the criminals deserving of their execution, and the corrupt who'd sent them there. Like Nowell, now taking his place at the front of the crowd.

Demdike felt herself pulled upright once again. She lifted her head high, ignoring the spectators as best she could.

The views out there on the moors were almost as

striking as those of their home in Pendle, though she would have preferred to be looking out across more familiar terrain. Still, she was glad to be back amongst nature after the long hours in the dungeon. She raised her eyes skywards. A buzzard circled the blue, like the shadow of Death himself.

Rope slithered around her neck. The hangman's noose sent her attention plummeting back to earth, and the grim reality each of them faced.

Still standing in the back of the cart, the younger prisoners appeared fearful and full of grief for the lives they might have known, while the two other older women drew themselves up as tall and proudly as they were able. If they had any fear, they didn't show it.

As for herself, Demdike felt a strange calmness. She had died once already and knew what to expect. But her anger had burnt out again. There was only the calm acceptance of a fate she couldn't change.

On her left stood Chattox, also taking in the beautiful view. "I know what you did for the last poor souls condemned to hang as witches, seeing them freed from their torment and taken to the next life so that they might know peace. And I wonder, will any now do the same for us?"

Demdike did not answer. On her right stood Alizon, who gripped her hand tightly as if she was but a child again, seeking the comfort of an adult to take away her fear and make everything right with the world. The girl might have spent most of her adolescence insisting she was an adult ready for all the responsibilities of adulthood, yet here was a poignant reminder of her youth and the life that was about to be taken long before her time.

That brought Demdike's need for vengeance blazing through the calm.

Tibb! she called once more.

This was it, her last chance to strike down at least some of those who had wronged them. Her last chance to save her family and their allies – even if it meant they would be on the run for the rest of their lives. But her faithful familiar remained absent. Desperation took hold.

Fancie! We had a deal. Where are you?

"I am sorry, Elizabeth," the demon's voice whispered in her ear. She turned her head and caught a glimpse of him standing behind her, in his human form. "But this was not part of our agreement. I honoured my end of the bargain in giving you more life to do with as you pleased, and not only restoring that, but also your sight and your health. And I would have protected the other 'witches', had you made your move as intended. But you did not, and I made no promises to keep them from harm in any other instance. I helped you have your revenge on the gaoler because I chose to, not because I am bound to follow your commands. Your chance for revenge in this life has passed. Now it is time for you to honour your end of the bargain, and so I await to collect your soul once the hangman claims your life."

"You lying, cheating varlet," she hissed in a low voice, so only he could hear. "You knew Jennet would be at the assizes and that our deal would change nothing. You knew fate would still lead us here, and yet you let me believe I had a chance to save my family if I sacrificed my soul. And I was fool enough to be deceived by such trickery."

"You know what I am. You know my nature. Can any of us truly change the essence of who we are?"

"So it is my own fault for allowing my heart to rule my

judgement and not my head? Oh the irony, after all my years of advising against just that!"

"Hush now. It will be over soon, and then all will become clear, I promise."

Fancie vanished just as the cart began to move beneath their feet. Demdike closed her eyes, forced to accept her fate then. Without the power of the spirits, her curses were just words, and with no tools to focus the power of her will it was nothing more than meaningless wishes, as unlikely to come true as those of the next woman. The cart rolled forward, and one by one their feet lost their purchase.

Pain erupted where the noose tightened around Demdike's neck. She tried to breathe, but the air refused to enter her brain. Panic took hold. Her legs kicked uncontrollably, her feet searching for something – anything – to stand on. There was only empty space.

The panic intensified, and Demdike struggled against the bonds round her wrists, desperate to free her hands and relieve the pressure around her throat. They refused to loosen. Her heart fluttered in her chest, her lungs gasping for breath. New pain began building in her head, and there came the terrible feeling it would explode. She opened her mouth to scream. No sound came out.

The noose twisted and Demdike spun to one side, to see Chattox performing a similar silent jig. Their gazes met and they were no longer rivals – just two terrified women facing their own mortal end.

Demdike spun towards the audience again. Her eyes found her son's face in the crowd, wearing a sad smile. It brought her no comfort while the panic flooded her brain. Christopher Bulcock was with him and many of the Nutters, their eyes wide and staring in horror. Her gaze returned to the nearest row of faces, where Nowell continued to watch with the same triumph he'd had during the trial. Jennet was nowhere to be seen.

A ringing started in Demdike's ears. The noise of the crowd faded away, and black spots appeared in her vision. She ceased her struggles. New calmness replaced the panic and her noose twisted again, this time to face her granddaughter – her legacy. The girl was still fighting, still very much in the grip of terror. A tear rolled down Demdike's cheek, and she mouthed "Don't fight, lambkin."

Alizon's gaze met hers but her granddaughter showed no sign she'd understood.

"Sleep now."

The darkness closed in. Her granddaughter's face faded, and Demdike died a second time.

New light flooded Demdike's vision, and she found herself standing beside her limp corpse, still swinging from the gallows at the top of Gallows Hill. Death was already waiting patiently, but he was not there for her this time.

"You could have had eternal peace, if only you had come with me," he said. "But you chose to deal with Fancie, and now you must pay the price. As must Anne Whittle."

The rest of the hanged were only just beginning to still. Demdike watched the inevitable happening with grim acceptance, as one by one they each lost their hold on life. Their battles did not end there, though. Ghostly shadows kicked violently into action, taking up the same struggle their earthly bodies could no longer make. Demdike's gaze hardened and she turned to the Reaper.

"Just see that these nine are able to move on, and not trapped in the torment of their final days on this earth."

"You presume to command me yet again?" Death hissed.

"Please. There are none left to free them if you don't do it now."

"Fear not, that is why I came. But you would do well to remember your place in the universe, Elizabeth Southerns."

With a swing of his scythe, nine of the ten souls were released from all that bound them to their mortal remains. They went with Death willingly, the familiars by the sides of those who had been cunning folk – even the hellhound Alizon had never had chance to make a pact with. Demdike's family stopped when they realised she wasn't following. They looked back expectantly.

"Go on now, you three," she said. "Do not worry about me. I have a different path to take, that's all."

"Will we see you again?" her daughter asked.

"I do not know," she answered truthfully.

Tears welled in Elizabeth's eyes, no longer mismatched. Her face reflected the beauty of her soul now. James wrapped a strong arm around her and gave Demdike a grim nod.

"Oh, Gran, don't leave us again!" Alizon cried, running over and pulling Demdike into a hug.

Demdike held her granddaughter tight, fighting back her own tears.

A bony hand landed on Alizon's shoulder. "Come."

Reluctantly, Demdike pulled away. "Go on, lass. Find your eternal peace."

Death steered the girl over to Elizabeth and James, and together they started on their final journey. Alizon gave Demdike one last tear-filled look over her shoulder, then they vanished. Demdike barely had time to process that final goodbye before Death returned to free Chattox. She was surprisingly quiet as her soul fell forward, out of the earthly remains yet to be cut down and moved to Pendle. Death caught her arm and helped her keep her balance. Then he vanished a second time, leaving Demdike alone with the woman she had once called friend and then rival, and ally in the end. But what was to become of them in death?

"Elizabeth," Fancie breathed into her ear, his voice seductive and full of forbidden promises.

Demdike's gaze hardened again. "Enough games, demon." She turned to face him. "You promised answers."

"Yes, and here they are. It has always been about you, Betsy."

They were no longer out on the moors but in a place that resembled the inside of Malkin Tower, though she felt certain they were not in her actual home. Chattox was gone; the two of them were alone in Demdike's bedroom. An involuntary shiver ran through her at hearing him call her 'Betsy', that endearing form of her name only ever used by Tom before. Fancie spoke it with the same sense of affection as her late husband. If she'd still had a beating heart, she suspected it would have quickened in response, but such sensations had died with her body.

"Why? Why am I so special?"

"So modest," he laughed. "You know you have a natural talent for the craft, Demdike. I would not offer the pact to just any wise woman, though when you refused me you forced my hand. Anne Whittle was a means to an end, nothing more. It was easy enough to turn her against you over the years, and her resulting hatred proved most useful in the end. I could not have forced you into giving up your soul without her, for I knew you would never part with it unless the lives of your family were at stake."

"Even so, if you are as powerful as you say then what need could you possibly have for our mortal souls?"

The demon laughed again. "Your gift of sight is restored, but still you do not see. There was never any magic of old woven into Lancaster Castle – it was my ancient power you sensed. Banishing a spirit as young as Dandy is nothing to one such as I, but Tibb would have been another matter, if it were not for the hold I have over him already. For I am his true master."

"No," she breathed, not wanting to believe it.

"The night you made your pact, I had already foreseen two possible futures. Either you would succumb to the temptation of power and be mine, or you would find the strength to resist, and so I had Tibb ready to approach you in my place. There was no future in which you did not choose him."

Shock gripped her. His words were clear and yet she struggled to understand them. How could Fancie command Tibb? Tibb was loyal to her. Tibb loved her!

"Yes, I had overlooked the sense of loyalty he would develop." Fancie's eyes glittered with cruelty, his lips twisting into a cold smile. "So I was especially hard on him when I needed to make you believe he had been driven off and perhaps even killed during the Samhain of 1609. Yet still he continues to test and challenge my hold over him, though it is one he ultimately cannot break." His smile widened. "Even when I forbade him to answer your calls."

"No," Demdike repeated, shaking her head.

"Yes." Fancie clicked his fingers. The hellhound she had always thought of as hers appeared beside him in his human shape, his face downcast and his head bowed with sadness and regret. "Why do you think, of all the hell-hounds you have dealt with over the years, he alone has the ability to take the shape of a man?"

"No!" she said again, backing away.

"But your soul will make a greater servant than even this cunning man, and doubtless Old Chattox will also have her uses. Perhaps in time you will learn to forgive me for all I did to bring us here, into this moment, but ultimately it matters not. It is not your forgiveness or understanding I need. You will come to realise how I could not let such a powerful soul slip through my fingers, and so here we are. Though it is a shame I could not lay claim to your daughter and grandchildren as well."

Fancie's eyes began to bleed to their true colour, until the two pupils floated in a sea of crimson. Demdike continued to back away as the skin of that deceptively handsome face darkened and became black as the depths of the abyss that spawned him; blacker than a moonless night and the shadows extending out around his shifting form. His ears grew pointed and his face distorted into something more bestial. Teeth lengthened into sharp points, his canines becoming as impressive as those of his hound, and his nails turned to claws. Wings stretched out behind him and a tail whipped into being.

Demdike turned and ran. She threw open the door to the outside world, only to find herself in that same hellish part of the spirit realm she'd visited during her astral travel.

The tunnel ahead sloped downwards, deeper into Hell – the last direction she wanted to go in. But the demon and his servant were behind her, blocking her way up towards the light. There was nowhere else to run.

Down Demdike went, silently praying for a passage to one of the other spiritual planes. A large cavern loomed ahead, a fire burning within. She was almost inside when Tibb began to close the distance, a hellhound once more, snapping at her heels. Fancie wasn't far behind, but it was her very own Tibb who caught her leg in his jaws. Tibb, who she had always trusted and believed in. Tibb, her loyal companion who had always been there when she'd needed him the most. Except he had never been hers at all. That hard truth was more painful than the reality of the fate she had been tricked into, and the sense of betrayal she felt wounded her more deeply than anything she'd ever known before.

Anguish filled her as she crashed to the ground. She struggled to free herself from the hellhound's iron grip, but it was a fight she was never going to win. His jaws didn't even loosen.

Fancie stalked towards her on clawed feet closer to the paws of his hound than a human's. A pit of hopelessness and despair engulfed Demdike then. Once again she was forced to accept defeat, made worse by the sight of the very thing she'd been praying for just beyond the flames – a passage that may well have led to freedom.

"It's over, Betsy. You can fight it all you want but your soul belongs to me, and you only make this harder on yourself the more you resist it. You know you cannot win."

She flinched at the touch of his clawed finger on her cheek, tender as any lover. Those two blood-red orbs locked gazes with her, and his cold, cruel smile was back. Demdike whimpered.

Tibb, she tried, with the last ounce of strength she had left. *Tibb, I want you to know I forgive you. I understand you had no choice, and I believe you were as faithful to me as Fancie's hold over you allowed. I ask only that you give me a chance to escape the demon's clutches now. Do this one last thing for me, Tibb. Please.*

Tibb didn't answer. Malevolent laughter oozed from Fancie's mouth and filled the cavern, wrapping around her soul and making her feel violated; unclean. Tibb glanced at his true master. Demdike felt another wave of despair. But then the pressure on her leg lifted, and she was able to scramble to her feet.

Fancie made no move to grab her. Demdike turned and started running again. She barely made it three steps before her soul froze in place. The cavern darkened, the flames all but dying out. She was given a clear view of the sunlight filtering through the passage she'd spotted, teasing her with the freedom that was so close she could almost have cried. But try as she might to keep running, her legs refused to obey.

Her spirit began to take on a new shape, and she realised then she had never had any hope of escaping. Fancie hadn't needed his hound to run her down, or even his own demonic body to catch her. The power he'd been granted over her soul was absolute, and he'd allowed her to run purely for his own amusement. Her will was no longer her own, and her eternity of servitude had begun.

EPILOGUE

F ive years passed. Richard had thought the death of the witches would bring him peace and an end to their wicked spell, and yet his misery endured. Not even the sight of Old Demdike and her family rotting atop Pendle Hill could bring him any satisfaction in the days following their execution, nor the destruction of Malkin Tower after it was set alight and burnt to the ground. A strange cry could be heard from somewhere within the flames, and charred animal bones were found among the ruins. Yet the noises the thing made sounded unlike any of God's creatures.

The taint of the witches lingered for a time after that, but they had long since been cut down and buried in an unmarked grave somewhere on the hill, and the fear of their evil had waned. Yet even with that victory, the emptiness from the loss of his lover gaped as wide as ever. Ale remained his only solace.

All Hallows' Eve had come again – the anniversary of Rob's death. The rest of Pendle were gathering in St Mary's to observe their usual customs, but Richard still could not bring himself to join them, no matter how many years went by. Life had lost all meaning. With the death of the witches, his purpose was gone. He had completed the great task God had trusted him with and freed the land from their blight, so what more was there for him to accomplish in this life?

Darkness had already fallen, the night sky as black and empty as the miller making his way across the moors. The dim glow of a lantern lit his path once more.

In the distance, he heard the tolling of St Mary's bells. But he had his own vigil to keep now. He had developed his own customs in remembrance of the lover he still longed to hold one last time, and so he risked roaming the shadows for his annual pilgrimage to the old barn where they used to meet. There he would drink to Rob's memory until the pain numbed and sleep took him. It was the only way he had found to make the night bearable.

A chill wind picked up, howling in his ears as Richard battled against it. For the briefest of moments, he fancied it was someone screaming, but he quickly chided himself for allowing his imagination to get the better of him. The witches were gone, taking their foul magic with them. The wind was just wind, and he still had his faith in God, even after all else was lost to him, and he trusted Christ to protect him from any evil spirits out there with him that night. That didn't stop the chill creeping down his spine. Henry Mytton's screams echoed inside his skull, still as loud as the night he'd murdered him.

It was that terrible night the wind took him back to then. He could almost feel the blood on his hands, could almost see the life he'd ended still leaking out on the ground around him. Mytton had not deserved his fury, and it was the one unforgivable act for which he felt remorse.

The shape of something large passed just on the edge of

the lantern's light, bringing him to an abrupt stop. Heart quickening under the whip of fear, Richard stood there in the darkness, alone and vulnerable as he scanned the shadows for any sign of a threat. Whatever it was had retreated into the cloak of night. Shaken and wary, he continued on towards the barn, his nerves taut and his senses strained to their limits.

There came the thunder of a storm roaring into life, spurring Richard onwards. Aside from the terrifying possibility of a dread thing stalking him, it seemed the weather was about to turn. The last thing he wanted was to be caught out in it.

Another rumble sounded. Not thunder this time. It was a low, distinctive growl, like that of a dog. Richard knew for certain then the threat was more than just the weather.

He stopped again, swinging his lantern round. Nothing. The night remained empty of unnatural beasts, and all was quiet once more. That did not bring the reassurance it should have. Richard stood with his heart pounding, scanning the darkness for any hint of movement. Where was it?

More thunder sounded. Richard broke into a run, determined to reach the shelter of the barn before anything else happened. He told himself he would be safe in there, with its four walls to hide in and only one direction for an attack to come from. Out in the open, he had no chance of defending himself from whatever might be lurking in the darkness, but once he was under cover he could not be caught unawares at least. Perhaps he could also bar the door and prevent anything following him in altogether.

The shape of the barn was just visible when he heard another growl. Lightning tore the night asunder, revealing the identity of the creature to be a huge black dog, with eyes ablaze and fangs bared. And it was standing right in the doorway of the building he'd thought to be his salvation.

Screaming himself now, Richard turned and ran back the way he'd come. He didn't get far. Fangs pierced the flesh of his calf, dragging him to the ground with such force that the skin was stripped from his palms and forearms, and both knees. The lantern was torn from his hand, the small flame winking out of existence and plunging them into total darkness.

Richard cried out and kicked with all his might, landing a lucky blow on the creature's muzzle. Those deadly jaws released their grip and he scrambled to get back to his feet. The hellhound was quicker. Suddenly it was standing over him, and running ceased to be an option. His only hope was to fight.

The miller managed to roll onto his back, bringing his bloodied arms up to defend himself. He could feel the thing's breath breaching those weak defences, the stench assaulting his nostrils and making him gag. Another flash of lightning showed him the terrifying scene of its gaping maw poised just above his outstretched hands, and with a whimper he closed his eyes and waited for sharp teeth to clamp down once more.

Minutes trickled by, but the attack never came. With the next streak of lightning the beast was gone.

Richard struggled to stand, wincing at the aches and pains caused by the encounter. If it hadn't been for the throbbing of his various wounds, he might have thought he'd imagined it all. For although the storm lit up the night like the coming of a second sun, the moors stretched empty and desolate in every direction for as far as his eyes could see.

Instinctively he reached for the tankard at his belt. It

was empty. The force of his fall had blown the lid open and spilled the entirety of its contents down his trousers and over the earth. That gave him another reason to hurry to the safety of the barn, limping back towards it as fast as his wounds allowed. He'd hidden plenty enough ale in there to see him through the rest of the night, even without the tankard he'd intended on drinking first. He just had to reach it.

Another figure appeared in the doorway, one to strike an even greater terror in him than the appearance of the black dog. He came to another stop, scarcely able to believe what he'd just seen. But more lightning confirmed it. He had not imagined her.

"No," he whispered. "You're dead."

Richard jumped when the old woman cackled in his ear, suddenly beside him.

"But this is Samhain, All Hallows' Eve, the night of the dead," she said. "We are free to cross the veil as we please, and meddle in the affairs of mortals as we see fit. You might have played your part in seeing my physical body destroyed, Richard Baldwin, but my name lives on and Old Demdike is not forgotten. I promised the day would come when the bloodlines of the cunning folk would know true justice. That day is now upon us, and our justice begins with you."

"No!" he screamed. "Stay back, hag. The Lord watches over me, and He will not suffer your evil to return to these lands."

The miller backed away as he talked, but he did not get far before he felt the same unnatural affliction take hold as she'd cursed him with eight years ago, that fateful night when last they'd met on those very same moors. He was back on his hands and knees, drowning in his own blood as

515

it frothed up in a raging torrent which spilled from every opening in his body.

The next flash of lightning revealed Demdike to be standing over him. A wicked light glinted in her eyes as she inflicted her cruel torment on his poor flesh. He was already struggling to breathe, the crimson liquid pouring out of him like a river bursting its banks, his body growing weak from the loss of his precious life's fluid. But it kept on streaming out of him, even after he reached a hand out towards his tormentor – just as he had the last time – trying to appeal to her sense of mercy.

How long he suffered Richard did not know, though it felt like an age as he crouched on all fours in the spreading pool of his own blood. The taste of it was foul on his tongue, and the feel of it passing through his orifices was unpleasant. His heart was a ball of agony in his chest as it strained to keep pumping the rapidly depleting fluid through his veins. Darkness beckoned. Still he suffered, long after he should have passed out. Only with death came release, and finally his hand fell back to the ground, his desiccated body collapsing in the mud a moment later. And thus ended the life of Richard Baldwin, miller of Wheathead.

Demdike lingered over his corpse, savouring the moment. There were some benefits to becoming a creature of spirit after all, especially during Samhain. It might take years, but she would have her revenge on all those who'd had a hand in sending the eleven of them to their deaths. Baldwin was to be but the first of many. She would have come for him sooner, but between the limits the universe placed on how much a spirit could meddle in the earthly realm, and the period of adjustment to her new existence, the wait had been necessary.

Now that she had mastered her new abilities and learnt to work within the boundaries both the universe and Fancie had placed on her, there would be no stopping her wrath. She would see that her family's memory was given the respect they deserved, if not for the sake of the dead then for Jennet, who she continued to watch over from the spirit realms. Little Jennet, who had been tricked into betraying them by men as evil as the demon she'd been tricked into serving. That was one thing she could take comfort in, at least. For her new powers had granted her the ability to look further than ever before, and she had seen the truth of Jennet's role in their deaths. It had been as she'd chosen to believe. Nowell had not made it clear the price of all he promised was the blood of all those the little girl loved.

She left Baldwin's cadaver, her dark desires satisfied for one night. The rest would follow in time, but she could be patient a while longer. They were only mortal after all, while she was so much more than that now, and there would be no escaping when she hunted each and every one of them down. Nor would she let them rest in death. The land remembered, and Pendle would know true justice. It was only a matter of time.

DEAR READERS

Thanks for reading The View from Gallows Hill. I really hope you enjoyed my version of the Pendle witch story and will check out my other works.

As you might have already gathered from my note at the start of the book, The View from Gallows Hill has been a real labour of love over the six years it's taken to get to this published version, and is the result of hundreds of long hours spent at my desk.

If I could ask a few moments of your time in return, please would you write me a review?

It doesn't have to be detailed. In fact, you don't even have to write anything if you don't want to – even a star rating is a big help! But reviews are really important for bringing new readers to my works, and bringing me a step closer to my dream of quitting my day job and becoming a full time author.

I'm always grateful to my readers who take the time to do this for me, and I do read each and every one of them. A good review always makes my day, and a critical review can provide the feedback I need to keep on improving and growing as a writer.

So if you wouldn't mind heading over to Amazon, all you need to do is click:

- https://Amazon.com/orders for US Orders
- https://Amazon.co.uk/orders for UK Orders

Then click 'write a product review' next to your The View from Gallows Hill order.

If you're on Goodreads and wouldn't mind going to https://www.goodreads.com/author/show/14138888.Nick_Stead and clicking the star rating on the right hand side, and then if you want to write a review to go with your rating it will invite you to do just that.

Thanks again!

ABOUT THE AUTHOR

A lifelong fan of supernatural horror and fantasy, Nick spends his days prowling the darker side of fiction, often to the scream of heavy metal guitars and the purrs of his feline companions.

Fate set him on the path of the writer at the tender age of 15. The journey has been much longer and harder than his teenage self ever anticipated, but 20 years later he is still forging ahead.

Nick is best known for his Hybrid series. He has also had short stories published in various anthologies, and will soon be releasing another non-Hybrid novel inspired by the legend of the Heart of Midlothian in Edinburgh and the history of The Old Tolbooth prison, as well as his own journey as a published author.

For more information about Nick, Hybrid, and other works visit: www.nick-stead.co.uk. Don't forget to sign up to his newsletter to keep up to date with upcoming releases and signing events, and receive a free short story, exclusive to the mailing list.

To receive notification direct from Amazon, simply click the Follow button on his Amazon Author Page to be informed when new books are out.

US: amazon.com/Nick-Stead/e/B010LSHNJ6
UK: amazon.co.uk/Nick-Stead/e/B010LSHNJ6

Or check out his Goodreads page:
goodreads.com/author/show/14138888.Nick_Stead

He's also on social media:

 facebook.com/officialnickstead
twitter.com/nick_stead

Also by Twisted Fate Publishing

THE HYBRID SERIES - Nick Stead

Book 1 - Hybrid

Book 2 - Hunted

Book 3 - Vengeance

Book 3.5 - Ascension (A Lady Sarah Novella)

Book 4 - Damned

Book 5 - Exiled

CHRONICLES OF THE FALLEN - Gareth Clegg

Vol 1: The Crowman

Vol 2: Babylon

Vol 3: Revelations

Compilation: Vol 1-3

CHARITY COMPILATIONS

Darkness (An anthology of Dark & Twisted Tales)

Light (An anthology of Light & Twisted Tales)

Printed in Great Britain
by Amazon

36398524R00294